ALSO BY BEATRIZ WILLIAMS

Along the Infinite Sea
The Secret Life of Violet Grant
A Hundred Summers
Overseas

Tiny Little Thing

BEATRIZ WILLIAMS

BERKLEY BOOKS
New York

BERKLEY

An imprint of Penguin Random House LLC
375 Hudson Street, New York, New York 10014

ISBN: 978-0-425-27886-4

The Library of Congress has catalogued the G. P. Putnam's Sons edition as follows:

Williams, Beatriz.
Tiny little thing / Beatriz Williams.
p. cm.
ISBN 978-0-399-17130-7
I. Title.
PS3623.I55643T56   2015   2014049848
813'6—dc23

PUBLISHING HISTORY
G. P. Putnam's Sons hardcover edition / June 2015
Berkley trade paperback edition / February 2016

PRINTED IN THE UNITED STATES OF AMERICA

Cover design by Lisa Amoroso.
Cover photograph © Frances McLaughlin-Gill, Condé Nast Archive / Corbis.
Interior text design by Amanda Dewey.

Penguin
Random
House

Praise for Beatriz Williams and her novels

"Sparkles like the New England summer sun."
—Karen White, *New York Times* bestselling author of
The Sound of Glass

"One of those addictive stories that grabs you and doesn't let go."
—Lauren Willig, *New York Times* bestselling author of
the Pink Carnation series

"[A] great summer read." —*People*

"Will keep the reader so engrossed, multiple applications of sunscreen
will be required." —*USA Today*

"[A] fast-paced love story." —*O, The Oprah Magazine*

"Blends history, romance, and social commentary into a very potent novel
that is much more than a summer guilty pleasure." —*Connecticut Post*

"One-stop shopping for fans of mysteries, romance, historical fiction, and
time travel. Williams's genre mash-up will hook you from page one."
—*Ladies' Home Journal*

"Mysterious, passionate, and engrossing." —PopSugar

"Smart, delicious writing." —*Library Journal*

"Every once in a while you stumble across the perfect summer beach read.
For me, that book is *A Hundred Summers*." —Examiner.com

"One of the best romantic novels I've read . . . Williams is an impressive
storyteller . . . I'll be first in line for whatever she writes next."
—Historical Novel Society

"With her gift for humor, snappy dialogue, and swooning romance,
there's plenty to enjoy." —*Kirkus Reviews*

To all those who return from war not quite whole
and to the people who love them

Tiny Little Thing

Tiny, 1966

CAPE COD, MASSACHUSETTS

The first photograph arrives in the mail on the same day that my husband appears on television at the Medal of Honor ceremony. It's accompanied by the customary note written in block capital letters. By now, I know enough about politics—and about my husband's family, I suppose—to suspect this isn't a coincidence.

There's no return address (of course, there wouldn't be, would there?), but the envelope was postmarked yesterday in Boston, and the stamps are George Washington, five cents each. A plain manila envelope, letter size, of the sort they use in offices: I flip it back and forth between my fingers, while my heart bounds and rebounds against my ribs.

"Tiny, my dear." It's my husband's grandmother, calling from the living room. "Aren't you going to watch the ceremony?"

She has a remarkable way of forming a sociable question into a court summons, and like a court summons, she can't be ignored. I smooth my hand against the envelope once, twice, as if I can evaporate the contents—*poof, presto!*—in the stroke of a palm, and I slide it into one of the more obscure pigeonholes in the secretary, where the mail is laid every day by the housekeeper.

"Yes, of course," I call back.

The television has been bought new for the occasion. Generally, Granny Hardcastle frowns on modern devices; even my husband, Franklin, has to hide in the attic in order to listen to Red Sox games on the radio. The wireless, she calls it, a little disdainfully, though she's not necessarily averse to Sinatra or Glenn Miller in the evenings, while she sits in her favorite chintz chair in the living room and drinks her small glass of cognac. It drowns out the sound of the ocean, she says, which I can never quite comprehend. In the first place, you can't drown out the ocean when it flings itself persistently against your shore, wave after wave, only fifty yards past the shingled walls of your house, no matter how jazzy the trumpets backing up Mr. Sinatra.

In the second place, why would you want to?

I pause at the tray to pour myself a glass of lemonade. I add a splash of vodka, but only a tiny one. "Have they started yet?" I ask, trying to sound as cool as I look. The vodka, I've found, is a reliable refrigerant.

"No. They're trying to sell me Clorox." Granny Hardcastle stubs out her cigarette in the silver ashtray next to her chair—she smokes habitually, but only in front of women—and chews on her irony.

"Lemonade?"

"No, thank you. I'll have another cigarette, though."

I make my way to the sofa and open the drawer in the lamp table, where Mrs. Hardcastle keeps the cigarettes. Our little secret. I shake one out of the pack and tilt my body toward the television set, feigning interest in bleach, so that Franklin's grandmother won't see the wee shake of my fingers as I strike the lighter and hold it to the tip of the cigarette. These are the sorts of details she notices.

I hand her the lit cigarette.

"Sit down," she says. "You're as restless as a cat."

There. Do you see what I mean? Just imagine spending the summer in the same house with her. You'd be slipping the vodka into your lemonade in no time, trust me.

The French doors crash open from the terrace.

"Has it started yet?" asks one of the cousins—Constance, probably—before they all clatter in, brown limbed, robed in pinks and greens, smelling of ocean and coconuts.

"Not yet. Lemonade?"

I pour out four or five glasses of lemonade while the women arrange themselves about the room. Most of them arrived as I did, at the beginning of summer, members of the annual exodus of women and children from the Boston suburbs; some of them have flown in from elsewhere for the occasion. The men, with a few exceptions, are at work—this is a Wednesday, after all—and will join us tomorrow for a celebratory dinner to welcome home the family hero.

I pour a last glass of lemonade for Frank's four-year-old niece Nancy and settle myself into the last remaining slice of the sofa, ankles correctly crossed, skirt correctly smoothed. The cushions release an old and comforting scent. Between the lemonade and the ambient nicotine and the smell of the sofa, I find myself able to relax the muscles of my neck, and maybe one or two in my back as well. The television screen flickers silently across the room. The bottle of bleach disappears, replaced by Walter Cronkite's thick black eyeglass frames, and behind them, Mr. Cronkite himself, looking especially grave.

"Tiny, dear, would you mind turning on the sound?"

I rise obediently and cut a diagonal track across the rug to the television. It's not a large set, nor one of those grandly appointed ones you see in certain quarters. Like most of our caste, Mrs. Hardcastle invests lavishly in certain things, things that matter, things that last—jewelry, shoes, houses, furniture, the education of the next generation of Hardcastles—and not in others. Like television sets. And food. If you care to fasten your attention to the tray left out by the housekeeper, you'll spy an arrangement of Ritz crackers and pimiento spread, cubes of American cheese and small pale rubbery weenies from a jar. As I pass them by, on my return journey, I think of my honeymoon in the south of France, and I want to weep.

"You should eat," Constance says, when I sit back down next to her. Constance is as fresh and rawboned as a young horse, and believes that every thin woman must necessarily be starving herself.

"I'm not hungry yet. Anyway, I had a large breakfast."

"Shh. Here they are," says Granny. Her armchair is right next to my place at the end of the sofa. So close I can smell her antique floral perfume and, beneath it, the scent of her powder, absorbing the joy from the air.

The picture's changed to the Rose Garden of the White House, where the president's face fills the screen like a grumpy newborn.

"It looks hot," says Constance. A chorus of agreement follows her. People generally regard Constance's opinions as addenda to the Ten Commandments around here. The queen bee, you might say, and in this family that's saying a lot. Atop her lap, a baby squirms inside a pink sundress, six months old and eager to try out the floor. "Poor Frank, having to stand there like that," she adds, when it looks as if President Johnson means to prolong the anticipation for some time, droning on about the importance of the American presence in Vietnam and the perfidy of the Communists, while the Rose Garden blooms behind him.

A shadow drifts in from the terrace: Constance's husband, Tom, wearing his swim trunks, a white T-shirt, and an experimental new beard of three or four days' growth. He leans his salty wet head against the open French door and observes us all, women and children and television. I scribble a note on the back of my brain, amid all the orderly lists of tasks, organized by category, to make sure the glass gets cleaned before bedtime.

Granny leans forward. "You should have gone with him, Tiny. It looks much better when the wife's by his side. Especially a young and pretty wife like you. The cameras love a pretty wife. So do the reporters. You're made for television."

She speaks in her carrying old-lady voice, into a pool of studied silence, as everyone pretends not to have heard her. Except the children, of course, who carry on as usual. Kitty wanders up to my crossed legs and strokes one knee. "I think you're pretty, too, Aunt Christina."

"Well, thank you, honey."

"Careful with your lemonade, kitten," says Constance.

I caress Kitty's soft hair and speak to Granny quietly. "The doctor advised me not to, Mrs. Hardcastle."

"My dear, it's been a week. I went to my niece's christening the next *day* after *my* miscarriage."

The word *miscarriage* pings around the room, bouncing off the heads of Frank's florid female cousins, off Kitty's glass of sloshing lemonade, off the round potbellies of the three or four toddlers wandering around the room, off the fat sausage toes of the two plump babies squirming on their mothers' laps. Every one of them alive and healthy and lousy with siblings.

After a decent interval, and a long drag on her cigarette, Granny Hardcastle adds: "Don't worry, dear. It'll take the next time, I'm sure."

I straighten the hem of my dress. "I think the president's almost finished."

"For which the nation is eternally grateful," says Constance.

The camera now widens to include the entire stage, the figures arrayed around the president, lit by a brilliant June sun. Constance is right; you can't ignore the heat, even on a grainy black-and-white television screen. The sweat shines from the white surfaces of their foreheads. I close my eyes and breathe in the wisps of smoke from Constance's nearby cigarette, and when I open them again to the television screen, I search out the familiar shape of my husband's face, attentive to his president, attentive to the gravity of the ceremony.

A horse's ass, Frank's always called Johnson in the privacy of our living room, but not one member of the coast-to-coast television audience would guess this opinion to look at my husband now. He's a handsome man, Franklin Hardcastle, and even more handsome in person, when the full Technicolor impact of his blue eyes hits you in the chest and that sleek wave of hair at his forehead commands the light from three dimensions. His elbows are crooked in perfect right angles. His hands clasp each other respectfully behind his back.

I think of the black-and-white photograph in its envelope, tucked away in the pigeonhole of the secretary. I think of the note that accompanied it, and my hand loses its grip, nearly releasing the lemonade onto the living room rug.

The horse's ass has now adjusted his glasses and reads from the citation on the podium before him. He pronounces the foreign geography in his smooth Texas drawl, without the slightest hesitation, as if he's spent the morning rehearsing with a Vietnamese dictionary.

". . . After carrying his wounded comrade to safety, under constant enemy fire, he then returned to operate the machine gun himself, providing cover for his men until the position at Plei Me was fully evacuated, without regard to the severity of his wounds."

Oh, yes. That. *The severity of his wounds.* I've heard the phrase before, as the citation was read before us all in Granny Hardcastle's dining room in Brookline, cabled word for word at considerable expense from the capital of a grateful nation. I can also recite from memory an itemized list of the wounds in question, from the moment they were first reported to me, two days after they'd been inflicted. They are scored, after all, on my brain.

None of that helps a bit, however. My limbs ache, actually *hurt* as I hear the words from President Johnson's lips. My ears ring, as if my faculties, in self-defense, are trying to protect me from hearing the litany once more. How is it possible I can feel someone else's pain like that? Right bang in the middle of my bones, where no amount of aspirin, no quantity of vodka, no draft of mentholated nicotine can touch it.

My husband listens to this recital without flinching. I focus on his image in that phalanx of dark suits and white foreheads. I admire his profile, his brave jaw. The patriotic crease at the corner of his eye.

"He does look well, doesn't he?" says Granny. "Really, you'd never know about the leg. Could you pass me the cigarettes?"

One of the women reaches for the drawer and passes the cigarettes silently down the row of us on the sofa. I hand the pack and lighter to Granny Hardcastle without looking. The camera switches back to a close-up of the president's face, the conclusion of the commendation.

You have to keep looking, I tell myself. You have to watch.

I close my eyes again. Which is worse somehow, because when your eyes are closed, you hear the sounds around you even more clearly than before. You hear them in the middle of your brain, as if they originated inside you.

"This nation presents to you, Major Caspian Harrison, its highest honor and its grateful thanks for your bravery, your sacrifice, and your unflinching care for the welfare of your men and your country. At a time when heroes have become painfully scarce, your example inspires us all."

From across the room, Constance's husband makes a disgusted noise. The hinges squeak, and a gust of hot afternoon air catches my cheek as the door to the terrace widens and closes.

"Why are you shutting your eyes, Tiny? Are you all right?"

"Just a little dizzy, that's all."

"Well, come on. Get over it. You're going to miss him. The big moment."

I open my eyes, because I have to, and there stands President Lyndon Johnson, shaking hands with the award's recipient.

The award's recipient: my husband's cousin, Major Caspian Harrison of the Third Infantry Division of the U.S. Army, who now wears the Medal of Honor on his broad chest.

His face, unsmiling, which I haven't seen in two years, pops from the screen in such familiarity that I can't swallow, can hardly even breathe. I reach forward to place my lemonade on the sofa table, but in doing so I can't quite strip my gaze from the sandy-gray image of Caspian on the television screen and nearly miss my target.

Next to him, tall and monochrome, looking remarkably presidential, my husband beams proudly.

He calls me a few hours later from a hotel room in Boston. "Did you see it?" he asks eagerly.

"Of course I did. You looked terrific."

"Beautiful day. Cap handled himself fine, thank God."

"How's his leg?"

"Honey, the first thing you have to know about my cousin Cap, he doesn't complain." Frank laughs. "No, he was all right. Hardly even limped. Modern medicine, it's amazing. I was proud of him."

"I could see that."

"He's right here, if you want to congratulate him."

"No! No, please. I'm sure he's exhausted. Just tell him . . . tell him congratulations. And we're all very proud, of course."

"Cap!" His voice lengthens. "Tiny says congratulations, and they're all proud. They watched it from the Big House, I guess. Did Granny get that television after all?" This comes through more clearly, directed at me.

"Yes, she did. Connie's husband helped her pick it out."

"Well, good. At least we have a television in the house now. We owe you one, Cap buddy."

A few muffled words find the receiver. Cap's voice.

Frank laughs again. "You can bet on it. Besides the fact that you've given my poll numbers a nice little boost today, flashing that ugly mug across the country like that."

Muffle muffle. I try not to strain my ears. What's the point?

Whatever Caspian said, my husband finds it hilarious. "You little bastard," he says, laughing, and then (still laughing): "Sorry, darling. Just a little man-to-man going on here. Say, you'll never guess who's driving down with us tomorrow morning."

"I can't imagine."

"Your sister Pepper."

"Pepper?"

"Yep. She hopped a ride with us from Washington. Staying with a friend tonight."

"Well, that's strange," I say.

"What, staying with a friend? I'd say par for the course." Again, the laughter. So much laughing. What a good mood he's in. The adrenaline rush of public success.

"No, I mean coming for a visit like this. Without even saying anything. She's never been up here before." Which is simply a tactful way of saying that Pepper and I have never gotten along, that we've only cordially tolerated each other since we were old enough to realize that she runs on jet fuel, while I run on premium gasoline, and the two—

jets and Cadillacs—can't operate side by side without someone's under-carriage taking a beating.

"My fault, I guess. I saw her at the reception afterward, looking a little blue, and I asked her up. In my defense, I never thought she'd say yes."

"Doesn't she have to work?"

"I told her boss she needed a few days off." Frank's voice goes all smart and pleased with itself. Pepper's boss, it so happens, is the brand-new junior senator from the great state of New York, and a Hardcastle's always happy to get the better of a political rival.

"Well, that's that, then. I'll see that we have another bedroom ready. Did she say how long she was planning to stay?"

"No," says Frank. "No, she didn't."

I wait until ten o'clock—safe in my bedroom, a fresh vase of hya-cinths quietly perfuming the air, the ocean rushing and hushing outside my window—before I return my attention to the photograph in the manila envelope.

I turn the lock first. When Frank's away, which is often, his grand-mother has an unsavory habit of popping in for chats on her way to bed, sometimes knocking first and sometimes not. *My dear*, she begins, in her wavering voice, each *r* lovingly rendered as an *h*, and then comes the lecture, delivered with elliptical skill, in leading Socratic questions of which a trial lawyer might be proud, designed to carve me into an even more perfect rendering, a creature even more suited to stand by Franklin Hardcastle's side as he announced his candidacy for this office and then that office, higher and higher, until the pinnacle's reached sometime before menopause robs me of my photogenic appeal and my ability to charm foreign leaders with my expert command of both French and Spanish, my impeccable taste in clothing and manners, my hard-earned physical grace.

In childhood, I longed for the kind of mother who took an active maternal interest in her children. Who approached parenthood as a kind of master artisan, transforming base clay into porcelain with her own strong hands, instead of delegating such raw daily work to a well-trained and poorly paid payroll of nannies, drivers, and cooks. Who rose early to make breakfast and inspect our dress and homework every morning, instead of requiring me to deliver her a tall glass of her special recipe, a cup of hot black coffee, and a pair of aspirin at eight thirty in order to induce a desultory kiss good-bye.

Now I know that affluent neglect has its advantages. I've learned that striving for the telescopic star of your mother's attention and approval is a lot easier than wriggling under the microscope of—well, let's just pick an example, shall we?—Granny Hardcastle.

But I digress.

I turn the lock and kick off my slippers—slippers are worn around the house, when the men aren't around, so as not to damage the rugs and floorboards—and pour myself a drink from Frank's tray. The envelope now lies in my underwear drawer, buried in silk and cotton, where I tucked it before dinner. I sip my Scotch—you know something, I really hate Scotch—and stare at the knob, until the glass is nearly empty and my tongue is pleasantly numb.

I set down the glass and retrieve the envelope.

The note first.

I don't recognize the writing, but that's the point of block capital letters, isn't it? The ink is dark blue, the letters straight and precise, the paper thin and unlined. Typing paper, the kind used for ordinary business correspondence, still crisp as I finger the edges and hold it to my nose for some sort of telltale scent.

DOES YOUR HUSBAND KNOW?

WHAT WOULD THE PAPERS SAY?

STAY TUNED FOR A MESSAGE FROM YOUR SPONSOR.

P.S. A CONTRIBUTION OF $1,000 IN UNMARKED BILLS WOULD BE APPRECIATED.

J. SMITH

PO BOX 55255

BOSTON, MA

Suitably dramatic, isn't it? I've never been blackmailed before, but I imagine this is how the thing is done. Mr. Smith—I feel certain this *soi-disant* "J" is a man, for some reason; there's a masculine quality to the whole business, to the sharp angles of the capital letters—has a damning photograph he wants to turn into cash. He might have sent the photograph to Frank, of course, but a woman is always a softer target. More fearful, more willing to pay off the blackmailer, to work out some sort of diplomatic agreement, a compromise, instead of declaring war. Or so a male perpetrator would surmise. A calculated guess, made on the basis of my status, my public persona: the pretty young wife of the candidate for the U.S. House of Representatives from Massachusetts, whose adoring face already gazes up at her husband from a hundred campaign photographs.

Not the sort of woman who would willingly risk a photograph like this appearing on the front page of the *Boston Globe*, in the summer before my husband's all-important first congressional election.

Is he right?

The question returns me, irresistibly and unwillingly, to the photograph itself.

I rise from the bed and pour myself another finger or so of Frank's Scotch. There's no vodka on the tray, under the fiction that Frank's wife never drinks in bed. I roll the liquid about in the glass and sniff. That's my problem with Scotch, really: it always smells so much better than it tastes. Spicy and mysterious and potent. The same way I regarded coffee, when I was a child, until I grew up and learned to love the taste even more than the scent.

So maybe, if I drink enough, if I pour myself a glass or two of Frank's aged single malt every night to wash away the aftertaste of Granny Hardcastle's lectures, I'll learn to love the flavor of whiskey, too.

I set the glass back on the tray, undrunk, and return to the bed, where I stretch myself out crosswise, my stomach cushioned by the lofty down comforter, my bare toes dangling from the edge. I pull the photograph from the envelope, and I see myself.

Me. The Tiny of two years ago, a Tiny who had existed for the briefest of lifetimes: not quite married, slender and cream-skinned, bird-boned and elastic, silhouetted against a dark sofa of which I can still remember every thread.

About to make the most disastrous mistake of her life.

Caspian, 1964

BOSTON

Eleven o'clock came and went on the tea-stained clock above the coffee shop door, and still no sign of Jane.

Not that he was waiting. Not that her name was Jane.

Or maybe it was. Why the hell not? Jane was a common name, a tidy feminine name; the kind of girl you could take home to your mother, if you had one. Wouldn't that be a gas, if he sat down at Jane Doe's booth one day and asked her name, and she looked back at him over the rim of her coffee cup, just gazed at him with those wet chocolate eyes, and said *I'm Jane,* like that.

Yeah. Just like that.

Not that he'd ever sit down at her booth. When, every day at ten o'clock sharp, Jane Doe settled herself in her accustomed place at Boylan's Coffee Shop and ordered a cup of finest Colombian with cream and sugar and an apricot Danish, she enacted an invisible electric barrier about herself, crossable only by waitresses bearing pots of fresh coffee and old Boylan himself, gray-haired and idolatrous. Look but don't touch. Admire but don't flirt. No virile, young red-blooded males need apply, thank you terribly, and would you please keep your dirty, loathsome big hands to yourself.

"More coffee, Cap?"

He looked down at the thick white cup in the thick white saucer. His loathsome big hand was clenched around the bowl. The remains of his coffee, fourth refill, lay black and still at the bottom. Out of steam. He released the cup and reached for his back pocket. "No thanks, Em. I'd better be going."

"Suit yourself."

He dropped a pair of dollar bills on the Formica—a buck fifty for the bacon and eggs, plus fifty cents for Em, who had two kids and a drunk husband she complained about behind the counter to the other girls—and stuffed his paperback in an outside pocket of his camera bag. The place was quiet, hollow, denuded of the last straggling breakfasters, holding its breath for the lunch rush. He levered himself out of the booth and hoisted his camera bag over his shoulder. His shoes echoed on the empty linoleum.

Em's voice carried out behind him. "I bet she's back tomorrow, Cap. She just lives around the corner."

"I don't know what the hell you're talking about, Em." He hurled the door open in a jingle-jangle of damned bells that jumped atop his nerves.

"Wasn't born yesterday," she called back.

Outside, the Back Bay reeked of its old summer self—car exhaust and effluvia and sun-roasted stone. An early heat wave, the radio had warned this morning, and already you could feel it in the air, a familiar jungle weight curling down the darling buds of May. To the harbor, then. A long walk by civilian standards, but compared to a ten-mile hike in a shitty tropical swamp along the Laos border, hauling fifty pounds of pack and an M16 rifle, sweat rolling from your helmet into your stinging eyes, fucking Vietcong ambush behind every tree, hell, Boston Harbor's a Sunday stroll through the gates of paradise.

Just a little less exciting, that was all, but he could live without excitement for a while. Everyone else did.

Already his back was percolating perspiration, like the conditioned animal he was. The more vigorous the athlete, the more efficient the sweat response: you could look it up somewhere. He lifted his automatic hand to adjust his helmet, but he found only hair, thick and a little too long.

He turned left and struck down Commonwealth Avenue, around the corner, and holy God there she was, Jane Doe herself, hurrying toward him in an invisible cloud of her own petite ladylike atmosphere, checking her watch, the ends of her yellow-patterned silk head scarf fluttering in her draft.

He stopped in shock, and she ran bang into him. He caught her by the small pointy elbows.

"Oh! Excuse me."

"My fault."

She looked up and up until she found his face. "Oh!"

He smiled. He couldn't help it. How could you not smile back at Miss Doe's astounded brown eyes, at her pink lips pursed with an unspoken *Haven't we met before?*

"From the coffee shop," he said. His hands still cupped her pointy elbows. She was wearing a crisp white shirt, a pair of navy pedal pushers, a dangling trio of charms in the hollow of her throat on a length of fine gold chain. As firm and dainty as a young deer. He could lift her right up into the sky.

"I know that." She smiled politely. The ends of her yellow head scarf rested like sunshine against her neck. "Can I have my elbows back?"

"Must I?"

"You really must."

Her pocketbook had slipped down her arm. She lifted her left hand away from his clasp and hoisted the strap back up to her right shoulder, and as she did so, the precocious white sun caught the diamond on her ring finger, like a mine exploding beneath his unsuspecting foot.

But hell. Wasn't that how disasters always struck? You never saw them coming.

Tiny, 1966

TINY LITTLE THING 27

W hen I come in from the beach the next morning, Frank's father is seated at the end of the breakfast table, eating pancakes.

"Oh! Good morning, Mr. Hardcastle." I slide into my chair. The French doors stand open behind me, and the salt breeze, already warm, spreads pleasantly across my shoulders.

My father-in-law smiles over his newspaper. "Good morning, Tiny. Out for your walk already?"

"Oh, you know me. Anyway, Percy wakes me up early. Wants his walkies." I pat the dog's head, and he sinks down at the foot of my chair with a fragrant sigh. "You must have come in last night."

"Yes, went into the campaign office for a bit, and then drove down, long past bedtime. I hope I didn't wake anyone."

"Not at all." There's no sign of the housekeeper, so I reach for the coffeepot myself. "How was the trip? We were watching on television from the living room."

"Excellent, excellent. You should have been there."

"The doctors advised against it."

Mr. Hardcastle's face lengthens. "Of course. I didn't actually mean that you *should* have been there, of course. Air travel being what it is." He reaches across the white tablecloth and pats my hand, the same way I've just patted Percy. "How are you feeling?"

"Much better, thank you. Are you staying long?"

"Just for the dinner tonight, then I have to get back in Boston. Campaign's heating up." He winks.

"I'm sure Frank appreciates all your help."

"He has a right to my help, Tiny. That's what family is for. We're all in this together, aren't we? That's what makes us so strong." He sets down his newspaper, folds it precisely, and grasps his coffee cup. "I understand they had plans last night. Frank and Cap and your sister."

"Did they?"

"Oh, they were in high spirits on the plane from Washington. Nearly brought the old bird down a couple of times. I wouldn't expect them here until afternoon at least."

"Well, they should go out. I'm sure Major Harrison deserves a little fun, after all he's been through. I hope Frank took him somewhere lively. I hope they had a ball."

"And it doesn't bother you? All that fun without you?"

"Oh, boys will be boys, my mother always said. Always better to let them get it out of their systems."

The swinging door opens from the kitchen, and Mrs. Crane backs through, bearing a plate of breakfast in one hand and a pot of fresh coffee in the other. The toast rack is balanced on a spare thumb. "Here you are, Mrs. Hardcastle," she says.

"Thank you so much, Mrs. Crane."

As I pick up my knife and fork, my skin prickles under the weight of someone's observation. I turn my head, right smack into the watchful stare of my father-in-law. His eyes have narrowed, and his mouth turns up at one corner, causing a wave of wrinkles to ripple into his cheekbone.

"What is it?" I ask.

The smile widens into something charming, something very like his son's best campaign smile. The smile Frank wore when he asked me to marry him.

"Nothing in particular," he says. "Just that you're really the perfect wife. Frank's lucky to have you." He reaches for his newspaper and flicks it back open. "We're just lucky to have you in the family."

Frank's yellow convertible pulls up with a toothsome roar and a spray of miniature gravel at one o'clock in the afternoon, just as we've finished a casual lunch in the screened porch propped up above the ocean.

I've promised myself not to drink nor smoke before his arrival, whatever the provocation, and I managed to keep that promise all morning long, so my husband finds me fresh and serene and smelling of lemonade. "Hello there!" I sing out, approaching the car in my pink Lilly shift with the dancing monkeys, flat heels grinding crisply against the gravel. I rise up on my toes to kiss him.

"Well, hello there!" He's just as cheerful as the day before, though there's clearly occurred a night in between, which has taken due toll on his skin tone and the brightness of his Technicolor eyeballs. "Say hello to your sister."

"Be gentle." Pepper climbs out of the passenger seat, all glossy limbs and snug tangerine dress, and eases her sunglasses tenderly from her eyes. "Pepper's hung, darling."

Do you know, I've never quite loved my sister the way I do in that instant, as she untangles herself from Frank's convertible to join me in my nest of in-laws. A memory assaults me—maybe it's the tangerine dress, maybe it's the familiar grace of her movements—of a rare evening out with Pepper and Vivian a few years ago, celebrating someone's graduation, in which I'd drunk too much champagne and found myself cornered in a seedy nightclub hallway by some intimidating male friend of Pepper's, unable to politely excuse myself, until Pepper had found us and nearly ripped off the man's ear with the force of her ire. *You can stick your pretty little dick into whatever poor drunk schoolgirl you like*—or words equally elegant—*but you stay the hell away from my sister,* capiche?

And he slunk away. *Capiche,* all right.

Pepper. Never to be trusted with boyfriends and husbands, mind you, but a Valkyrie of family loyalty against outsider attack.

I step forward, arms open, and embrace her with an enthusiasm that astonishes us both. What's more, she hugs me back just as hard. I kiss her cheek and draw away, still holding her by the shoulders, and say something I'd never said before, on an instinct God only knows: "Are you all right, Pepper?"

She's just so beautiful, Pepper, even and perhaps especially windblown from a two-hour drive along the highway in Frank's convertible. Disheveled suits her, the way it could never suit me. Her eyes return the sky. A little too bright, I find myself thinking. "Perfectly all right, sister dear," she says, "except I couldn't face breakfast, and by the time we crossed the Sagamore Bridge I was famished enough to gobble up your cousin's remaining leg. No matter how adorable he is."

I must look horrified, because she laughs. "Not really. But a sandwich would do nicely. And a vodka tonic. Heavy on the vodka. Your husband drives like a maniac."

"Make it two," says Frank, from behind the open lid of the trunk, unloading suitcases.

"But where is Major Harrison?" I can't bring myself to say *Caspian*, just like that. I feign looking about, as if I'd just recognized his absence from Frank's car.

"Oh, we dropped him off already, next door. That's a lovely place he's got. Not as nice as yours." She nods at the Big House. "But then, his needs are small, the poor little bachelor."

"Well, that's a shame. I was looking forward to meeting him at last."

Frank ranges up with the suitcases. "That's right. He missed the wedding, didn't he?"

"Oh, I can *promise* he wasn't there at your wedding." Pepper laughs. "You think I'd forget a man like that, if he were present and accounted for?"

Even battling a hangover, Pepper's the same old Pepper, flirting with my husband by way of making suggestive remarks about another man. I take her arm and steer her toward the house, leaving Frank to trail behind us with the suitcases. The act fills me with zing. "But he's still coming for dinner, isn't he?"

Franks speaks up. "He'd better. He's the guest of honor."

"If he hasn't come over by six o'clock," says Pepper, "I'd be happy to pop next door and help him dress."

Guests first. I lead Pepper upstairs to her room and show her the bathroom, the wardrobe, the towels, the bath salts, the carafe of water in which the lemon slices bump lazily about the ice cubes. I'm about to demonstrate the arcane workings of the bath faucet when she pushes me toward the door. "Go on, go on. I can work a faucet, for God's sake. Go say hello to your husband. Have yourselves some *après-midi*." She winks. Obviously Mums hasn't told her about the miscarriage. Or maybe she has, and Pepper doesn't quite comprehend the full implications.

Anyway, the zing from the driveway starts dissolving right there, and by the time I reach my own bedroom, by the time my gaze travels irresistibly to the top drawer of my dresser, closed and polished, it's vanished without trace.

Frank's in the bathroom, faucet running. The door is cracked open, and a film of steam escapes to the ceiling. I turn to his suitcase, which lies open on the bed, and take out his shirts.

He's an efficient packer, my husband, and most of the clothes have been worn. Hardly an extra scrap in the bunch. I toss the shirts and the underwear in the laundry basket, I fold the belt and silk ties over the rack in his wardrobe, I hang the suits back in their places along the orderly spectrum from black to pale gray.

I make a point of avoiding the pockets, because I refuse to become that sort of wife, but when I return to the suitcase a glint of metal catches my eye. Perhaps a cuff link, I think, and I stretch out my finger to fish it from between Frank's dirty socks.

It's not a cuff link. It's a key.

A house key, to be more specific; or so I surmise, since you can't start a car or open a post office box with a York. I finger the edge. There's no label, nor is it attached to a ring of any kind. Like Athena, it seems to have emerged whole from Zeus's head, if Zeus's head were a York lock.

I walk across the soft blue carpet to the bathroom door and push it wide. Frank stands before the mirror, bare chested, stroking a silver razor over his chin. A few threads of shaving cream decorate his cheeks, which are flushed from the heat of the water and the bathroom itself.

"Is this your key, darling?" I hold it up between my thumb and forefinger.

Frank glances at my reflection. His eyes widen. He turns and snatches the key with his left hand, while his right holds the silver razor at the level of his face. "Where did you get that?"

"The bottom of the suitcase."

He smiles. "It must have slipped off the ring somehow. It's the key to the campaign office. I was working late the other day."

"I can go downstairs and put it back on your ring."

He sets the key down on the counter, next to his shaving soap, and turns his attention back to his sleek face. "That's all right. I'll put it back myself."

"It's no trouble."

Frank lifts the razor back to his chin. "No need."

By the time I've emptied the suitcase and tucked away the contents, careful and deliberate, Frank has finished shaving and walks from the bathroom, towel slung around his neck, still dabbing at his chin.

"Thanks." He kisses me on the cheek. His skin is damp and sweet against mine. "Missed you, darling."

"I missed you, too."

"You look beautiful in that dress." He continues to the wardrobe. "Do you think there's time for a quick sail before dinner?"

"I don't mind, if you can square that with your grandmother. Naturally she's dying to hear every detail of your trip. Especially the juicy bits afterward."

He makes a dismissive noise, for which I envy him. "Join me?"

"No, not with the dinner coming up, I'm afraid." I wind the zipper around the edge of the empty suitcase. Frank tosses the towel on the bed and starts dressing. I pick up the towel and return it to the bathroom. Frank's buttoning his shirt. I grasp the handle of the suitcase.

"No, no. I'll get it." He pushes my hand away and lifts the suitcase himself. It's not heavy, but the gesture shows a certain typical gallantry, and I think how lucky I am to have the kind of husband who steps in to carry bulky objects. Who invariably offers me his jacket when the wind picks up. He stows the suitcase in the wardrobe, next to the shoes, while I stand next to the bed, breathing in the decadent scent of hyacinths out of season, and wonder what a wife would say right now.

"How was the drive?"

"Oh, it was all right. Not much traffic."

"And your cousin? It didn't bother him?"

Frank smiles at me. "His name is *Cap*, Tiny. You can say it. Or Caspian, if you insist on being your formal self."

"Caspian." I smooth my hands down my pink dress as I say the word.

"I know you've never met him, but he's a nice guy. Really. He *looks* intimidating, sure, but he's just big and quiet. Just an ordinary guy. Eats hamburgers, drinks beer."

"Oh, just an ordinary beer-drinking guy who *happens* to have been awarded the Medal of Honor yesterday for valiant combat in Vietnam." I force out a smile. "Do we know how many men he killed?"

"Probably a lot. But that's just war, honey. He's not going to jump from the table and set up a machine gun nest in the dining room."

"Of course not. It's just . . . well, like you said. Everybody else knows him so well, and this entire dinner is supposed to revolve around him. . . ."

"Hey, now. You're not nervous, are you? Running a big family dinner like this?" Frank takes a step toward me. His hair, sleeked back from his forehead with a brush and a dab of Brylcreem, catches a bit of blond light from the window, the flash of the afternoon ocean.

"Don't be silly."

He puts his hands around my shoulders. "You'll be picture-perfect, honey. You always are." He smells of Brylcreem and soap. Of mint toothpaste covering the hint of stale cigarette on his breath. They were probably smoking on the long road from New York, he and Pepper, while Caspian, who doesn't smoke, sat in the passenger seat and watched the road ahead. He kisses me on the lips. "How are you feeling? Back to normal?"

"I'm fine. Not quite back to normal, exactly. But fine."

"I'm sorry I had to leave so soon."

"Don't worry. I wasn't expecting the world to stop."

"We'll try again, as soon as you're ready. Just another bump on the road."

"If you tell me you're just sure it will *take* this time," I tell him, "I'll *slap* you."

He laughs. "Granny again?"

"Your impossibly fertile family. Do you know, there are at least four babies here this week, the last time I counted?"

Frank gathers me close. "I'm sorry. You're such a trouper, Tiny."

"It's all right. I can't blame other people for having babies, can I?"

He sighs, deep enough to lift me up and down on his chest. "Honey, I know this doesn't make it any better. But I promise you we'll have one of our own. We'll just keep trying. Call in the best doctors, if we have to."

His kindness undoes me. I lift my thumb to my eyes, so as not to spoil his shirt with any sodden traces of makeup. "Yes, of course."

"Don't cry, honey. We'll do whatever it takes."

"It's just . . . I just . . ." Want it so badly. Want a baby of my own, a person of my own, an exchange of whole and uncomplicated love that belongs solely to me. If we have a baby, everything will be fine, because nothing else will matter.

"I know, darling. I know."

He pats my back. Something wet touches my ankle, through my stocking, and I realize that Percy has jumped from the bed, and now attempts to comfort my foot. Frank's body is startlingly warm beneath his shirt, warm enough to singe, and I realize how cold my own skin must be. I gather myself upward, but I don't pull away. I don't want Frank to see my face.

"All better?" He loosens his arms and shifts his weight back to his heels.

"Yes. All better." But still I hold on, not quite ready to release his warmth. "So tell me about your cousin."

"Cap."

"Yes, Cap. He has a sister, doesn't he?"

"Yes. But she's staying in San Diego. Her girls aren't out of school for the summer until next week."

"And everything else is all right with him? He's recovered from . . . all that?"

"Seems so. Same old Cap. A little quieter, maybe."

"Anything I should know? You know, physical limitations?" I glance at my dresser drawer. "Money problems?"

Frank flinches. "*Money* problems? What makes you ask that?"

"Well, I don't want to say anything awkward. And I know some of the cousins are better off than the others."

He gives me a last pat and disengages me from his arms. "He's fine, as far as I know. Both parents gone, so he's got their money. Whatever that was. Anyway, he's not a big spender."

"How do you know?"

"I went out with him last night, remember? You can tell a lot about a man on a night out."

Frank winks and heads back to the wardrobe, whistling a few notes. I look down at Percy's anxious face, his tail sliding back and forth along the rug, and I kneel down to wrap one arm around his doggy shoulders. Frank, still whistling, slips on his deck shoes and slides his belt through its loops.

Don't settle for less than the best, darling, my mother used to tell me, swishing her afternoon drink around the glass, and I haven't, have I? Settled for less, that is. Frank's the best there is. Just look at him. Aren't I fortunate that my husband stays trim like that, when so many husbands let themselves go? When so many husbands allow their marital contentment to expand like round, firm balloons into their bellies. But Frank stays active. He walks to his office every day; he sails and swims and golfs and plays all the right sports, the ones with racquets. He has a tennis player's body, five foot eleven without shoes, lean and efficient, nearly convex from hip bone to hip bone. A thing to watch, when he's out on the court. Or in the swimming pool, for that matter, the one tucked discreetly in the crook of the Big House's elbow, out of sight from both driveway and beach.

He shuts the wardrobe door and turns to me. "Are you sure you won't come out on the water?"

"No, thanks. You go on ahead." I rise from the rug and roll Percy's silky ear around my fingers.

On his way to the door, Frank pauses to drop another kiss on my cheek, and for some reason—related perhaps to the photograph sitting in my drawer, related perhaps to the key in Frank's suitcase, related perhaps to my sister or his grandmother or our lost baby or God knows—I clutch at the hand Frank places on my shoulder.

He tilts his head. "Everything all right, darling?"

There is no possibility, no universe existing in which I could tell him the truth. At my side, Percy lowers himself to the floor and thumps his tail against the rug, staring at the two of us as if a miraculous biscuit might drop from someone's fingers at any moment.

I finger my pearls and smile serenely. "Perfectly fine, Frank. Drinks at six. Don't forget."

The smile Frank returns me is white and sure and minty fresh. He picks up my other hand and kisses it.

"As if I could."

Caspian, 1964

H e avoided Boylan's the next day, and the next. On the third day, he arrived at nine thirty, ordered coffee, and left at nine forty-five, feeling sick. He spent the day photographing bums near Long Wharf, and in the evening he picked up a girl at a bar and went back to her place in Charlestown. She poured them both shots of Jägermeister and unbuttoned his shirt. Outside the window, a neon sign flashed pink and blue on his skin. "Wow. Is that a scar?" she said, touching his shoulder, and he looked down at her false eyelashes, her smudged lips, her breasts sagging casually out of her brassiere, and he set down the glass untouched and walked out of the apartment.

He was no saint, God knew. But he wasn't going to screw a girl in cold blood, not right there in the middle of peacetime Boston.

On the fourth day, he visited his grandmother in Brookline, in her handsome brick house that smelled of lilies and polish.

"It's about time." She offered him a thin-skinned cheek. "Have you eaten breakfast?"

"A while ago." He kissed her and walked to the window. The street outside was lined with quiet trees and sunshine. It was the last day of the heat wave, so the weatherman said, and the last day was always the worst. The warmth shimmered upward from the pavement to wilt the new green leaves. A sleek black Cadillac cruised past, but his grandmother's sash windows were so well made he didn't even hear it. Or maybe his hearing was going. Too much noise.

"You and your early hours. I suppose you learned that in the army."

"I was always an early riser, Granny." He turned to her. She sat in her usual chintz chair near the bookcase, powdered and immaculate in a flamingo-colored dress that matched the flowers in the upholstery behind her.

"That's your father's blood, I suppose. Your mother always slept until noon."

"I'll take your word for it."

"Trust me." She reached for the bell on the small chinoiserie table next to the chair and rang it, a single ding. Granny wasn't one for wallowing in grief, even for her oldest daughter. "What brings you out to see your old granny today?"

"No reason, except I'll be shipping out on another tour soon."

Her lip curled. "Why on earth?"

"Because I'm a soldier, Granny. It's what I do."

"There are plenty of other things you could do. Oh! Hetty. There you are. A tray of coffee for my grandson. He's already eaten, but you might bring a little cake to sweeten him up."

Right. As if he was the one who needed sweetening.

He waited until Hetty disappeared back through the living room doorway. "Like what, Granny? What can I do?"

"Oh, you know. Like your uncle's firm. Or law school. I would say medicine, but you're probably too old for all that song and dance, and anyway we already have a doctor in the family."

"Anything but the army, in other words?" He leaned against the bookcase and crossed his arms. "Anything but following in my father's footsteps?"

"I didn't say that. Eisenhower was in the army, after all."

"Give it a rest, Granny. You can't stamp greatness on all our brows."

"I didn't say anything about greatness."

"Poor Granny. It's written all over your smile. But blood will out, you know. I tried all that in college, and look what happened." He spread his hands. "You'll just have to take me as you find me, I guess. Every family needs a black sheep. Gives us character. The press loves it, don't they? Imagine the breathless TV feature, when Frank wins the nomination for president."

"Oh, for heaven's sake. You're not a black sheep. Look at you." She jabbed an impatient gesture at his reclining body, his sturdy legs crossed at the ankles. "I just worry about you, that's all. Off on the other side of the word. Siam, of all places."

"Vietnam."

"At least you're fighting Communists."

"Someone's got to do it."

The door opened. Hetty sidled through, her long uniformed back warped under the weight of the coffee tray. He uncrossed his legs and pushed away from the wall to take it from her. He couldn't stand the sight of it, never could—domestic servants lugging damned massive loads of coffee and cake for his convenience. At least in his father's various accommodations, the trays were carried by sturdy young soldiers who were happy to be hauling coffee instead of grenades. A subtle difference, maybe, but one he could live with.

"Thank you, Hetty. What about this photography business of yours?" She waved him aside and poured him a cup of coffee with her own hands.

"It's not a business. It's a hobby. Not all that respectable, either, but surely I don't need to tell you that?"

"It's an art, Franklin says. Just like painting."

"It's not just like painting. But I guess there's an art to it. You can say that to your friends, anyway, if it helps." He took the coffee cup and resumed his position against the bookcase.

"Don't you ever sit, young man?"

"Not if I can help it."

"I guess that's your trouble in a nutshell."

He grinned and drank his coffee.

She made a grandmotherly *harrumph*, the kind of patronizing noise she'd probably sworn at age twenty—and he'd seen her pictures at age twenty, some rip-roaring New York party, Edith Wharton she wasn't—that she would never, ever make. "You and that smile of yours. What about girls? I suppose you have a girl or two stringing along behind you, as usual."

"Not really. I'm only back for a few weeks, remember?"

"That's never stopped the men in this family before." A smug smile from old Granny.

"And you're proud of that?"

"Men should be men, girls should be girls. How God meant us."

He shook his head. The cup rested in his palm, reminding him of Jane Doe's curving elbow. "There *is* a girl, I guess."

As soon as the words left his mouth, he realized she was the reason he came here to lily-scented Brookline that hot May morning, to its chintz upholstery and its shepherdess coffee service, to Granny herself, unchanged since his childhood.

Jane Doe. What to do with her. What to do with himself.

"What's her name?" asked Granny.

He grinned again. "I don't know. I've hardly spoken to her."

"Hardly *spoken* to her?"

"I think she's engaged."

"Engaged, or married?"

"Engaged, I think. I didn't see a band. Anyway, she doesn't seem married."

"Well, if she's only engaged, there's nothing to worry about." Granny stirred in another spoonful of sugar. The silver tinkled expensively against the Meissen. "What kind of girl is she?"

"The nice kind."

"Good family?"

"I told you, I don't know her name."

"Find out."

"Hell, Granny, I—"

"Language, Caspian."

He set down the coffee and strode back to the window. "Why the hell did I come here, anyway? I don't know."

"Don't blaspheme. You can use whatever foul words you like in that . . . that *platoon* of yours, but you will not take the Lord's name in vain in my house."

"Yes, ma'am."

"Now. To answer your question. Why did you come here? You came here to ask my advice, of course."

"And what's your advice, Granny?" he asked the window, the empty street outside, the identical white-trimmed Georgian pile of bricks staring back at him.

The silver clinked. Granny, cutting herself a slice of cake, placing it on a delicate shepherdess plate, taking a bite. "I am amazed, Caspian, so amazed and *perplexed* by the way your generation makes these things so unnecessarily complicated. The fact is, you only have one question to ask yourself, one question to answer before you do a single first thing."

"Which is?"

"Do you want her for a wife or for a good time?"

The postman appeared suddenly, between a pair of trees on the opposite side of the street, wearing short pants and looking as if he might drop dead.

Caspian fingered the edge of the chintz curtain and considered the words *good time*, and the effortless way Granny spoke them. What the hell did Granny know about a good-time girl? Not that he wanted to know. Jesus. "There's no in between?"

A short pause, thick with disapproval. "No."

"All right. Then what?"

"Well, it depends. If you want a good time, you walk up to her, introduce yourself, and ask her to dinner."

"Easy enough. And the other?"

Granny set down her plate. The house around them lay as still as outdoors, lifeless, empty now of the eight children she'd raised, the husband at his office downtown, if by *office* you meant *mistress's apartment*. She was the lone survivor, the last man standing in the Brookline past. The floorboards vibrated beneath the carpet as she rose to her feet and walked toward him, at the same dragging tempo as the postman across the street.

She placed a hand on his shoulder, and he managed not to flinch. "Now, don't you know that, Caspian? You walk up, introduce yourself, and ask her to dinner."

Tiny, 1966

At half past five o'clock, I push open the bottom sash of the bedroom window and prop my torso into the hot salt-laden air to look for my husband.

The beach is crammed with Hardcastle scions of all ages, running about the sand in skimpy swimsuits. Or *frolicking*: yes, that's the word. A cluster of younger ones ply their shovels on a massive sand castle, assisted by a father or two; the younger teenagers are chasing one another, boys versus girls, testing out all those mysterious new frissons under the guise of play. Hadn't I done that, between thirteen and sixteen, when the Schuylers summered on Long Island? I probably had. Or maybe my sisters had, and I'd watched from under my umbrella, reading a book, safe from freckles and sunburn and hormonal adolescent boys. Saving myself for greater things, or so I told myself, because that's what Mums wanted for me. Greater things than untried pimply scions.

A cigarette trails from my fingers—another reason for opening the window—and I inhale quickly, in case anyone happens to be looking up.

Of the seven living Hardcastle children, six are here today with their spouses, and fully thirteen of Frank's cousins have joined them in the pretty shingle and clapboard houses that make up the property. A compound, the magazines like to call it, as if it's an armed camp, and the Hardcastles a diplomatic entity of their own. I know all their names. It's part of my job. *You're the lady of the house now,* Granny Hardcastle said, when we joined them on the Cape for the first time as a married couple. It was August, a week after we'd returned from our honeymoon, and boiling hot. Granny had moved out of the master suite while we were gone. *You're the lady of the house now,* she told me, over drinks upon our arrival, and I thought I detected a note of triumph in her voice.

At the time, I'd also thought I must be mistaken.

You're in charge, she went on. *Do things exactly as you like. I won't stick my nose in, I promise, unless you need a little help from time to time.*

I spot Frank, tucking up the boat in the shelter of the breakwater, a couple of hundred yards down the shore. At least I assume it's Frank; the boat is certainly his, the biggest one, the tallest mast. At one point he meant to train seriously for the America's Cup. I don't know what became of that one. Too much career in the way, I suppose, too much serious business to get on with. There are two of them, Frank and someone else, tying the *Sweet Christina* up to her buoy. No use calling for him, at this distance.

I draw in a last smoke, crush out the cigarette on the windowsill, and check my watch. Five thirty-five, and no one's getting ready for drinks. Everyone's out enjoying the beach, the sun, the sand. Below me, Pepper reclines on a beach chair, bikini glowing, head scarf fluttering, every inch of her slathered in oil. Pepper has olive skin, so she can do things like that; she can bare her shapely coconut-oiled limbs to the sun and come out golden. She's not hiding her cigarette, either:

it's out there in plain sight of men, women, and children. Along with a thermos of whatever.

Everybody's having a sun-swept good time.

Well, good for them. That's what the Cape is for, isn't it? That's why the Hardcastles bought this place, back in the early twenties, when beach houses were becoming all the rage. Why they keep it. Why they gather together here, year after year, eating the same lobster rolls and baking under the same sweaty sun.

Just before I duck back into the bedroom, a primal human instinct turns my head to the left, and I catch sight of a face staring up from the sand.

For an instant, my heart crashes. Giddy. Terrified. *Caught*.

But it's only Tom. Constance's husband, Tom, a doctoral student in folk studies—whatever that was—at Tufts and now at leisure for the whole lazy length of the summer, with nothing to do but collect his trust fund check, tweak his thesis, and get Constance pregnant again. He sits in the dunes near the house, smoking and disgruntled, and that disgruntled face just so happens to be observing me as if I'm the very folk whereof he studies. He's probably seen my unfastened dress. He's probably seen the cigarette. He'll probably tattle on me to Constance.

Little weasel.

I smile and wave. He salutes me with his cigarette.

I withdraw and pretzel myself before the mirror to wiggle up the zipper on my own. (A snug bodice, miniature sleeves just off the shoulder: really, where was a husband when you needed him? Oh, of course: tying up his yacht.) I swipe on my lipstick, blot, and swipe again. My hair isn't quite right; I suppose I need a cut. So hard to remember these things, out here on the Cape. It's too late for curlers. I wind the ends around my fingers, hold, release. Repeat. Fluff. The room lies silent around me. Even Percy has dozed quietly off.

As I finger my way around my head, the face in the mirror seems to be frowning in me. The way my mother—passing me by one evening on her way to someone's party—warned me never to do, because my skin might freeze that way.

Wrinkles. The bitter enemy of a woman's happiness.

Frank bursts through the door, smiling and wind whipped, at ten minutes to six, a moment too late to fasten my diamond and aquamarine necklace for me.

"Had a nice sail?" I say icily.

"The best. Cap joined me. Just like old times, when we were kids. Went all the way around the point and back. Record time, I'll bet. Goddamn, that man can sail." The highest possible praise. He blows straight past me to the bathroom.

"Even with one leg?" I call out.

"It worked for Bluebeard, didn't it?" He laughs at his own joke.

I screw on the last earring and give the hair a last pat. "I'm needed downstairs. Can you manage by yourself?"

Frank walks out of the bathroom to rummage in his wardrobe. "Fine, fine." His head pokes around the corner of the door. "Need help with your zipper or anything?"

My shoes sit next to the door, aquamarine satin to match my dress and jewelry, two-inch heels. I slip my feet into one and the other. The added height goes straight to my head.

"No," I say. "I don't need any help."

On my way downstairs, I stop to check on Pepper.

"Come in," she says in reply to my knock, and I push open the door to find her belting her robe over her body. I have the impression, based on nothing but instinct, that she's been standing naked in front of the mirror in the corner. It's something Pepper would do, admiring her figure, which (like that of our youngest sister Vivian) belongs to a different species of figures from mine: tall, curved like a violin, colored by the same honey varnish. It's the kind of figure that inspires men to maddened adoration, especially when she drapes those violin curves as she usually does, in short tangerine dresses and heeled slippers.

All at once, I feel flat and pale and straight-hipped in my aquamarine satin, too small, insignificant. A prissed-up girl, instead of a woman: a rigid frigid little lady. What's happened to me? My God.

"Aren't you dressed yet?" I ask.

"I've just come in from the beach. So hard to leave. I haven't lain out on a beach in ages."

"All work and no play?"

"Oh, you know me." She laughs. "It's killing me, this crazy Washington life. It's so lovely to be idle again. I know you're used to it, but . . ." She turns away in the middle of an eloquent shrug and looks out the window.

"Not that idle."

"A lady of leisure, just like Mums. I can't tell you how jealous I am." She stretches her arms above her head, right there before the window, not jealous at all. Nor in any hurry to dress herself for the party, apparently.

I cast a significant glance at my watch. "I'm on my way down, actually. Can I help you with anything? Zipper?"

She turns back.

"No, thanks. I can manage. There's not much to zip, anyway." Another low and throaty laugh, and then a sniff, incredulous. "Tiny! Have you been *smoking*?"

As she might say *swinging*.

I consider lying. "Just one," I say, flicking a disdainful hand.

"Good Lord. I never thought I'd see the day. Poor thing. I guess this family of yours would drive anyone to debauchery. Don't worry." She zips her lips. "I won't say a word to Mums. Is Major Gorgeous here yet?"

"Nobody's here yet. We still have a few minutes."

"You sound awfully cold, Tiny. Maybe you should sit out on the beach for a few minutes and warm up your blood. It works wonders, believe me."

I gaze at my sister's playful eyes, tilted alluringly at the corners. Her curving red mouth. The old Pepper, now that it's just the two of us, alone in her room. Her claws, my skin. We do so much better when there are others around. Someone else's family to distract us, someone else's irreversible birth order: flawless first, naughty second, locked in timeless conflict.

At my silence, Pepper pulls the ends of her robe more closely together. "So. I saw your husband and the major out there on the water, sailing a boat. Did you get your *après-midi* after all? It must have been a quick one. Not that those aren't sometimes the best."

"Actually, I had another miscarriage eight days ago," I say. "I don't know if Mums told you. So, no. No *après-midi* for a few more weeks yet, unfortunately. Quick or not."

Pepper's arms uncross at last. Her tip-tilted eyes—the dark blue Schuyler eyes she shares with Vivian, except that hers are a shade or two lighter—go round with sympathy. "Oh, Tiny! Of course I didn't know. I'm so sorry. What a bitch I am."

I turn to the door. "It's all right. Really."

"My big fat mouth . . ."

"You have a lovely mouth, Pepper. I'm going downstairs now to make sure everything's ready. Let me know if you need anything."

"Tiny—"

I close the door carefully behind me.

D ownstairs, everything is perfect, exactly as I left it three quarters of an hour ago. The vases are full of hyacinths—my first order, as lady of the compound, was nothing short of rebellion: I changed the house flower from lily to hyacinth, never mind the financial ruin when hyacinths were out of season—and the side tables are lined with coasters. All the windows and French doors have been thrown open, heedless of bugs, because the heat's been building all day, hot layered on hot, and the Big House has no air-conditioning. Mrs. Crane and the two maids are busy in the kitchen, filling trays with Ritz crackers and crab dip. If this were a party for outside guests, I'd have hired a man from town, put him in a tuxedo, and had him pour drinks from the bar. But this is only family, and Frank and his father can do it themselves.

Frank's father. He rises from his favorite chair in the library, immaculate in a white dinner jacket and black tie, his graying hair polished into silver. "Good evening, Tiny. You look marvelous, as always."

I lean in for his kiss. "So do you, Mr. Hardcastle. Enjoying your last moment of peace?"

He holds up his cigar, his glass of Scotch. "Guilty as charged. Anybody here yet?"

"I think we'll be running late. I stuck my head out the window at five thirty, and nobody was stirring from the beach."

"It's a hot day."

"Yes, it is. At least it gives us a few moments to relax before everyone arrives."

"Indeed. Can I get you a drink?" He moves to the cabinet.

"Yes, please. Vodka martini. Dry, olive."

He moves competently about the bottles and shakers, mixing my martini. You might be wondering why Frank's mother isn't the lady of the house instead of me, organizing its dinner parties, decreeing the house flower, and you might suspect she's passed away, though of course you're too tactful to ask. Well, you're wrong. In fact, the Hardcastles divorced when Frank was five or six, I can't remember exactly, but it was a terrible scandal and crushed Mr. Hardcastle's own political ambitions in a stroke. You can't run for Senate if you're divorced, after all, or at least you couldn't back in the forties. The torch was quietly tossed across the generation to my husband. Oh, and the ex–Mrs. Hardcastle? I've never been told why they divorced, and her name isn't spoken around the exquisite hyacinth air of the Big House. I've never even met her. She lives in New York. Frank visits her sometimes, in her exile, when he's there on business.

There is a distant ring of the doorbell. The first guests. I glance up at the antique ormolu clock above the mantel. Five fifty-nine.

"Thank you." I accept the martini from my father-in-law and turn to leave. "If you'll excuse me. It looks like somebody in this family has a basic respect for punctuality, after all."

I nearly reach the foyer before it occurs to me to wonder why a Hardcastle would bother to ring the doorbell of the Big House, and by that time it's too late.

Caspian Harrison stands before me in his dress uniform, handing his hat to Mrs. Crane. He looks up at my entrance, my shocked halt, and all I can see is the scar above his left eyebrow, wrapping around the curve of his temple, which was somehow hidden on the television screen by the angle or the bright sunshine of the White House Rose Garden.

A few drops of vodka spill over the rim of the glass and onto my index finger.

"Major Harrison." I lick away the spilled vodka and smile my best hostess smile. "Welcome home."

Caspian, 1964

When Cap arrived at the coffee shop the next morning, nine thirty sharp, the place was jammed. Em rushed by with an armful of greasy plates.

"What gives?" he called after her.

"Who knows? There's one booth left in the corner, if you move fast."

He looked around and found it, the booth in the corner, and moved fast across the sweaty bacon-and-toast air to sling himself and his camera bag along one cushion. Em scooted over and set a cup of coffee and a glass of orange juice on the table, almost without stopping. He drank the coffee first, hot and crisp. You had to hand it to Boylan's. Best coffee in Back Bay, if you liked the kind of coffee you could stand your spoon in.

He leaned against the cushion and watched the hustle-bustle. A lot of regulars this morning, a few new faces. Em and Patty cross and recross the linoleum in patterns of chaotic efficiency, hair wisping, stockings sturdy. Outside, the pavement still gleamed with the rain that had poured down last night, shattering the heat wave in a biblical deluge, flooding through the gutters and into the bay. Maybe that was why Boylan's booths were so full this morning. That charge of energy when the cool air bursts at last through your open window and interrupts your lethargy. Blows apart your accustomed pattern.

"What'll it be, Cap? The usual?" Em stood at the edge of the table, holding a coffeepot and a plate of steaming pancakes. They had an uncomplicated relationship, he and Em; no menus required.

"Well, now . . ."

"If you love me, Cap, make it snappy."

"Bacon, four eggs over easy, lots of toast."

"Hungry?" She was already dashing off.

"You could"—Em was gone—"say that." Across the crowd, someone dropped a cup loudly into its saucer, making him jolt. He converted the movement into a stretch—nothing to see here, folks, no soldier making an idiot of himself—and plucked the paperback from his camera bag, but before he could settle himself on the page the goddamned bells jangled again, clawing on his nerves like a black cat, and he jerked toward the door.

His chest expanded and deflated.

Well, well. Jane Doe. Of all the girls.

She took off her sunglasses to reveal an expression of utter, utter dismay. (With another girl he might simply have said *total dismay*.) Her shiny dark hair bobbed about her ears as she looked one way and the other, searching for a booth around which to enact her invisible force field. She wore a berry-red dress, sleeveless, a white cardigan pulled around her shoulders. Her face glowed with recent exercise, making him think instantly of sex (vigorous, sweaty morning sex on white sheets, while the early sunlight poured through the window, and a long hot shower afterward that might just end up in more sex, if luck were a lady, and if the lady could still walk).

Em passed by. Miss Doe tapped her on the elbow and asked her a question; Em replied with a helpless shrug and moved on.

Miss Doe's elegant eyebrows converged to a cranky point. She had expected better than this. To her left, a sandy-haired boy about four years old started up a tantrum, a real grand mal, no holds barred, a thrashing, howling, fit-to-be-tied fit over a glass of spilled milk. In the same instant, the door opened behind her, and a large man barged through, smack between Miss Doe's white cardiganed shoulder blades. She staggered forward, clutching her pocketbook, while the man maneuvered around her and called for Em in a loud Boston twang.

At which point, Cap raised his hand into the crowded air.

Not a wave. Not a beckoning of the fingers. Just a single hand, lifted up above the sea of heads, the way he might signal noiselessly to another soldier in the jungle. I'm here, buddy. At your back. Never fear.

Miss Doe wasn't a soldier. She saw his hand and ducked her head swiftly, pretending she hadn't noticed. But an instant later, her eyes returned to his corner. He lowered the hand and shrugged, pretending he didn't care.

But his heart was bouncing off his rib cage, and it wasn't just the crash of the coffee cup and the jingle of bells. Miss Doe was slender and gently curved, almost boyish, not his preferred figure at all, and still he couldn't remove his mind from the belly of that berry-red dress, the tiny pleats at her tiny waist, the rise of her breasts below the straight edge of her collar. The pink curve of her lips, slightly parted. The suggestive flush of her cheeks. Flushed with what? Did she spend the night with her fiancé? Did she shed her immaculate clothes for him, her immaculate hair and lipstick? Did she let down her force field and allow him inside?

What was she like, inside her force field?

She lifted an uncertain eyebrow. He held up his hands before his chest, palms out, and sent her his best crooked smile, the one that never failed. No threat here. Just helping a girl out, the goodness of his heart.

Miss Doe hoisted her pocketbook up her shoulder, the same gesture as before, and walked poker-faced toward his booth. He liked the way she moved, sinuous and gymnastic in her matching berry-red kitten heels, not the usual mincing gait you saw around town. Girls with no stride at all, no swing, no natural grace.

You could always see the real girl in her walk, couldn't you? The one thing she couldn't make over.

She arrived at the booth, smelling of Chanel.

"Caspian," he said, without standing up.

She slid in across from him, holding her dress beneath her. She settled her pocketbook on the seat, well away from his grasp, and folded her hands on the edge of the table. Her engagement ring glittered just so in the yellow light from the hanging lamp. Mother of God. Three carats at least. Almost as big as his grandmother's rock.

"Tiny," she said.

"Tiny?" he said. "Is that a nickname?"

She fixed him a steely one. "Yes, it is."

She studied the menu carefully, considered each item, and raised her head at last to order her usual coffee and an apricot Danish. Em hid a smile and scooted obediently off, tucking her pencil between her ear and her graying brown hair. She scooted right on past the boy with the tantrum and his harried mother, who cajoled and scolded in alternating beats.

"Please go ahead," Tiny said, gesturing to Cap's plate. "Don't let it go cold on my account."

"I won't." He picked up his fork with one hand and his paperback with the other, and commenced—against every instinct, ground in him since childhood—to shovel and read, having rolled the cover carefully around the back so she couldn't see the title.

"I appreciate your offering me a seat, Caspian," she said. Elocution lessons, no doubt at all. The vowels so terribly well-rounded, the consonants crisp enough to shatter on contact. That kind of expensive vocal delivery didn't just occur by accident.

He loaded his fork with eggs, gestured prong first to the paperback, and said, "Sorry. Do you mind?"

Her pink lips compressed into a straight line. "I beg your pardon."

He pretended to read amid the fracas. Tiny tapped her finger on the edge of the table and glanced back at the screaming boy.

"She should take him outside," she said softly. Not the way most women would say something like that, all pursed lips and disapproval. Curious. You'd think the impeccable Miss Doe would regard the mothers of misbehaving children in the same class as criminals.

"What's that?"

"She should take him outside. The boy. He'll settle down sooner without an audience, where it's calm."

He shrugged and turned his eyes back to the paperback.

Tiny's coffee and Danish clattered down before her. She added a dainty few grains of sugar, a precious few drops of cream.

"Refill, Cap?" asked Em.

He looked up. Em winked and tilted her head at the berry-red figure across from him, sipping her coffee.

Cap held out his cup and pointed his thumb at Tiny's Danish. "Yes, ma'am. And I'll have one of those, too."

"Well, and who's the hungry one today? Exercising again?"

"Yes, ma'am. Fit for service."

Em set down the coffeepot on the edge of the table. She was the kind of waitress who could ignore the breakfast rush when it suited her. He liked that about her. "C'mon, then," she said. "What did you do this morning?"

Ran eight miles. Lifted dumbbells in the attic. Climbed the stairs, wearing his pack, bottom to top, seventy-five seconds flat. Five times.

He shrugged. "Some running, some weights."

Em stuck out her hand and tried to measure his left bicep with her hand. "Flex for me, Cap."

He obliged.

"That's not bad. They grow 'em big where you come from, huh?"

"Just elbow grease, ma'am. Works every time."

Em winked again and turned to Tiny, who sat there razor straight, face frozen in a prim pink smile. Em nudged the nearby air with her coffeepot. "You watch yourself with him, ma'am. He'll charm your socks off if you're not careful."

"Oh, don't worry about me."

Cap returned his attention to his book. Tiny sipped her coffee, and when Em arrived back with Cap's apricot Danish she asked for a fork, so she could eat her own, which she did in small bites, each one passed gracefully from her plate to her mouth, as if she were eating lunch in the Oak Room at the Copley Plaza.

Cap pointed his forefinger at a remaining crumb. "You going to finish that?"

"Yes, as a matter of fact."

"Aha. So you're hungry, too, only you won't admit it. Reducing for the wedding?"

"I'm not reducing."

"When's the big day?"

"June." She said it reluctantly, as if she were worried he'd use the information against her.

"Oh, really? Right around the corner, then. My cousin's getting married in June."

"How lovely."

"He's a lucky man, your fiancé."

"I like to think so."

Across the room, the toddler was wailing now, down on the floor with his arms and legs waving. *Want more syrup! Want more syrup!* And the mother hushing, flushing, red-faced, helpless, trying to peel his boneless body off the linoleum.

Cap tapped the corner of his mouth with his finger. "You've got a bit of apricot jam, there."

The tip of her tongue flashed out, remembered its manners, and disappeared. She picked up her napkin and dabbed instead.

"Nope, the other corner. Here, I've got it." Before she could react, he reached across and swept away the dot from Tiny's mouth. Her lip was softer than he expected. He licked the sweet jam from his finger and smiled at her shocked expression. "You look as if you've never been on a date with a man before."

"This isn't a date!" she gasped, and touched her ring with her thumb.

"Hey," he said gently, losing the wicked smile. "Relax. I'm just playing with you a bit. Tiny." He tried out her name on his tongue, and it tasted good. "Come on. You've seen me every day for a month. Just an ordinary guy, eating his eggs. You can relax, all right? Just relax. Not going to bite, I swear."

Her brow worried. Her lips parted, and then squeezed back into that tense pink line.

"Let's put it this way," he said. "If I were going to make a move on you, I'd have done it last week, when you were wearing that pink number, the one with the . . ." He gestured to his neck.

"Lace." She exhaled audibly, a whoosh of apricot air. And she smiled. And holy God, that smile, like she'd just swallowed the sun. Where had she been hiding that smile?

He smiled back. "You see? One of the good guys."

"All right, Caspian." She held out her hand. "Let's start again."

He set down his cup and reached for the handshake that would start things all over again, down the road he wanted to take her. But in the instant before his fingers touched hers, the bells jangled furiously, like they meant business this time, and a man in a dark suit walked through the door, drew a gun from his pocket, and stepped to the register at the front.

"Hands in the air! Everyone!"

The little boy stopped crying midwail.

Tiny, 1966

aspian Harrison holds my outstretched hand. "Thanks. You *can* call me Caspian. Or just Cap, like the rest of the family."

He looks the same. Of course he does. Men like him aren't made for changing. The taut face, the pale green eyes with the serious creases at the corners. The dark hair shorn to a bristle, emphasizing the bones of his face.

Except for the scar. Though my eyes remain locked politely with his, I still see it at the periphery, long and thick, pink against his tan. (Where *had* he found a tan like that, after all those months in the hospital? Or has the sun of Southeast Asia burned permanently into his subderma?)

The thing about faces, though, is that when your emotions are tangled up in a person, your memory can't quite draw up a picture of him. You can't remember exactly what he looks like. It's a scientific fact; I read it somewhere. Something to do with the neural connections of the brain. So as Caspian stands before me, two years later, the very familiarity of his image shocks me. *It's you!* says the startled jump of my pulse, remembering, and yet the absolute warrior rawness of his beauty still shaves my breath, as if I'm observing him for the first time, that very first time I walked into Boylan's Coffee Shop, all innocent and unsuspecting, clutching my pocketbook, and there he sat in a booth in the corner, exotic and feral, eating his eggs.

I remember the photograph now sitting in an envelope at the bottom of my underwear drawer. Not the wisest place to hide something like that, I realize now. My fingers grip the sides of the glass. For an instant, his face blurs in front of me, as if the resentment and anger have formed a film atop my eyeballs.

And then he comes back into focus.

"Caspian. Of course. Come in. You didn't need to ring the doorbell."

"I thought I should. It's been a while."

I motion in the direction of the library. "Would you like a drink? Frank's father is standing by. You're the first to arrive."

"Sorry. Army habit."

"Yes, of course."

We stand there suspended for an instant, not quite sure what to say. I'm afraid I'll burst out with some question about the photograph. I'm afraid I won't, that I'll just let this awful thing dangle unspoken between us.

Well, maybe I should. Maybe if I ignore it long enough, leave it in its drawer upstairs, untouched, unspoken, it will disappear. It will never have existed to begin with.

A hand falls on my shoulder. Caspian's eyes shift to the right.

"Cap! You're early!" says my husband, Frank.

"I'm on time, actually. Which is early, in this crowd."

"You can take the boy out of the army . . ." Frank shakes his head and applies a kiss to my cheek. "I see you've finally met my lovely wife."

Caspian's gaze travels from my cheek to Frank's hand on my shoulder, and finally to Frank himself. He smiles. Not a happy smile. "The pleasure was mine."

I raise the glass to my lips for a sip that turns into a gulp. My nose bumps against the olive. I'll say, I think.

"Wow," says Frank. "Did I miss something?"

I realize I've said it aloud.

"I'll have that drink now, if you don't mind," Caspian says quietly.

His voice is the same, too, formal and easy at the same time, rumbling naturally from his throat. Two years ago, dizzy with the newness of infatuation, I had adored that voice. What wouldn't you confess, to a voice like that? What wouldn't you reveal of yourself? No, I can't blame that old Tiny, that young Tiny, two years younger, two years fresher and so damply naïve.

I turn for the library. "Of course. Right through here."

I leave Caspian in the library with my father-in-law, drink safely in hand, talking about Vietnam and the politics of war by proxy, and by this time the house is filling up at last. Frank pulls me aside and wraps his hand around my elbow.

"What was that all about?" he asks.

"What was *what* all about?"

"Between you and Cap. Did he try something?"

We're standing in a shadowed corner, so it's hard to see Frank's expression. His brows are down low over his blue eyes, which doesn't happen often. I put on my cheerful face. "Why, no. Just the usual hello."

"Because he can be a bit funny sometimes. He's been away awhile, and—well, you know." He delivers the *you know* in a masculine growl that runs the gamut of possibility.

I edge my body to the right, so that the light from the opposite window finds my husband's face, and I can determine whether he's angry or worried. Whether this is my fault or Caspian's fault. What exactly he means by that *you know*.

"Are you saying your cousin can't be trusted?" I ask.

"I'm just saying he can be a little direct. Army guy."

"Is this something to do with last night? When you went out?"

Frank pauses. "What do you mean by that?"

"I mean, did something happen last night that made you think he couldn't be trusted with women? You said, in the bedroom just now, you said that you could always tell about a man, on a night out."

I don't know quite what I'm fishing for. From the look on Frank's face, which has shifted from concern to wariness, he has a better idea than I do.

"Look," he says. "He's a bachelor. Red-blooded. You can read all you want between the lines of that. I just want to make sure he was a gentleman."

I smile. "Darling, I was just making a little joke back there. I guess I need to work on my delivery. If Pepper had said the same thing—*I'll say*—you'd have thought she was just flirting."

His brow flattens out, his smile returns. "All right, all right. I just want to make sure you're okay."

"I'm more than okay. Perfectly capable of fending off ungentlemanly behavior at cocktails."

"I know you are. My perfectly capable wife."

I reach up and brush his lapel with my thumb. "Don't worry about me. I won't let you down."

He kisses the thumb and pats my behind. "You never do. Now go spread some of that charm around."

Over his shoulder, from the additional height of my two-inch heels, I see a familiar face part from the crowd and turn in our direction. The words *bachelor* and *red-blooded* float in my head. *Read between the lines*, Frank said, whatever that meant. And I think I do. I think I do know what that means. After all, Caspian *is* a bachelor, isn't he? An attractive, red-blooded bachelor, strong and scarred and so on, tall and wounded, the kind that women hang all over at nightclubs and cocktail parties.

Well, who can blame them? Here *I* am, a wife and hostess, a straight young pillar of society, and my face warms right up when Caspian turns to me. My blood rises obediently under the touch of Caspian's attention.

I wrap my empty hand—the left hand, crowned by a triumphant engagement ring and wedding band—around the back of Frank's neck. I pull him down for a lingering kiss.

He lifts his mouth away, bemused. "What was that for?"

"For calling me charming." I press the tender crease of his lips with the index finger of my right hand, the hand holding the martini.

The vodka hits fast and hard. I step outside for a breath of the fresh stuff, and nearly stumble over Kitty, Constance's daughter, who sits cross-legged on the terrace, staring at the wall.

I catch her shoulder just in time. "Oh, I'm sorry, darling. Are you okay?"

"Yes." Her arms are crossed.

I bend down next to her. "Why aren't you over by the pool, with the other kids?"

She shakes her head.

"Would you like me to get Mommy for you?"

She presses her lips together and shakes her head again.

"Okay, then." I ease myself down next to her on the stones, careful not to snag my stockings. "We'll just sit here."

We stare companionably at the beach, where the seagulls seem to have found an object of dispute, some rotting marine carcass or another. The air fills with acrid squawks. Vicious things, seagulls. I wiggle my toes inside my satin shoes and wonder if I could possibly take them off. (The shoes, not the toes.)

"What's that smell?" says Kitty.

I cup my hands over my mouth and puff out a breath. "It's my martini, I think."

"It's yucky."

"Yes. Yes, it is, isn't it?"

"Then why do you drink them?"

"Oh, it's just what grown-ups do, I guess. We do a lot of silly things. Maybe we just wish we were still kids, like you."

She chews on this for a moment. "Mommy drinks martinis."

"Does she?"

"She drinks them in the nighttime. Then she takes her pills and sometimes she gets mad at Daddy." She says this in the same matter-of-fact way she might describe a game of marbles with her cousins.

"How do you know this, honey? Shouldn't you be in bed at nighttime?"

"Sometimes I need a glass of water."

I draw an invisible circle on the stone next to my foot and think of Mums and Daddy, sometimes getting along and sometimes not, lubricating the Fifth Avenue evenings with vodka and courtesy. "Well, you know. Grown-ups fight sometimes."

"One time they took off their clothes and Mommy kissed Daddy's wee-wee."

I open my mouth and nothing comes out.

"Nancy wouldn't let me play with her horse." She starts to cry.

"Oh, honey. Is that why you're sitting here, all by yourself?"

Sniff. "Yes. She said I couldn't play with it because I had germs."

"We all have germs. It's okay."

"Do you have germs?"

"Yes. We all do. I think Nancy just didn't want to share her horse."

"That's not very nice."

"No, it isn't." I rise on my knees and take her hand. "Let's go over to the pool with the other kids, and I'll tell Nancy she has to share her toys with her cousins."

"Okay." She jumps up and tows me along the terrace at a skip. The afternoon sun lights her hair like a nimbus. "It's a white horse with black dots on its bottom."

"An Appaloosa."

She swings our linked hands. "Sometimes Daddy kisses Mommy's pagina."

"Her *what?*"

Kitty chants, "Boys have penises, girls have paginas."

"Oh. *V*agina, honey. With a *V*."

"Vagina, vagina!" she shouts, all the way to the pool, while I try to shush her. Probably not hard enough.

When I return to the party, fully refreshed, Pepper has just descended the stairs in splendor, her bosom not quite overflowing from an iced violet dress cut on an extremely expensive bias that ends a good four inches above her knees. She looks even more delicious than usual.

Delicious, that's the word for Pepper. If I were a man, I'd want to gobble her up and lick my chops afterward. Nature's just devious that way, giving Pepper all the sex appeal, as if to lock us in our preordained places and watch, breathless, to see if we can break loose.

To the Hardcastles, Pepper is a rare dish, never before seen at the table. *This is my younger sister Pepper,* I say, by way of introduction, presenting her with garnish.

Why do they call you Pepper? the men usually ask.

She usually winks. *Because I'm that bad.*

As a rule, the women don't see the satirical curve of her lip when she says this, and they harden up instantly into those frozen polite expressions you get when a wind-and-surf clan of females like the Hardcastles—no makeup, horsey leather faces—encounters the cultivated variety.

I watch Kitty's mother, Constance, tighten her mouth at Pepper, and I realize in that instant that I have more in common with my sisters than I realize, and that I've really never liked Constance at all. Constance, who threw an aggressive baseball into my unsuspecting stomach that first summer, soon after I knew for certain I was pregnant, and who apologized too profusely afterward. *I should have known better,* she said, shaking her head, and what could I do but accept her apology and tell her it was nothing? The first miscarriage began soon after, but of course I couldn't blame Constance for that. It was an accident, after all.

I should have kept my eyes on the ball.

The Hardcastle *men,* on the other hand. Well, well. *They* interpret Pepper exactly the way they want to, don't they? Men always do. Pepper's happy with this arrangement. She's never had much use for women. Even when we were kids, her friends were mostly boys. Our sister Vivian's the only glittering double X wiggling her shapely fins in the sea of Y chromosomes surrounding Pepper, and maybe that's only because they're sisters, united in their disdain for me, the uptight and obedient Tiny, no fun at all.

"Honestly, Constance—it's Constance, isn't it? There's so many of you, and you all look alike!"

Constance's mouth screws into an anus.

I have to bite my lip to hold back a hysterical giggle, because Pepper's exactly right. They do look alike, the Hardcastles. There's just this look, a distinctive shape of the eyes, the wild thickness of the hair, the relation of nose to mouth to cheekbones. (Caspian, perhaps, is the only exception—in him, the Harrison genes seem to have triumphed.) On the men of the family, the Look is dashing and gloriously photogenic, redolent of football games and windswept sailboats, apple pie and loving your mother. On the women, the proportion is wrong somehow. Coarse, a bit goggle-eyed. *Handsome* is the best you can say of any of them.

Or is that ungenerous of me?

Pepper doesn't care whether she's ungenerous or not. She doesn't care that Constance's poor mouth is about to grow a hemorrhoid.

What would that be like, not to give a damn what the other women think?

I observe Pepper, whose head is tossed back in laughter, exposing the peachy column of her throat to the dying afternoon light. (We're all out on the terrace now; the house is really too hot.) Pepper, in the very throes of not giving a damn.

It would be fucking wonderful, wouldn't it?

Yes. It *would* be wonderful. For a short hour or two, a long time ago, it *was* wonderful. It was freedom.

I swallow the last of my drink and head into the kitchen to give the orders for dinner.

Dinner, I'll have you know, is a smashing success, right up until the point when the fight breaks out.

Emboldened by two expert martinis—I usually drink only one—and smothered by the persistent stuffiness indoors, I order the dining room table to be brought out through the French doors onto the terrace, overlooking the ocean. The last-minute change rattles Mrs. Crane, but with a few soothing words and the assistance of the doughty Hardcastle men in dragging around the furniture, the table and chairs are soon set, every fork and wineglass in place, candles lit, bowls of priceless purple-blue hyacinths arranged at even intervals down the center of the tablecloth.

"It's brilliant!" says Pepper. She floats to her seat. The breeze is picking up, rustling her hair.

"Oh, I'm sure the bugs are delighted." Granny Hardcastle drops into the chair at Frank's left and casts me a look.

I turn to Mrs. Crane. "See if Fred can dig out the tiki torches from the pool house, please." Fred's the groundskeeper. "I think they're on the right-hand side, near the spare umbrellas."

Mrs. Crane is always happy to score a point against Granny. "Right away, Mrs. Hardcastle. Shall I tell the girls to start serving?"

"Yes, please. Thank you, Mrs. Crane."

The maids start serving, and Frank pours the wine. I take my seat at the opposite end, and Cap, waiting for this signal with the other men, lowers himself into the chair at Frank's right with only the slightest stiffness. Pepper has somehow negotiated the seat to Caspian's right, directly across from Frank's father, and before long the torches are lit, the bugs have scattered, the empty wine bottles are piling up at the corner of the terrace, and Pepper and Caspian have struck up the kind of rapport of which dinner party legends are made.

Well, why shouldn't they? They're both unattached. Both attractive and red-blooded. Bachelor and fashionable Single Girl.

"How long is your sister planning to stay?" asks Constance, from two seats down on my left.

I plunge my spoon into the vichyssoise. "Why, I don't know. Wouldn't it be lovely if she stayed all summer?"

Constance turns a little pale.

"Sadly, however, she works as an assistant to a certain senator in Washington, and I'm afraid he can't do without her for long." I lean forward, as if in conspiracy. "Though I suppose that possibly qualifies as aiding and comforting the enemy, doesn't it?"

From the other side of the house comes the sound of raucous laughter. The younger Hardcastles are eating dinner by the pool, under the supervision of a pair of gossiping nannies, and the teenagers have quite possibly found the stash of beers and liquors in the pool house bar. I motion to Mrs. Crane. "Could you ask Fred to keep watch over the young ones at the pool? Perhaps lock up the pool house?"

She nods and disappears.

Through the soup course and the appetizer, the scene is one of convivial amity, ripe with wholesome feeling, perfumed with hyacinth, lubricated by a crisp white wine and the warm undercurrents of a family welcoming home its prodigal son. The breeze surges in from the Atlantic, soft with humidity. The tomato aspic is a perfect balance of sweetness and acidity, the shrimp firm and white pink. To my right, Frank's handsome younger brother Louis keeps up a stream of earthy conversation. To my left, Pepper's laughter rises to the pale evening sky. Nearby, Constance's diamonds glitter atop her leathery collarbone, having caught the light from a nearby torch.

I look at her and think, *pagina*.

The shrimp and aspic are cleared away. The bottles of red wine are placed, already open, on the table. I signal to Louis at my right, and Louis signals to Frank's cousin Monty, across the table, and together they pour out the wine, one by one, filling every glass.

When they're done, Frank rises to his feet, clinks his glass with his fork, and smiles at me down the long reach of the Hardcastle table.

"Ladies. Gentleman. In-laws." He grins at Pepper. "Outlaws."

"Hear, hear," says Louis.

"First of all, I'd like to thank my lovely wife, Tiny, for arranging this wonderful dinner here tonight, this dinner that brings us all together, decently clothed for once. Tiny?" He picks up his glass and gestures in my direction.

I pick up my glass and gesture back.

"Hear, hear," says Pepper. "To the miraculous Tiny!"

The chorus of agreement. The crystalline clinking. The works.

"And now, for the real business of the evening. Not quite two years ago, the man seated next to me, whom we all know, though he wasn't around as much when we were all kids, army brat that he was . . ."

Caspian turns his shorn head and says something to Frank, something in a low voice that I can't quite pick up at this distance, though Pepper tilts back her head and laughs throatily.

"All right, all right," says Frank. "Anyway, this kid grew up into a soldier while we were all going to law school, to medical school, and it turns out he's got a lot of Hardcastle underneath that unfortunate Harrison exterior. . . ."

Another muttered comment from Caspian, and this time all the men around him laugh, though Pepper—yes, *Pepper*—actually looks a little mystified.

"Anyway, as I said, and seriously now, while we were home, stateside, safe and sound, our cousin Cap here was fighting for his life, for *our* lives and freedom and way of life, way off in the jungles of Vietnam. Fighting against the enemies of freedom, fighting against those who would see America and all it stands for wiped from the face of the earth. While we gentlemen were safe abed, to paraphrase, he put himself in danger every day, under fire every day, and one day last year all hell broke loose, and—well, we all know what happened that day. As of yesterday, the whole country knows what happened that day."

The last traces of jocularity dissolve into the evening air, which has just begun to take on the bluish tinge of twilight.

I look down at my empty plate. My shadow is outlined on the gossamer porcelain.

"Cap," says Frank gravely, from the other side of the table, and I close my eyes and see an unscarred Caspian, a pair of trustworthy shoulders in a shaft of May sunshine, drinking coffee from a plain white cup. "Cap, there's no way to thank you for what you did that day. What you sacrificed. Medals are great, but they're just a piece of metal, a piece of paper, a few speeches, and then everyone goes home and moves on to the next thing. We just want you to know—we, Cap, your family—we love you. We're proud of you. We're here tonight because of you, and whenever you need us, we'll band up for you. The whole gang of us. Because that's what we do, in this family. Cap? Come on, stand up here, buddy."

I force myself to look up, because you can't have Franklin Hardcastle's wife and hostess staring down at her plate while Franklin Hardcastle polishes off the toast to the guest of honor.

Frank stands at the head of the table, and his arm climbs up and over the trustworthy shoulders of his cousin, who stares unsmiling and unfocused at a point somewhere behind me. "Cap. To you." Frank clinks Caspian's glass.

The chorus starts up again, *hear hear* and *clink clink*, and then Louis stands up and claps, and we all stand up and clap, until Caspian raises his wide brown hand and hushes us with a single palm.

"Thank you for coming here tonight," he says, all gravel and syrup, vibrating my toes in their square-tipped aquamarine shoes. "Thank you, Tiny, for the superb dinner. Thanks for the speech, Frank, though I really don't deserve it. We're all just doing what we have to do out there. Nothing heroic about it. The real heroes are the men I left behind."

He breaks away from Frank's encircling arm and sits back down in his chair.

For some reason, I cannot breathe.

There are twenty-two people seated around the baronial dining room table of the Big House, and all of them are quiet: so quiet you can hear the teenagers squealing secrets by the pool, you can hear the bugs singing in the dune grass.

Until Constance's husband, Tom, throws his napkin into his plate.

"Goddamn it," he says. "I can't take it anymore."

"Tom!" snaps Constance.

"No. Not this time." He turns and tilts his head, so he can see down the row of Hardcastle cousins and in-laws to where Caspian sits, staring at a bowl of hyacinths, as if he hasn't heard a thing. "I'm sorry, I know you lost a leg and everything, and you probably believe in what you're doing, God help you, but it's fucking *wrong* to award a medal in *my* name—because *I'm* a citizen of this country, too, man. I'm an American, too—award a fucking *medal* for invading another country, a third world country, and killing its women and children just because they happen to want a different way of life than fucking capitalism."

The silence, frozen and horrible, locks us in place.

"I see," says Caspian, absorbed in the hyacinths.

Frank rises to his feet. His lips are hung in a politician's smile, so slick and out of place it makes me wince. "Tom, why don't you go back in the house and take a little breather, okay?"

"Oh, come on, Frank," says Constance. "He's allowed an opinion. Tom, you've had your say. Now calm down and let's finish our dinner."

Tom stands up, a little unsteady. "Sorry, Connie. I can't do this. I can't sit here and eat dinner with you people. You fat, satisfied pigs who give medals to fucking murderers—"

"Jesus, Tom!"

"Now, Tom . . ." I begin.

He turns to me and stabs a hole in the air between us with his rigid index finger. "And *you*. Sitting there in your pretty dress and your pretty face. You're a smart girl, you should know better, but you just keep smiling and nodding like a pretty little fascist idiot so you can get what you want, so you can smile and nod in the fucking White House one day . . ."

Somewhere in the middle of this speech, Caspian wipes his mouth with his napkin and stands up, sending the chair tumbling to the stone rectangles behind him. He walks down the line of chairs and yanks Tom out of place by the collar. "Apologize," he says.

The word is so low, I read it on his lips.

Tom's face, looking up at Caspian, is full of vodka and adrenaline. "Why? It's the truth. I can speak the truth."

"I said. Apologize."

Just before Tom replies, or maybe too late, I think: Don't do it, Tom, don't be an idiot, oh Jesus, oh Caspian, not again. I think, simultaneously, in another part of my head: Dammit, there goes dinner, and also: Should we try serving afterward or just put everything in the icebox for a cold buffet tomorrow at lunch?

"Oh, yeah? And what are you going to do if I don't? Knock me out in front of everyone?"

Caspian lifts back a cool fist and punches him in the jaw.

Caspian, 1964

Well, hell.

If it were just Caspian occupying that diner booth, he'd be on the guy's ass in a second, two-bit potbellied crook waving a gun like that. Wearing a goddamned *suit*, for God's sake, like he was a wiseguy or something.

But Tiny.

He reached across the table, grabbed her frozen hand, and slid the engagement ring off her finger and into his pocket. She was too shocked to protest. She stared at the crook, at flustered Em trying to open the cash drawer.

"Get down," he muttered.

She turned her head to him. Her face was white.

"Get down!"

The man waved his gun. "Hey! Shut up back there!"

From underneath his mother's protective body, the little boy started to cry.

"Shut that kid up!"

The boy cried louder, and the man fired his gun. The mother's body slumped.

Em screamed, and the man lost his cool, flushing and sweating. "Shut up! Shut up!"

Em tried to dodge around him, to the mother on the floor covering her boy, but he grabbed her by the collar and held the gun to her forehead. "Nobody move, all right? Or the waitress gets it. You!" He nodded to the frozen-faced couple in the first booth. "Put your wallet on the table! Right there at the edge!"

Em squeaked. Looked right across the room at Cap and pleaded with her eyes.

Damn it all.

Cap reached for Tiny and shoved her bodily under the table. In the next second, he launched himself down the aisle toward the man, who spun around and hesitated a single fatal instant, trying to decide whether to shoot Cap or to shoot Em.

As Cap knew he would. Because only training—constant, immersive, reactive training—can counter the faults of human instinct.

Or anyway. Cap was willing to take the chance.

He aimed for the gun first, knocking it out of the wiseguy's hand in one swift strike of his elbow. He howled. Em fell free. Cap reached back for a killer punch to the man's saggy jaw.

Jingle, jingle. The door swung open. Cap released the punch regardless. The man dropped like a sack of vanquished flour.

Cap turned to the door, expecting to see a flood of dark blue, Boston's finest, but instead there's another man in a dark suit and a brown fedora, pointing a gun straight to his chest.

The lookout.

"Hands in the air."

Cap lifted his hands slowly. He couldn't see the back booth from here. He cast out the net of his senses, hearing and smell and touch, the vibration in the air, searching for some sign that Tiny was still crouching unseen underneath the table, where he left her. Her three-carat engagement ring still sat in his inside jacket pocket. A stupid place to put it, but what else was he going to do?

"Take off his hat." The lookout nodded to the man in the first booth, whose wallet sat on the edge of the table.

"His hat?"

"Take it off. Nice and easy."

The gun was pointed straight at Cap's heart. This man knew what he was doing, didn't he? Not like the fleshy idiot lying motionless on the floor. Why was this one, the competent one, stuck with lookout duty? Lookout was the idiot's job.

Cap reached for the hat and lifted it gently from the man's head.

"See? That wasn't so hard. No one needs to be a hero. Now put the wallet in the hat."

Cap picked up the wallet and dropped it in the hat.

"Atta boy." The man raised his voice. "Now, all of you, take your wallets out of your pockets and put them on the table. Nice and easy, so this nice man here can put them in the hat."

There was a second of shocked silence.

Where the hell were the police? Hadn't someone called from the kitchen in the back?

The man fired his gun into the ceiling. "Now!"

A shower of plaster fell on his shoulders. A woman screamed, a faint pathetic little noise. He pointed the gun back at Cap. "No funny business, either!"

Okay, then. Keep the man's focus right here, on Cap, until the police arrive. No one gets hurt, that's the main thing.

Let the police take care of it, Cap. Don't be a hero. We don't need a hero, here. Just a regular guy to keep the gun occupied, to drag his feet until the police saunter on up.

The man jiggled the gun. Under his fedora, a faint sheen of sweat caught the light.

"Go on. Next booth. Keep it moving."

Cap dragged his feet to the next booth. The woman there, a woman in a cheerful yellow suit, dropped a little coin purse into the hat with shaking fingers.

"Open the pocketbook, lady," said the man at his side.

"But . . ."

"Open the pocketbook."

She unhooked the clasp and opened her pocketbook.

Someone was whimpering behind him. The little boy. *Mommy, Mommy,* he whined.

The man nudged Cap with his gun. "Empty it out."

Cap took the pocketbook and shook it out over the table. A wad of Kleenex, a tube of lipstick, a battered compact, a pen, a couple of rubber bands. A neat roll of dollar bills, the housekeeping money.

"What have we here," said the man. He picked up the roll and dropped it neatly in the hat. "Next."

Two more booths, three more wallets. The whimpering was getting louder now, accompanied by a low and constant moan, the boy's mother. The only sounds in the coffee shop, except for the gravelly hum of some electric appliance he'd never noticed before. He and the crook were getting closer to the booth in the corner now, where Tiny was hiding.

Where the sweet hell were the police? Cap glanced at the door.

"Lady! What the *fuck* do you think you're doing?"

Cap turned his head, and Jesus H. Christ.

There she was, Tiny idiot Doe, shoeless, crawling as silently as a berry-red cat across the floor toward the heap of whimpering child and moaning mother.

Afterward, Cap found Tiny in the kitchen, cradling the little boy in a soft woolen blanket. God knew where she found it. He'd gone to sleep against her shoulder, slack and blissful, his eyelashes like tiny feathered crescents against his pink cheeks. Above, a single bare bulb cast a glow over them both.

Cap swallowed back the ache in his throat.

"His grandmother's here. Police want you."

She turned her pale face toward him. "How's his mother?"

"Ambulance took her. I think she's all right. I've seen worse." A hell of a lot worse. "Looks like the shoulder. No organs."

She rose to her feet, lifting the sleeping boy without a sign of effort. Stronger than she looked, Miss Tiny Doe. "Will you take him?"

"Sure. If you want." He held out his arms. "You okay?"

"Yes. I just don't want to see the police, that's all." She laid the child in his arms, taking care as the small head transferred from her slim shoulder to Cap's. She tucked the blanket around the little boy and wiped away a small smudge of dried blood from his forehead. "Careful."

"You have to see the police, you know. Give a statement."

She hesitated. "Are there reporters there?"

"They're not letting them in. But, yeah, they're outside the door."

She unbuttoned the cardigan from around her shoulders and stuck her arms through the holes, one by one, putting it on properly. The flush was returning to her skin. "Can the police come back here for their statement?"

"I don't see why not. I'll tell them you need some quiet."

"And are they finished with you?"

The boy stirred, made a small noise in his throat. Cap hoisted him up higher to get a better grip. "I'll probably have to go back to the station later for more questioning. Because of everything."

Everything. Cap's instant reaction when the second man turned toward Tiny, the swift strike to his arm, the struggle for the gun, the snap of bone. Capitulation. Sending Em to the phone to call the police, because the kitchen was empty; the cook and his assistant had fled through the open back door. Waiting, waiting, trying to keep everybody calm while the police came. Tiny taking the child, calling for help for the mother, taking out her own handkerchief and showing someone how to hold it on the wound. Jesus, what a morning. He was getting a headache now, the hangover of battle. Like the melancholy you got after sex sometimes, the departure of adrenaline, leaving only yourself and the paltry contents of your soul.

"I see. Yes, of course you will. Thank you," she said, as an afterthought. "Thank you for . . . well, for saving us. It could have been so much worse."

He studied her wide-open eyes, the length of her eyelashes. She looked sincere, and humble. No frostiness now, here in the kitchen of Boylan's Coffee Shop.

"You're welcome," he said, and walked back into the dining area.

The grandmother let out a cry when she saw him. She rushed forward and engulfed the boy into her arms, without so much as a word to Cap. Not that he minded. He could take Tiny's thanks, but not a stranger's. He kept his hand on the boy's back until he was sure the old lady had him firmly, and then he turned to one of the cops standing around with notepads.

"Well? Do you need anything else?"

"Yeah, we're gonna need you down at the precinct, buddy. Standard procedure."

"Can you give me a lift?"

"Sure thing."

Another cop walked up. "I thought you said the broad was in the back."

"Yeah. The kitchen. Red dress."

The cop shrugged. "She's not there now."

By the time Cap turned the corner of Marlborough Street, it was nearly three o'clock in the afternoon, and the sun hit the fourth and third floor windows of his parents' house in six blinding rectangular patches. A slight figure in a berry-red dress sat at the top of the stoop, hands folded neatly in her lap. She rose at the sight of him.

"I thought you'd never get here."

He slung his camera bag to the pavement and fished for his key. "How did you find me?"

"The waitress told me. The dark-haired one."

"Em? Huh. Wonder how she knew."

Tiny didn't reply. She stood on the top step, watching him as he climbed. He tried not to look at her, though his body was light with relief at the sight of her slim figure, the gentle swell of her hips beneath the fabric of her dress. He stuck his key in the lock. "Are you coming in?"

"No, I just . . . I just wanted to have . . ." Her voice was breathless with nerves. "Have a word with you."

"More comfortable inside. You look like you could use a drink."

She paused. "I don't really drink."

"A good time to start, I'd say."

Unexpectedly, she laughed. A beautiful laugh, deeper and heartier than you'd think, a tiny girl like her. Her brown hair had come a bit disheveled. The curls fell more loosely about her ears and the top of her neck, so you could run your hands right through them, testing for strength and silkiness, right before you leaned in and kissed her.

As if she caught the drift of his thoughts, she lifted one hand to her head. The back of her arm was smooth-skinned and taut, an athlete's arm. Honed by tennis, probably. Or golf. Girls like her played golf, didn't they? In pink argyle sweaters.

Her laughter faded, but the smile remained. "All right, Caspian. I guess you're not going to bite."

He opened the door and stood back to usher her through. "Only if you beg me."

Tiny, 1966

om waves away his wife's anxious fingers and holds the bag of ice to his jaw. "You see? He proved my point. Just a killing machine, paid for by our own tax dollars."

I wipe my fingers on the kitchen towel and think, What tax dollars? Your trust fund's in nice sweet tax-free municipal bonds, yielding three and a half percent, or I'll eat my stockings.

I say, "Actually, Tom, if he'd wanted to kill you, he would have punched a lot harder."

"Are you saying *this* isn't bad enough?" Tom points to his jaw, which sports a thick purple bruise but appears otherwise intact.

"I'm saying he could have done worse. A lot worse. I *assure* you."

Constance looks up from her fervid examination of Tom's jaw. "I can't believe you're defending him."

"I'm not. For one thing, my dinner party is ruined." *Ruined*, I tell you.

I wrestle down a smile.

She turns back. "He's a bully. He always was. For God's sake, Tom, let me have that. You're not supposed to *dab* it." She snatches the pack of ice, braces the other side of his face with her hand, and smashes the cheesecloth against his jaw. "Anyway, good riddance. Between you and me, he never did fit in around here. Even as a kid, he didn't."

"Good riddance?"

Constance nods to the open door of the kitchen. "I saw him leave, just now."

I throw down the towel on the counter. "Excuse me."

Just before I cross the threshold, I remember something. I pause and turn my head over my shoulder. "Oh, and Constance? The two of you might want to start making sure you've locked your bedroom door at night, if you're thinking of getting frisky."

Outside, Fred and Mrs. Crane are still picking up the broken china, and the ocean crashes on regardless. "I'm sorry, Mrs. Crane," I say, "but did you see Major Harrison go by?"

"Yes, ma'am." She straightens. Her face is expressionless. "He came through a minute ago and went off that way." She waves to her right, toward the old Harrison house.

"His house, or the beach?"

"I couldn't tell. Is everybody all right, ma'am?"

"Everybody's fine, Mrs. Crane. Thank you so much for cleaning up like this. I'm awfully sorry."

"It's no bother, Mrs. Hardcastle. Oh, and ma'am?"

I pause on my way to the stone steps, down to the beach. "Yes, Mrs. Crane?"

"He did apologize, Major Harrison did. Just now. I thought you should know that."

I smile. "I certainly hope he did."

The beach is dark, except for the phosphorescent waves kicking energetically to my right. Behind me, in the distance, Frank's voice rises in laughter. He's taken the men down to the flat patch of sand near the breakwater, where they're playing a drunken game of blind midnight football, patching up any hurt feelings after the brawl. The women, of course, are putting the children to bed. And the teenagers? God only knows.

Brawl. Not a brawl, really. Most of them were on Cap's side, after all. But there was some pushing and shoving, some broken crockery, some feminine panic and some masculine settling of various scores. Any pretext for that, among the competitive Hardcastles and their competitive spouses.

I look up the dunes to the Harrison house, just as the porch light flicks on.

Apologize, Caspian says again, this time in my own head, and the word sends another surge of feeling in my veins, the familiar crazy hope, and I tell my veins sternly: *Stop it. You know better.* And: *You have too much to lose, this time.* And: *Think of Frank.*

And finally, when even that didn't work: *The photograph, damn it.*

My veins settle down. But my legs carry me in the direction of the Harrison house, guided by the light on the porch.

By the time I reach the steps, the light is off again. I pound on the door anyway.

The tread of footsteps, and the door opens.

"Tiny."

"Caspian."

He opens the door wider and slips through to stand on the worn entry mat, shutting the faint light of the entryway firmly away behind him. His body fills the porch. My pulse falls into my fingertips. Veins again. The last glass of wine seems like a very long time ago. I can't even taste it in my mouth anymore, which is now dry and sticky, perched above my strangled throat.

Why am I here?

Worse. What if someone sees me?

"I'm sorry about what happened," he says. "I was going to tell you before I left, but you were busy in the kitchen."

"Oh, that's all right. I couldn't blame you for that. Tom's a . . ." I search for the word, but it seems to have escaped me.

There's not much light, but his smile makes itself seen. "Yes, he is."

He's taken off his magnificent dress coat, the one with the medals. I picture it lying across the back of the chintz chair in the living room, where he's tossed it. Or—more likely, knowing Caspian—hanging up neatly in the entry closet, behind a white-painted door, between an old mackintosh and a plaid beach blanket. His shirt is stiff and white, smelling of laundry starch. And of him. Caspian. I breathe through my mouth, to inhibit the flow of scent to my brain: scent, after all, is the sense most directly linked to the brain's emotional centers. Or is it memory? Well, either one, emotion or memory, they're the last things I need stimulated just now.

But I can't quite shut it all off entirely.

I lift up my chin. "Are you sorry for anything else?"

There is a pause, a sort of expressionless instant that might mean anything, and then he shakes his head. "Everything seems to have turned out all right, after all."

"Oh, yes. Turned out *perfectly*."

"I was just thinking that, actually. At the exact second you knocked on the door. How well things turned out for you. How perfect you looked tonight. And Frank. The two of you headed for big things, exciting times, just as you always wanted."

"All's well that ends well, as they say." I hold out my hand. "No more hard feelings. You're forgiven."

He gives my hand a single shake. His palm is dry and warm. "Forgiven. Good. Now, if you'll excuse me?"

I withdraw my hand behind my back. "Of course. Just . . ."

He's already turned back to the door, already placed his hand on the knob. "Just?"

I haul in a deep breath and smash my hands together, in the small of my back. I say, in a rush: "The photographs. The ones you took. What did you do with them?"

There is a small half-crescent window above the door, and the entry light spills through and falls on his brow, illuminating his forehead and nothing else. An eyebrow lifts, out of the shadow and into the glow. "The *photographs?* Why do you ask?"

I shrug. "Just curious."

I watch his face carefully, but when did Caspian Harrison ever leave anything lying about unguarded? When could I ever have trusted the expression on the outside of him?

He shifts his weight and turns his head to the beach. The sight of his profile hurts my ribs. His hand still rests on the knob. "I packed them up. Haven't looked at them since."

"Really?"

He looks back at me. "Really."

I want to probe further. Well, what did you do with the boxes? Are they sitting in a Hardcastle attic somewhere? Could anyone have found them? Broken in and stolen them? Sent one to me enclosed in a manila envelope, with a friendly note included free of charge?

Or was that *you*, Caspian? The man I trusted once.

Surely not. Surely Caspian would never do that.

I press my damp palms against my dress and try one more time. "So you never looked at them? Never showed them to anyone?"

"Jesus. Of course not."

"All right, all right."

The floorboards creak under his shifting feet. "Something going on, Tiny? Does Frank know something?"

"No! No. I just . . . I was thinking. When I heard you were coming. Obviously it's not something I'd care to have spread around."

"And you really think I'd do that? You think I'd goddamned *tell* about us? Breathe a single word?" He slams a fist against the doorjamb. Not too hard, but enough to rattle the frame a bit.

I look downward, to the tips of his shoes. Slippers, actually. He's changed from his shiny black dress shoes into worn gray slippers, scuffed in all the usual places.

"No. I guess not."

"Okay, then. Anything else?"

"No," I say. "That's all. Good night."

He hesitates, as if he's about to say something more. My veins, my stupid blood lightens again, the way it did as I looked out the window this afternoon, the way it did just now on the beach, the way it did when Caspian held out his hand and introduced himself in the humid air of the coffee shop, eight million lifetimes ago.

And then: "Good night, Tiny."

He slips back inside the house, as noiselessly as a six-foot mouse, and I am left alone on the porch, in the darkness, drenched in disappointment.

I return home through the terrace doors, patting my wind-blown hair as I step over the threshold. The rooms are still, except for the distant crashes in the kitchen. Granny has probably gone upstairs to her cold cream and her Gothic paperbacks.

As I pass the library entrance, however, I catch the rumble of a man's voice, the faint smell of fresh cigarettes. I can't hear the words. It's a hushed sound, a compression of urgent words: the sound of someone who doesn't want to be overheard. Frank's voice. I push the door open.

Frank stands next to the window, staring at the darkened beach, talking quietly into the telephone receiver. The box dangles from the opposite hand, hooked by his first two fingers, which also contain a nimble white cigarette.

He glances at me, and I can't decide how to read his expression. Startled? Guilty? Annoyed?

"Sorry. I've got to go. I'll call you later. Yes. Me, too." He settles the receiver back in the cradle and returns the telephone to the round table next to the armchair. A faint *brrring* echoes back from the startled bell. Frank smiles. "Campaign staffer."

"They must be hard workers, taking phone calls at this hour."

"Campaigning's a twenty-four-hour job, these days." He takes a swift drag on his cigarette and stubs it out in the ashtray next to the telephone. "Drink?"

"No, thank you."

He heads for the drinks tray anyway and pours himself a neat Scotch in a lowball glass. The ice bucket is empty. He takes a sip and turns in my direction, and it seems to me that his face is stiffer than it should be. That his brow is hard with tension. "You're quiet," he says. "Something wrong?"

I fold my arms and laugh. "Other than your cousin starting a fight at his own celebration dinner?"

"That Tom. Jesus." Frank shakes his head and laughs, too, a dry laugh. "I don't know what Connie was thinking when she married him."

"She was in love, I guess. We can't always choose whom we fall in love with."

He finishes off the whiskey and clinks the glass down on the tray. He stares at it for a second or two, bracing his fingers on the rim, like he's expecting it to do something, to sprout legs and jump off the tray and run down the hall to the kitchen for Mrs. Crane to clean. He says softly, "No. That's true. I'm just lucky I fell in love with you, I guess. All those years ago."

"We're both lucky. Lucky to have each other."

"Sweetheart." Frank approaches me and puts his hand behind my head. He kisses me on the mouth. His lips are soft and smoky. "Going upstairs?"

"Yes."

He follows me to our bedroom, footsteps heavy and quiet on the stairs behind me. When we reach the door, his arm stretches out before my ribs to turn the knob. The room is dark and warm, a little stale with the dregs of the afternoon.

"Could you crack open a window?" I ask.

Frank heads for the window. I reach for my earlobes and turn to the mirror above the dresser. Frank's reflection appears behind me. He unfastens my necklace; I take off my earrings. When the jewelry is safely stowed in the inlaid mother-of-pearl box in the center of the dresser, Frank puts his hands around my shoulders. The warmth of his skin shocks me.

"I was so proud of you tonight," he says. "You looked so beautiful. So composed. You handled everything perfectly."

"Oh, I have my uses."

"You certainly do. You're a miracle. My one true love." He bends his head and kisses me, first in the hollow where my throat meets my collarbone, and then another kiss an inch farther down, and then once more, right at the neckline of my dress. I sift my hand through his sunbrushed hair, while he lingers on me, holding his warm mouth against my skin for an age or two, like a lover tasting his mistress after a long absence. My belly blossoms. A final kiss, and he looks back up to study me in the mirror. "Happy?"

I gaze at Frank's mouth. The safe, familiar dent above his upper lip. "Of course I am. Dear Frank."

"Good," says Frank. "Anyway, I thought I'd take a walk for a bit. Clear my head. Are you all set? Any zippers needing attention?"

"Just the one in back."

He unzips my dress, fondles my waist, kisses my temple. "Good night, then, darling. I'll try not to wake you up when I get back."

When I startle awake the next morning, seized by a newborn determination to confront Caspian about the photograph, Frank grunts and throws an arm across my middle, enclosing me in a haze of stale booze and dried-up ocean. Percy's face regards me hopefully from the edge of the bed.

The beach is deserted at this hour. I remove Percy's leash and watch the exuberant pattern of his paw prints form on the flat damp sand, the receding tide. It takes me two miles up the beach and back to screw up the necessary courage, but on my return I march up to the door of the old Harrison cottage and knock, *bang bang bang.*

There is no answer.

At breakfast, Mrs. Crane tells me that Major Harrison already left, that Fred drove him to the station at dawn, both suitcases packed, wearing plain civilian clothes.

No, he didn't say where he was going. Or if he'd be back at all.

Caspian, 1964

When Cap was five years old, his family moved abruptly from some foreign posting (Frankfurt, maybe? He had a vague recollection of a corner shop selling German candy) and returned to Boston, to the handsome brownstone on Marlborough Street that had been his parents' wedding present from the Hardcastles.

He still carried a vivid memory of driving down the street in the middle seat of the moving van, next to his father in the passenger seat. "There it is," Dad had said, lifting Cap onto his lap, and Cap had caught sight of his mother waving joyously from the stoop, bundled in a blue coat, holding his three-year-old sister's woolly hand in hers. Dad was smoking his pipe, and somehow the smell of his tobacco burrowed its way into the memory of that afternoon, so that even now, as Cap opened the front door and followed the carpeted stairs stretching to the upper floors, as he smelled the familiar combustion of warm plaster and old wood, he thought of Dad and his pipe and his clean-shaven jaw. A sense of rightness stole over him, of impending happiness, just out of reach.

The happiest days of his life.

When he'd returned to Boston on furlough a month ago, he'd recognized the old place the instant he'd turned the corner and beheld it in the afternoon light. It was home. It was childhood, those few precious years between, say, five and eight, when they had all lived there together and Mother was alive. The large bay window on the parlor floor, overlooking the street, where Mother kept the piano. The paneled pocket doors to the dining room, endless fun. Dad's study. Cap's old bedroom on the third floor, at the back, which had been let out for years, like the other floors, bringing in money that he didn't really need, money that went straight into his savings account, zeros adding up magically to some sum he refused to acknowledge.

Now, of course, in the hindsight of adulthood, he knew that they had returned because of his mother's sickness, and that his father had been granted some sort of compassionate leave. That was why they had all lived with such furious domesticity in those years, such determination to love every moment together, to squeeze the day of every last drop of joy.

He led Tiny up to the fourth floor, his own floor, the attic floor. A tidy little bachelor pad with plenty of light: the old boxroom converted to a darkroom, a kitchenette in the corner, a sofa in the front room, and his own bedroom in the back. "It's not much, but it's home," he said, opening the door, flinging his hat on the stand, conscious suddenly of the mismatched furniture, the walls covered in thumbtacked black-and-white photographs.

Neat, of course. Military neat. The bed made in hospital corners, the furniture exactly squared, the floor bone clean and smelling sternly of soap.

Tiny wandered to the window like a woodland deer. Her eyes were huge and glossy dark as she swiveled her head about, taking in the details of her surroundings. Her pocketbook dangled from her hand, the cardigan slung between the straps.

He set down his camera bag in the hall. "What's your poison?"

"I don't mind. Whatever you've got."

Not much. He preferred to do his drinking elsewhere. Still, there was vodka, there was lime juice in the ancient Frigidaire. He poured out a pair of gimlets and carried them into the living room.

Tiny stood with her hands braced on the windowsill, staring at the green-leafed tips of the trees that lined the sidewalk below. The slanted sunlight just touched the back of her neck. He could trace the perfect arcs of her shoulder blades through the material of her dress, the flex of her calves, and he realized she'd taken off her shoes and risen up high on the balls of her feet.

There were a thousand questions he wanted to ask her, a thousand things he wanted to know about her. He advanced across the old wooden boards and placed the drink on the sill, next to her long-fingered hand. "What's he like?"

"Who?"

He was close enough to smell the faint perfume on her skin, to detect the movement of her back as she breathed, the whisper of fabric. Close enough to realize, in shock, just how small she was, how delicately made, each bone and curve of her tuned in fine precision. "The man you're marrying."

She picked up the drink and turned her face away from the window glass to sip. She made a little moue, swallowed, and sipped again. An amateur. "He's lovely. Handsome and brilliant. Harvard. He's a lawyer, going into politics eventually. Or that's the plan, anyway. Big things."

"A real catch."

"I like to think so."

"How did you meet?"

She drank again, more deeply this time, and moved away from the window. "Oh, you know. I was at Radcliffe. We met at a mixer, my sophomore year. He was a senior."

"Fell in love?"

"Yes, I guess. If that's the word. *Fall* in love." She shook her head and reached for her pocketbook, which was slung over the arm of the sofa.

"Well, you love each other, don't you? That's why you're getting married."

She took out a pack of cigarettes and a slim gold lighter. "Do you mind?"

He shrugged. "It's your funeral."

"Oh, a clean liver. My fiancé would approve, when he isn't out enjoying a smoke himself, on the sly." She set down her drink to light the cigarette. "Don't tell on me."

"Your secret's safe with me." He leaned back against the window-sill and crossed his arms. "You didn't answer my question, though."

She blew out a slow cloud of smoke and waved it away with her hand. "Look, can we not talk about the wedding for a single damned minute? I've been living and breathing it for the past six months."

"All right. What *did* you want to talk about?"

She was wandering the room again, in quick little strides, searching him out. A bundle of nerves now, Miss Tiny Doe, her hair ruffled, her drink and cigarette in hand. A current of restless energy surrounded her, vibrating with possibility, with the potential for a rare and shattering explosion, a shower of sparks, the Fourth of Tiny July.

She stopped by the wall of photographs and touched the edge of one with her finger, which was manicured in berry red, matching her dress. "Yours?"

"Yes."

"They're very good. This one here, the vagrant, with the sunlight glittering on his stubble. Very good. Are you a professional?"

"It's just a hobby. I'm a soldier, actually."

She turned her head. "I might have guessed. That, or an ex-cop. The way you acted in there. What branch of the service are—?"

He snapped his fingers. "Yeah, that reminds me. So about what happened today. Any particular reason you gave them the slip?"

"Who?"

"The *police,* Tiny."

She stared down at her cigarette. "Do you have an ashtray?"

He sighed and heaved himself away from the window to the kitchenette, where he found one of his mother's teacups at the back of the shelf, an old-fashioned red-hued pattern, chipped and scarred. "You can use this," he said, turning the corner to hand it to her.

She took it without looking at him and dropped a long crumb of ash inside, just in time, followed by a single wet drop.

"Oh, Jesus." He touched her elbow. "Are you all right?"

"Yes!" She jerked her elbow away and turned her shoulder, but it was all a lie. She wasn't all right. The tears tracked right on down her pristine cheeks, to be whisked instantly away in furious strokes of her fingers.

"Shh. It's okay. It's done. You're okay here." He rested his hands on the balls of her shoulders.

"Stop it. I don't— I never cry—" She tried to juggle the drink and cigarette and teacup, and the drink lost out, dropping in a wet crash to the wooden floor. "Oh, damn, I'm so sorry—"

"Forget the drink. Jesus. You can cry. Cry all you want. Here's my handkerchief." He pulled it out of his jacket pocket and held it out to her, but she still had the cigarette and the teacup left. He took the smoke from her unresisting fingers and crushed it out in the teacup, and he set them both down on the floor next to the broken glass. "Come here, before you cut yourself."

"I'm— I'm all right. I'll get a—get a—cloth or something. Clean up. I'm sorry. I'm a—such a klutz—"

He picked her up and carried her to the sofa, where she hiccuped and buried her head in his shoulder and cried in earnest, soaking his jacket and the shirt beneath. His hand absorbed the tremors of her back. He closed his eyes and sat absolutely still, waiting out the storm, tracking its arc in the strength of her sobs, the pace, until bit by bit she blew herself out, ebbing and ebbing, a final gust, and quietude, except for the low parabolic roars of the passing cars.

He fingered her hair, which smelled like a garden. A garden at night. Gardenias? He didn't know much about flowers.

Without lifting her head, she said, muffled in his jacket, "You probably hate crying women."

"You'd be surprised. A lot of men cry out there. In the field. At night. The younger kids, missing their mothers."

"But women. Women crying. Most men hate that."

"I don't give a damn. Cry all you want. Anyone would cry, after a thing like that."

"But not you."

"Well, I've seen worse. But if I hadn't, I'd probably be crying right along with you."

She didn't answer, only sat there curled up into his shoulder, as if she were too embarrassed by the loss of composure to lift her head. Cap went on stroking her hair, and not just because it felt so damned good, because *she* felt so damned good, firm and soft and dainty and strong and wet and fragrant, a gardenia-scented bouquet of tender female limbs tucked into his sofa and his body. No, not just because of the pleasure of stroking her hair, but because it was the only thing keeping the awkwardness at bay, between two strangers like them. The only thing to comfort her.

She could be crying with anyone. She could have gone to her mother or her best friend, she could have gone to a grandmother or cousin or sister or brother, if she had them. She could have gone to her fiancé. She *should* have gone to her fiancé, a day like today.

Why had she come to him?

She shivered a little, the way you sometimes did after a long cry, when the heat and the energy fled and you were left with nothing to keep you warm. He went on stroking her hair, feeling her breath in his shoulder, trying not to think about having sex with her.

She turned her head, freeing her face, and sighed. "I guess you're probably wondering why I'm here."

"The question crossed my mind."

Tiny sat up. "Do you still have that handkerchief?"

"Right here."

"Thanks." She stood up, with her back to him, while she made busy with the handkerchief, fixing her face. His gaze fell to her calves, slender and graceful, curved with firm muscle beneath her stockings. He closed his eyes and tried not to picture them wrapped around his back.

"So. I was wondering, Cap . . . I was hoping . . ."

He opened his eyes. She was facing him again, eyes red and puffy but surprisingly composed, surprisingly put back together. You couldn't ruffle Miss Tiny Doe's dignity for long. Even her hair seemed to have fallen back into place, or maybe that was the stroking of his hand.

"Yes?" he prompted, when her voice faded away.

Her shoulders rose bravely. She knit her hands together in front of her tiny waist, folding the handkerchief in the smallest possible square between them.

"Do you know how to make a person disappear?"

Tiny, 1966

When I was about five years old, my parents nearly divorced. I doubt either of my sisters remembers this; they were practically in diapers still. Daddy had come back from the war, shot in the groin, and for a long time, he didn't seem to be getting any better. I remember how he used to sit in his chair atop some sort of odd-shaped blue cushion, drink in one hand, cigarette in the other, looking as if he might curl up against the upholstery and die at any moment. I wanted to climb on his lap and hug him, but I couldn't. His wound.

Eventually he started getting up and about, and went back to work at the law firm in which he was a partner, and that was when he found out Mummy was having an affair. (This part was explained to me later; at the time, all I knew was that there was fighting and tantrums, that Mummy and Daddy didn't seem to like each other anymore, and I had to remain very, very quiet in my room or I might make it worse.) After they went to bed, invariably in separate rooms, I would slip out and clean up all the messy cocktail glasses and the cigarette butts. I would get up early and bring Mummy her coffee, I would tidy my room, I would mix Daddy his martini, because you never knew what might help. You never knew what might make them love you enough to stay together.

Looking back, as a worldly adult, I suspect Daddy was so upset because of the injustice. Due to the nature of his injury, sexual activity was impossible for some time. I think there were specialists involved, delicate surgeries, until things were back in working order, but in the meantime he was unmanned, and there was Mums, dissatisfied as ever, seeking satisfaction the only way she knew how. The only way they both knew, really, because I also happen to know that he slept with other women when he was overseas: Mums once told me about the letters she found in his kit that came back with him. (They liked to do that with me, amassing evidence against each other, in case I should ever find myself having to choose sides.)

Anyway, Mums had her revenge, and Daddy couldn't revenge her revenge, and everything balanced precariously for a while, and I don't know why they didn't divorce. People were divorcing by then, it wasn't all that big a scandal anymore. Maybe Mummy and Daddy had married into an expectation of discreet infidelity, as rich people did back then, and they came at last to an understanding. Maybe they really loved each other, and found the grace for forgiveness. Or maybe neither of them wanted to give up the apartment on Fifth Avenue. (New Yorkers are practical like that, especially when it comes to real estate.) Who knows, really? Only the two of them. Eventually the fighting simmered down, the balance of power was restored, and life went on. They remain married to this day, God help them both, and are even sometimes happy with each other.

But I've never forgotten that year on the brink. I've never forgotten what a small thing I was, tiny and powerless in my bedroom, afraid to shout out and ruin everything. And I've always been amazed by my younger sisters, who are never afraid to shout for anything they wanted, not the least little bit.

Take Pepper, now. Pepper walks into the Hardcastle breakfast room four days later like she owns the joint. She kicks off her shoes and settles in, beneath a watercolor seascape executed by Granny Hardcastle herself in 1934, during her blue phase, and she says, loud and fearless: "Did you know there's an old car out there, buried in the shed?"

I look up from my coffee. "What shed?"

"The one near the elbow of the driveway. Covered in brambles." She reaches for the toast rack. She smells fresh and salty. Her hair is done up in her cheerful yellow head scarf, and she hasn't taken off her sunglasses. A good thing Granny Hardcastle eats breakfast in her room. "Where is everybody, anyway?"

"It's Monday morning, darling. Frank's gone into Boston, trawling for campaign money, and his father's back at his desk. For work," I add, with a slight emphasis on the word *work*, because isn't that what Pepper's supposed to be doing right now? Working. In Washington. Not here.

She peels off her sunglasses—masculine wire-rimmed ones, like those worn by fighter pilots—and smiles. "Don't you fling those dirty four-letter words at me."

"You're welcome to stay as long as you like, of course," I say. "But aren't they expecting you back in the office by now?"

"Oh, we understand each other, Washington and me." Pepper gnaws her toast, glances at the buffet laid out behind us, and reaches for the coffeepot. "About this car, though. I think you should have a look. It's very old and lovely. I'll bet it's worth a mint."

"What do you know about cars?"

"More than you think." The old sidelong wink.

It occurs to me, as we strike out across the damp grass of the driveway oval, that if you told me a week ago I'd be tolerating this—striking across grass with Pepper, striking across anything and for any length of time with Pepper, for that matter—I'd have smiled politely and reached for the telephone to dial up the loony bin. Percy trots at our heels, in the wary wedge of space between us. "Just how did you happen to be poking around there, anyway?" I ask.

"I'm nosy."

"Well, I knew *that*. But you've only been here four days. Don't tell me you've already exhumed the Big House of all its secrets." I picture my underwear drawer. Surely not.

Pepper waves this away. "I might have made a wrong turn last night, coming back from the tennis courts."

"I can't imagine how."

"Anyway, I came back this morning with a crowbar—"

"You didn't!"

"Useful little darlings, crowbars. And look!" She points across the remaining few yards of grass and into a patch of brambles, which, on closer inspection, obscures the gray weathered boards of an old shed.

"I'll be damned," I say.

"Tiny!" Pepper is shocked. Shocked.

I pace a slow half circle around the bramble patch. Why have I never seen this before? Or perhaps *noticed* is a better word. After all, I've driven past these brambles countless times, in Frank's yellow roadster, in my own staid blue Cadillac. (And then in another car entirely, on another day I would rather not recall.) The bushes tangled into vines, which tangled into the shade of the birch trees that protected the Hard-castle property from the curious public road, from the photographers looking to make a buck. For some reason, the groundskeeper has simply allowed this descent into wilderness.

"Well, it's odd," I say. "This isn't like Fred at all."

"Not a bramble man, our Fred?"

"It's not the brambles themselves. You perceive this whole mess is supposed to block the view from the road, after all." I wave my hand in the direction of the pavement, on the other side of the trees, from which a telltale drone of engine obligingly raises its voice to a roar. "The more brambles, the merrier."

"The shed itself, then?"

"Yes." I pick my way through the brambles to the wide door, which stands ajar, presumably because of Pepper's crowbar. The air is cool on my bare arms, shaded by the layers of vegetation. "If Fred weren't using the shed, he'd have had it torn down, instead of letting it collapse on its own."

"It isn't collapsed."

"Not yet. Was it locked?"

"Yes."

I turn my head and raise my eyebrow at her. She shrugs an innocent pair of shoulders. "That's what crowbars are *for*, Tiny."

"I suppose you'd know." The door is only cracked open. One of a double set, taking up almost the entire end of the shed. The other door still lies flush with the wall, held in place by the encroaching brambles. The doors are made of vertical boards, in contrast with the rest of the shed, clad horizontally. A rusty lock lies in the matted grass at my feet, still attached to its mottled metal plate. I can see the scars on the edges of the doors: fresh unpainted wood against the peeling gray.

"Well, go on." Pepper prods my back. "Open it."

Like when we were girls. Like when she or Vivian would dare me to peek in on Grandmother Schuyler swimming naked in the pool on

Long Island, or to lick the frozen lamppost outside our Fifth Avenue apartment. A rush of trepidation overcomes me, a premonition of . . . no, not evil, not exactly. But *something.* Something behind that door. Something rather formidable, something complicated. Something I'd really rather not face at the moment.

But it's too late for nonsense. I stick out my hand and haul open the door.

The hinges shriek in shock. A gust of air greets me, cool and musty, smelling of black grease. I wave my hand in front of my nose, imagining mildew. "I can't see anything."

Pepper is struggling with the other door, pushing hard against the brambles. "Hold on. Here comes the sun. Ouch! God *damn* it!"

"Splinter?"

"No. Thorns." She sucks on the pad of her thumb and gives the door a last almighty shove, and lo! like magic, or divine benediction, a shaft of pale morning sun finds the exact angle between the branches and brambles and open door, and turns the air to gold.

Illuminates the dusty chrome points of the object that fills the shed.

"You weren't kidding," I say.

"Would I jest?"

I step forward and rest my hand on the hood ornament, a delicate three-pointed star enclosed in a circle. "It's a Mercedes-Benz."

"You don't say."

I turn my head. Pepper's still standing near the door, backlit by the sunshine, one leg propped against the doorjamb, her arms crossed beneath her breasts. A speculative posture.

"Oh? And what do you know about Mercedes-Benzes?" I ask.

She pushes off from the doorjamb and strolls along the side of the car, drawing a trail along the endless black hood. "Oh, this and that.

Not the sort of machine a Schuyler would be caught driving, would it? Rich and glamorous."

"And terribly German. The wrong kind of German."

"That, too."

"How old do you think it is?"

Pepper circles the sloping rear like a trainer inspecting a Thoroughbred. "Oh, thirty years at least. It looks like the kind of thing Göring would have driven around Berlin, doesn't it? Look at the curve of the fender. The way it swoops down from the front tires like that. It absolutely screams sex, doesn't it?"

I release the star and step around the left front wheel. Two slender exhaust pipes extend from the side of the hood and into that glorious swooping fender, like Adam's ribs. A canvas sheet is draped atop the open cockpit. "Hard to tell under all that dust," I say.

"Oh, you're better than that, Tiny. Even you can see what's beneath. The curve of this rear." She shapes it in the air with her hands, just so. "Can't you just imagine driving this gorgeous beast down some lovely old road? Miles and miles. To the middle of nowhere."

"*You?* The middle of nowhere?" I lift the canvas sheet. A slow drift of dust slides down the other side, like snow. "Anyway, it can't possibly start."

"Who says? Let me help you with that." She moves to the passenger side and grasps the opposite end of the canvas.

"In the first place, the gas tank will be empty."

"How can you be sure of that?"

"Evaporation, darling. Thirty years of it, probably." We fold up the sheet in perfectly synchronized movements, lengthwise and lengthwise again, and then we meet at the top of the hood to bring the edges together. "And oil."

"What do you know about oil?"

"I know cars need it, so the parts don't stick together."

"Oh, an expert, then."

I fold the sheet over my arm and turn back to the car. "I suppose we'll have to call somebody in to fix it. Or else tow it to a garage."

"Don't you dare!" Pepper walks back down the hood to the passenger door. "Just look at this leather, Tiny. All brown and soft. The dials."

"Don't open it!"

But it's too late. Pepper tries the handle and—much to my surprise—the door gives way fluidly, without a squeak, a miracle of Teutonic engineering. She lowers her body inside and closes her eyes. "Oh, *Tiny*. Come inside."

"You're a dope."

My sister leans her head back, eyes still closed, mouth curved in a luxurious smile. "Better than sex," she says.

"Surely you're having better sex than *that*, Pepper darling."

She cracks open an eyelid. "Better than what you're having with old Frank, I'll bet. Nice married under-the-covers missionary sex." She pats the driver seat. "Come on in. You know you want to."

I swallow back my outrage—well, she's right, isn't she? Hit the old nail smack on the head—and set the thick square of folded canvas on top of the hood, just behind the ornament. "I do have work to do, you know. At least a dozen notes to write, and Frank wanted me to look over his speech while he's away—"

"Oh, screw the housewife routine, just once." She pats the seat again.

I exhale the heavy sigh, just to show her how large a favor she's asking, and swing around the side of the car to the driver's side. This door sticks a little, or maybe it's just me, sticky and incompetent, but Pepper reaches over and gives it a shove, while I tug, and at last the latch gives way and the door glides weightlessly outward. I hold my skirt beneath my thighs and slide downward into the driver's seat.

"You see what I mean?" says Pepper.

The scent of leather rolls around me in a masculine fog. I place my hands on the steering wheel, two o'clock and ten o'clock. The thick dust on the windshield obscures my vision. Behind me, the seat molds itself around my back and legs, the curve of my buttocks, like a pair of large and skillful hands.

"I see what you mean."

Pepper's opening the glove compartment, the ashtray. "Look at this!" she exclaims, holding up a cigarette butt, rimmed in pink lipstick.

"Good Lord."

She revolves it between her fingers. "Can you imagine? I wonder who owned it."

"One of the Hardcastles, obviously."

"Do you think so? A German car like this? A special order, I'm sure, right from the factory. You would have had to be some sort of European aristocrat to get your hands on this. Anyway, the Hardcastles were like the Schuylers, especially in those days. Nice reliable Packards and Cadillacs and Oldsmobiles. Nothing too flashy."

I run my hands along the white steering wheel. Pepper sets the cigarette back down in the ashtray and starts rummaging through the glove compartment. I say, "It's not flashy, exactly."

"All right. Sexy. Glamorous."

"Well, Granny Hardcastle was a bit more fun before she married. So they say. You know she brought money into the family. Her father was in textiles, a self-made man."

"Hmm. I didn't know that. *In*teresting." Pepper's curious head is still tucked down, at a level with the glove compartment. The yellow ends of her scarf slide around the nape of her neck. "I guess it fits. I always thought there was something not quite *us* about her. The way she works at it all."

"We're not allowed to talk about it, of course. The great myth of the Brahmin Hardcastles would be exploded. What's that?"

"A glove, I believe." She dangles it before her, a short tan kidskin number, a lady's driving glove. "But that would have been ages ago, wouldn't it? Before the war. The First World War, I mean. This was built in the thirties."

"Around the time Frank was born."

"So she would have been a grandmother already."

"A young one."

"Still. This isn't her car, I'm sure of it. Which begs the question: Whose?" Pepper folds up the glove and places it back in the compartment. "There aren't any documents here. So somebody's hiding something."

"Why do you say that?"

"Why else would you take the papers out of the car, silly?"

"I don't know. Safekeeping."

"Take the papers, but leave the cigarette butts?" She shakes her head and leans back against the seat again, with her eyes open this time, staring at the low beams of the roof. "No, there's a secret here somewhere."

"You're so suspicious, Pepper. I'm sure there's a straightforward explanation."

"Tiny, darling. Everyone has secrets. Even you, I'll bet."

I flex my fingers around the steering wheel a final time, and let my hands fall into my lap. From the corner of my eye, I sense that Pepper has rolled her head to the side, watching me. I run my forefinger along the rim of the opposite cuticle. "Not as many as you do, I'll *bet*."

The edge to my words, the crisp emphasis on the word *bet*—especially on that final consonant *t*, scattering the dust—makes me realize, too late, how easy we've been with each other. How relaxed the air between us. How I've just hardened it, back into the familiar permafrost.

Pepper turns her gaze back to the roof beams and says in a worldly voice: "When it comes to secrets, darling, it's not how many. It's how big."

I'm sorry, I want to say. I flatten out my palms and smooth away the wrinkles in my skirt. "Is that so."

"Oh, that's so, all right. Want to hear something funny?"

"I could use a laugh."

"For a second there, I mean a moment ago, I almost called you *Vivian.*"

Do you know what? I really do laugh at that.

For all the car's enormous proportions, its length and copious breadth, the cockpit has an intimate feel, a soft brown leather cocoon, edged in chrome and dirty glass. The sun's moved on already, shifting its angles, and you can't see the individual motes of dust any longer, the living quality of the air. I nudge my sister with my shoulder. "You really are a dope."

We sit there, a pair, watching the shade progress until the last of the sun has disappeared behind some vegetable obstacle outside. Pepper lifts one elegant sandaled foot and places it against the dashboard. "So," she says. "What did one dehydrated Frenchman say to the other dehydrated Frenchman?"

"I can't imagine."

"What do we do now, Pierre?"

A giggle slips out of me, and another. Pepper joins me, her pretty chest heaving with giggles, her sundress shivering, her perfect golden calf swooping into her slender ankle, like the fender over the front wheel of a vintage Mercedes-Benz roadster.

"Actually, I do have something you could help me with," I say at last, placing my hand against my stomach to stop the laughter.

"What's that, honey? Seducing someone's husband? Arsenic in Constance's tea?"

I place my two hands on the top edge of the windshield and heave myself out of the seat.

"I need you to help me sell some jewelry."

You won't be surprised—I certainly wasn't—to learn that Pepper is an expert appraiser of fine jewelry.

"This bracelet here should do it." She dangles it from her fingers. "It's better to sell off a bracelet, anyway. They don't usually notice."

"You're assuming Frank gave me the bracelet."

"Didn't he?"

"Well, yes. But it *might* have been someone else."

She gives my injured air the old wise eye, and I think, This is what it's like to have a sister.

"Anyway, it's perfect. Valuable enough, but not too valuable. No engraving to give you away. Nothing particularly special." She taps it with the other finger, sending it swinging. "Actually rather boring. What was the occasion?"

"I don't remember. Christmas, maybe."

"Well, next time send him out shopping with me."

The day has grown sinfully warm, the morning dew burned thoroughly away, and I go so far as to put the top down on the car. "I don't suppose you're going to tell me what this is for," says Pepper, examining her fingernails as we rush down the highway, a little too fast.

"Just a little temporary emergency."

"Lost money at bridge?"

"Bite your tongue. I never lose at bridge."

She looks out the side. "Of course not."

There is a dealer she knows in Boston. Don't ask why, she says, and I park the car obediently outside and don't ask why. We seem to be getting along so well, after all. I set the brake with a flourish. Pepper takes the box from me as we approach the door. "I think you'd better let me handle this."

"With pleasure."

The building seems respectable enough, the storefront modest red brick, next to a bookseller on one side and a delicatessen on the other. A. R. GOLDFARB, says the lettering on the window. ESTATE JEWELRY. I follow a half step behind Pepper and admire the brilliant red highlights in her chestnut hair, the narrowness of her rib cage, the mannequin profile of her. She looks like trouble at any angle, Pepper, even in the harshness of noontime, even in her shabby beach clothes.

"I'm looking for Mr. Goldfarb," she tells the man at the counter, a tall fellow in his early twenties or even younger. His loose brown suit hangs from the bones of his shoulders, hoping for more.

He speaks up in a faulty tenor. "I'm sorry, Mr. Goldfarb's in the back. Can I help you?"

The brilliant Pepper smile, the one that can't be denied. She places the box on the counter in front of her. "I'm afraid I absolutely *must* speak with Mr. Goldfarb."

Ten minutes later, Pepper and I climb back into the sun-warmed Cadillac, together with one thousand four hundred dollars in neat crisp Franklins, folded into a corner of my pocketbook. I turn the ignition. Pepper loops the yellow scarf back around her hair. The pocketbook sits on the bench seat between us, loaded with cash.

I put the car in reverse, back up, and put on my turn signal, preparing to enter traffic.

"Something wrong?" Pepper asks, when the car doesn't move.

I change gears and pull out. "Nothing."

"Come on. Tell me. Are you in trouble?"

"It's nothing."

"Because I'm an expert. Trouble's my middle name. My first name, if you think about it."

I slow down for the red light ahead. "Nothing, I said."

"That kind of trouble, is it?" She lays her forearm along the side of the car, right along the slit of the rolled-down window, and fingers the triangle of glass at the corner of the windshield. "You know, we *could* just take off."

The light turns green. I press down on the gas pedal. "Take off?"

"Split. Evacuate. Disappear. We've got the cash. We've got the car."

At the word *disappear*, my fingers squeeze the steering wheel. "Oh, come on."

"I'm not joking. Not exactly."

"What makes you think I want to disappear?"

"Just a guess. I've been thinking, over the past couple of days, that maybe my sister's perfect little life isn't so perfect after all. That maybe you've finally figured out that your world-class husband isn't worth what you're paying for him."

"That's just stupid." I glance down at my pocketbook. "Anyway, I already tried disappearing, and it didn't work so well."

"Really? When was that?"

"A long time ago. Sometimes, Pepper, you just have to face your problems. To accept what God's given you and make the best of it. Give up and grow up."

Pepper doesn't reply. The car floats through the hot sunshine, down the long road. The buildings shimmer by, the other cars, the other people, limping down the sidewalks under the weight of the building heat. I'm wearing a large-brimmed hat to keep the sun from my skin, and it flutters in the draft, almost but not quite ready to blow off.

"So why do *you* want to disappear?" I say. "Speaking of perfect lives. Working for a hotshot senator. The high life in Washington and New York."

"I'll tell you if you tell me."

"Pepper . . ."

"Stop here," says Pepper.

"What?"

"Pull over, right here." Her voice is urgent.

I swerve the car to the curb. Someone lays on the horn, long and hard.

"What is it? Are you all right?"

Pepper points her long finger to a storefront just behind us. "It's a garage."

"What?"

I follow her finger. JOE'S GARAGE, says a grubby sign above a wide carriage entrance, AUTO PARTS AND SERVICE. DOMESTIC AND FOREIGN. An old-fashioned gas pump sits outside. Probably a box of buggy whips in the basement somewhere.

"I don't need any auto parts," I say.

"Yes, you do," she says. "Gas, oil. Repair manual. God knows what. Or Joe. Joe knows what." She giggles.

I gaze at her laughing face in bemusement. The pretty, wagging ends of her yellow scarf. Her unguarded nose, kissed by the sun. "Are you talking about the *Mercedes*? The Mercedes in the shed?"

Pepper spreads out her hands. "Sure, why not? If we're going to disappear, we might as well do it in style."

"But you don't know a thing about fixing cars."

"We're a couple of smart girls. How hard can it be?"

"You," I say, "are completely nuts."

She picks up my pocketbook and peels off a hundred-dollar bill from the wad. "That's why they love me."

Caspian, 1964

ap rose from the sofa and found his drink on the window-sill. He finished it off and held the glass against his stomach. "Depends, I guess. On what you mean by disappear. And who."

"Me." Her voice was determined. Clear of tears.

He needed another drink. He took his glass to the kitchenette and refilled it. When he turned, Tiny was still standing in place, swiveled to follow his progress. She'd unfolded the handkerchief again, and it dangled like a doll's bedsheet before her, held up at each corner by her elegant fingers.

"Cold feet?" he said.

"No. I don't know. It's been building for a while. All my life."

"You've wanted to disappear all your life?"

"Yes!" She collapsed back on the sofa and stared at the ceiling, pressing the handkerchief into her ribs.

He propped his shoulder against the doorway to the kitchenette. "Then why haven't you?"

"You don't know. You don't understand."

"Of course I don't know. We've only just met this morning."

"But you've been watching me all month, at the coffee shop. Watching me carefully."

Cap shrugged his other shoulder. "So I like watching pretty girls. Sue me."

Tiny lifted her head and looked at him. "Why do you do that? Pretend you're someone you're not."

He snorted. "Glass houses, Tiny."

"Look. Can I just have the other Caspian back for a second, please? I can't explain anything to this one."

The rush of adrenaline caught him by surprise, filling his bones with air. He ducked back to the kitchenette and set his glass on the counter, breathing slowly, in one, two, three, out one, two, three. His brain was already giddy with vodka. Empty stomach. They hadn't offered him anything to eat at the police station.

He picked up the broom and dustpan and stepped around the corner to sweep away the shards of Tiny's broken glass. The bin was empty, the garbage put out this morning before he left, a lifetime ago. The thousand pieces shivered against the bottom.

"All right," he said, returning to the living room. Tiny occupied the sofa, cradling his handkerchief in her hands, her dress bright against the old olive-green upholstery. He sat down next to her. "Why do you want to disappear?"

"No. Say something to me first. Something real."

He picked up her left hand. "I still have your engagement ring in my pocket. Do you want it back?"

"Oh, my God! The ring!" She straightened herself and looked down at her empty hand. "I'd forgotten all about it!"

"How could you forget a rock like that when it's missing from your finger?"

She fell back against the sofa cushion, but she didn't pull her fingers away, even when he placed his other hand on top, sandwiching her inside. She said, "Well, that's it, isn't it? Maybe I didn't want to remember."

"Cold feet," he said again.

"Maybe. I don't know. Haven't you ever felt—" She paused, collecting her thoughts. Her lashes were long and curling, a natural black, since she must have cried away all her mascara into his shoulder. He wanted to take her picture, to capture the extraordinary shadow of her eyelashes on her skin, the angle of her cheekbone in the slanting afternoon sun. "Haven't you ever felt trapped inside yourself, like you want to do something else, *be* someone else, and you can't break free, you can't loosen yourself from the—I don't know—this *thing* you're supposed to be, this public facsimile of yourself?"

"I don't know. Maybe." He ran over the words again. "Why don't you start from the beginning?"

"You don't want to hear all this."

"I'm used to it. All the other guys used to come to me with their stuff. Don't know why. I was the goddamned father confessor out there, sometimes. The things I heard, hell."

"You see? That's what I thought, when you walked in the shop that first day. I knew I could trust you."

"Just by looking at me?"

"Well, you were different from everyone else. You were reading Thomas Hardy. I thought, any guy *that* size who reads Thomas Hardy of his own free will, in paperback, curling back the cover so no one can tell, well, you can trust a guy like that. And then the waitress said—"

"Em?"

"Yes, Em. The dark-haired one. She said you were a good guy. A gentleman, she said. She also said you liked me." She nudged him with her elbow.

"Well, hell. That's the last time I tell her my secrets."

"So you *do* like me?" Tiny asked the ceiling.

"I'm crazy about you."

There. *Crazy about you.* The words were out, floating in the air, no sucking them back in.

"Oh, my God." She closed her eyes. "I can't believe this. I can't believe this is happening. I'm going to hell, aren't I?"

"Nothing's happening, Tiny. Nothing's happening unless you say so."

And for God's sake, *say so.*

She absorbed this information, turning it this way and that inside her perfect head, examining its possibilities and nuances. "Okay," she said at last.

"Okay, what?" he said, trying not to think about having sex.

"Okay, that makes me feel better. Even though it shouldn't matter, feeling better. I mean the point of all this, the point of disappearing, is to get away from that."

"From what, exactly?"

"From what everyone else expects of me. From worrying about pleasing everyone. Playing my little role. Living up to their expectations. Letting their expectations become my expectations, until I can't tell what's real, what I really want, because it's all wrapped up in *my* wanting what *they* want. A big, exciting life, the wife of a big, exciting man." She paused. "Does that make sense?"

"Sort of." He lifted away his topmost hand, his right hand, and propped his elbow on the back of the sofa. Maybe that would help him focus on something other than Tiny's nearby skin.

"I mean, why did you join the army?"

This was firmer ground. "Because I liked it. Because I knew it.

Knew I could do it well. Suits me. My father was a soldier. He stayed on after the war, made a career of it."

"But did you really want to be a soldier? Or had you never considered anything else? I mean, did your family want you to sign up, or did *you* want to sign up? For yourself?"

He thought about Granny and law school. "The opposite, I'd say. I don't have much to do with Dad's family, he was an only child. But my mother's family . . . well, I wouldn't say they disapprove, exactly. But they think I could do better. Be more ambitious."

"Oh." Her forefinger rubbed against his forefinger. Did she realize she was doing it? Did she feel the same friction of nerve endings, all the way to her backbone? Her gaze traveled back to the wall of prints. "What about your photographs? Did you ever think of doing that instead?"

"I *am* doing that."

"But if you had to make a choice. Between photography and the army. If the army told you you couldn't pick up a camera again, ever, what would you choose?"

He returned the caress of her finger. He couldn't help it. "What are we talking about, exactly?"

"When you walked into my coffee shop, a month ago—"

"*Your* coffee shop?"

She opened her eyes—she'd held them closed, all this time—and tilted her head to look at him. "Yes, *my* coffee shop. I've gone there for years, during breaks between classes."

"What classes? Aren't you done with college?"

"Dance classes. I'm a dancer. I dance with this amateur group, teach the younger kids."

Her slender calves, curved with muscles. The lithe grace of her back. The taut arms, the elegant enigma of her, delicate and rope strong at the same time.

"Of course," he said. "Jesus, of course. I should have guessed."

"Yes, well, I love it. It's the only thing I've ever done that made me feel right. Made me feel myself. And Mums said fine, live in Boston and do your dancing, the perfect way to wait him out until he proposes . . ."

"Damn it."

"So I did, and I just thought—well, it never occurred to me—"

"What?"

"That I was supposed to stop, once we got married."

"Who says you have to stop?"

"No one *said*. It's just assumed, by all of them. I realized it about a month ago, just before I saw you for the first time. I'd had tea with his grandmother a couple of days before, and she said something—I don't remember exactly, she's so elliptical, she sneaks everything in until you realize too late that she's been scolding you all along or committed you to some awful thing or another—anyway, just what a relief it must be, giving up the dancing, all that hard work, I could concentrate on getting our house set up and having babies, helping my husband with his work. . . ."

"Damn it."

"And it's not that I don't want any of it. I want babies, I love babies. That little boy today . . ." Her eyes welled up at the corners.

"What does he think? Your fiancé?" Strange, that he could talk about this fellow as if he were an inanimate object of some kind, a cipher, when in fact Tiny had promised to marry him. Had known him for years, had gone to endless dinners and picnics and football games, probably frolicked in the Cape Cod sand with him. Probably even had sex with him. He existed. A real person whom Tiny, this tempting Tiny sitting by his side, inches away, was supposed to be in love with.

"He assumes it, too. Of course he does. They all think alike in that family. Single-minded."

He swore again.

They sat quietly, without saying anything. Cap thought about his drink in the kitchenette, but he couldn't move an inch, couldn't direct his body to exist anywhere else than right here, next to Tiny, her steady pulse, the slow dance of their fingertips revolving around each other. He'd given up trying not to think about sex. He'd given his imagination all the rein in the world, picturing her naked beneath him, writhing on top of him; now he added in the intoxicating element of her dancer's athleticism, the sensuality of dance itself. Ballet, he was sure of it. Tiny was the ballet sort of girl. Christ almighty. He was sitting on the sofa, screwing fingers with an engaged ballet dancer.

She wasn't the only one going to hell.

"But it's not just that," she said. "*That* was only the moment of realization, the moment I knew I had to escape somehow. It's been building all year, ever since the night we got engaged."

"Then why did you do it? Get engaged? Say yes?"

"Because that's what I *do.*" Softly. "I do what I'm supposed to do. Girls like me, we wear our pearls and we write our thank-you notes the very next morning, and we fall in love with only the best sort of young man, the kind of man who's going places and will take us with him. And when he asks us to marry him, we say *yes*."

"But why? That's the part I don't understand. Anyway, I've seen girls like that, I *know* girls like that, and you're not one of them." He pauses. "On the outside, maybe, but even then . . ."

"You don't understand. There's this allure. It's like a scientist striving for the Nobel Prize, the ultimate mark of success in your chosen field. You won't just be any old wife, living out in the suburbs, same thing every day. You'll be *his* wife, meeting exciting people, doing exciting things. The night he proposed, it was the night of my dreams. The night I'd been waiting for all along. The culmination of all my efforts, right? And it was. It was a hell of a night."

"I'll bet."

"Oh, it was the limit. The absolute limit. Do you know how he did it?"

"No idea."

"You'll love it. Picture this. It was the night after he graduated from law school. I'd been waiting for years, you know. I almost gave up on him a dozen times, but . . . well, he was . . . he *is*—you'd have to know him, I guess—he's dazzling. He holds you in his palm. He's the one, there's no one else close."

She spoke in a curiously emotionless voice, echoing Cap's own attitude: as if her fiancé's charms were something you might read about in a magazine profile, unconnected with a breathing human being. Cap wanted to ask if she loved him, *really* loved him, but it seemed clumsy somehow. A vulgar question to ask, in the middle of such a confession.

"I knew everyone was expecting him to propose," she said. "My girlfriends were starting to laugh behind my back: *Oh, he'll never ask her, she'll be waiting till she's sixty.* Most of them were already married or engaged. It was humiliating. I forgot why I wanted to get married, or why I wanted *him*, I just wanted the damned ring already. God, I'm so lousy, aren't I? How did I get this way?"

Without warning, she yanked her fingers away from his and jumped to her feet. She crossed the floor, rubbing the knuckles of her left hand, while Cap leaned forward on the sofa cushion and measured her elastic stride, the length of her neck.

She stopped in front of the wall of photographs. The sunlight hit her profile head-on, draping her in gold. "Anyway. We went out to a big dinner with his family to celebrate the graduation—top of his class, of course, he gave a speech and everything, a grand speech, oh yes, *stirring*, they all told me that, see, he's a great one for speeches—and everyone toasted him, his grandmother and aunts and uncles and cousins, the whole clan of them. Admiring their crown prince. So proud. We took up an entire banquet room at the Copley Plaza. Champagne and caviar and filet. A great big chocolate cake, his favorite. They don't splash out often, his family, but when they do . . . well, they make their point. I sat next to his sister. She took my arm and talked about how happy they all were. *Grateful,* she said. That was the word. How much everyone loved me. How good I was for him. The perfect girl to settle him down. Can't you just hear it? What a hoot."

She laughed and shook her head and reached out to smooth down the edge of one of the photographs, which was curling at the corner. "God, the lights were so bright. I don't know why I remember that. All those chandeliers. Anyway. Afterward, he took me out for a drive in his convertible—it was midnight, by then—and somewhere in Wellesley we stopped by the side of the road, in the moonlight, and there was this picnic basket waiting for us with a bottle of champagne. And the ring. Glittering there at the bottom of my glass. Can you believe it? He'd left the ring there at the roadside, the whole time we'd been eating dinner. A ring like that."

"Jesus."

"Well, that's him all over. Nothing bad can touch him, can it? The bill never comes due. So I was thrilled and said yes and we drank down the whole bottle, there by the road. In the moonlight. I don't know how we made it home. And I woke up the next morning with the worst hangover in the world and thought, Now what? Mother's happy. He's happy. The families are happy. Well, not my sisters, I imagine, but they're never happy with me. So why aren't *I* happy? I mean, my exciting life is about to begin at last. Why aren't I *happy*, for God's sake?" Her voice died away. She braced one hand on the wall and lifted the other to shield her eyes. "And I've been trying to figure that out ever since."

What was that about a force field? It was down without a trace, every barrier zapped out, the electric fence switched off, leaving only her tender and vulnerable skin between them.

Why aren't I happy? He considered the words, which might mean anything. Might mean a spoiled girl doesn't know happy when it spills champagne at midnight on her pretty young bosom. Might mean a restless soul yearns to break free of her gilded shell. What *was* happy, anyway? Was *he* happy? Did it matter? Or did you just keep on doing the thing you were supposed to do, whatever it was: did your duty, did your part to keep the whole vast machinery of the world clicking along, and leave all the happiness bullshit to bored housewives and college students with too much time on their hands?

Her head was bowed. He wanted to walk over and take her in his arms.

"All right." He wove his fingers together. "Fine. So you don't want to get married after all. Why not just call it off? Tell them you can't go through with it. Call it all off."

"Oh, God. You don't understand my family. You don't understand *his*. They'll talk me out of it. They'll tell me it's cold feet. Every bride feels this way. Nerves. And then they'll say I can't back out. Everyone's counting on me, everyone believes in me. He needs me. He's the perfect match. And that's the thing, you know." A burst of half-hysterical laughter. "He is! The absolute perfect match. I might be First Lady one day, I'll bet, if we play our cards right. If we put every foot right. Imagine that! What a triumph, what a life we'll have."

A queasy feeling stirred the bottom of Cap's belly. The rear lobes of his brain.

But she was turning now, turning toward him, and her face was so bleak and pleading he couldn't think of anything else. Just her. Tiny, in her berry-red dress, her luminescent sun-draped skin.

"And I'll suffocate," she said softly. "Worse. I'll become one of them. This is my last chance, Caspian."

He rose and walked to the kitchenette to fetch his drink, which he finished in a long and greedy gulp. He slammed the glass back down on the counter. Hard enough to make the cupboards rattle. Make the Frigidaire gasp and sneeze.

"You'll help me, won't you? I saw you at the coffee shop today. You knew what to do."

He looked up. She stood right there where his living room met his kitchenette, braced with her white palm high against the wall, just above the top of her head. One stocking foot was curled around the other calf. He wondered if he could span her waist with his hands, like a girl from another century.

"Yes," he said. "I know what to do."

Tiny, 1966

Pepper wants to know how long it's been since I last made love. (That's not the term she employs.)

I lean against the wall of the shed and cross my arms. "What the hell kind of question is that?"

"A simple, direct one. With a simple, direct answer. Come on. A week? A month?"

"It's not a fair question and you know it. I lost a baby, remember?"

"Four weeks ago."

"And Frank's away."

"What's that? I can't hear you when you mumble like that."

I push myself off the wall and walk forward to the front end of the Mercedes-Benz. The hood is up, and Pepper's legs emerge from the side, clad in old blue dungarees and salt-stained sneakers. Her torso is buried deep, lost to view behind the raised metal hood. I place my hands on the edge of the grille. "Frank's away," I repeat.

"Oh, yes. *Campaigning.*"

"It's his job, Pepper."

"It's July. The election's in November."

"The primary's in early September. And there's fund-raising. That's the big thing, fund-raising. You can never have too much money."

"Well, he was back last weekend. Did you do it then?"

"I'm not going to answer that."

"So you didn't. Why not?"

"Pepper!"

"All right, then. Forget the past four weeks. When was the last time you did it? When he got you pregnant to begin with? Oh, shit. Can you find me a wrench?"

I stalk to the toolbox. "What kind of wrench?"

"I don't know. Any old wrench. But answer the question."

I grab one of the rusty metal wrenches—at least I think it's a wrench—and carry it back to the gaping, oil-smelling hole in which my sister is immersed. "Here you are."

Without looking, she thrusts a dirty palm in my direction and plunges the wrench into the hole with her.

"Are you sure you know what you're doing?" I ask.

Pepper's head pops out from the German innards. Her valuable chestnut hair is wrapped up in a checkered cloth, like Rosie the Riveter. A tiny smear of grease forms a fetching beauty spot at the corner of her mouth. She holds out the wrench. "Tiny, this is a screwdriver."

I snatch it back and head for the toolbox again. "You would know."

You might perceive how expertly I avoided Pepper's last question. The truth is, we've had this conversation before, or something like it. Pepper—I don't mean to shock you—she loves to talk about sex. I let her rattle on, up to a point. Why not? It's all about the intimacy of watching her work in the dilapidated old shed, brashly taking apart a delicate, high-performance Mercedes-Benz engine and attempting to put it back together again, all the while keeping the whole affair secret from the nosy big noses of the Hardcastle females. (Well, Tom, too.) I keep a bucket of suds (soap, not beer) next to the door, so she can wash off the grease before she emerges, and even then I live in delicious terror of her being found out by that fetching smear of black grease on her cheek.

As to why, I have no idea.

It's not as if I'm actually planning to drive off with Pepper, should she miraculously succeed in getting the damned automobile running again. (No, don't worry, I won't bore you with the entire tragic list of casualties and snafus; let's just say that thirty years of idleness isn't good for a delicate high-performance Mercedes-Benz engine, especially when tended by one young woman with plenty of moxie but no previous mechanical aptitude, reading from a disintegrating old manual written in German and obtained by Joe's Garage at great expense from God knew what channels.) It's not as if I'm not already busy. It's not as if I haven't got a million ties binding me to my promising life, to my marriage, to this summertime patch of Cape Cod and its winter cousin on Newbury Street.

Maybe I just enjoy spending a few leisured minutes with my sister, every so often, for the first time in my life.

Pepper's voice continues, muffled by metal. "So. Poor old you. Pretty Franklin's a dud in bed. Or else the spark's just gone. Have you thought about swinging?"

"*Swinging?*"

Pepper leans her elbows against an exhaust pipe. She takes the wrench—at least, I hope it's a wrench—from my hand. "You know. You meet at someone's house, you have a few drinks, you eat a few canapés, you switch husbands . . ."

"I know what swinging *is*, Pepper. I'm just not going to discuss this with you. You're not even married. You have no idea . . ."

"I'm just trying to help, darling. Trying to pry the old prude out of you."

"You're trying to pry, period."

"Well, I'm curious to know why my sister isn't in love with her dazzling husband."

"I *am* in love with my husband."

"Then why aren't you out on the campaign with him, smiling pretty for the cameras and the big-pocket donors and then screwing like rabbits in the hotel afterward?"

"For heaven's sake, Pepper!"

"Politicians are sexy, Tiny. It's a fact. If you don't, some other girl will." She laughs and waggles her wrench. (I'll say that again: *waggles her wrench.*) "Hell, even if you *do,* some other girl might. He's only human."

I have no answer for that. I turn away and wipe my hands on my apron.

"In fact, I wouldn't be surprised if he's up inside some tart from his campaign office right this minute, you know, in the back room where they keep the VOTE FRANK bumper stickers, some shapely little tart like me . . ."

There is a cough from the doorway of the shed.

I spin. Pepper bangs her head on the hood of the Mercedes and drops the wrench—*clangedy-clang-clang*—on the pile of delicate high-performance Mercedes-Benz engine parts scattered next to the front fender.

My hands freeze inside the folds of my skirt. My throat freezes, too. It falls to Pepper to greet the new arrival, which she does in typical Pepper fashion, throaty on the vowels, double on the entendre.

"Well, hello there, Frank. We were *just this second* wondering where you might be."

I must have been seventeen or eighteen, still in school but nearly a woman. I went to the kitchen in my old quilted dressing gown, looking for a glass of milk from the icebox. It was late, which was unusual for me, so I suppose I'd been up reading. Anyway, I didn't need to go hunting in the icebox, because the milk bottle was on the kitchen table, and Daddy was pouring himself a glass. He looked up, surprised, as if it were some extraordinary thing, finding your own daughter in your own kitchen.

"What's the matter, Daddy?" I asked, reaching for a glass from the cabinet, because I saw from his face that he was drinking the milk because he was trying not to drink the Scotch.

"Oh, nothing," he said, and then, as an afterthought: "Lost another case."

I sat down and poured the milk into my glass. "You win some, you lose some, I guess."

"But I lose a lot of them, don't I?" His hair was rumpled, his eyes bruised.

I remember wondering why he cared. It wasn't as if Daddy's career was anything more than a hobby; it wasn't as if the family's capital wasn't safely invested in nice straight government bonds, yielding just the right amount, enough to pay the maintenance on the apartment and the house in East Hampton, enough to pay the housekeeper and cook and driver, the school fees and the dresses, the club dues and the fresh weekly flowers.

I ventured: "If you don't enjoy it, you could always retire, couldn't you?"

He laughed deep. "Quit! That's right, I could quit, couldn't I?

Before they ask me to resign from the partnership. I could just god-damn quit. Wouldn't your mother be so proud." He drank the milk. "Proud as ever."

I covered his hand. "But she *is* proud of you."

"No, my dear, she is not. Why should she be? If she'd married the right man, she could have been First Lady. She could really have been somebody. Instead she married me."

"Mummy loves you, though. She does."

At this, my father leaned forward, and though he was not a man of strong passions, though he was not an intimate kind of daddy, he looked at me like he meant it, and his eyes became fierce. I had never seen his eyes like that. I had always thought of my father as a man without any fire at all.

"Listen to me," he said. "A little fatherly advice. You're a lovely girl, Tiny, a good sweet girl, but you're tender. Your sisters, they can take care of themselves, they'll be happy running around town mak-ing trouble all their lives, but you need a husband like a vine needs a tree. So I'll tell you this. You want to be happy? Marry a man who can take you places. Marry a man you can be proud of, a man with a future ahead of him. A woman's never happy if she can't respect her husband."

"But Mummy does respect you."

He leaned back and smiled and shook his head, and that was all. Fatherly advice, over and out. We finished our milk and went to bed, and I lay awake on my pillow, staring at the ceiling, until I heard my mother arrive home, the sound of her heels skidding on the parquet hall, and I thought, for the first time, My God, she's miserable, isn't she?

And then: Maybe he's right. Maybe I'm just a vine after all, a vine in search of a tree.

You can't tell Granny Hardcastle about the car," I say.

Frank cranes his neck toward me, keeping his eyes carefully on the road. The engine of his little yellow roadster is loud; the wind is even louder. "What's that?"

I cup my hand around my mouth and lean toward his ear. "The car! You can't tell Granny Hardcastle!"

"Wouldn't dream of it!" he shouts back. "But why not?"

"She'll put a stop to it."

"Why do you say that?"

"She puts a stop to everything."

"What's that?"

"Everything!"

He makes a sort of half smile and nods, at the same time straightening himself before the windshield to end the conversation. To save his voice, which he'll need tonight.

I want to say: How much did you hear? Do you agree? Are we having enough sex? Are we in love? Were we ever in love? Are you having sex with other women? Because politicians are sexy, and you're only human.

I want to say: I have something to tell you. A few tiny little things to tell you. A bit of a confession, in fact.

I look down at my lap. My pocketbook rests in the crease of my thighs, which are covered in a skirt of blue linen, below a neat square jacket of blue linen and a necklace of fat irregular freshwater pearls. Matching earrings, of course. Shoes of blue. Stockings of nylon. Gloves of white kid. Legs long, waist trim, lipstick pink. Bones dainty and symmetrical, hair dark and obedient. *You'll have to hurry and get ready, I'm afraid,* Franklin had said, as we strode across the driveway oval to the

Big House. *Cocktails start at six. I'm sorry to have to drag you out, I know you're happier here, but Dad thinks you need to be there.* So considerate, Frank. Not a single allusion to Pepper's provocative conversation. Not a single raised eyebrow, not a shared conspiratorial wink, husband to wife: *We know better, don't we, darling?*

I say, "Do I look all right?"

He doesn't hear me. His hands are steady on the wheel; the hot wind ruffles his hair. I think, That's odd, he looks a little pale. A little tense around the mouth. The eyes, squinting intently at the windshield, focused on some detail far away from the two of us.

I lean closer. "Are you all right?"

"What's that?"

"Are you *all right*?"

He reaches for my hand and squeezes it. "Yes, all right! You?"

"Yes!"

There's no point saying anything else, when he can't hear me.

Frank's father is waiting for us in the hotel suite, drink in hand. I set my pocketbook on the coffee table and kiss his cheek.

"I'm sorry to drag you into town," he says. "Hot day like this. Drink?"

"Yes, please. Vodka tonic."

He turns to the cabinet and unscrews the top of the vodka bottle. Frank walks to the window and lights a cigarette. The room is full of polished brown furniture. A stack of briefing folders sits in the center of a rectangular sofa, upholstered in the kind of murky florals that can disguise any stain, no matter how guilty. Frank always likes to overnight in a hotel when he's campaigning, even when we're in Boston. The separation from our domestic environment puts him on his game, he says.

"Photo call at five," says Mr. Hardcastle, as he plucks ice cubes from the bucket, one by one, "and then the donors come in. Cocktails at six, then dinner. You brought evening clothes, I hope?"

"Yes. Frank filled me in. I'm all packed and ready."

Frank turns around and leans against the windowsill. "She knows what to do, Dad. Don't worry about Tiny."

Mr. Hardcastle smiles and hands me the drink. "I never do. Thanks for coming in, my dear. I hope it wasn't an imposition."

"Not at all." I sip and swallow. My gloves are still on, my hands sweating beneath.

"You're feeling better, then? Join us on the campaign trial?"

"Of course. You only have to ask, you know."

"Well, we appreciate it. It looks a hell of a lot better, you know, when the wife's by his side. To say nothing of your personal charm with these donors we've got tonight."

"Oh, I don't know about that." The room is hot. I set down my drink, take off my gloves, and unbutton my jacket. The blouse beneath is silk, pale cream. Mr. Hardcastle glances briefly at my chest, at the spot of dampness between my breasts.

"Franklin, open the window," he says. "The other thing is, the poll numbers are slipping."

I look between Mr. Hardcastle and Frank, who has turned to open the window. His suit jacket is off, his sleeves rolled up to the elbows. "I didn't realize that."

"We didn't want to worry you. It's this goddamned Murray, he's hitting hard on Vietnam, rousing the fucking—excuse me—rousing the rabble." He slams his drink onto the cabinet and looks at Frank, who has turned around again and propped himself against the open window, the yellow afternoon sun. "Nothing we can't handle. We have a plan. You're part of it, if you don't mind. For one thing, you photograph like a dream. Murray's wife can talk, all right, she can talk your fucking ear off, but she looks like a constipated rat."

"*Dad.*" Frank shakes his head and nods at me.

"I beg your pardon, my dear. You'll excuse the plain speaking; we were up late last night. Strategy meeting." He lifts one hand to his forehead and massages the loose skin with his fingertips.

I swirl the liquid around the glass. Frank's face is still pale, the cigarette still jerking up and down. Mr. Hardcastle's anxious fingertips rise from his forehead to his hair, raking through the gray threads. Son and father. Their stares, as they regard me, are curiously alike: the same blue eyes, the same expressions of wary calculation.

To be perfectly honest, I haven't given this campaign much thought. It's the maiden race, a gimme, Frank the Thoroughbred against a pack of anonymous local nags. He's supposed to win handily. Going away. Outclassing the field in a single blinding Hardcastle smile. The idea of Frank failing at this—failing at the first hurdle, the September primary, Frank who has never failed at anything—causes the world to turn upside down before my eyes.

"How bad is it?" I ask.

"We're six points behind at the moment," says Frank. He reaches for an ashtray and crushes out the cigarette.

"I see."

"We're not sure why," says Mr. Hardcastle. "Just looks like they don't trust us. The old story: rich boy from Brookline, buying his seat. That's the view."

I allow a smile. "Imagine that."

Mr. Hardcastle's face reacts as if it's been dipped in wet cement and left to dry. "So we want to humanize him. Bring out the wife. You've been almost invisible this summer."

"I didn't realize I was needed."

"Frank insisted we didn't push you. He wanted you to stay put out there. On the beach." Mr. Hardcastle's voice is very soft, in contrast to his eyes, which penetrate the space between my eyebrows.

I look at Frank's creased forehead and back at my father-in-law's hard squint, and my organs shrivel up inside my belly. This failure of Frank's—a failure saturating the atmosphere with cigarette smoke, creasing Hardcastle foreheads and squinting Hardcastle eyes—spreads across the room to sink down upon my head. It's *my* failure. I've failed them. A good wife belongs at the candidate's side, well-groomed and smiling. A good wife follows the candidate's campaign, familiarizes herself with his constituents and their concerns, knows every minute fluctuation in the polls. A good wife poses for the camera with her best foot forward (to elongate the leg, you see, and emphasize the curve of hip) and her best smile hiding her troubles. A good wife produces equally photogenic children to illustrate the candidate's qualities as a family man. A good wife conceals no shaming secrets, sells no affectionate Christmas jewelry, admits to no untoward desires.

For some reason, the accusation in Mr. Hardcastle's gaze is easier to bear than Frank's worried sympathy. I turn back to my husband anyway. "I'm so sorry. I didn't realize." I manage a smile. "My first campaign, after all. Push me all you like."

Before Frank can reply, Mr. Hardcastle says, "Good. The *Globe*'s been asking to do a feature on the two of you. You'll be hosting a reporter at your table tonight. Tomorrow morning at ten, they're sending the same reporter and a photographer to Newbury Street to do the usual piece, candidate and his family at home."

"If that's all right," says Frank. His arms are crossed, one finger tapping the other elbow.

"Of course it's all right. We haven't any groceries, but . . ."

"I've sent over one of the staffers already to fix things up. Fill the icebox, plump the pillows. Put out fresh flowers."

"I see." Failure, failure. Now one of the campaign staffers is filling in, performing the duties I should have overseen myself. I add, a little desperate, sinking fast: "I'll be up early, of course, to make sure everything's in order."

"There's no need. Better you get plenty of rest."

I think of the floor of the shed, scattered with car parts. My room in the Big House, which I left in disorder, in the frantic haste of showering and packing but also the unsupervised laziness of the past few weeks. A jar of face cream sits open on the counter. My earrings were left out on the bureau last night. Worse: a dress, unironed, stained with red wine, lies casually over the top of the slipper chair in the corner.

"I've had plenty of rest. I'm ready to work." I lift the sweating glass to my lips.

"Good girl," says Mr. Hardcastle. "We'll put our best foot forward tonight. The lovely wife. The wounded cousin."

I cough up a drop or two. "The *what*?"

"Cap." Frank pushes himself off the windowsill to reach for the cigarettes. "We've asked Cap to join us tonight."

"*Caspian?*"

"You don't mind, do you, darling? I've told him to be on his best behavior. No throwing punches, no matter what the hecklers say. Not that there'll be hecklers tonight."

I finish my drink and set it down on the coffee table next to my pocketbook and gloves. "Not at all. If you'll excuse me, I think I'll just freshen up a bit before I change."

I n the white marble bathroom, I drop my skirt and blouse in a pile and stare at myself in the mirror. My dewy white skin, my clinging silk slip. My eyes, large and round and brown. Like a doe, my mother used to say, appraising me like a fine painting, adding up my market value as a series of individual components. Pretty face equals x. Delicate figure equals y. Air of virgin innocence equals z.

But she was wrong. It isn't just an algebra of components, is it? It's the whole package. It's how you hold it all together.

There is a knock on the door. For an illogical instant, known only to my subconscious, I imagine it's Caspian Harrison.

"It's me," says my husband.

"Come in."

Frank appears behind me in the mirror, so suddenly that I'm startled by his good looks, by the width of his shoulders in comparison to mine. He only seems large to me like this, when I see us together in the mirror, the physical difference between my body and his. Or maybe it's just that I'm such a small and insignificant creature. *Such a tiny little thing,* my mother used to say, giving my cheek an approving caress.

He smiles. "I have something for you."

His hands appear, and with them a slim rope of diamonds alternating with glittering navy stones, sapphires probably. Before I can gasp, he loops them around my neck.

"My *God,* Frank!"

He fastens the necklace at my nape with his expert fingers. I touch the stones in the hollow of my throat, which are larger than the others, anchored by a central sapphire the size of a dime.

Frank kisses my earlobe and stares in the mirror. "Beautiful. Just as I thought."

"What's this for?"

"For being you. For putting up with your busy old husband and his busybody family."

My eyes are already filling up, all wide and oily in the mirror, and I hardly ever cry. Tears never got you anywhere in the old Schuyler apartment on Fifth Avenue. "Of course," I say stupidly. "Of course."

"I didn't mean to put you on the spot like that. Back there with Dad."

"You should have told me things weren't going well."

"I didn't want to push you, after what happened. Anyway, it's only summer. We have months to go."

"But I'm your wife. I'm supposed to be helping you."

"You *are* helping me. You're a wonderful wife." He kisses the side of my neck, above the diamonds and sapphires. His lips are cool and worried. "I'm sorry I've been neglecting you like this."

The shed is so far away, Pepper's conversation is so far away, that I stare at the glint in Frank's sandy hair for a few seconds before I catch his meaning.

"Oh, God. Don't listen to my sister. She's just oversexed, that's all."

"You know I'm just giving you time to get better, don't you? After what happened. Trying to be a respectful husband." He smiles into the mirror.

I lay my hand on one of his. "Of course I know that."

He squeezes my arms gently. "*Are* you feeling better, Tiny? I know it's still soon."

Here's the thing about drought: when the rain comes again, you're not quite sure what to do with it. The drops fall on your dry skin, scattering the dust, and you don't know how to absorb it. After the first miscarriage, the doctor told me I could resume relations with my husband as soon as the discharge (yes, that's exactly what he called the remains of my pregnancy, the *discharge*) had finished. You need to get right back in the saddle after a fall, he said. I did as he instructed, I followed his prescription because he was a doctor, and because a good wife doesn't refuse her husband, and as soon as my uterus was demonstrably empty again I reported this fact to Frank—we were just climbing into bed, I in my nightgown and he in his silk pajamas—and he said *All right* and settled in closer, and I thought, No, this is wrong. He kissed me, and my mouth, which was filled with grief, found him intolerable. He took off my nightgown, and in that instant, as the lamplight struck my body, my flesh cringed away from his, my whole heart screamed, *No, I don't want you, I don't want you inside me, I only want my baby back, my precious little baby who never had a chance, who is gone without a trace, never to return, never to be known to me.*

But here's the thing: I never said it out loud.

Well, you know me. I do my duty. I do what makes people happy. So I lay there while Frank made love to me, his silk pajama shirt flapping valiantly against my chest, his eyes screwed shut in concentration, and I hated him for doing it, and myself for letting him, and when I thought he fell asleep I curled into a ball and cried carefully into my pillow. I didn't think he heard, but we didn't make love again for a month and a half, and it took a lucky accident, a combination of too much champagne and a sultry bitch making her move on Frank at a cocktail party one night, to unfreeze my body and lock us back together, panting, reckless, on the living room sofa at midnight, a thing we had never done before or since.

After the second miscarriage—which occurred shortly after the telephone jangled with the news that Frank's cousin Caspian had been airlifted from the Laos border two days earlier with critical injuries, and was not expected to survive—Frank was more careful. My God, I don't think he even hinted at sex for two months, and even then we endured several awkward efforts before we were back to normal. Twice a week or so: a pleasant, steady matrimonial rhythm for an attractive young couple hoping for a baby.

"I know it's soon," Frank says, and you can't blame him for that, poor man.

I don't know how to soften my body, how to receive him. I need champagne, I need a woman in a black dress putting her hand on my husband's chest in the corner of a drunken room. I need to silence the back of my brain, whispering, *Caspian's here, Caspian's back, you'll see Caspian tonight.* I need to concentrate on this, my marriage, the two of us, Frank and Tiny. What is real. What exists. What cannot be altered.

"You're so good to me," I say, to drown out the whisper. "You really are."

"God. Don't say that. It's the other way around. You're good to *me*."

"I've been wallowing in self-pity. I should have been here in the city, with you."

"Don't listen to my father. I have plenty of help here. Too much. Anyway, it's early days. We have weeks until the primary."

"No, it's true. I've let you down, and I promised myself, I promised myself when we got married, that I'd never, ever do that. I'd *never* let you down."

He turns me around. "Jesus, no, don't cry, Tiny." He bends down and kisses my eyes, my cheeks. "Remember the photographers."

Remember the photographers. Downstairs in the ballroom, waiting, flashbulbs poised. The photo call at five, the reporter at our table, ready to take every note. To document the perfect young life of the perfect young couple.

"What time is it?" I ask.

He checks his watch. "A quarter past four."

"I've got to start getting ready."

"All right." But he doesn't let go. He raises his hands and strokes my hair, over and over, smoothing it flat against my head, except that the flip at the bottom insists on springing free whenever his palms lift away. "I *do* love you, Tiny. I do. Don't ever think I don't."

"I'd never think that."

"Poor Tiny."

"I'm fine, Frank. Really."

"No, you're not." He kisses me again, warm and deep. "I'll make it up to you tonight. If you want me to."

"Of course I want you to."

"I owe it to you. You've been so good to me. I'll make it up to you. You'll fall in love with me all over again." The dazzling smile breaks out, the gleaming teeth, while his hands keep stroking, stroking, down my throat and over the glittering necklace to cover my breasts.

"What makes you think I ever stopped?" I say.

Caspian, 1964

When Cap returned from the French bakery on Beacon Street the next morning, bearing breakfast in one hand and a newspaper in the other, music was floating through the walls and under his door, colored with the scent of coffee.

He paused at the top of the stairs. It was a waltz of some kind, tinnily rendered, probably Strauss, not that he'd listened to the pile of old disks under the record player in years. Not since he was a kid. He shifted the bag of croissants from one hand to the other—oh, the *look* the girl had given him at the bakery, the raised-eyebrow-curled-lip look, a look pregnant with *Entertaining a lady friend this morning, are we?*—and fished for the key in his pocket.

No, not Strauss, it was Tchaikovsky, he decided, as he juggled the newspaper and croissants and opened the door; but before he could explore this thought any further, it more or less fell to pieces and dissolved into the ripples of his gray matter, because right bang before his dazzled eyeballs, Miss Tiny Doe was dancing across the length of the living room, wearing one of his shirts *and nothing else.*

He knew his jaw was dangling somewhere around his sternum, and the bakery bag and the newspaper clung for dear life to the tips of his slack fingers, but he couldn't summon the strength to put any of them back in proper place.

All right. Jesus. *Yes*, she was wearing something else. Her—what did girls like her call them?—her foundation garments were right in place where they should be, thank God, flashing beneath the ends of his white shirt as she performed an exuberant series of pirouettes on the balls of her beautiful feet. Her eyebrows were screwed in concentration, but her mouth smiled as it flashed past and past, like a singularly arresting strobe light.

Cap knew nothing about ballet, but he recognized the tireless perfection in the movements of her right leg, fully exposed, flicking elegantly back and forth as it propelled her around. And her left leg, long and straight, holding her up atop an impossibly miniature ankle, the foot pumping up and down like a slender piston in the rhythm of her rotation. He couldn't even breathe, looking at her like this.

He moved like a robot to the kitchenette and set the croissants and the *Boston Globe* on the scrap of empty Formica, and then he headed to the darkroom.

Two days, he told her last night, as they shared an omelet and a pair of vodka gimlets for dinner. She had two days to decide what she wanted to do. She was still in shock from the coffee shop robbery, after all. She had to think about this carefully. Rationally. With a cool head. The stakes were high. Her entire life, in fact. She realized that, didn't she?

Oh yes, she'd said. Her eyes gleamed.

Fine, then. She could sleep in his room, he told her. He'd take the sofa and a blanket.

The loneliest damned night of his life, including the ones he'd slept in the jungle.

He found his camera, his flash. The morning light didn't reach the living room, which faced west. He'd need his fastest film, to catch those flashing legs. Or maybe the blur would look even better. Capture that floating quality in her movement.

She was still dancing when he returned, but she caught sight of him this time, or else the sight of him actually registered on her brain, and she stopped almost midleap.

He lifted the camera. "No, keep going."

"I can't with you standing there, taking pictures."

"Pretend I'm not here."

She walked over to the record player, lifted the arm, and switched off the turntable.

"Nice shirt," he said.

"I'm sorry. Do you mind?"

"Not at all. It suits you. I don't suppose any of my trousers will fit?"

She laughed. She was still facing the record player, one hand on the edge of the box. "Not a chance. I made coffee."

"Good. I brought breakfast. I hope you like croissants." He replaced the lens cap, set down the camera, and headed for the kitchenette.

"You bought croissants?" She pronounced the word with a marked Parisian accent.

"You seem like the croissant kind of girl. Was I wrong?"

"No." She laughed again. "I like croissants. Here, I'll pour the coffee."

She came up behind him while he reached for the plates, faintly humid with exercise, breathing quickly. The mugs were on the top shelf. He pulled down a pair and handed them to her, trying not to breathe her in too deeply. In the absence of perfume, she smelled of skin and female perspiration, and a familiar scent he recognized as his own laundry soap. The combination unnerved him.

"Thank you," she said, taking the mugs and filling them from the shiny stainless-steel percolator, the only object he'd bought new for the apartment. "I hope you like it strong."

"Black and thick."

"I thought so." She handed him his mug and opened the Frigidaire for the milk. He had to turn away, at the sight of Tiny Doe's half-dressed limbs poised in front of his icebox light. She moved about his kitchenette without the slightest self-consciousness, adding milk and sugar to her coffee, stirring, joining him at the little table with her breakfast. The shirt, thank God, was buttoned almost to the collar. "Thank you for running out so early," she said.

"I was up."

"Oh, was that you, thumping up and down the stairs? I had to put my head under the pillow."

He shrugged. "Morning exercise. Why didn't you let me take the picture?"

"I don't like having my picture taken. I never have." She tore off a section of croissant with unnecessary vigor.

"What, are you part Indian?"

"I beg your pardon?"

"Well, some of them don't like having their pictures taken, apparently. Because if you capture an image of someone, it's like you've taken a part of his soul. Or so I'm told."

She lifted the mug of coffee to her lips. "Well, they're right. That's exactly how I feel."

"What if I promise to give you the prints afterward? And the negatives?"

"Then what's the point of it? For you, I mean."

"Just to see if I can do it, I guess. Capture you, capture the essence of the dancing. On film."

"And why do you want to do that?"

He finished his croissant and swallowed it down with a gulp of coffee. "Because it's the most beautiful thing I've ever seen."

Her long fingers went still around her coffee mug. She stared down at them, at the coffee, brown and milky. "Me, or the dancing?"

"Both."

She made a choking sound.

"I'm sorry, I didn't mean . . ."

"No! No. Thank you. It's a very nice compliment."

"It's not a compliment. It's just . . ." He'd finished his croissant, his coffee, too. Tiny sat with her head bowed, across from him. He rose and took his empty dishes to the sink. "It's just what I thought, when I came in. That's all."

"Well, thank you for telling me."

"Don't thank me."

His belly rumbled softly. He was still hungry; a single croissant and a cup of coffee didn't go far when you'd already pushed your body to the far limits of human endurance by six o'clock in the morning.

"Would you like the rest of my croissant?" Tiny asked quietly.

"No, thank you."

"Well, if you've been climbing stairs all morning, when any sane person would be lying asleep in his bed, you're going to need some protein, aren't you?" She rose from her chair. "I'll make eggs."

"You don't need to . . ."

But she was already bustling about the kitchenette, dragging a pan out of the miniature cupboard, jerking open the Frigidaire door. He stood back against the wall and watched her, arms folded, while she beat the eggs with a vengeful fork and added milk.

"The secret is to cook them slowly," she said, "and keep stirring."

"You don't say."

"Sometimes—" Her voice caught. "Sometimes I put in a little cheese, at the end."

"I'm not sure I have any cheese."

"Well, you should. It's a—" Again. "It's a staple."

She stirred the eggs quietly. At one point she lifted her left arm and brushed the cuff against her eyes, a furtive gesture. She was so small and graceful, hovering domestically over his breakfast. So vulnerable in his laundered white shirt, buttoned all the way up to the collar. Her thighs were peach-pale and firm beneath the hem.

Cap rested his head back against the wall and thought, *I'm falling in love with you.*

"What was that?" Tiny turned her head, and he realized he'd whispered the words aloud.

"Nothing."

He ate his eggs standing up, drinking another cup of coffee. Tiny refilled her own cup and nibbled a few bites of scrambled egg, straight from the pan, sitting at the table.

"Good idea," he said. "You need to eat, too. All that dancing."

"I know."

He placed the empty plate in the sink. "Listen. I'm going to go out for a bit. Take some pictures. Bring back a few groceries. I think you need some time to yourself."

"I was going to suggest the same thing, actually." She wiped her mouth with a paper napkin. "Do you have any writing paper? I thought I'd start by writing a letter to him. Letters to both the families."

He turned on the faucet and reached for the dish soap. "You've decided, then?"

"Yes. I think I have. I slept on it, like you said. And I woke up feeling exactly the same way as yesterday."

"Which is?"

"That I've been happier in the past twenty-four hours than I have in the past twenty-four years."

She appeared beside him, without warning, and set the pan and her empty cup in the enamel sink, right next to his. She went on: "Freer. More myself. As if I've finally figured out what I really want from life. What's really important, and it's not *being* important. Or being married to someone important, which according to my mother is the same thing, only better, because you don't have to do all the work yourself." She laughed. "Anyway, I don't have to send the letters until I'm ready, right? And then . . ." She picked up a dish towel and took the wet plate from his hands.

"Then what?"

"Well, that's where you come in. Show me how to disappear, so they can't find me and try to change my mind."

"Tiny, I have to report for duty in two weeks. I'll be heading out to Indochina. Do you know where that is? How far? Playing hide-and-seek with Vietcong for another year. This nice little strip of land on the Laos border, a real paradise, eight thousand miles away."

Eight thousand miles away. The words, now that he said them, sounded inconceivably distant. Eight thousand miles away from Boston. Eight thousand miles away from Tiny Doe, dancing in his white shirt, stirring his eggs.

"Caspian, really." She wiped the mugs dry and set them back in the cupboard, side by side. "Cool your jets. I'm not asking you to marry me, for God's sake. I just need a little—I don't know, whatever you call it, in the army—tactical assistance. And maybe some moral support."

He unplugged the drain and dried his hands. "Are you sure you need it?"

"Well, you're the one who's done this already, aren't you? You've escaped. Made your own life. I could use a tip or two from an expert." She flicked the dishcloth at him. "Now, off with you. Go wander around Boston and take your marvelous pictures. I'll be just fine."

She looked up at him with those huge brown eyes, and he no longer wanted to wander the city and take pictures of bums and street corners and swan boats. He wanted to stay right here.

Tiny reached up and touched the corner of his mouth with her dishcloth. Wiped away some particle of breakfast. "That wouldn't be wise, though, would it?"

This time, he was sure he hadn't said the words aloud.

"Off you go," she said. "I mean it. I promise I'll be here when you get back."

He levered himself away from the wall and went to put his camera in its bag, his film, his extra flash, his notebook, his dog-eared copy of *The Mayor of Casterbridge*, nearly finished. "Don't mess with my darkroom," he said, hoisting the bag over his shoulder.

"Wouldn't dream of it. And, Caspian?"

He paused at the door. "Yes?"

"I might let you take my picture, when you get back."

Tiny, 1966

When I was about eight years old, my mother, in a rare fit of maternal attention—she must have been between lovers—enrolled me in my first ballet class. Why do you think? To make me graceful.

Actually, it was the three of us, me and Pepper and Vivian, but my sisters dropped out within a month. Or maybe they were kicked out. Anyway. They hated it, and I loved it: the discipline, the method, the way you had to combine strength with grace, science with art. The way you could, for a single soaring instant, set yourself free. You could articulate an emotion without saying a word. You could use your body, you could push and punish your muscle and bone and hone them into something magnificent, something that had purpose. Something that was no longer tiny but colossal. No longer delicate but strong.

I attended my last formal dance rehearsal on the morning of the coffee shop robbery, over two years ago, but I still practice sometimes, in my room, before any sort of significant performance: a wedding, a formal party, a photo call. On the morning I married Franklin Hardcastle, I spent two hours in a ritual of pliés and arabesques, pas de chat and grands jetés, until my nerves were taut and secure, until I knew I could do what I had to do that day, to secure my brilliant future. I still remember the pleasant pull in my hamstrings as I walked down the aisle, that familiar ecstasy of a rope that has been stretched too tight and finally allowed to relax. I really don't remember the ceremony itself, except for the glint of the candles on Frank's hair.

Today, at twelve minutes to five o'clock, dolled up in my strapless raspberry satin, gloved to the elbows, wearing my new diamond and sapphire necklace, stockings and makeup in place, matching raspberry satin pocketbook packed with lipstick and tissue and compact and a few sneaky cigarettes, I rest my hand on the back of the chair and arrange my feet in first position.

Frank drifts between bedroom and bathroom, getting himself ready. It's a high-roller crowd tonight, and he's dressed the part: black tails, stiff shirt. His white bow tie forms a pair of flattened white triangles under his chin. He stops in the middle of the room. His head is bowed over his forearm. "Can you do these cuff links for me? My fingers won't behave."

I rise from a plié and reach for his left wrist. "Nerves?"

"I guess so."

"Don't worry. They'll love you. They always do." I straighten the cuff and pat his hand. "Everybody loves you, Frank. You just have to show them the real you."

"Whatever that is," he mutters.

I lift my head. Frank's face is turned away, but the expression there is entirely unlike the Frank I've always known. The Frank who knows who he is. The scent of cigarettes drifts from his clothes. His breath delivers a pungent fist of Scotch.

"Is something wrong, Frank?" I ask.

He looks at me, and the tension melts into a warm smile. "Nothing's wrong, darling. Put those pretty shoes on. It's time to go downstairs."

Photo call at five. I don't know if you've ever had the pleasure. You pose in front of a line of men (it's almost always men) in your best dress, you freeze your body and your face into the preferred ideal, into the woman the world expects you to be, and let the flashbulbs pop away like the Fourth of July, capturing this frozen and artificial you for the eager consumption of the general public. It's a real gas. God forbid you should overlook a wrinkle on your dress or your forehead.

They pose me with Frank first. I'm familiar with the drill by now. I tilt my body at the exact correct angle toward him and disappear my gloved arm into his. Chin down, shoulders back, stomach in. Don't blink. Never, ever blink. The massive camera lenses point toward us like a cluster of erect phalluses, while the men behind them shout instructions—*To the right! A little more smile! Put your arm around her!*—and the flashbulbs make their ecstatic little explosions against my skin.

Beautiful, shout the photographers. *Beautiful.*

Frank's father joins us, Hardcastles to the right and left of me, and then Frank by himself, solid and presidential, while I stand to the side with my father-in-law and long for a cigarette. "He looks well," says Mr. Hardcastle, arms crossed and appraising, and then, "Oh! Hello, Cap. You're late."

Caspian's voice, on the other side of my father-in-law: "You said six o'clock, sir."

"You didn't get the message? You're wanted for the photo call." Mr. Hardcastle nods toward the flashing bulbs. "Say hello to Tiny."

"Hello, Tiny."

"I believe Major Harrison prefers to *take* pictures. Not to *be* taken," I say.

"Well. I guess my cousin-in-law knows me already."

"It's not a question of what Cap *wants,*" says Mr. Hardcastle. "It's a question of what's required."

"Of course." Caspian takes off his hat and smooths an unnecessary hand over his short hair. "Whatever you need, Uncle Franklin."

Well, at this angle I can't see much, and I'm not going to step out of line to get a better look at him, not if you offered me a priceless diamond-and-sapphire necklace. I can't afford to lose my composure when the cameras are nearby. Still, there's no avoiding the awareness at my periphery, the Caspian-shaped imprint on my senses. He's wearing his dress uniform again. A few inches of his head rise above Mr. Hardcastle's silvering hair. Some bit of gold braid on his hat keeps catching the explosions of light, and then casting its reflection on the sides of his large fingers. The constant soft pop of the bulbs can't disguise the tone of his voice, which is low and genial.

I want to say, Where have you been for the past few weeks? Why did you disappear like that?

I want to say, The photograph. I know it wasn't you. It can't have been you, blackmail's not your style, but in that case, how did the photo end up in a manila envelope, addressed to me? Who did you show it to? Who did you give it to? Why would you share such an unbearably intimate moment with someone else? Why would you not guard it against all other eyes, for my sake? Why would you betray me? When I trusted you.

"I hope we haven't inconvenienced you," I say. "I'm sure you have a thousand things you'd rather be doing."

"Family first," says Caspian.

Mr. Hardcastle holds up one hand. "All right. You're on."

"Hat or no hat?"

Mr. Hardcastle considers. "No hat."

Caspian turns to me, hands me his hat, and walks toward the dais without a single hint of a limp. The hat is still warm from his head, even through the silk fibers of my gloves, and I hold it against my stomach and finger the gold braid.

By five thirty, the photographers are finished, and Frank's campaign staffers step in to brief me. The donors are the usual mix of businessmen and wives, the prominent and the ambitious and the curious, the old guard and the rising middle, linked by money and a weakness for glamour and an evangelical faith in Frank. I know many of them already. A piece of cake. The reporter from the *Boston Globe*, now. Had I met him before?

"No," I say. "Is he new on the society page?"

"He's not on the society page," says the staffer, a pretty girl named Josephine with startling auburn hair and streaks of dark mascara on her daring loop-the-loop lashes. She rims her upper eyelids with swooping lines of kohl for that catlike effect that's all the rage. "He's on the political beat."

"Really? But this is a soft piece, isn't it? The candidate and his wife at home."

The other staffer, a young man in his very early twenties, shrugs his shoulders. "Wants to do his background, I guess. The business is changing. People want to know about the candidate's life. Character, style, personality. People want mystique. The Camelot effect." He checks his watch, taps it, and looks back up into my silence.

I say: "Well, I don't suppose it makes much difference, as long as he knows the rules. Is he bringing his wife?"

"He's not married." This from Josephine, who is smiling at me. Smugly, I think.

"Are you familiar with Frank's positions, Mrs. Hardcastle?" asks the young man. What's his name? I'm supposed to be better at this. Stephen. That's it, Stephen.

"Of course I am, Stephen," I say. "You might be surprised to know that my husband and I discuss politics frequently."

"It's Scott," he says, "Scott Maynard, and I'm sure you do. But just in case, I've prepared a brief for you. Very simple, one page, lays out the key points of the platform in clear language."

"Thank goodness." I take the paper from him, fold it into tiny squares, and tuck it into my pocketbook. "We wouldn't want my poor little brain to be overwhelmed, would we?"

"We just want to make sure you're up to date," says Josephine. "Frank's been on the road a lot, after all. You've hardly seen each other. In fact, that's a question that might come up. The strain of campaigning on a marriage. You know the rumors about Jack Kennedy."

Did I know the rumors.

"Well, I'm sure my poor little brain will find a way to answer that one, too, if you give me enough time to think about it." I rise from the chair. My shoes are new and a little stiff, not quite molded to my feet. I feel like a mouse on stilts. "After all, Frank and I have been intimate for many years. We have such a solid foundation together."

Scott and Josephine rise in unison. Josephine's wearing an elegant dress, a short silver halter overdraped by a tent of shimmery translucent chiffon, and a pair of expensive diamond stud earrings, at least a carat each. Though the heels of her silver shoes are a fashionably modest inch and a half, she's nearly as tall as Scott. "Perfect," she says. "That's exactly how we want you to answer."

The *Globe* reporter arrives late, just after the salad is removed and the filet arrives under silver domes. He begs our pardon. He's younger than I expect, fresh of face and sleek of hair, and the hand he holds out to me appears to have been manicured.

"A pleasure, Mr. Lytle. Don't give it another thought." I look up at his rather handsome face, his sharp hazel eyes, and think, This is a man I can do business with.

"A newsroom is a dangerous place to be when you've got a pressing engagement," he says. "I hope I haven't missed the speech."

"No, we're running late. You know how these things are."

He nods at my neck. "Red, white, and blue. The patriotic touch."

I glance down at my priceless new necklace, at the diamonds and sapphires hovering above the raspberry satin. "Isn't it, though. Do you like it?"

He flips up his tails and takes the seat next to me. "I do indeed."

I signal to the nearby waiter for wine—an excellent Bordeaux has just replaced the white Burgundy—while Mr. Lytle arranges himself. Frank's still deep in conversation with his neighbor, the frosted wife of an extremely wealthy financier, who smiles and nods in rapture as he speaks to her. I glance across the table at Caspian, who has just turned away from some distant contemplation to catch my gaze.

"Have you met my husband's cousin, Major Harrison?"

"I haven't had the pleasure. Major Harrison? Congratulations. I saw the ceremony on TV. An honor to meet you."

"Caspian," I say, "this is Mr. John Lytle, a political editor at the *Globe*. He's doing a background feature on Frank."

Caspian catches my drift. He smiles, all toothsome and welcoming. Even Caspian knows what's required at a moment like this. "Mr. Lytle. Welcome. You've come to the right place. I can tell you all his buried secrets, for the right price."

Lytle laughs. "Music to my ears."

By the time Frank steps up to the podium, we're all pleasantly drunk and ready to laugh at his jokes, good and bad. In Frank's case, of course, they're all good. The dessert has been set, the cigarettes have come out, the lights are dim and alluring. Frank looks terribly handsome, up there with the microphone. Handsome and energetic. He speaks about taxes, about the importance of prosperity, about the necessity of ensuring a just society in which opportunity is the birthright of each and every citizen. He slides smoothly into the subject of Vietnam, the link between our national security and the threats to personal and economic freedom around the globe, and then he introduces Caspian.

As soon as Frank uttered the word *Vietnam*, Caspian took his cue. He laid his napkin in neat folds alongside his plate, took a last sip of wine, and rose to his feet. He stands now near the podium, at the perfect respectful distance, hands folded modestly behind his back. Attentive to Frank.

"... my cousin, of whom I believe you've all heard, or should have heard, Major Caspian Harrison of the Special Forces. Caspian?"

My God, I think, as Caspian strides to the podium, as he shakes Frank's hand and turns to the audience. He looks seven feet tall, even though he isn't. He looks like a warrior king, like he could snap the metal arm of the microphone in half and toss both ends like javelins into the crowd. He doesn't belong here, he doesn't belong in the same universe as these people. How had I forgotten that about him? Forgotten the magnitude of him, when seen from a distance.

Frank is an inch or two shorter. Caspian tilts his neck downward to meet the microphone. "Good evening. I'm honored to be here tonight, honored to have the opportunity to speak to all of you about my cousin Franklin Hardcastle, one of the best men I've ever met."

The edges of my vision grow a little blurry, and Caspian's image swims in the middle. I reach for my wine. At my side, Lytle crushes out his cigarette in the ashtray and leans into my ear. "Holy cow. He almost looks as if *he* should be the candidate."

I pick up my raspberry satin pocketbook from the edge of my plate. "Excuse me."

Outside, the air is still hot and stale, and the sun hasn't quite set. I stand on the balcony, staring at the pinks and purples rimming the nearby rooftops, the square penthouse of the hotel itself, while I suck on my cigarette. The faint drone of Caspian's voice drifts through the open door. I can't quite pick out the words. There is applause, and more heroic, low-pitched Caspian eloquence, and a final rolling thunder of clapping hands, scraping chairs, approval. Then Frank's voice, briefly, and just as the cigarette burns out between my gloved fingers, the opening notes of the orchestra, to start the dancing. I drop the stub just in time and crush it under the square heel of my shoe.

I dance with the financier first, while Frank dances with his wife. I smile and flirt and thank God for the wine. Then we switch partners, and Frank asks me if I'm enjoying myself. "Very much," I say.

"How did I sound up there?"

"Perfect. You hit all the right notes."

"Cap did all right. God bless him. People were practically pulling out their checkbooks as he spoke."

"Yes, the *Globe* reporter was awfully impressed."

Frank leans in. "Have you been smoking?"

"Just one."

The orchestra is playing an old standard, and we dance automatically. Frank's eyes wander the crowd around us, the people standing at the edge. A high pitch of energy surrounds him, a pitch I recognize from other nights, other events. I suppose we all recognize it, we wives of performers (and that's what politics is, isn't it—performing, I mean): celebrity or charisma or plain old razzle-dazzle, a brilliance that you might call artificial, a masquerade, but really it isn't. The mask is part of the person. That's why it's so compelling. I grasp his chin and tug him back to face me. "You should be careful, though. Lytle said that it almost looks like Caspian should be the candidate."

Frank frowns down at me. "What the hell does that mean?"

"Just that he's very impressive up there. He's a natural leader."

"I can hold my own against fucking Cap."

"Shh." I glance to either side. "Of course you can. But you don't need to have him following us around at every fund-raiser, either."

A flashbulb pops nearby, and another.

"Not that you weren't wonderful up there," I say. Smiling.

"Cap's loyal. Cap's not going to burn me."

"Of course not. Politics is the last thing he's interested in."

"How do you know?"

"You know how I can size people up."

Frank looks past my ear, over my shoulder to the rim of the dance floor. "Well, you're right. Cap doesn't know jack about politics."

"Not like you," I say, but it's too late. My husband's arm is stiff around my waist, his hand touching mine only at the necessary fingertips.

The music concludes. Frank leads me to the side, where Josephine waits, talking and laughing with the financier from our table. Her hair is much longer than mine, a shiny loose auburn mess that hovers casually over her bare shoulders. The bangs are pulled back into a sparkling clip at the top of her head, very mod. The thick kohl around her lids reminds you of Bardot, or maybe Fonda. She seems remarkably self-possessed for such a young woman, just out of college, twenty-two years old. Where did my husband find her?

Frank's smile breaks out. "Ah, Jo! There you are. How are we doing tonight?"

She looks up at him like he's Moses. "*You*, Frank Hardcastle, are a *star*. You had me in tears."

"All credit to my crack campaign staff."

"Hardly." Josephine reaches up and caresses the diamond stud in her left ear. I can't quite be certain in this light, but I think she's blushing.

My husband holds out his arms. "Dance?"

Off they go. "She's a pretty thing, isn't she?" says the financier.

"She's very good at her job," I say. "Frank does have an eye for talent."

"I'll say."

I open my mouth to change the subject, but someone addresses him from the other side, and he turns away, leaving me suspended and solitary at the edge of the dance floor.

You know, it's funny. When I first met Frank at a Radcliffe mixer seven years ago, he was dancing with another girl. A blonde, that time, but otherwise a lot like this one: swollen of bosom, smoky of eye. The hair was perhaps a few shades too bright for credibility. She wasn't even a Radcliffe girl at all; she was somebody's friend or cousin, I found out later. A ringer. Anyway, he caught my eye, because how could Franklin Hardcastle not catch your eye when you're nineteen and he's twenty-one, and you've never kissed a boy and he's the handsomest man you've ever seen? All that razzle-dazzle. I turned away. He went on dancing, and then the two of them disappeared from sight for an hour or so. When I saw him next, his hair was tousled, his skin was a little flushed, and I was struggling with my coat in a dank linoleum hallway, preparing to head back to my dormitory before curfew. A pair of hands appeared on my sleeves, helping me in, and I looked up and there he was, Franklin Hardcastle, Harvard senior, radiant in blue eyes and sandy tousled hair. A smooth brown tweed jacket cradled his shoulders. He said, *Who's the lucky fellow?* and I said, *Who do you mean?* and he said, *The one you're hurrying off to meet,* and I said, *Nobody, actually, just heading to my dormitory,* and he said, *You're Tiny Schuyler, aren't you?* and I said, *How did you know?* (heart galloping), and he said, *Because I've spent the last six months hoping I'd run into you like this,* and I said, *Well, here I am,* and long story short, I never saw that other girl again, though I saw plenty more of Frank.

But I do think of her often, that platinum ringer at the Radcliffe mixer, and I think of her now as I watch my husband wing around the dance floor with his campaign staffer. Josephine. I turn the name over in my head, as her bright head revolves in and out of sight, twenty or thirty yards away from me. Frank's arm is around her back, his hand is splayed wide at the far quadrant of her back, so that the extreme tips of his fingers curve around her trim young waist. His gold wedding ring gleams against the silver halter. They are both smiling.

"You look as if you could use a drink," says a male voice at my elbow, and for an instant my heart gallops, but it's only Lytle from the *Boston Globe*, handing me a glass of champagne.

"Thank you."

He watches me gulp it down. "A hell of a life, isn't it, for a nice girl like you."

"How do you know I'm a nice girl?"

"Just a guess. Dance?"

I place the empty glass on a nearby table and take Lytle's outstretched hand. The song is just ending, so we hang on into the next. He's an easy man to talk to, John Lytle—"Call me Jack, Mrs. Hardcastle"—really terribly personable.

He delivers me back to my seat and I reach for my pocketbook, a smidgen unsteady, and that's when I notice the manila envelope tucked underneath the raspberry satin, with my name, MRS. FRANKLIN

HARDCASTLE, JR., printed in black block letters, a quarter-inch high, in the corner.

'm Tiny Schuyler, I'm Mrs. Franklin Hardcastle, Jr., and for the first time in my whole square life, I'm thoroughly drunk.

I have had several too many. (I couldn't give you an exact count, but *several* should cover it.) I have rolled up the manila envelope into a stiff little tube and shoved it into my raspberry satin pocketbook, and I have marched to the nearest waiter and taken a glass of champagne and bubbled it merrily down my throat while that dear Jack Lytle tagged affectionately along behind me. I have had a sophisticated conversation with him, while smoking the remaining cigarettes in my pocketbook. *They're all bores, you know. Rich, contemptible bores. The women are the worst.*

Lytle has handed me another glass and a *Really? How so?*

Such a dishy fellow, Lytle. So easy to talk to. You can confide in a man like that; he knows exactly what you mean when you say something you can't quite remember exactly, the morning after, but goes something like, *They've forgotten all they ever learned at college, even if they went, and even if they learned anything to begin with. They haven't got a single ambition of their own. They married fat successful men so they could be thin successful wives.*

Lytle has thoughtfully pulled me to the bar, where we can be comfortable. *You think they all married for money?*

I have waved my hand expressively. *Oh, I'm sure they'll say they were in love, and maybe they were, but did they fall in love with high school math teachers and policemen and engineers? No, they did not.*

Lytle has seen fit to wonder why I'm here, then, if I despise events like this and people like this.

I have then sighed and stared into my empty glass and said something like, *Well, I guess I'm one of them, aren't I?*

And then, on reflection, *Besides, wouldn't they just kill me if I asked for a divorce?*

And Lytle has said, *Who?* and I have said something like (hand waving to the dais), *Them. Frank, his father. The whole damned Brahmin mob,* and Lytle has said, *Well, well. Aren't you such a surprise, Mrs. Hardcastle,* and I have said (looking up gratefully), *Aren't you such a dear, Mr. Lytle.*

So. Here I am, the elegant Mrs. Franklin Hardcastle, Jr., gloved to the elbows, savoring all these brand-new sensations, this pleasant sloppy lightness of passage, Lytle's sympathy, the pretty faces and so on, and a large hand appears out of nowhere to cover the satin fingers that cover my guilty pocketbook.

"Tiny," says the hand's owner.

Now, two guesses. Does the hand in question belong to my devoted husband, Mr. Franklin S. Hardcastle, Jr., he of the burnished hair and the burnished smile? I'll give you a hint: it does not. No, no. Frank Hardcastle has disappeared, poof, just like that, no burnished head to be found in this merry old ballroom at midnight. Cinderella the lowly campaign staffer seems to have disappeared, too, and her dainty glass slippers with her. Franklin Senior is working the crowd to my left—far to my left—and nowhere in that thick Boston fog of cigarette smoke and cocktail breath do I know a single friend.

Except this one. Your second guess. Caspian, whose hand lies atop mine.

In the slow and drunken moment that passes between his word—*Tiny*—and mine, I ponder the nature of that thought. Caspian, a friend? An hour or two ago, clean and sober, I wouldn't have put those two words together. At most, I consider Caspian an unpredictable ally, bound to me by the accident of my marriage, our interests momentarily aligned. But I know for a fact—I know by solemn experience—where Caspian's real loyalties lie. He's a Hardcastle, and the family business comes before everything else. Including himself.

Including me, if I should be so careless as to stand in opposition.

"Caspian," I say. "I thought you were long gone."

"Your father-in-law called my room."

"I can't imagine why."

He turns to Jack. "Lytle, isn't it?"

Jack holds out his hand. "From the *Globe*. Loved your little speech. You have a gift."

"Not really. I'm just eager to see my cousin doing what God put him on this planet to do."

"A true believer."

"I've known Frank since we were kids, Mr. Lytle, and I can't think of a better man for the job. And, trust me, I know a little bit about character, by now." Caspian winks.

"I'm sure you do. Three tours in 'Nam. Jesus. And then you come home to this." Jack waves his drink.

"This? This isn't so bad."

Jack laughs. "Not here. Tonight. I mean the protests, the students. *LBJ, LBJ, how many kids have you killed today?* That kind of thing. Any rotten eggs thrown at your head yet?"

Caspian's face turns to stone. "No."

Another laugh. "Well, I don't suppose anyone would dare. Still. You've heard what's going on. What do you think?"

"People have a right to their opinions, Mr. Lytle, at least those of us lucky enough to be standing here in an American ballroom instead of a Vietnamese rice paddy. Now, if you'll excuse me, I haven't had the pleasure of dancing with my cousin yet." His hand slides up my forearm to grasp my elbow.

"You can dance?" Lytle asks.

"I can try."

Caspian leads me to the dance floor, which has grown looser and more dangerous since I left it an hour ago, jiving with couples dancing a little too close and laughing a little too loud. I shift the pocketbook to my left hand and clasp Caspian's hand with my right. "Can you really dance?" I ask.

"We're about to find out."

"You don't need to do this."

"I had to get you away from that reporter somehow."

We execute a turn, which Caspian manages better than most of the men around us.

"I can handle myself," I say.

"Uncle's orders."

"And we all know you do *exactly* what the family tells you to do."

I'm peeking steadily over his shoulder, watching the pleasant kaleidoscope pass by, because his face is too much. He's too much, and I, Mrs. Franklin Hardcastle, Jr., have had *much* too much champagne.

"In this case, yes." His voice is low and rumbles from his chest, just a few inches from my ear. "But mostly, I just want to do what's best for you."

"Oh, I see. And obviously *this* is what's best for me," I say bitterly.

"This? This is *your* choice, Tiny. What you chose."

I step unsteadily back, away from his chest. The champagne bubbles have all died away. "I think it's time I went to my room."

"I think that's an excellent idea."

Caspian keeps my hand in his and threads me through the crowd to one of the double doors at the other crimson end of the ballroom. Down the corridor, the lobby opens like a new marble world, containing its elevator banks and its grand staircase, but Caspian steers me in the other direction. "Let's get a little air first," he says.

Outside the cool breath of the air-conditioning, the courtyard is dark and hot, but the change in atmosphere does clear my head a degree or two. I put my hands on the railing and stare down at the pocketbook clenched between them. Wishing I had a cigarette inside. Something to do.

"Can we clear something up?" Caspian says. "Just one thing."

"And what's the point of that, exactly?"

"Because we're living side by side now. We can't just keep avoiding each other."

"Then go back to Vietnam." The words are out, sharp and awful. I bend my head to the railing. "I'm sorry. I'm sorry. I didn't mean that."

He answers me far more gently than I deserve. "Why the hell do you think I stayed on in the first place?"

"I don't know. To save the world."

"Jesus. All right. Yes. To save the fucking world. Because anything was better than coming back to you and Frank."

"Then why are you here now? Go to your sister in San Diego. I'm sure she could use a man around the house."

"Because I'm needed here."

"Oh, yes. I forgot. Frank's campaign."

Caspian's hand finds my shoulder. I've forgotten how large his hand is, how thoroughly it covers my skin. "Tell me the truth. Why you're unhappy."

Two years ago, I would have confessed to that voice. How couldn't you confess to a voice like that? To a hand like that, steady and reliable on your shoulder?

I made a mistake, Caspian. I've failed. My life isn't quite so perfect as it seems. The bargain I made, it hasn't quite turned out the way I dreamed.

Or better yet: *You know those pictures you took? I need to know how they might have gotten in the hands of a filthy blackmailing scoundrel.*

But now? Confess all *that*? Now there's a good one. To Caspian, of all people. Caspian with his direct line to the senior Hardcastles, Caspian who had been sent tonight to clean up the drunken mess of me by none other than Mr. Franklin Hardcastle, Senior. *Uncle's orders,* he said.

Sure, maybe he wouldn't rat on me. The odds, I figured, were maybe fifty-fifty. But even sloppy with champagne, I wasn't the kind of girl to take those odds.

I certainly wasn't the kind of girl to tell her problems to any old stranger.

"I'm not unhappy. I am . . ." I curl my fingers around the pocketbook and draw it into my belly. "I am *perfect*. I'm perfect."

Caspian's hand remains on my shoulder. I can feel his fingertips in the hollow. I can count each one.

"All right," he says. "I'll take you upstairs."

I turn, dislodging the hand. "I can find my own way."

"I promised your father-in-law I'd make sure you got to your room safely."

"That's noble of you."

I try to walk past him, but he starts first, drawing my hand into the crook of his elbow, and owing to some failure of backbone, some surfeit of champagne, I let it stay.

Caspian takes me up in the metal service elevator, tucked out of sight. I can't blame him. I suspect my lipstick is askew, my hair disturbed. I wonder if my face has taken on that florid quality I regard with such pity in other women. Beside me, Caspian is utterly still. I look down at our feet, lined up in a row, in and out of focus.

"I'm sorry about your leg," I say.

Caspian reaches forward and presses the emergency stop. We stagger to a halt. I throw my hand out to the wall to steady myself, while an alarm bell gives off two demented rings.

"It's just a leg," he says.

An ominous quiet fills the car. An absence of hydraulics. I have never noticed how noisy elevators are until now. Caspian's body dwarfs mine, filling up all that silent space, and the impression—Caspian's reliable size, his quiet fortitude—is so familiar, I stare at our aligned feet and think, *It doesn't matter*. Doesn't matter why we fell apart two years ago. He's here now. He came back.

I say softly, "That's what I told myself, when I heard the news. I thought it was a fair trade. I told God he could keep the leg, as long as you came home alive."

"You could have saved yourself the trouble. At the time, I didn't care one way or another."

His shoes are black and polished, rounded at the tips, almost liquid in their military perfection. Identical in every detail. You would never guess, if you didn't already know, that one of them contains a mechanical contraption, a bang up-to-date marvel of bionics or whatever they called it, instead of a living human foot.

If I were his wife instead of Frank's, I'd weep for that foot. Weep that I'd never have a chance to see it wiggle next to mine, to feel it curl around my leg at night, to rub it when it's weary, to tickle its sole, to kiss every toe. I'd mourn forever for Caspian's lost foot. Where were its remains, anyway? Did they cremate amputated limbs? Throw them out with the trash? Where were the rotting molecules that had once been Caspian's beloved left foot? So lurched my champagne-drenched thoughts, in the grim-bright metallic interior of the hotel service elevator.

"How are they treating you, Tiny?" says Caspian. "The family, I mean."

"Just fine."

"Because I've been wondering. I've been hoping they're making you happy. That they appreciate you, the real you."

"I'm happy."

"If you need me, you know, I'm right here."

"Yes. Yes, indeed. You're right there."

He persists, in a gruff voice: "I'm not going to get in the middle of your marriage. I'd never do that. I'm just . . . well, if you ever need help, that's all. Help of any kind."

"What makes you think I need any help?"

"I just have a hunch. I guess I knew you pretty well, for a few days."

"For a few days, yes. You did."

The intercom explodes. "Everything okay in there?"

"Yes!" Caspian barks. "My mistake. Just turn us on again."

There is a static curse and a grinding noise, and the elevator lurches into motion. I stumble out of alignment with Caspian's feet, and he puts out a hand to steady me.

"You probably think you can't trust me," says Caspian, watching the numbers light up above the door, "but you can, Tiny. You can trust me. I'm on your side."

I tighten my hands around the pocketbook. "Since when is that?"

"Since always."

The car bangs to a stop. The doors kick open. Caspian's hand touches the small of my back, urging me forward, and I step onto the worn crimson carpet of the service hallway. My feet totter and ache in their pretty raspberry satin shoes.

I tuck the pocketbook bravely under my elbow and turn to Caspian. He regards me with the same expression he once wore inside the sacred rectangle of his Marlborough Street living room, as if he would like to surround me with his long limbs and burrow through the pores of my skin and invade me.

I'm not sure whether the fluttering in my belly is champagne or melancholy, flirtation or guilt. Anticipation or dread.

"Well, then. Can I trust you to walk me to my door, Major Harrison?"

TINY LITTLE THING

Caspian, 1964

This time, Caspian climbed the three flights of stairs at a run, while his camera bag banged against his hips and his heart banged against his ribs. He could hardly resist the urge to shout, *Honey, I'm home!* as he threw open the door, knowing that Tiny existed beyond it, waiting for him to return.

He'd pushed the whole dilemma out of his mind all day. He'd focused on his camera, on picking out subjects, setting scenes, considering light and angle and perspective. It was too much to think about, really: the ethics of making his move on another fellow's girl, even a girl who'd taken shelter under his roof and asked for his help. Once she'd written that letter, was she free? Was *he* free, considering he was leaving for the other side of the world in two weeks? The honorable thing was to wait until he was back from his tour, alive and whole, the both of them having had time to consider things rationally, to write a few letters, to get to know each other better. In her case, to get over this fiancé of hers, to maybe date a guy or two on the rebound, to settle herself in her newfound life. Then they'd see how things went. Try each other out. Inch by careful inch into intimacy.

But he didn't feel rational—let alone honorable—by the time he threw open the door to his apartment and cast about for Tiny's sun-draped shape to rise from the sofa. He only knew that he had two weeks, fourteen days left, before he put eight thousand miles between the two of them, and he had to touch her, he had to kiss her, he had to leave some physical imprint on her, and she on him, or he couldn't possibly endure the lonely year ahead.

When he stepped through the doorway, though, Tiny didn't rise from the sofa, sun-draped or otherwise.

The room was empty.

He dropped his camera bag carefully to the floor and called out her name.

No answer.

He looked around the corner of the kitchenette, not really expecting to see her. He walked down the hall and glanced inside the darkroom, which lay untouched and acrid.

The door to the bedroom was closed. A sliver of light showed beneath. Cap felt the blood rushing in his veins, the wind in his lungs. He placed his knuckles against the old wood and knocked softly. "Tiny?"

He didn't hear a reply, but the door was thick, a hundred years old, solid chestnut like they didn't make anymore. Once, his father said, you could crawl from Boston to Washington across the limbs of giant American chestnut trees, but the Japanese blight took care of that romantic notion a generation or two ago. He turned the knob and pushed it open, inch by careful inch.

"Tiny?" he said again.

She sat in the middle of the bed, neatly made, with her knees tucked up under her chin and her dancer's arms wrapped around it all. A few papers lay in front of her, and a ballpoint pen with its cap on.

"Are you all right?" he said.

"Not really."

He pushed the door open the rest of the way and walked into the room, light with relief that she was talking, at least. That she was there, sitting on his bed. He lowered himself into the wooden chair.

"Did you write the letter?"

She picked up the pen and hurled it against the wall. The cap broke away on impact. "I can't do it. I can't. I couldn't even find the words."

He didn't know what to say. Something was crushing his shoulders, a metal safe with a ton of precious bullion inside. "All right."

"All right? Is that all?" She stuck her hands in her hair, which was fully disheveled, a shining brown mess. "I tried, and do you know how it sounded? Vain. And weak. And self-centered. I've got no earthly reason to break off this engagement, have I? It's everything I ever wanted, isn't it? An important life, the wife of someone extraordinary. And I knew what the trade-offs were. I knew what to expect. I was *bred* to expect them."

"What trade-offs, Tiny? What are you trading off?"

She moved her head from side to side. "After all this time, pretending to be happy, pretending to be the perfect wife to be. All my life. My mother. The look on her face. I can't stand it, I can't! She's pinned everything on me, her perfect little virgin daughter, her last hope for redemption, so she can believe . . . she can think that she did *something* right at least . . ."

He lurched forward and grabbed her hand. "Take it easy. Whoa."

"I'm just being selfish and ungrateful. Lots of girls— I've been so lucky—and I don't— I can't *prove*—" She stopped.

"Prove what, Tiny?"

"Nothing. Nothing I can write down, anyway. Nothing that doesn't sound like paranoia." She bit back a hysterical sound. "Tell me about yourself, Cap. Tell me about your family. I want to know what that sounds like, a normal family."

He tightened his fingers about hers, as if that could stop her slipping away. "I don't know about normal. My mother died when I was eight. My father never remarried. We went from base to base, me and my sister and him. All around the world, no real home. Not very normal at all."

She looked up. Her eyes were dry and white; she hadn't been crying. For some reason, that seemed worse to him. As if her grief lay in some territory beyond tears, some unreachable region of despair. "Why didn't your father remarry?" she asked.

"I don't know. You don't meet a lot of suitable women on a foreign army base, I guess."

"I suppose he loved her. Your mother."

"Yes. He didn't talk about her much. But he kept her picture by the bed. On his desk. He took leave when she was sick, an extended leave. I don't remember it very well. I was pretty young. But . . . yes, I guess I knew how much he loved her. I don't think he ever stopped."

"He never had any other women."

"Not when she was alive. I'm sure of that."

"How can you be sure?"

"I just am. That's who he was, my dad. He mated for life. And my mother—well, she was exceptional."

"And afterward? After she died? Were there other women?"

"If there were, he kept it away from us."

She was looking not at Cap, but at their hands, roped together. "Of course," she said. "Some men are like that, I guess."

His knees hurt, pressed against the floor by the side of the bed. "What exactly are we talking about, Tiny?"

She shook her head.

"Look, I'm not here to break up anyone's engagement. Not here to undermine a man I don't even know. But I think— Hey, look at me a minute, all right?"

She looked up miserably.

"I want you to be happy, that's all. With him, if that's what you want. Or without him, if that's what you want." *Him*: Cap felt it should be capitalized, this unknown Him who bestrode the two of them, Cap and Tiny, like a colossus. Like a giant metal safe full of bullion. "You're a beautiful girl, a—" He reached for words, words that sounded right, not too smarmy, not too melodramatic, not too alarmingly worshipful at a moment like this. "A girl in a million. So it's not for you to prove to him why you shouldn't get married. If he doesn't deserve you, if he makes you unhappy, like *this*—"

"Oh, God, Caspian!" She tossed herself back on the bed and stared at the ceiling, her arms and legs spread out like a starfish. She'd found a pair of his pajama pants, thank Christ, which she'd somehow managed to fit to her frame by tightening the drawstring and rolling up the waistband several times. "Stop making this so easy for me. Stop showing me what I'm missing. What's been missing from my life all these *stupid fucking years*!" She shouted the last words, making the windows ring.

He rose to his feet. "What the hell does that mean?"

She rolled her head on his pillow and smiled at him. "It means I'm ready for you to take my picture."

S he took off the pajama pants—*I can't dance in these things*— while he opened the window shades all the way, letting the five o'clock May sunshine flood unchecked through the watery old glass.

"You're sure?" he said. "There's no pressure."

She held up a disk from the pile and examined the label. "I want to."

"All right, then." He took out his camera, changed lenses, checked the film. No flash, this time. The sunlight was pure and plentiful. His fingers tingled: that rising anticipation of a perfect photograph hovering nearby, waiting to be snatched from the air and made real.

He heard the scratch of the needle, the first few notes as they emerged from the speaker, reedy and contained. He took off the lens cap and smiled. "The *Pastoral*?"

"You like it?"

"A favorite."

She lifted one leg to the back of the sofa and stretched her body to a breathless length. Her fingers wrapped around her toes. "I didn't know you liked musty old composers. I would have pegged you for rock and roll. No. Wait. *Jazz*." She said it like a sex word.

"I'm full of surprises. Though I like jazz, too."

"Hardy. Beethoven. What next?"

He lifted the camera to his eyes and observed the flex of her arms through the lens. "Ibsen."

"Oh, a radical! Or are you trying to tell me something?"

He snapped the shutter. "What do you think?"

"For the record, I think Nora's an irritation. Just because you're a housewife doesn't mean you lack any sense at all. Anyway, she was stupid to marry a man like that, wasn't she?" She switched legs, and this time she faced him as she stretched, and her smile was relaxed.

"It was a hundred years ago, right? Things were different. Anyway, there wouldn't be a play if she hadn't made that mistake. And she does realize the mistake, in the end."

"At least you call it a mistake. Some men wouldn't. Some people wouldn't."

He snapped another shot. "Like who?"

She smiled enigmatically and turned about into an arabesque, bracing her hands on the back of the sofa. "Let's start," she said.

"Already have." He snapped again.

The music was building now, the oboes revolving intricately upward to the crest, the violins answering back. Tiny rose up on her toes and lifted her arms into a graceful arc. Her hair was wrapped back with Cap's monogrammed linen handkerchief, one of a set given to him by his grandmother several Christmases ago, and her exposed cheekbones attracted luminous stripes of sunlight as she held herself in position, smiling, waiting for the joyous wave to break.

Cap dropped to one knee, a few yards away, and adjusted the aperture. A little more light. That was it. Dazzling.

Just as he took the picture, she looked down at him and winked.

The violins burst free, and so did Tiny.

It was like a feast, like a hotel banquet, dish after dish placed before you, each one better than the last, until you almost lost track of what you were eating. Thank God for the camera, because he could never have found the necessary thousand words to describe Tiny's grace as she danced the length and breadth of his living room, the flash of her legs in the sunlight, the liquid strength of her movement. More than that. The way each attitude presented itself to his lens in flawless balance, a ready-made composition. The art of the photograph, the science, the framing: Tiny accomplished all these by herself, and he, Cap, only had to open the shutter at the right instant, to manage the flow of light around her body.

Until he lay on his stomach, pointing the camera at an acute angle, trying to reveal the length of her neck, the line of her jaw, before the movement pounced to its end. Too late, he realized she was drawing near him, and too late, she realized it, too. She corrected her trajectory, dragged her toe an instant too long on the wooden floor, and staggered.

For an instant, it looked as if she'd recover. Her long legs assembled beneath her, sounding out her center of gravity, while the oboes and the violins exchanged a last conversation, a final farewell. But just as she pitched upward again, safe and sound, her face turned horrified, and she crumpled back down to land with a thud on the century-old chestnut boards.

"Tiny! Jesus!" He sent the camera skidding and leaped to her motionless body.

She lay sprawled on the floor with her eyes ominously closed, one leg bent beneath the other. Here below the furniture, the windows were too high and the sun too low, and his light-blinded eyes couldn't quite focus on her. He grabbed her hand. "Are you all right? Tiny, come on!"

Was it the shadow, or had her lips turned gray? He slapped her cheeks gently, once each side.

"Tiny! For God's sake! Wake up!"

Her eyelashes wavered. A pathetic little groan emerged from her throat.

"Tiny! Talk to me, love. Wake up."

The eyelids swept up, revealing the rich brown of her irises. Her forehead creased, bewildered.

"Thank God! Tiny, it's me, it's Cap. Can you hear me? You've had a fall."

Her lips moved. "I don't— I—"

"It's me. I've got you. Just don't move. Does anything hurt?"

"I—don't understand—"

"That's okay. You're going to be a bit confused. Just lie still, okay? You were dancing, you fell—"

"No." She pulled her hand away. "I don't understand. Where am I? And who are *you*?"

As if his heart stopped beating.

He set his palms on the floor, next to her shoulder, and tried to keep his voice steady. "It's Caspian. Caspian, from the coffee shop. We're in my apartment. You're staying here, remember? To think things over."

Her brow was still puzzled. She tried to lift herself on her elbows, winced, and eased back down.

"Lie still, sweetheart. It'll come back to you. Just rest for a second." He wasn't even sure what he was saying. Like he'd speak to a hurt dog or a startled horse or an injured soldier. The words didn't matter. Just the stream of them kept her calm, kept him calm, kept the whole world propped up around them long enough for him to gather his wits. To start his heart beating again.

With a single weak finger, she motioned him closer.

"What is it? Do you need something?" He bent his head toward hers and inhaled his own scent, his soap and his laundry and his bed. The peculiar scent of his apartment, absorbed into Tiny's hair.

She whispered in his ear. "Are you still crazy about me?"

He closed his eyes. "Christ."

Her laughter was golden, like the aging sunlight above them. He grabbed her with both arms and hauled her delicate form against his chest, while the last gentle chords of the opening movement dissolved into scratches.

Tiny, 1966

The tuft of hair on the nearby pillow might belong to anyone.

Oh, you know how it is. You crack your eyes open into the dawn, and your senses are still so crusted with sleep, your brain is still so immersed in the Stygian netherworld of the unconscious, that you don't even know your own name. You don't know who you are, or where you are, or whose bed and whose life you now occupy. You don't know if you're four years old or a hundred and four. You don't know if this is yesterday or tomorrow, America or Pangaea.

That tuft of hair, you know, represents some sort of clue. Tugs an association of some kind. Something to do with the day before, or the night before.

"Caspian?" I whisper. The first name that pops into my head.

The hair doesn't move, not by a ripple.

But I'm on to something, I know it. If I keep on staring at the tuft, the idea will take shape. A glass of water and an aspirin. Hands adjusting me into the white sheets. Yes. Caspian's hands. The light clicking off. The familiar voice, wishing me good night.

More.

Caspian standing next to me in the space just outside my hotel room door. I am opening my pocketbook to find the key. *What's in that envelope,* he asks, and *Wouldn't you like to know,* I say. This memory is astonishingly clear, in fact. Caspian is frowning in the dim overhead light of the elevator car. I am waggling my finger at him. *Just whom did you give those photographs to?* And he shakes his head. *We'll talk when you're sober, Tiny.*

Sober, Tiny.

Sober. Jesus. I was drunk, wasn't I? That was what drunk was, waggling my flirtatious finger at my husband's strapping cousin, hoping he might take me to bed with him.

I heave myself upward, to the displeasure of my head. Oh, my God. The champagne. The ballroom. The pretty faces, sliding past; the sympathetic knowingness of that *Globe* reporter. Caspian's hand on mine, pinning me down against my satin pocketbook. Caspian's hand on my bare shoulder.

There is movement from the bundle of masculine hair and limbs lying beside me. The owner flings out an arm, finds me, and makes a noise of possession. "Tiny," he says.

Frank's voice.

I sink back down under the weight of my husband's arm. My eyes are wide open, staring at the far-away ceiling; I think my heart must be about to beat itself right out of my chest. The covers open, releasing the familiar warm smell of Frank's skin, the scent of matrimony.

He rises a little, hovering over me.

"I'm sorry," he mutters. He pushes back my hair from my face.

"Sorry for what?"

"I meant to . . . last night . . ." He kisses my chin, my throat.

"You're such a good wife, Tiny, you're perfect. You looked so beautiful. It was the drinks, I guess. The pressure. You can't imagine the pressure right now. My dad—"

I lift my hands around his head and smooth his hair. "It's all right."

"No, it's not. Shouldn't have snapped at you like that. Gone off in a huff like that. You don't deserve that, you don't deserve any of it. I promised myself I'd . . . ." His mouth climbs on mine, soft and unwashed and comfortable. "That was the last time. Promise you."

My heart is cold. My head pounds. I need another aspirin, another glass or two of water. A cigarette, a drink, anything.

"The last time *what*, Frank?"

"Nothing."

In that instant, as Frank tugs down the straps of my slip and starts making love to me—good, warm, respectable married sex—I know exactly what Frank was doing last night.

Well, it isn't as if I haven't always known, haven't I? The clues were all there. The history of infidelity was there, discreet maybe, but adding up and up into a number that couldn't be dismissed.

And that word—*nothing*—confirms it. *Nothing* can only mean one thing.

I wonder where they did it, he and his latest girl, his campaign girl—her name escapes me right now—when they had sex last night. Did they do it in her room? In the stairwell? On the elevator, while the emergency alarm rang in the background? Did he use a rubber when he had sex with her, or did he release his reckless Hardcastle sperm directly into her pagina?

Or her mouth. It might have been her mouth. I remember the look in her eyes last night, the puppylike adoration, and I know she'd do anything to please him, anything he wanted. Girls like that, they didn't play fair.

"You have the nicest breasts," Frank says, kissing them. "I love those sweet little tits of yours."

Now, Tiny. This is the exact moment when I should kick him off the bed, headfirst (either head would do). God knows he deserves it. God knows I'm angry enough.

But you know me. I do what I'm supposed to do, damn me to hell, damn my goddamned innate stupid nature, my guilt, my yearning to please. I do what a good wife should, even a betrayed one. I sublimate my anger into something more suitable. I take Frank on with a defiant passion instead, I clutch his head and call out, I thrash and rock and heave with the best of them, because maybe—just maybe—I, Tiny Schuyler Hardcastle, am no slouch either. Maybe I'm not Frank's brand-new girl Friday, voluptuous and vibrant, desperately devoted. But beneath my porcelain exterior, I, too, am packed tight with sexual longing, with a craving for sexual release that my anger—pure, frustrated, helpless, perverse—only intensifies. I imagine Caspian's dark head, Caspian's looming shoulders, Caspian's sure and rhythmic hips, and release—oh God, *release!*—ah, yes, gorgeous, long-lived release is my revenge.

It's only afterward, as the orgasm recedes and my husband slumps his panting body across mine, that the nausea climbs into my belly and the headache returns to throb between my ears.

Josephine. Her name pops up like a cork into my hangover.

And I'm no better than Josephine, am I? I succumbed to the Hardcastle allure. I made my own bargain with the status and the promise of it all. The razzle-dazzle. Being Frank Hardcastle's wife, being the chosen one of the chosen man. Pepper had me there. *Politicians are sexy, Tiny. It's a fact.* The price of marrying the man everybody wants.

You don't complain when the bill arrives. You rise above it all, pure and perfect.

I push Frank away and slide across the mattress to safety.

Now, when I say I've never been drunk before, I don't mean to imply that I've never had a bit more than I should. Everyone does, don't they, from time to time? I've gone to bed a little tipsy, I've woken up a bit hairy the next morning. But this is something else. I want to vomit.

I stagger around the bottom of the bed and find the bathroom, where I do just that. Vomit, into the elegant white porcelain toilet, just missing the elegant white marble floor. I kneel down carefully after the first heave or two, one tender patella and then the other, and I heave a little more, nothing too voluminous, until I reach a burning concentration of bile and call it a day.

How strange, that a body can feel so muddled and cloudy, and yet so exquisitely sensitized. The marble floor penetrates my kneecaps, cold and hard. A distant thumping from some other room knocks against my eardrums like an iron mallet. I can identify each individual follicle of hair on my skin, and they all hurt.

I grip the toilet seat and lever myself upward. I flush without looking and turn to the sink. A washcloth has been laid out on the counter, and a pair of toothbrushes on either side of a small untouched tube of Colgate. I run my furry tongue along my furry teeth and set to work, avoiding my reflection in the mirror, scrubbing my face with the dampened washcloth and scrubbing my teeth with a pungent excess of toothpaste.

I'm in the bathtub, taking a shower, curtain drawn tight, when Frank knocks on the door.

"Tiny? Is that you?" he asks, through the wood.

"Who else would it be?"

"Are you all right?"

"I'm perfectly fine, Frank." It's not my usual day to wash my hair, but I'm shampooing anyway, scrubbing away on my second *rinse, repeat*. As if I could just wash everything down the drain and leave myself unstained. Lily-white. Error free.

"Can I come in?"

"Suit yourself."

The door squeaks. A pause of footsteps. The tinkle of rain on porcelain, and a deep Franklin sigh of relief.

I lean my head back, let the suds fall away, and reach for the cream rinse. Through the patter around me, I hear Frank open the faucet of the sink. The shower is hot and delicious. If I could fall asleep like this, standing here as the water sizzles down the corrupt channels of my body, I'd do it.

"Are you going to be out soon?" Frank asks, through a muddy foam of toothpaste.

"Not if I can help it."

"Because the car arrives in half an hour."

I lift my head out of the stream. "What car?"

The faucet goes off again. *Whoosh whoosh.* Frank spits into the sink.

"The car to Newbury Street," he says, all clear now. "For the interview."

The front door swings open as we climb up the steps of our house on Newbury Street, Frank and I, his hand at my back in case I should stumble.

Josephine pops into view. "Hello, there! Everything's just about ready. Flowers everywhere, coffee's brewing."

"Thank you. I'll have a cup right now, if you don't mind." I hand her my gloves and hat and keep my pocketbook tucked safely under my arm. "A teaspoon of sugar and just a splash of cream."

She turns to my husband. "Can I get you anything, Frank? Coffee? I baked up a little cinnamon coffee cake, so the house smells welcoming."

"Coffee cake! I'd love a slice."

All the chirpy talk is jangling the interior of my skull. I skim through the hallway to the front parlor, which I left in spotless condition six weeks ago, lemon scented and beeswax polished, and everything remains exactly so, like fruit preserved in a jar, except for the fresh bouquets of yellow roses in my every available vase. A miasma of warm cinnamon invades the air, conquering the flowers.

The Hardcastles presented us with the town house on Newbury Street right after our honeymoon. A little gift, they said, to start out married life on the right foot, which is to say well shod. The joint came complete with Mrs. Crane, who had worked for Granny Hardcastle for years and was probably a spy. Or at least, she started out that way; she's surely given it up long since. I'm just too dull.

Was too dull.

I arrange my pocketbook on the table under the garden window, right in front of the wedding photos in their silver frames, and admire the geometry. The juxtaposition: innocent tulle against sultry leather.

Tiny Hardcastle has a secret.

Frank's voice appears over my shoulder. "Are you okay, Tiny? You seem a little funny this morning."

"I'm fine."

He clears his throat. "Were you all right about . . . you know . . ."

"Making love?"

"I know it wasn't very gentlemanly of me, but—"

I pick up the pocketbook again and tuck it back under my arm. "Can I ask you a question, Frank?"

"Sure." He looks wary.

"What time *did* you get to bed last night?"

He shrugs his gray shoulders—he's wearing a smart suit of light summer wool, the same color as a sky full of snow, above a pristine collared shirt and no tie—and shifts his vision to the window behind me. "I don't know. Two o'clock, three maybe. You know how it is."

"Yes, I know."

His eyes return to mine, all blue and boyish, a bit bruised underneath the lower lashes. "But it won't happen again. Never. I promise. This morning, when I looked over and saw you lying next to me—"

"You *promise*, do you?"

He holds up a hand. "Promise. You're the most important thing, Tiny. We're a team, aren't we? The greatest team in the world."

"I don't know, Frank. Are we?"

"Don't be sore. If you knew how sorry I am. I'm ashamed, if you want to know the truth. I acted like a spoiled kid instead of a husband." He touches the pearls at my neck, smooths the skin of my collarbone. "Did you get back to your room all right without me?"

"Yes. Fine. Your father sent Caspian to make sure I behaved myself. I'd had a bit too much champagne, apparently. Caspian made me drink some water and take an aspirin."

"Good old Cap." Frank smiles the old smile and puts his hand on my shoulder. "So that's what the problem is? A bit hungover?"

"Oopsy-daisy."

"Poor Tiny."

"Poor little me."

His fingertips rub the back of my neck. Tender itty-bitty circles. "Well, try not to let it happen again, okay? You don't want to get a reputation."

"Oh, my goodness, no. God forbid *that*. If you'll excuse me, I'm just going to freshen up before the reporter gets here."

"Good idea." Frank leans forward to kiss my forehead. As I turn to head down the hallway, he delivers my bottom a friendly conjugal pat.

The bathroom is clean and white and free of cinnamon, thank God. The door must have been closed while Josephine was baking her coffee cake in my oven. A bowl of yellow roses sits on the windowsill, quietly perfuming the room. I lean against the wall and draw deep gusts of air into my lungs. The pocketbook is clutched to my stomach. There are no cigarettes inside, just a manila envelope, still unopened, with my name on it.

You know how it is in families. Vivian was the smart daughter, Pepper was the beautiful daughter. I was the good daughter. Not that Vivian isn't gorgeous, and Pepper isn't terribly clever; not that I'm a dunce or a plain Jane. It's just the division of labor. On the other hand, Vivian, the *soi-disant* smarty-pants, got Bs and Cs all the time, and once a horrifying D (it horrified *me*, anyway) which she taped to the wall of her bedroom in a place of pride: *I hated that teacher, I would have gone ahead and flunked, except I'd have had to take the damned class again.*

Me, though. My report cards were perfect, perfect, an uninterrupted column of A A A A into the distance. Except one quarter. My junior year at Nightingale-Bamford. I wrote an essay on a nice safe subject, Jane Austen and the marriage of convenience, boilerplate and elegant, not a word out of place, and the teacher returned it with a red letter C disfiguring the top margin. *Not original*, she wrote beneath, as if originality were the only thing that mattered. She wasn't particularly impressed with my insights into Thackeray and Trollope, either, and when I returned home from school on the last day before the Christmas recess and saw my report card in its envelope (unopened, of course, since Mums couldn't care less about things like grades, though I brought her my flawless reports every quarter, with a freshly shaken martini on the side), I knew that uninterrupted column of As would contain a most unwelcome intruder. Maybe a B, if I were lucky. More likely a C.

I took that envelope and hid it in my desk. (Mums never noticed.) All Christmas vacation it sat in the bottom drawer, stalking me through a half-inch layer of polished nineteenth-century mahogany, and I couldn't open it. Couldn't face the news. If I didn't open it, if I didn't see the awful ink with my own eyes, it wouldn't be true. The agony of failure wouldn't sear my belly. You know, like the old tree falling in the forest, with no one to witness.

You're probably expecting me to conclude this little story with the usual tidy moral. *On the last day, just before I returned to school, I finally gathered my courage, opened that envelope, and faced the Awful Truth. And I became a stronger woman for it!* Well, I didn't. I never did open that envelope. I believe it still sits in the bottom drawer of the desk of my old bedroom on Fifth Avenue, overlooking the park. I wonder if the grade was a B or a C, after all.

I open my eyes and unhook the clasp of my pocketbook. The manila envelope, still rolled into its snug little tube, sits at the bottom, beneath my lipstick and compact.

I set it on the windowsill and touch up my lips. Powder my nose. My eyes are tinted red at the rims, my skin a shade too pale. Is that what a hangover does? Reverses your colors? My pearl earrings nestle into my earlobes, matching the fat strand that dwarfs the bones of my neck.

Little Tiny has a big fat secret.

Perfect little Tiny is cracking apart.

The thing about a report card, though, is that it doesn't matter. Who gives a cluck whether you got a B or a C instead of an A. It's just your own pride at stake.

But *this* mistake. This one stupid mistake. It could ruin me. The whole world would see me unmasked, stripped bare, on the front page of the newspaper, if I ignore the contents of that envelope.

Of course, it could also ruin Frank.

The wide-eyed woman in the mirror stares back at me, terrified, reproachful. This is what happens, Tiny, when you walk off the pavement. When you let down your guard. Let this be a lesson. That impulse that slams into your body, has always slammed into your body, under the pressure of Caspian's heroic hand?

Resist it.

I pinch my cheeks and reach for the envelope.

It's a different photo from the first, a close-up. Caspian has caught the vulnerability in my huge brown eyes, beneath the bravado. Something about the light makes my eyelashes look twice as long as they really are. Every detail is so keen, every line of me so familiar, I can almost smell Caspian's apartment. The warm sunlight on the sofa cushions. The thoughts in my head, the magnetic fizzle of anticipation in the air.

Probably the creep got his hands on the entire roll of film. The note says:

WHAT A GOOD GIRL YOU ARE

HOW ABOUT TWO THOUSAND THIS TIME

MAYBE YOU CAN SELL AN OLD JEWEL OR TWO

NEXT THURSDAY

DON'T BE LATE

I expect to feel fear at the physical sight of the photograph, at the sharp block letters of the note: the limb-melting kind of fear, a liquidity of terror. (Like the Eskimos and their snow, I have a name for each different type.)

Instead I'm assaulted by anger.

The scintillating kind. An electricity of fury.

I can scarcely control the shake of my fingers as I shove the photograph into the envelope and the envelope back in my pocketbook. I snap the closure like a rifle shot. The bathroom door nearly rips off its hinges as I march back into the hallway.

Josephine is just walking out of the parlor, smiling, hair swinging. I take her by the elbow.

"Had a nice evening yesterday?"

Her limbs are larger than mine, but my grip is stronger. She tries to pull her arm away. "Yes, I did, thank you."

"Good." I wink. "So did I. Frank is always so full of energy after these little affairs."

I release her astonished arm and stalk like Pepper into the parlor, where the coffee is waiting and so is a grinning Jack Lytle.

I don't know what devil possesses me. Until now, I didn't know the devil even bothered with the likes of me. I toss my guilty pocketbook on the table and pick up my coffee—Frank and Lytle are already drinking theirs—and say, "Jack! You recover quickly, if you don't mind my saying so."

He shakes my hand, still grinning. "Mrs. Hardcastle. So do you, if you don't mind my returning the compliment."

Frank waggles back and forth between the two of us. "Did you two have a good chat last night?"

"We did indeed. Mrs. Hardcastle gave me her unedited opinion of the nice folks financing your campaign, Frank. She's got a lot of spunk, your wife. I congratulate you."

Frank nearly spits out his coffee. "Thank you." The words tilt ever so slightly upward at the end, like a question.

"I have to say, I agree with her a hundred percent," Lytle says, offering me a chair. "You just don't usually hear it from the horse's mouth, as it were. Not that Mrs. Hardcastle is anything like a horse."

"No, no," says Frank. "Not at all."

"Well, maybe an Arabian." Lytle slings himself into the opposite chair, while I cross my legs and raise my cup. "A fine white Arabian. Clever, beautiful, elegant. Minds of their own. Not afraid to let you know what they really think."

Frank eases downward onto the sofa, next to me, and takes my hand. "Is that so."

"Oh, you know how it is." I lock eyes with Lytle. "When you're speaking off the record, in a social setting, for background only."

Lytle lifts his eyebrows. He really is a handsome man, even in daylight, better groomed than your average newspaper columnist. His eyes are darkish, some middle ground between brown and hazel, and his fingers contain the cup and saucer like a man who knew his tea from his coffee. He reaches for his inside pocket. "Do you mind if I smoke?"

I set down my coffee and hold out my hand. "Do you mind if I join you?"

"Don't be silly, darling." Frank squeezes my hand. "Mrs. Hardcastle doesn't smoke."

"She does among friends." I take the cigarette from Lytle, place it between my lips, and lean forward for him to light it up. "And I consider Jack a friend. Don't you, darling?"

Frank's sitting next to me, so I can't see where he's looking, whether it's me or Lytle. His legs shift. "Of course."

"Allow me to say, Mrs. Hardcastle, that your husband intrigues me even more than you do." Lytle lights his own cigarette and blows the smoke to the side. "How did the two of you meet?"

"At a Radcliffe mixer, when I was nineteen." I turn my head to look adoringly at Frank. "We've been together ever since."

"Indeed." Lytle sends my husband a wise-eyed look, just between men. "I see."

"What can I say? I looked at her and said to myself, Frank Hardcastle, she's the one."

"Any plans for kids?"

Frank catches himself and looks at me.

"Not yet," I say. "We're still so in love."

Lytle winks. "Isn't that how you end up with kids? If you're doing it right, that is."

"We certainly hope to have children soon," Frank says hurriedly.

"Well, that's good. Very good." Lytle lifts his cigarette. "The perfect family man, then. Beautiful wife, kids on the horizon. Just a normal, happy, well-adjusted guy."

Frank makes a self-deprecating chuckle to acknowledge the truth of Lytle's words. "If you say so. I'm the luckiest man on earth, that's for sure, and that's why I'm eager to go to Washington on behalf of the people of Massachusetts, the people who work hard and—"

"And you, Mrs. Hardcastle? Normal, happy, well adjusted? Handsome husband, kids on the horizon?"

I lean forward to tap a bit of ash into the tray, to pluck my coffee cup and take a sip. Too much sugar, I think. "Well, now. That's an excellent question, Jack."

"What?" says Frank.

"Really?" says Lytle. "How so?"

"I mean, who's really happy? Well adjusted, that's a laugh. Now, I'm awfully lucky, I admit." I wave my cigarette hand to indicate the roses and the polish. "And my husband certainly *is* handsome, isn't he? The cream of the crop. No, I did well for myself. Top-drawer, absolutely."

"Tiny—"

"But here's the thing, Jack. Are we on the record or off?"

"Whatever you want us to be, Mrs. Hardcastle."

He leans forward, and I lean forward, connecting over the tops of the yellow roses.

"Tiny—"

"Jack, the thing is, while I believe absolutely in my husband's ability to represent the Commonwealth of Massachusetts, to fight for justice and opportunity, et cetera and so on—"

"Jesus, Tiny—"

"I really sometimes wonder whether the whole system is broken. Because, really, isn't it all for show? Isn't everything just for show? The donors last night, they were putting on a show for us. They were putting on a show for one another. We were damned sure putting on a show for them. The all-American candidate and his all-American wife, clean as a whistle, the good-looking masquerading as the good. And what in God's name does any of *that* have to do with natural law and civil rights, with the conflict in Vietnam and the larger problem of the spread of Communism and nuclear capability, with what we believe and who we are as a country, and the right way forward on any number of critical issues . . ."

Frank stands up and calls out to the crack in the pocket doors. "Josephine! How about bringing in that coffee cake?"

Caspian, 1964

Tiny spoke into his shirt, still laughing. "You should have seen the look on your face."

"You're going to hell for this." His relieved mouth had somehow found its way into her hair, at the edge of the monogrammed handkerchief that held it all back. He kissed her there. She'd never know, right?

"I'm already going to hell for this. Didn't I tell you?" She stopped laughing and lay there, pleasantly slack, her hands tucked up between his chest and hers. "Did you get enough pictures? Or should I keep going?"

The camera.

He put his hands around her arms and set her away. The camera sat on the floor, a few feet from his knee, miraculously intact. "I think that's plenty," he said. He picked up the camera and examined it knob by knob, giving it his full attention. His heart had resumed beating by now, though at an unnaturally quick pace, throbbing in his neck.

"Can I see them?" There was a brief scratch as she lifted the needle away from the record, interrupting an arpeggio in the second movement.

"I'll have to develop them first." He got up and went to the darkroom—a closet, really, the old boxroom where steamer trunks and other bulky clutter used to be kept, perfect for his purposes once he'd hired a plumber to run a pipe in for running water—and there in the utter darkness, as he worked by touch, unspooling the film from the roll, loading it onto the reel, lowering the reel into the film tank, his heart returned to normal. His breathing slowed. He flipped on the lights and went through each methodical step, until the negatives hung drying from the rack and he returned to the living room.

Tiny had made coffee. She gave him a cup and curled up on the sofa, still wearing his shirt, her long bare legs tucked up beneath her. He wanted to join her, but instead he went to the window and stared down at the sporadic pulse of traffic, the motionless trees. A woman walked by, leading a small and reluctant poodle. He could see the long, straight part of her hair, all the way up here. When he turned to speak to Tiny, her head had fallen back on the sofa, and she was asleep.

Tiny slept quietly, as still as a bird. He tried not to watch her, but as he read his book in the chair across the room, his eyes kept lifting away from the page, as if to reassure himself that she was still breathing. The minutes ticked softly by. He checked his watch, set aside the book, and rose to his feet.

She must have felt the vibration through the floorboards. Her eyes opened. "What are you doing?"

"The film should be dry. I'm going to process the negatives."

"Can I help? I've never seen pictures developed before."

"If you like."

He headed for the darkroom without looking back.

He told himself he didn't want her to follow, but when she stepped inside the room right behind him, he admitted that the warm feeling in his chest was one of elation, not despair. Yes, he was happy she was there. Just her presence, nothing more. What was wrong with that?

"Close the door," he said.

"Oh! Of course."

He switched on the red lamp and pulled the film from the drying rack to examine the negatives.

"I thought this was a darkroom. You know, *dark*?"

"The black-and-white paper isn't sensitive to red light." He held up the negatives and peered carefully, one eye closed.

"I see. And you only work in black-and-white?"

"I like black-and-white. You can fiddle with light and shadow more. You can see things that color obscures."

"Like what?"

"Details."

Usually, the process of selecting the right negative to develop was fairly straightforward. In an entire roll of film, he might have two that looked promising. Two that might be worthy of the trouble of printing, if he were lucky. As he scanned the long strip of film, his pulse ratcheted upward. One, two, three. Okay, not four. Five maybe. Six. Oh, God, *seven*. Eight. She was turned the wrong way in nine, but even there, if he cropped it . . .

"What's wrong?" asked Tiny. She stood against the door, hands folded behind her back, in stock-still observation.

"Nothing's wrong."

"You're frowning."

"I'm concentrating. They're all good, actually. They're amazing." Forget ten. But eleven and twelve. Fourteen. Sixteen, seventeen. Christ, she was good. "I'll be up all night."

"Um . . . I'm sorry?"

He turned to her and grinned. Elation again. "Don't be sorry."

"A smile! Finally. I was beginning to think you'd run out of them."

He stepped to the cutting counter and picked up the scissors, slicing the negatives into strips of five. "I've got a few left in here."

"For the photographs, or me?"

"Both. Now look here. These are the negatives, see?" He held up a strip and beckoned, though in the warm confines of the darkroom she was only a couple of steps away. "I go through these and decide which ones are good enough to print, except in your case, they're all good."

She pushed herself from the door and joined him. "Can you really tell which ones are good? I can hardly see what they are."

"I've had practice. Look for yourself."

She took the strip from his fingers and held it against the red darkroom light. Her eyes narrowed. Cap watched her irises flick from image to image, the little purse of her lips. She came to the end and shook her head. "You're a better man than I am, Gunga Din."

"Well, take this one right here, for starters. You're filling the entire frame, a nice arc to your body, your face half-turned to the camera. You can see a good balance of light and dark areas. Those are some of the things you look for. So you take the negative and move over here, to the enlarger . . ."

She watched with apparently avid interest as he showed her how to create the image, how to focus and enlarge until it was just right, exactly as it should be, and how to make a test strip on photographic paper, to find the correct exposure. In the red wash of the light, her lips disappeared, and her eyes looked even larger than before, like a young animal's. The top button of her shirt had come undone, baring a triangle of volcanic skin that pointed downward to the slopes of her breasts. He managed resolutely to ignore the provocation. They moved to the chemical baths.

"Oh, I see!" she exclaimed, when the test strip emerged from the developer. "Oh, look! There I am!"

"There you are." He held up the strip to examine the prints. "I think the second one is about right, don't you? Ten seconds of exposure, maybe eleven. I want these really light. Almost overexposed. I want to grab the radiance."

"Radiant, am I?"

He sank the test strip into the fixer bath. "You know you are."

When she didn't reply, he looked over his shoulder. She stood with her back against the cutting board, her fingers curled around the edge of the counter. It was hard to tell in this light, but she might have been crying. Or else holding the tears back. Suffocating in them.

He said, "Can you give me a hand over here? Rinse this off in the last tub?"

"All right."

She took the test strip from him and plunged it into the rinse bath with the tongs, tilting her face downward so he couldn't see her expression. He stepped back to the enlarger and opened the box of photo paper. From behind him came a careful sniff, a woman gathering her composure.

"What are you doing now?" she asked.

"Making a print."

"I think this is rinsed off. What should I do with it?"

Without turning his head, he said, "Grab one of the clothespins and hang it on the line above your head."

A pause. "I can't quite reach."

"Oh. Sorry about that."

He reached above her, careful not to touch so much as the edge of her shirt, the tender curve of her ear, and clipped the test strip to the drying line.

"Caspian . . ."

He returned to the enlarger, made a final adjustment. "Count with me," he said, and opened the aperture. "One . . . two . . . three . . ."

She joined in softly. "Four . . . five . . . six . . ."

Seven. Eight. Nine.

Her voice was breathy, full of exercise and emotion. Before him, her image soldered invisibly to the photographic paper, her body stretched into a promising white curve, elastic control, sexy as all burning hell.

Ten. Eleven.

He closed the aperture and handed her the paper. "Now put it in the developer."

"I really don't—"

"Go ahead. It's your picture. Just hold it by the very edges with the tongs."

She took it from his hand. "All right. But you have to tell me when to take it out."

She dipped the paper into the developing bath. Cap stood nearby, just close enough to feel her without touching her. Above her collar, her dark hair escaped from his handkerchief to lie in wisps against her long red-tinged neck.

"Close your eyes," he said.

"Why?"

"You'll see."

She closed her eyes. "When do I take the photograph out?"

"Thirty seconds."

"But I haven't been counting."

"I have." He reached around her and closed his hand about her wrist. Next to the tongs, her image materialized like a ghost on the white paper.

"Caspian?"

"Keep your eyes closed." He was counting in his head, holding on to his sanity in the slow tick of numbers. Her bones were light in his hands, her body stiff. Twenty-two. Twenty-three. Her anxious metacarpals shifted beneath his fingertips. "*Shh,*" he said.

Twenty-nine. Thirty.

"Now take it out," he said, guiding her hand, "and dip it in the fixer." He nudged her sideways within the cage of his arms and pressed again with his fingertips, quite gently, and she followed him downward until the photo was fully immersed in the fixing solution. "Eyes still closed?"

"Yes."

"I'm amazed."

"Well, I trust you. Besides"—she laughed, a shallow laugh—"it's fun, really. Like when my sisters and I would blindfold each other and stick our hands in all sorts of disgusting messes from the kitchen to guess what they were. Vivian once put my fingers in a bowl of macaroni and cheese and told me it was brains. I almost believed her."

"You have a strange idea of fun, you and your sisters."

"Why? What do boys do?"

"Cowboys and Indians. Stickball." He lifted her hand with the tongs out of the fixing bath. "Now the rinse."

They moved like dancers to the last tray, which was equipped with running water to clean all the chemicals away from the photograph. He set aside the tongs and moved her hands about in the tray, showing her how to rinse the paper thoroughly, but mostly to enjoy the gentle sway of their fingers in the water, the way her shoulders had now relaxed into his ribs, just above his heart.

"Can I open my eyes now?"

"Almost." He lifted her hands, until the photograph hovered dripping before her face, and then he released her. "Now."

She gasped, a wondrous little intake of air.

"That's you. Look how strong you are. How beautiful. Look at your arms, the way they're curved. That muscle there, in your calf. Your fearless eyes. Your mouth."

"It doesn't look like me."

"Yes, it does. It looks exactly like you. The real you. The true Tiny. Radiant. The way I picture you, when you're not in front of me."

She shook her head.

"So you have to promise me, love, that *whatever* you do with yourself in this life, *whoever* you do it with, you won't stop *this*. All right?" He tugged the picture from her fingers and hung it up above her head with a clothespin, next to the test strip. "You won't stop dancing."

"Caspian," she whispered.

He looked down.

She stared right back up at him, a few inches away, bathed in red. Her eyes brimmed, luminous, about to spill over. She lifted her hands and cradled his face, and before he could react to this unexpected caress, before he could even bring his own hands down from the drying line to grab her waist or her shoulders, to pull the handkerchief from her hair and anchor his fingers in her, she dragged him to her lips and kissed him.

She kissed hard but not deep, as if she were afraid of opening him up, of opening herself up. The tip of her nose brushed the tip of his nose, and her breath tasted like coffee. His hands hovered around the back of her head, at the place where her hair curled away from the handkerchief, slippery as old silk, radiant with the warmth of her scalp. He tried gently to open her mouth a little more, but she pulled away and dropped her fingers away from his face.

"Come back here," he said, reaching for her. Soft in his head. Hard as stone down below.

Her chest moved quickly. "Thank you. Thank you for this."

"Tiny—"

He reached again, but she moved too fast. She cracked open the door of the darkroom and slipped through in a flash, shutting it behind her, and he needed to follow her, he needed to take her back and make her stay, but what right did he have to her? None.

What right did he have to stop her going? Not the slightest.

Only the longing in his chest, the longing in his belly, the longing in his balls. And that was his problem, not hers.

He reached for the next negative and fit it into the enlarger, and when he heard the front door open and close a moment later, he knew she was gone.

Tiny, 1966

TINY LITTLE THING

t seems I'm in disgrace," I tell the man seated beside me.

Mr. Hardcastle's thumbs press into the steering wheel, until the nail beds turn white. "Of course not. We just think it might be best if you spent a little more time at the Cape before returning to the campaign."

"But I'm perfectly fine."

The radio, humming a pleasant background scenario of careless woodwinds, finds a patch of static. Mr. Hardcastle leans forward and fiddles with the knob, until at last he gives up and switches it off entirely. "Of course you are."

"You're speaking to me as if I'm a child. Or a lunatic."

"We understand it's been difficult—"

"But a Hardcastle wife is expected to keep her mouth shut, isn't she? Not to discuss any uncomfortable truths."

He strikes a fist against the steering wheel. "The *press*, Tiny! You should know better than to say things like that in front of a reporter. I don't know what's come over you."

"I was upset. I just couldn't take it anymore."

"That's no excuse. Your personal feelings are irrelevant."

His anger blisters the air. I turn my head to the half-open window and attempt to relieve the sting in my eyeballs. To peel the frustration from the lining of my throat.

"I'm sorry," he says. "I spoke sharply just now. I understand you're not yourself."

The trees pass by, the long straight stretch of highway leading into the shore. A layer of clouds has spread overhead, sagging with heat. I can smell the impending shore, the grassy rot of the salt marsh. "It's not the baby," I say.

"We quite understand how desperately you wanted this child, Tiny . . . ."

"It's not the baby!" I shout out the window.

Mr. Hardcastle presses a button near his door handle, and the glass draws silently up, shutting off the salty draft in an instant. He leans forward and switches on the air-conditioning. "I see."

"No, you don't. I've *had* it, do you understand? I've *had* it with working so hard to get things right, not putting a foot wrong, smiling for the cameras and pretending to have the perfect marriage—oh the hypocrisy—while we all pretend Frank isn't sleeping with other women—"

"You believe Frank is sleeping with other women?"

"You know it's true. He always has."

The car in front of us, a ten-year-old Buick sedan the color of new lichen, draws closer and closer, foot by foot, until we're so close that the brilliant chrome of the rear bumper hurts my eyes. Until I can sketch the outline of the driver through the glass, and the pair of dice dangling from his rearview mirror. He glances into it, sees our looming reflection, and panics. The brake lights flash on, red and bright against the chrome. I shove my right foot against the floorboard and strangle the gasp in my chest.

At the last instant, Mr. Hardcastle pulls to the left and overtakes the Buick.

"Frank loves you," he says.

"That has nothing to do with it."

The thumbs are drumming now. The car's accelerating, the engine droning heavily. "Tiny, the wife of a politician, of any great man, has to understand how the world works. A leader naturally attracts followers. It doesn't mean he loves you any less. You're the woman he comes home to, the bulwark, the virtuous center around which his life revolves. Actually"—he gathers strength from some inner reservoir of self-righteousness—"you should count yourself lucky he doesn't do it more often. I'm sure you've heard the stories about Jack Kennedy. The psychology of leadership almost requires that—"

"That he gets into bed with his campaign staffers? That he's habitually and cheerfully unfaithful to his wife?"

"It's not *infidelity*, Tiny. Infidelity is when a wife strays from her husband."

"*What?*"

He explains calmly: "Because a woman takes a lover when she's in love. Her heart's involved. Frank's *heart* isn't involved with this . . . this girl, or any other. It's just physical release. A boost to the ego, every man needs that. His heart is all yours. You know that. He *needs* you, Tiny. He loves you."

I lean forward and wrap my gloved hands around my knees, almost unable to breathe. The engine roars at the pace of my heart, hurtling down the highway toward the Atlantic, passing cars like an ocean liner passing a fleet of fishing smacks.

Mr. Hardcastle continues. "If *you* were to stray, now. That would present a more serious problem. Your loyalties divided, your emotions committed elsewhere, outside the family. To say nothing of the question of parentage, if you were to have a child. An unforgivable breach. I speak hypothetically, of course, to illustrate the point."

"So Caesar's wife must be beyond suspicion, while Caesar can sin all he likes?"

"Men are different, Tiny."

"*People* are different, Mr. Hardcastle."

The pistons call out as Mr. Hardcastle pulls around another car, eighty miles an hour at least. I grip the door handle. The pavement rushes by, the blurred and bony trees, like a movie reel run through the projector at high speed.

"I think you're a little overwrought, Tiny," says Mr. Hardcastle in a very low voice.

"I don't think I'm overwrought at all. I don't think my husband is constitutionally helpless to keep himself from cheating on me. Look at Caspian. Your nephew. I don't think he'd cheat on his wife."

"He doesn't have a wife."

"But if he did, he'd be loyal."

Mr. Hardcastle releases a giant sigh, the kind you spend on children and lunatics. "Caspian is not a great man, Tiny. He's not a mover of events. He's a soldier. A good one, but a soldier. The history books won't be written about him."

"He's a better man than any of you, I suspect. At least you can trust him."

Mr. Hardcastle switches back into the right lane, which is temporarily clear of opponents, but he doesn't slow down. "That's true. Cap's a loyal man. You're right about that."

"You see? It's possible. And I absolutely *refuse* to put up with . . ."

I hear the screech almost before I feel the pressure of deceleration against my chest. The heavy black car swerves to the side of the road in a series of fishtails, drowning out the sound of my scream. We stop in a lurch, and the sudden quiet turns me weightless with fear.

"Is that an ultimatum, Tiny?" Mr. Hardcastle asks softly.

"No. Not exactly."

"Then what is it? What do you mean, *refuse to put up with it?*"

I release the door handle and smooth my skirt about my legs. My hands flicker a little too quickly. "I mean Frank needs to understand that this behavior isn't acceptable. That I can't just go on being a . . . a good wife, a picture-perfect wife, if he keeps on humiliating me like this."

"Humiliating you? Surely he's been discreet."

"The campaign staffer. Josephine. He was with her last night, before he came to bed."

"*Josephine?* You're sure?"

"It's too obvious for words. The way she *looks* at me."

Mr. Hardcastle stares at my mouth. "Very well. Then she's gone."

The cold delivery of the words—*she's gone*—dissolves my last nerve.

"You don't need to fire her," I whisper. "I'm sure she's good at her job. The campaign part of it. It's Frank who needs to . . . to . . ."

He turns his head to gaze through the windshield. "I'll speak to him."

"But he's not going to change. He promised me, right before the wedding, that there wouldn't be any more women. He said marriage would change him. But it hasn't. It won't. It will only get worse, the more successful he gets, because that's what happens when you think you're invincible. You think you have a right to women."

The cars whoosh and rattle past us, making Mr. Hardcastle's black Lincoln sway ever so slightly as we sit there on the shoulder, staring together at the dark asphalt, the clean white stripe, the heavy gray sky above the treetops. The air conditioner whirs in the spaces between them.

"What about financial compensation?" says Mr. Hardcastle.

"I beg your pardon?"

"A settlement of some kind. In ten years, fifteen years, when we've gotten where we want to go—"

"You must be joking."

Mr. Hardcastle reaches across the bench seat and covers my fisted hands with his own. "I assure you, Tiny, I'm not. I will not allow my son's career to be derailed by some harebrained impulsive move on your part, made at a time when your emotions are running amok. Surely you've always understood that you'll be rewarded handsomely if you behave yourself. The sky's the limit, Tiny. Dream as big as you want. You could be the most famous, the most envied, the most photo-graphed woman in the world. I mean that literally. In the entire *world*, Tiny."

"Maybe I don't want that anymore. Maybe I only thought I did."

"Every woman wants that, if she dares to admit it."

"I'm quite sure I don't. In fact, I dislike it intensely. Being photo-graphed."

"You like having money."

"Money's lovely, I won't deny it, but there are more important things."

"I'm sure we can find them for you. But the reverse is also true, you know." He puts the car back into gear and checks the mirror. "The stick, as opposed to the carrot."

I want to tell him I'm not a donkey, and, in any case, I don't par-ticularly like carrots. But the urge is smothered by an instinct, a poker player's instinct, to hide my cards from the dealer. You don't try to beat the house, do you? You keep your head down and your cards close to your chest until you've gathered enough chips to cash in and walk out the door to a waiting automobile, packed and rumbling by the curb.

Mr. Hardcastle merges smoothly back into traffic. "Don't think I'm insensitive to your plight, my dear. I like you very much. We all do. We're here to make you happy, if you let us."

I say yes, of course I understand, and neither of us utters another word down the length of the highway, through the village and down the lane to the Hardcastle property. When we pull up before the entrance to the Big House, right between the stone urns of bright yellow marigolds, I take off my pointy shoes and tell Mr. Hardcastle that I think I'll take a little walk before lunch, to clear my head.

Pepper props her legs up on the dashboard and chews her sandwich. "And what brought about this sudden change of heart?"

"Frank's having an affair."

She swallows and tears away another bite. Peanut butter, no jelly, just like she used to eat when we were kids. The smell tweaks my nose like an old friend. She reaches for the bottle of Coke on the floorboards. "I'd say more than one."

"Why would you say that?"

"Just a hunch. Put it this way: you find out a lot about a man when you go out for the evening in his company." She waves the Coke bottle. "He wasn't turning them away at the door, if you take my meaning."

"Funny. He pretty much said the same thing about Caspian."

"Caspian?" She laughs. "No, the good major just sat there with a beer or two, fending them off with one arm. Frank was the one collecting votes."

"Yes. Yes, of course he was. How stupid of me."

"At least he had the decency not to make a move on *me*. Now that's a gentleman for you."

"Pepper, you've really got to raise your standards."

"As the kettle said to the pot." She sets the bottle back down. "He's *your* husband, after all."

"Yes, he is, isn't he?" I raise my stockinged feet to the dashboard, to the right of the steering wheel. The nylon slips against the liquid smoothness of the wood. "You don't happen to have a cigarette, do you?"

"Back at the house. Sorry. I suppose a good sister would be offering you a vodka and a smoke at a time like this. All I've got is peanut butter and a Coke."

"Well, it isn't as if I haven't always known. There were always other girls. I never saw them, he was decent enough for that, but I knew they were there."

"Then why did you marry him? Assuming you cared."

"*Because*, my dear Pepper, I didn't just want to be any old housewife. I wanted a life with purpose. I didn't want to be Mums, running around, drinking and sleeping around, doing absolutely nothing at all when I could have done so much. And—well, this is the stupid part. I thought he would stop when he got married. I really did. He sat me down and promised me, a week before the wedding, and I was so . . . so jangled up and just sick inside, at that particular moment, I decided to believe him."

"You're right. That was about as stupid as it gets."

"Yes, I realized that pretty quickly."

"So why didn't you divorce him then? At the first instance? Admit you were stupid?"

"What, admit I *failed*, Pepper?"

"Yes. Why not? Everyone makes mistakes."

I sigh. "Look, I know it's hard for you fearless and rambunctious girls to understand this, you and Vivian, but I'm very good at turning my head and pretending unpleasant things don't exist. It's how I survive. You survive by striking your own trail and climbing the mountain, I survive by finding the road around it." I pause. "I know you both sneer at me for it. I know you think it's a weakness. Trying to be good, trying to make the best of things."

She leans her head back and stares at the roof. Somewhere up there, tucked into a nook where one beam meets another, lodges a discreet nest of baby starlings, fed at intervals by an anxious mother starling. We noticed them last week. It's transfixing, the sight of those desperate little beaks. You can't help thinking, God, how fragile. I wonder if they make it.

Pepper says softly: "Maybe I understand that a little better than you think."

I wiggle my toes on the dashboard. "Do you mind if I finish your Coke?"

"Be my guest."

I pick up the bottle from the floorboard and lift it to my lips. The air in the shed brims pleasantly with grease and warm grass, with the faint whiff of the nearby ocean. Behind my back, the old leather seat is as comforting as ever. Pepper doesn't seem to have made much progress. The hood stands open, and the floor is littered with random bits of machinery, pretty much the way I left it yesterday.

"I'm pregnant," Pepper says to the starlings.

The Coke sputters from my lips.

"Isn't it stupid? Here you are, wanting a baby so much, Frank's messing around with other girls, and here am I, the fallen woman . . ." She shakes her head against the leather. "I'm sorry. I wasn't going to tell you. I haven't told anyone."

"Not even Vivian?" My voice lands somewhere between a whisper and a squeak. I wipe the Coke around my mouth with the edge of my dress. Surely I've misheard her. Or she's joking. One of Pepper's jokes.

"No. She's off in East Hampton for the summer. It's not the kind of thing you just bring up over the phone. Anyway, she's got her own bag now."

I set down the bottle and lay my forearms over my belly. "How are you feeling?"

"Oh, fine, actually. I'm like a peasant woman. A little woozy when I'm hungry. And I can't face bananas, for some reason. My boobs hurt, though. They've started busting right through my brassiere. Look." She unbuttons her blouse, and sure enough, her breasts are spilling out the top of the pretty lace-trimmed silk, plump and creamy, like a pair of overambitious soufflés.

I gaze at the abundance of her, the living proof, unable to look away. "Have you decided what to do?"

"Do you think I'd be hiding out around here if I had?"

"What about the . . . you know . . ."

"The father?" She laughs him away.

"Does he know?"

"Not yet."

"Is he married?"

"He might be."

"Oh, God, Pepper." I turn my head away from the mesmerizing sight of her pregnant breasts and look through the bars of the steering wheel to the dull curved metal of the Mercedes hood. Pepper has a baby inside her. A real live baby, the kind that didn't die in your womb. How could a baby possibly die, with vibrant Pepper to nourish its dividing cells?

Pepper pregnant. Pregnant by a married man, a man she probably knew from Washington. Maybe someone I know. Frank knows a lot of people."

"Well, anyway. I know you were wondering why I've been hanging around like this. I probably owed you an explanation."

"No. I mean, you didn't. But thank you for telling me."

"Thanks for not telling me how stupid I am. How I get what I deserve. *Oh, Pepper, how on earth could you get yourself into a mess like this?*"

"Well, I already *know* how you get yourself into a mess like this. I've been trying to get myself in the same mess for two years now."

"I've always been careful, you know. Honestly, it's a mystery. Some fucking determined little sperm."

"I always figured you were on the Pill."

"You'd think, wouldn't you? A fun-loving girl like me. My mistake."

"His mistake, too."

She shrugs.

"You have to tell him, Pepper. It's his responsibility. He should do something for you."

"Really? And if your husband was to get some girlfriend pregnant, you'd want him to do something for her?"

An image materializes before me: pretty Josephine, her triumphant belly curved with Frank's baby, her breasts spilling out of her expensive career-girl brassiere. Frank lifts her hair from her bare shoulder and kisses her skin. She gazes past his head and smiles smugly at me. My hands curve into fists.

"I'm sorry," says Pepper. "Jesus. What a dumb thing to say."

"No. Fair point."

"I'm going to hell, aren't I?"

"Probably," I say, "but we all make stupid mistakes, don't we?"

"Except you. My perfect sister."

"Oh, I'm not so perfect." I unclench my fists and raise them to the edge of the windshield to hoist myself up. "I think I'm going to go back to the house and get changed."

When I reach the front door of the Big House, shoes and stockings dangling from my fingers, Mrs. Crane is there to greet me.

"Oh, there you are, Mrs. Hardcastle! There's a Mr. Lytle on the phone for you."

I set down the shoes and roll my stockings into a ball. "Did he say why he was calling?"

"No, ma'am." She glances at the slender leather pumps on the floor, the stocking ball in my hand. "It's the second time he's called."

"Thank you, Mrs. Crane. I'll take it in the library."

Lytle's voice is low and confidential through the long-distance cables. "Mrs. Hardcastle. How are you?"

"I'm well, thank you, Mr. Lytle." I say his name with particular emphasis, to make it quite clear that *Jack* is an expedient of the past.

"Are you alone?"

"For the moment."

"I just wanted to let you know that I consider this morning's interview—the whole twenty-four hours, really—to be off the record. I mean that."

"Do you really?"

"Look, I know how it can be for you wives. I don't envy you. But I do have a job to do, Mrs. Hardcastle, and I'm working on a lead or two now that . . . well, you might not like what you hear."

"What sort of lead is that?"

"Like I said, I'm just doing my job. I like you, Mrs. Hardcastle, and I'd hate to see you get hurt, but that's the nature of the business.

I don't think it's any secret that I'm digging around, up here. I just wanted to let you know, as a courtesy . . ."

"I quite understand. Is that all?"

"Yes. Yes, I suppose it is."

"Thank you for calling." I pull the receiver away from my ear, which has taken on a kind of numbness, a cold cotton stuffing, and at the last instant I hear a faint *Wait!*

I return the receiver to my ear. "Yes?"

"Maybe you *can* help me with something, Mrs. Hardcastle."

"I can't imagine what."

"I don't suppose you've heard anything in the family, any explanation for a certain incident in Mr. Hardcastle's junior year at Harvard. Anyone ever discuss that with you?"

"What sort of incident?"

"A disciplinary incident, Mrs. Hardcastle. Surely you've heard about it."

I turn my gaze to the wall of the library, where Frank's Harvard degree hangs on the wall next to his father's, and his grandfather's, too, framed in burl wood. The comfortable Latin words are identical in all three, down to the typescript: OMNIBVS AD QUOS HAE LITTERAE PERVENERINT SALVTEM . . .

"Mrs. Hardcastle?"

"I'm sorry. I can't imagine what you mean. My husband's record at Harvard was exemplary. He was the salutatorian. He gave a speech at the commencement ceremony, a very stirring speech."

"No one's ever referred to any dealings with the dean's office?"

"The dean's office? What sort of dealings?"

"That's what I'm trying to find out, Mrs. Hardcastle, and I must say it's been slow going. Records missing, that sort of thing."

"I'm at a loss. I've never heard of such a thing. I'm sure you must be mistaken. Did the suggestion come from our opponent's office? Because it's completely out of—"

A shadow falls across the doorway, in the corner of my vision. I startle around to find Mr. Hardcastle standing just inside the threshold, hat in hand, jacket over his arm, watching me quietly.

"Mrs. Hardcastle?"

"Out of character. I really must go, however. Thank you for calling."

I settle the receiver in its cradle, straighten my skirt over my bare legs, and smile at my father-in-law.

"I hope I haven't interrupted," he says.

"Not at all."

"I'm just heading back into town. I've spoken with my mother to fill her in. We're both in agreement that you should continue here at the Big House for the time being, until you're feeling better."

"Actually, I'm feeling quite well. I—"

He steps forward, kisses my cheek good-bye, and puts on his hat. His hand lingers around my upper arm, and his smile is bland. "Don't try to sneak away, now."

He turns and leaves the room, and it isn't until the front door latches faintly from the hallway that I realize he never asked me who was on the telephone.

Caspian, 1964

The day Caspian's mother died, the principal came to his classroom and beckoned to the teacher, Miss Flaherty, and Miss Flaherty, after a whispered conference, had arranged her face into a sympathetic mask and walked up to his desk and said, "Caspian, gather your books; your father is waiting for you in the office," in a voice just short of a sob.

All the other kids had stared at him as he took out his notebook and pencil case and the lunch box he wouldn't need today. Everyone knew that his mother was sick, of course. That she was gonna croak. He had felt the eyes tracking him as he trudged to the door, to the waiting principal, whose face wore the same sympathetic mask as Miss Flaherty. Had felt those speechless young eyes transforming him forevermore into Cap Harrison, the Boy Whose Mother Died.

Now, be nice to Cap, their moms would say, as they handed out lunch boxes and pencil cases and mittens the next day, before the school bus trundled around the corner. *He has no mother now.* A motherless boy.

They had stopped at his sister's classroom first, before proceeding to the office. She had come out crying, and he had put his arms around her in the backseat of the car, as Dad drove them to Granny's house, where Granny was waiting in her chintz chair in the living room, wearing a navy-blue dress and flamingo-pink lipstick. By the time they reached Brookline, Cap's shoulder was wet through with his sister's tears.

He dialed her up now. "Janet?"

"Cap? Jesus! Hold on." A child was crying in the background. Her second, from the high-pitched sound of it, a girl improbably named Ursula. The older one never did cry much; she was too busy consoling her mother. Janet had gotten pregnant at age seventeen by a junior officer in Manila, a nice fresh West Point boy who did the right thing and married her, started sleeping with other women almost immediately, and then progressed along the spectrum of infamy until he was regularly hitting his wife by the time the baby was born. She'd hung around a year before she divorced him and started having a little fun herself, to make up for the misery. If she knew who fathered Ursula, now two years old and a sulky little beauty, she wasn't telling. The crying stopped, replaced by canned television laughter. "Where are you? What time is it?"

"I don't know. Seven o'clock, maybe. How are the girls?"

"They're great. They love California. Is everything okay?"

"Sure, everything's okay."

"Because you sound upset."

"Just wanted to check in. See how you're getting along out there."

"I'm good, Cap. I am. The job's going well. Night school's going well. Even Dad might be proud of me." She allowed a touch of sarcasm. She and their father had never really gotten along. He had been too taciturn, and she needed affection. She needed a mother. She needed a father who hugged her and called her his princess, not a man stuck in perpetual mourning for a woman his daughter could never match.

Cap sighed. "He always was proud of you, Janet."

"No, he wasn't, Cap. Let's not have this argument again. So why did you really call?"

He sighed again. The line crackled with his breath.

"Come on, big brother. This call is costing you. Coast to coast. Make it snappy."

What the hell was he doing here? Why was he calling Janet, of all people? He almost hung up, and then: "All right. There's this girl."

A shriek.

"Calm down. Christ. She's engaged."

"Oh, *engaged*. Well, that's nothing. You've got it all over the other guy."

"You don't even know the other guy."

"I know *you*."

He stared down at the beige box of a telephone, at the numbers and finger holes spaced evenly around the dial. The cradle beckoned, the twin plastic buttons. He could just press one down and end the call now. Save himself a few bucks. Janet's breath popped and crackled down the line, her faith in him. He closed his eyes.

"It doesn't matter anyway," he said. "She just left."

"Left for good?"

"I don't know."

"Aren't you going after her? Find this guy of hers and punch his lights out?"

"Hadn't planned on it."

"Then why the fuck are you calling me, big brother?" she said, exasperated, mindless as usual of the child in the room behind her.

He rose to his feet and walked to the limit of the cord. "I don't know. Shit. I don't know."

She laughed. The television noises were gone; maybe she'd moved to the kitchen. He pictured her tiny house in San Diego, the corner kitchen with the peeling fruited wallpaper, Janet carrying the telephone from one room to the other, the receiver cradled between her ear and shoulder, the line stretching out behind her to the jack in the wall of the living room, under the window. "Dad used to hate it when we swore," she said.

"Washed my mouth out with Ivory soap."

"Mine, too. Didn't help. So listen, Mr. John Wayne, strong and silent type. Your lips taped shut. I know you don't want to talk about it anymore, so I'll just say this. A woman wants to know you'll fight for her. That you want her badly enough. If she's going to leave this fiancé of hers, she wants to know it's worth her while. So *is* it worth her while?"

"Hell, no. I'm shipping out in two weeks. This guy's a prince. I'm just a soldier, blood all over my hands, a grunt with no—"

"Jesus, Cap. It was a rhetorical question. Of *course* it's worth her while. Soldier. Grunt. For God's sake, you're a decorated officer. You're the best. You're the best—" Her voice got all scratched up. "The best brother in the world. Rescued me over and over, when anyone else would have given up on me. You pay my damned rent every month. My girls, they fucking adore you. Shit, you're making me cry, Cap. Just go out and make some girl happy, okay? Some lucky girl."

"Janet, I don't know where she lives. I don't even know her last name."

"Go find out."

Go find out. He stared at the wall of photographs, on which he'd tacked a large print of Tiny in the upper right corner, soaring off the edge of the plaster in an arc of inexpressible grace. Her face turned away. "Are you coming to Frank's wedding?" he asked.

"Frank's wedding? You mean cousin Frank? Who's he marrying?"

"I don't know. Some Park Avenue girl, I think. Couple of weeks. New York City. I'm stopping there on my way out."

She chuckled feebly. "I guess I wasn't invited. Can't have the unwed mother hanging around the corner of the ballroom, eating up the canapés and disgracing the family name, can we?"

Damn it.

"I'm sorry, Janet."

"Don't be. Enjoy yourself. I'll see you in a couple of weeks, right? Before you report?"

"I'll be there."

"Bring your new girl so I can meet her."

"I'll try."

"What's this *try* business? That doesn't sound like my big old brother. Just do it, Cap. Execute." She said it just like their father used to, when confronted with disappointing report cards or cars that needed washing on a raw February morning. *Execute*. Get it done, no excuses.

Except that Tiny wasn't a report card or a dirty Chevrolet. She wasn't a problem that could be solved with a little determination and elbow grease. Just because he wanted her in his present bed, in his future life; wanted to write to her from the jungle and tell her every last thing, to write her his soul; wanted to read her letters, to tuck her picture in his pocket and stare at her image until he fell asleep and dreamed of her, too; wanted with an irrational fierceness to know that Tiny would be waiting for him, suntanned and bare-armed, in a small rented house in San Diego a year from now when he stepped off the

Lockheed C-130 a free man: just because he wanted all these things, didn't mean he should have them.

Didn't mean he *could* have them.

"All right, Janet," he said. "Whatever you say."

"Do you want to talk to the girls?"

"Sure. Put them on."

He spoke with his nieces for a few minutes, first an incomprehensible Ursula and then her more rational sister, Pamela, whose front teeth had come in at last and forced away the final traces of her lisp. He said good-bye and hung up the receiver, hard, so the bell gave off a startled ding, and he stared up at the ceiling—he was on the sofa, now, in the exact squishy spot he cradled a shuddering Tiny yesterday—and wondered what it would be like, having kids with Tiny.

That's how crazy he was.

B ut he was a man of action, after all. Not a man who sat on sofas and stared at the ceiling, kicking a beige telephone on the floor with his toe.

Execute. His father's voice, or his sister's?

It didn't matter. The echoed word in his head was enough to start the inevitable chain reaction, the chemical combustion that set him in motion. He jumped to his feet, grabbed his wallet and keys, slammed the door behind him. He thundered down the stairs and out on the sidewalk, where the sun was still high enough to be seen above the housetops, and the air had only just begun to cool.

He reached Boylan's Coffee Shop in four minutes flat, just as old Boylan was flipping the OPEN sign to CLOSED.

"What's up, Boylan? Closing early?"

"I'm too old for this shit. What the fuck was you doing, getting blood all over my nice clean floor the other day?"

"Just saving your customers from getting shot up, old man."

"The fuck you were. That nice Mrs. Larkin, the one with the big tits, she got a hole in her shoulder the size of a baseball, she says."

"She'll be all right. Give her a good story at the bridge club. Listen, I need your help."

"Cops all over the place, drinking all my fucking coffee. Are you coming in, or what?"

Cap stepped inside the restaurant and discovered he was starving. He made himself a sandwich in the back while Boylan hunted down Em's phone number in the office. Turkey and Swiss cheese. Mustard and mayo. He could have used a drink, too, but that'd have to wait. The kitchen reeked of Lysol. Maybe the cops took one look at the stove and sent over the health department.

"Here you go." Boylan shoved a piece of paper in his hand. "Andrew four-five-oh-two-six. You better not be messing with my waitresses, you dumb cluck."

"Can I use your phone?"

Em was surprised to hear his voice. No, she didn't know Tiny's address, the lady lived a few blocks away on Dartmouth, that's all she knew. Her last name? Not sure. Something to do with the sky. Skylark?

"Schuyler?" he said.

Schuyler. Tiny Schuyler. Her name.

"That's it. Now be gentle. She's a nice girl. And she's nuts about you."

The weight on his shoulders lifted a fraction. A few meager stacks of bullion. "I sure as hell hope so, Em."

Tiny Schuyler proved easier to find than he imagined. There were several Schuylers in the phone book, but only one Miss C. Schuyler resided on Dartmouth Street, at number 26, apartment 2B. He shut the directory and realized he'd just done the same detective work Tiny did, two days ago. The both of them, tracking each other down in turn, trying to find a way in.

He hoped Em was pouring herself a drink and putting her feet up.

In no time, in a lifetime, he wheeled around the corner of Dartmouth Street and into the volcanic glare of the dying sun. He wondered what the *C* stood for, but only for an instant, because number 26 stood only a couple of houses down the block, a regular door, a regular building. A genteel, well-kept old town house, divided into genteel, well-kept apartments, suitable for young women living alone. The front door was polished, the stoop clean, the knobs brass. He'd passed this door a dozen times in the past month, and probably a hundred since he was a kid, and what do you know? Tiny Schuyler's door. He found the button for 2B and pressed it. SCHUYLER, said the label above, in typed black capital letters. His pulse beat in his throat.

The intercom made a noise that might or might not have been a human voice.

"Hello?" said Cap. "Tiny?"

Static.

"Tiny? Tiny, it's me. Cap."

The door buzzed, and Cap threw it open before it shut off. The hallway smelled of old sunshine and cigarettes. He bounded up the stairs to the second floor. Apartment 2B. The B flat would be in the back, wouldn't it?

He turned his head, and there at the end of the hall leaned a beautiful woman in the open doorway of apartment 2B, one leg crossed over the other, holding a cigarette between the first and second fingers of a bejeweled right hand, and a highball glass in the bracelet-framed palm of the left hand.

Cap rested his hand on the bannister. "I'm sorry. I was looking for Miss Tiny Schuyler."

The woman straightened her elegant long body and crossed her arms, keeping careful hold of both drink and cigarette. "I'm Mrs. Schuyler. The mother of the bride. Who the hell are you?"

Tiny, 1966

The phone rings at dawn, just as I'm about to take Percy for his walk. I snatch it up on the first ring, because who dials a telephone at dawn? Only bearers of bad tidings.

"Tiny, darling. Thank God."

"Mums?" There's no point in trying to hide my astonishment. At five o'clock in the morning, my mother might just as well be heading for bed as rising from it.

"I just had the most awful dream about you. Are you all right?"

"Of course I'm all right." I wind the cord around my finger. "How are *you*? This isn't like you, calling so early."

"I couldn't go back to sleep. I thought you'd be up." She pauses. "Are you sure you're all right?"

"Absolutely. Just the usual summer nonsense."

A long sigh rushes down the copper wires, from the tip of Long Island to the tip of Cape Cod. "Well, then."

I hesitate, and then: "What was the dream about?"

"I don't remember exactly. It was terrifying, though. Absolutely terrifying. My heart's still thundering." A faint and familiar clink underlines her words.

"Go back to sleep, Mums."

She yawns. "No, I'm up now. How's Pepper?"

"Pepper's fine. Pepper's . . . Pepper's blooming."

"Pepper's *what?*"

"Groovy. Pepper's groovy."

"Is that some sort of slang? I wish you wouldn't use slang, darling. It doesn't suit you. God knows, Vivian's bad enough, but from *you?* I don't think I can take it. Not this early in the morning."

"Well, you were the one who called *me*, Mums."

More clinking. "Maybe I'll drive up and join you two for a bit. See for myself."

"Mums, I'm fine. Really. We're both fine. You're the last thing we need."

"I just can't get this out of my head. It's too awful."

I glance at my watch. "I've got to run, Mums. I love you. Smooches to Vivian and the boys."

I stare at the telephone for a moment or two after I've hung up, tracing the dial with my forefinger. Because I could call her back. I could tell her that I'm in trouble, that I've screwed up, that I've made a few mistakes, a few doozies, and need a little help from the old Schuyler matriarchy. That maybe her dream isn't so far out, after all. That maybe the good daughter, the tiny perfect one, is the greatest disappointment of all.

At my feet, Percy whines and nudges my ankles. I crouch down and take his soft bumpy head into my chest. I whisper into his ears, "You'll still love me, won't you, Percy? You're on my side."

The old house is silent as the grave. We hold our embrace for a moment or two, Percy and I, until at last he nudges me gently in the stomach to tell me it's time to get moving.

spot a swimmer, out past the breakers, stroking steadily from north to south while the sun nudges up the horizon. Percy wants to join him.

I whistle, and Percy bounds obediently out of the uncurling surf, back toward me. He shakes the water free in an expert rattle of fur, from tip on down to tail, and then he looks up and whines, all huge eyes and cocked ears and general canine persuasion.

"Come on, doggin-boggin. Let's not bother the poor guy. He's working too hard. Anyway, you can't swim out that far, you silly boy."

You see them from time to time, the ocean swimmers. They're the diehards, the merfolk, born with saltwater veins and seaweed hair; locals, usually. Sometimes I think there must be something addictive about it, plowing through the virgin sea, the gold water sunrise. My cousin Lily Greenwald swims out every morning, down the coast in Rhode Island, and it keeps her fit as a fiddle, though she must be in her fifties now. You have to be confident to swim like that. You have to have been doing such things all your life, to plunge so fearlessly through the waves of concussive surf and into the rollers beyond, to crawl atop the skin of the ocean while the vast volume teems beneath you.

This morning's swimmer trundles along in a steady rhythm. His arms pump as regularly as pistons, and as I watch him swim, as I calculate the unceasing beats of his progress, I perceive that he lifts his head to draw breath on every fourth stroke.

Percy pads along behind me, resigned. I keep up a brisk pace, as if I might possibly outrun my thoughts, if I move fast enough. Last evening, Granny Hardcastle invited Constance and Tom and the children for dinner, along with a couple of other cousins. A merry bunch. Pepper appeared about halfway through, still in her dungarees, dressed in dust and a smear of grease. She grabbed a chicken leg and went upstairs, without even looking at me, and I haven't seen her since. I couldn't; how could I? If I forgive Pepper, if I even acknowledge her, I must also acknowledge and forgive Josephine. I must acknowledge and forgive Frank. I must acknowledge and forgive myself. The awfulness is still sinking into my bones. The enormity of what I have to face. The mountain I have to scale, because there are no more roads around it. I stand before Everest, with no hobnails and ice pick, no oxygen tank, no rope and no parka, no wise Sherpa to advise me. Just myself. Tiny me.

The salty morning air fills my lungs. I stride faster and faster, until my legs sing and my feet almost break into a run. My canvas shoes fill with sand. Ahead, the jetty stretches out like a dark finger, made of large slippery rocks; the boats are moored on the other side. I usually turn here and head back to the Big House or, perhaps, if I'm feeling particularly energetic, strike out another lap up and down the Hardcastle beach. I reach the base of the jetty and pause, preparing to turn, when Percy lets out a soft call, more a yip than a bark, and I look down the length of the jetty to find the swimmer climbing up the rocks at the end.

Climbing: I should say hoisting. The tide is high; the jetty is low. The swimmer braces his palms on the topmost rock and launches his body upward, utterly naked, and as the new-risen sun finds his skin, and his torso unfolds, a gap appears between the bottom of his left knee and the jetty below.

Dive, Tiny. Run for cover.

But nothing moves, not a twitch.

He stands only fifty feet away, wet and white-backed. His face and front are charcoal with shadow, a classic Grecian silhouette, broad of shoulder and narrow of hip, balanced on the one whole leg. My instinct is that of a deer caught in the open: if I don't move, he won't see me. My body will remain camouflaged against the sand.

Well, it seems to be working. He hasn't noticed me yet. He reaches down for the towel on the rock—my God, did he simply dive off the jetty and into the water?—and rubs himself dry.

You should really go now, Tiny. You've mastered your shock. So Caspian's back here on the Cape, physically manifest, arrived in the night when you weren't watching. God knows why. Now turn around and steal off down the sand, and maybe he'll stop by for breakfast. Tell you why he returned, today of all days, when you have just been sent down in disgrace.

But like the sight of those baby starlings, like the sight of Pepper's swollen and guilty chest, the extraordinary balance of Caspian's body holds me fast. It shouldn't. I of all people know how the human body can align itself on a slender vertical axis, can spin and point and leap from a single well-trained toe. Why should I gaze in awe at the way Caspian dries his body with a towel, drapes the towel across a rock, and reaches for a tubular object that must be his artificial leg?

And then Caspian freezes altogether, for what I believe they call a pregnant instant. His hand is braced against a piling. His back is smooth. I wonder if he's breathing, if he's thinking, because I surely to God am not. I surely to God cannot move a single fiber, cannot connect a single synapse.

A pair of seagulls dispute a morning crab. The silence melts. Caspian lifts his head and then his torso, straightening and turning in my direction at the same time, I don't know how. The leg hangs from one hand. He stands at an angle, catching a bit of newborn sun on his front, and now I *know* I should turn away, I should hide my virtuous married eyes, but how can I do that? Turn away from Caspian, when he's showing me this? The stump ends in a curious round bump, a ball of unfinished tibia covered with skin.

Percy breaks away from my legs and bounds down the jetty toward Caspian, pumping his tail.

You can't hate a man like that, can you? You aren't allowed to hold any grudges when he's given his lower leg for his country. Given it for you, inasmuch as you're an American, too. One hundred millionth of that lost leg is for your sake. A single cell, maybe, but it's enough. The purest kind of restitution. And if you don't hate him, and maybe you never really did—maybe you just hated yourself, after all, transference or projection or whatever a shrink would call it—then what *do* you feel?

Percy reaches him. Sniffs at the leg dangling from his hand. How must that left foot ache, supporting Caspian's soldierly weight, all alone. He scratches Percy's ears.

I think, *This is absurd.* Caspian's standing there, naked as noon, staring at me, daring me. Anyone might be watching. You can see the pair of us from the ocean windows of just about every house on the property, if you happen to be peeping your bloodshot eyes through the curtains at half past sunrise on a Friday morning.

I open my mouth and call down the length of the jetty. "Good morning!"

"It certainly is."

He has the trick of making himself heard without shouting. Like an actor, whispering in such a way that the rear stalls can hear him.

I whistle for Percy. He lollops back toward me, grins his guilty canine grin. The sight of his face breaks the spell. I clip his leash to the collar and turn for the house.

"Tiny!"

I wave good-bye over my shoulder. But the image remains in my frontal lobe all through shower and breakfast, all through the morning, all through my life. You can't ever forget a sight like that.

Speaking of breakfast. Pepper doesn't come down. Strengthened by the image in my frontal lobe, I search her out in her room, where she's filling a blue suitcase and smoking a cigarette. A tall glass of tomato juice sits on the windowsill.

"You're packing."

"You don't say."

"You don't have to leave, Pepper."

She straightens from behind the suitcase lid and tips her cigarette into the ashtray. "Don't I? Surely you're not planning to convert the old place into the Hardcastle Home for Fallen Women and Found-lings."

"Look, I'm sorry. You caught me by surprise, that's all. The timing wasn't the best. To say the least."

"No, you're dead right. I'm the enemy, aren't I? The kind of woman who steals your husband and gets pregnant with his baby. The one who breaks up families at Christmas and makes wives and kids weep bitter tears into their pillows. You've got every right to shun me. You especially, Tiny dear. You *should* shun me." She reaches for her tomato juice and drinks it down in such a way that makes me suspect it isn't just tomato juice. I have the feeling she's not looking for sympathy. That she neither wants nor expects me to fold her in my arms and say, *Hush now, that's not true, you made a mistake, that's all, we shouldn't judge you like that, oh, society is so damned cruel and unjust to women like you.*

"All right." I round the corner of the bed and take the cigarette from the ashtray. I examine it from all sides, like a relic of an alien civilization, and then I lift it to my mouth and inhale. Tobacco, with a garnish of tomato juice and vodka. "You're the enemy. You're the predator. You're the bitch who stalked down some poor little innocent and well-meaning husband and slept with him and got herself pregnant. But you're also my sister. You're *my* predatory little bitch. And that baby is *my* nephew or niece. So you can stay with me as long as you need to." I grind out the cigarette into the ashtray. "As long as you want to."

Pepper sinks into the slipper chair and cradles her glass. One slender leg crosses over the other and bounces, bounces. Her face is so beautiful, you can't find a single flaw. The geometry of her cheekbones deserves its own mathematical theorem. "Is that so? Have you checked with your in-laws?"

"They can choke on it."

"I'm three months along. Can't hide it much longer."

"All the better. I can't wait to see their faces when they put one and a half together. We can invite the press. I happen to know this guy at the *Globe*, a sucker for a good story."

She props her head on one hand and laughs. "You've changed, Tiny. I didn't know you had a sense of fucking humor."

I turn to the suitcase, remove a jumble of shirts, and start to fold them into a neat stack on the bedspread. "You never fucking asked."

After a moment, I hear the raspy click of a cigarette lighter, and then Pepper joins me at the sleek blue Samsonite, casting me in her statuesque shadow. She picks up the stack of folded shirts. "My, my, Tiny girl," she says, around the cigarette that dangles from her lips. "What would poor old Mums say about the two of us?"

Caspian, 1964

Tiny's mother. The mother of the bride, as she so pointedly pointed out, dressed in a flawless white-trimmed navy blue suit with elbow-length sleeves, and a small navy blue hat that matched her navy blue shoes. The heels on those shoes must have been four inches at least. Four excessive inches, for she was already tall: as tall as a fashion model and just as sleek.

And who the hell was *he*?

"I'm a friend," he said. "Do you know where she is?"

Mrs. Schuyler lifted her cigarette. Just before it touched her lips, she said, "If I did, do you think I'd tell you?"

He shrugged. "I just want to make sure she's all right."

She blew out a long curl of smoke. "You tell me."

"Isn't she there with you?"

"No, she isn't." Mrs. Schuyler gestured over her shoulder, with her drink hand, into the apartment. "She hasn't answered her phone in two days, so I thought I'd come up and check on her. I don't suppose you happen to know where she's been?"

"She's been with me."

She raked him over, forehead to toe and back to forehead again, lingering expertly on the narrowness of his hips and the width of his shoulders. As she might have measured up a horse for the sixth race at Narragansett. "I see."

"I've slept on the sofa, Mrs. Schuyler."

"Have you? That's good of you. You do know she's going to be married shortly?"

"That's up to her, I guess."

She tapped her cigarette thoughtfully against the doorjamb and took a delicate sip of her drink. "I don't believe I caught your name, young man."

"It's Caspian, Mrs. Schuyler. Caspian Harrison."

She frowned. "That's an unusual name."

"My mother was a little unusual."

"No doubt." She lifted a telling eyebrow. "In any case, Mr. Harrison, I think I'm getting the picture here. I suppose every bride gets the jitters, even a girl like my daughter. And I suppose if she's going to get the jitters, she might as well do it in style. God knows I did."

"She hasn't got the jitters, Mrs. Schuyler."

"But I do think, Mr. Harrison, if you'll excuse me, that as her mother, I'm in a better position than you are to understand what constitutes my daughter's happiness. To know and want what's best for her. Do you know, she's been in love with her fiancé for four years now? No, five. They're the loveliest couple in the world. Really, you should see them together."

"I sincerely hope I don't."

She lifted her glass, but she didn't drink. Instead she held it there, next to her navy-blue bosom, while the smoke trailed lazily from the fingers supporting her elbow. "I do hope, Mr. Harrison, that you're not the sort of man to take advantage of a girl's perfectly natural nervousness on the eve of her wedding."

"I haven't touched her."

"I don't give a damn if you've touched her or not. She's entitled to enjoy herself a little, if she likes. God knows she's earned it. What concerns me, Mr. Harrison, is what you intend to do with her now."

"As I said before, that's up to her."

She considered him. The hallway swelled with afternoon warmth, and the ice in her glass had nearly melted. The condensation fell downward onto her fingers, which were white and well kept but not lacquered. Cap took in all these details in the dusky light and wondered how he would shoot her. From the side, maybe, to capture the queenly slant of those cheekbones, exactly like Tiny's, only sharper with age. He would maybe turn on the light overhead to make that shadow harsher, to etch out the fine lines at the corners of her eyes. If he turned her at just the right angle, with the light just so, and the focus just right, he could find the transparency of her irises. Could express the brittle character of her beauty, the enigma of what lay beneath.

Mrs. Schuyler lifted herself away from the doorjamb. "You might as well come in, Mr. Harrison."

Inside, Tiny's apartment was small and spotless. There was no sign of a roommate. The kitchen was no larger than his own, taking up a corner of the living room, and a door at the opposite end indicated a bedroom. Mrs. Schuyler stalked to the kitchen, stubbed out her cigarette, and poured another drink. She opened up the icebox and took out a tray of ice cubes from the freezer compartment. "Drink?"

"No, thanks." He leaned against the wall, next to the door, and folded his arms. "You don't know where she is, then? Has she been home?"

She dropped three cubes in her glass and stuck the tray back in the icebox. A bottle sat on the counter. Vodka, nearly full. She reached for it and unscrewed the cap. "You've misplaced her, I take it?"

"She left my apartment a few hours ago."

Mrs. Schuyler turned and leaned against the counter, holding her drink at her hip. "I don't know where she is, but she's taken a suitcase. I checked."

A suitcase. The air sucked from his chest, beneath his folded arms. "And no word where she's going?"

"Not a peep. No note. *Quite* unlike her." She sent him a gimlet look that placed the blame for this anomaly squarely on his shoulders.

He looked right back. The same way he looked at a colonel when they called him up before the brass. The same way he looked at his grandmother when she summoned him for a teatime chat about his future.

"You know, Mr. Harrison . . ."

"Captain Harrison."

"Oh, indeed? I *am* impressed. But the fact remains, *Captain*"—she said the word in a throaty purr—"I know my daughter a great deal better than you do. She might think she needs a few kicks before settling down, and maybe she's right. I've sheltered her, I admit it. Wanted to keep her from repeating a few of my more egregious mistakes."

"No doubt."

"But you must understand, Captain, that Tiny's a good girl. I mean that literally. She's *good*. She's far better, for example, than *I* am, and God knows I don't deserve her." She drank her vodka and reached for the pack of cigarettes on the counter. Parliaments. She didn't open them, however. She only tapped the cardboard with her long fingernail, like a spy signaling to another spy.

"Funny, I had the same thought," he said.

"I named her after my husband's aunt. Did you know that? Christina Dane. She died in a hurricane before Tiny was born. The most awful thing. They never even found the body. And I always thought—well, it was almost as if she *knew*, even when she was a baby."

"Knew what?"

Tap tap tap. The icebox—an elderly model—coughed wheezily behind her, held a perilous silence, and then resumed humming at a more subdued pitch.

Mrs. Schuyler set her glass on the counter. "I'll tell you a little story. You see, we didn't baptize her until she was almost two. I'm not the most religious girl in the world, I'll admit, and I wasn't on what you'd call speaking terms with God at the time—we have that kind of relationship, He and I, a real love-hate sort of thing—but the Sunday we finally chose just so happened to fall on the first Sunday after Pearl Harbor. The church was packed, as you can imagine." She stopped tapping at last, took out a cigarette, and casted about, frowning. "I don't suppose you have a light, Captain?"

"Afraid not."

She opened a drawer next to the tiny gas stove and found a book of matches. "Anyway, packed church, everybody scared out of their wits, war's arrived at last, and God knows we've all seen what Europe's been through already. France occupied, London in ruins. To say nothing of poor old Shanghai. And Tiny, she arrives at the altar, and she doesn't cry a bit, does she? She's an angel. She's wearing a lovely white silk dress, trimmed with lace, an heirloom. Her hair was much lighter then, when she was a baby. Almost gold. The minister reaches into the font for the water, and she holds out her little hand, Captain Harrison, her sweet little hand, and she catches the drops in her fingers and she laughs. *Laughs*. Golden laughter, like the goddamned bells of heaven. You should have heard the gasp from all those poor heartsick people in the church that day. She *cured* them. There's no other word for it."

Mrs. Schuyler struck the match and turned away as she held it to the cigarette, as if she were trying to hide something, tears maybe. "And we all knew, didn't we, in that second, that everything was going to be all right. That God maybe gave a damn after all."

"I think I can picture it," said Cap.

Mrs. Schuyler dropped the match in the sink and faced forward again. "Well, I saw right then that she was meant for great things. That she was going to be a queen among us, someone for the dirty masses to look up to and worship. Sixty, eighty years ago, I'd have taken her to Europe and married her off to a duke or a prince, but these are modern times, Captain Harrison, and nobody cares a damn about titles anymore, titles are a joke that isn't even funny, so when she found the next best thing, all by herself, you can imagine my delight. All those years, I'd raised her to be the perfect consort. I'd sheltered her, I'd educated her, I'd kept her safe until her prince found her. I'd done it, against the odds. Against, you might say, my own nature." Her hand was a little shaky, operating the cigarette back and forth, back and forth to her glossy pink lips. Short and deep. "And I really cannot see, Captain, how *you*, however handsome and broad-shouldered and concerned for her welfare, fit into the picture."

There was one window in Tiny's living room, double width, facing south over what should have been a garden below. Outside, the sunset transformed the sky, pink and brilliantly gold, still bright enough to spar by. It softened the lines of Mrs. Schuyler's face, so that if she were made on a more delicate scale, her mass reduced by perhaps a quarter, bones shrunk and skin tightened in exact proportion, she might almost have been her daughter.

Cap uncrossed his arms and straightened himself. "Well, then I guess we've got nothing else to say. If she turns up, do you mind letting me know?" He reached for his wallet and hunted down a card.

"I most certainly will not."

He handed her the card anyway. "Just let me know she's all right, Mrs. Schuyler. That's all I ask."

She slipped it into her jacket pocket without looking. "I don't suppose I can ask you to return the favor."

He placed his hand on the doorknob and stared at the curled fingers, as if he wasn't sure they belonged to him. "I can promise you one thing, Mrs. Schuyler. If Tiny's with me, nothing and no one is going to hurt her."

He opened the door and left the room. Just before he closed it behind him, Mrs. Schuyler's voice drawled across the stagnant indoor air.

"I can't tell you how much that comforts me, Captain Harrison."

He walked slowly, and by the time he reached his own house, the pinks and golds of the promising May sunset had dissolved into a bruised twilight. The hallway was dark. He didn't bother turning on the light. He climbed the stairs and pulled the key out of his pocket.

"Caspian?"

He held himself still at the top of the stairs. To his right, a shadow detached from the wall.

He looked down at his hand, and the faint glint of the key in his palm. The slow thud of his heartbeat surprised him. But maybe he knew she was there all along.

"Tiny," he said.

Tiny, 1966

A tall figure rises out of the armchair when I head into the library to mix myself a recuperative drink before dinner. I'm embarrassed to say he catches me off my guard, even and perhaps because I've been toying with the image of him all day.

Before Caspian can speak, Pepper pipes up from between another pair of armrests. "Tiny! There you are. Look who's come for dinner."

"Surprise," says Granny Hardcastle.

I put my smile in place and pivot to face them. Caspian holds out a grave and formal hand. "Good evening, Mrs. Hardcastle. Hope I'm not intruding."

Granny smiles over her drink. "I asked him over."

I place my palm against Caspian's palm and allow him to kiss my cheek. He smells like shaving soap, the genuine article, sandalwood and all that kind of old-fashioned thing, and his kiss is firm and no-nonsense. "Of course you're not intruding, Caspian. And it's Tiny. I thought I made that clear."

"Yes, ma'am."

"Can I pour you a drink?"

Pepper says cheerfully, "Oh, I've already taken care of that. In loco sisteris, as the Latins say. Which reminds me: Where have you been?"

"Frank called." I head for the drinks tray, because firstly I need a drink and mostly I need something ordinary for my hands to do, something easy and automatic, to shake out the vibration in my fingers. Caspian's wearing a navy-blue jacket and a necktie, and while the effect isn't as imposing as his dress uniform, he still makes my ribs creak. The tie's green, the same mossy shade as his eyes, and quite narrow, beginning with a strangulated knot and ending in a point just above his belt.

"What did Frank want?" asks Granny.

"Oh, the usual. Say hello, ask how the ocean's behaving itself. How I'm behaving myself." I pour a few drops of vermouth over the ice cubes in the shaker, swish delicately, and strain it back out.

"That's good of him. They must be terribly busy."

Pour vodka over ice. Shake. Strain vodka into martini glass.

"Well, that's the thing about these darling Hardcastle men. They like to keep an eye on you." Add olive. Turn, lift glass, smile. "Cheers all."

Dinner is intimate, dangerously so. Caspian to the right of me, Pepper to the left of me. Granny Hardcastle ahead of me, in Frank's usual spot, bending her gaze over us and maintaining an unnerving silence, a pastel-flowered sphinx, as cold poached halibut replaces iced gazpacho—the weather is hot as blazes—and the conversation rides bravely on.

"Weren't Constance and Tom supposed to have dinner here tonight?" I ask.

"The baby has a cough," says Granny Hardcastle. "Caspian, my dear, may I trouble you for the salt?"

Caspian passes the salt in silence. (His not to make reply, apparently.)

Pepper starts up an anecdote about some party in Washington, lousy with drunken interns and the senators who love them. She wheels to a halt in the middle of a double entendre and throws up a speculative eyebrow in Granny's direction.

"Yes, dear?" Granny drops an ice cube in her wine. "Don't stop there. Did the poor girl ever get around to enjoying her cocktail wiener?"

"Eventually," says Pepper.

Granny smiles benevolently. "I'm not surprised. I don't suppose your employer was attending this particular party? The distinguished senator from New York, I mean."

"Yes, he was."

"Oh, how lovely. Did you get to enjoy a wiener with him?"

Pepper, embarking on a runner bean, loses herself in a fit of coughing. Caspian discovers a flaw in his wineglass.

"After all," Granny continues, "no one likes to leave a party unsatisfied."

My sister sets her fork carefully on the edge of her plate and turns her head in Granny's direction. Her face, I notice, has gone a little pink. "You would know, I understand."

"I beg your pardon?"

Pepper folds her napkin. Her fingers are beautiful and trembling, which is so unlike her (the trembling, not the beauty) that I find myself riveted by her knuckles. She says, in a voice jam-packed with feeling: "Did you also know my great-aunt Julie has a very long memory, Mrs. Hardcastle? And we're very close."

"I'm not surprised."

"Well. Then you know she doesn't mince words. And I think my aunt would agree with me when I observe . . . I observe that the senator is a great man, a very great man, and your vulgar comments"—

her voice breaks—"your *vulgar* comments only show you're the same tasteless, social-climbing, *mean* little bitch you were back then."

She bolts from the table and out of the room. A few shocked seconds later, the front door crashes shut.

I dab my mouth with my napkin and rise from the chair. "Excuse me."

The shed is so dark, I wish I'd brought the cigarette lighter from my pocketbook. "Pepper?" I ask, though I can hear her breathing plainly.

"In the car."

The orange end of a cigarette flares in the middle of the gloom. I take a ginger step or two in its direction and grope for the hood. "I hope I don't trip over a piston or something."

"Be my guest. The whole damned shed can go up in flames, for all I care."

"Gosh, Pepper. Say what you really feel." I find the edge of the door with my fingers.

"*Gosh.* What person over the age of twelve says *gosh,* Tiny?"

"I do. Move over."

The leather creaks softly. I ease myself into the driver's seat and reach for Pepper's cigarette. "I don't think you're supposed to be smoking these anymore."

"Oh, you and the Surgeon General. Anyway, maybe I'm getting an abortion."

I allow myself a shallow drag and crush the rest out on the floorboards. "*Are* you getting an abortion?"

"It seems like the most sensible solution to the problem, doesn't it?

Nobody's feelings get hurt. Two families—what do they call us, the magazines?—two *important* families are saved from disgrace. And I don't have to find out what kind of a rotten mother I'd make."

"On the other hand, you could get arrested."

She snorts. "Somehow, I just don't think the charge would stick. Friends in high places, you know."

"Wow. Was there something in the wine?"

"Wow." Her voice mocks me, high and singsong.

"I'm just saying, you should take care of yourself, that's all."

"What are you, a fucking doctor?"

"No. But honestly? I'd give anything to be in your shoes right now, instead of mine."

My eyes are adjusting to the darkness. I can pick out the cracks of light through the boards, the shadows of the trees beyond the open doorway. Sunset is still maybe a half hour away, but the radiance of daytime is gone, finished, see you tomorrow. The world has gone flat. Directly before me, the steering wheel curves in a perfect white arc above the dashboard. I rest my two hands at the very top.

"In my shoes. Is that so?" Pepper says dully.

"You have no idea."

"I don't get it. Why do women want babies, anyway? They ruin your figure, they take up all your time."

"They haven't ruined Vivian's figure."

"Well, that's just Vivian. She only sits down to take a crap."

A dizzy pause, and then I explode into laughter, helpless gusts of it. "Oh, my God. Oh, my God, Pepper. *Where* do you learn these awful . . . these awful . . ."

"Spend enough time around Washington men, darling, and you can be just like me." She rummages in her pocketbook and comes out with another cigarette. "Knocked up and swearing like a sailor."

"Well, maybe I'll join you down there."

"But wasn't that the plan already? You and the Hardcastles."

"There seem to be a few hitches."

"Just as well. Impeccable Tiny. You'll be shocked out of your girdle, darling, and I mean that literally." She lights her cigarette and blows out a stream of smoke.

"You'd be surprised. I'm not quite as impeccable as . . ."

The bright beam of a flashlight slices the air in half between us. Pepper slides her feet off the dashboard and launches herself to an upright position.

"Hello?" I call out.

"Jesus. There you are."

Caspian's shoulders materialize out of the gloaming, silhouetted behind the circle of white from the flashlight. The beam switches back and forth between us. I hold up my hands in front of my face. "Stop that! Do you want to blind me?"

"Sorry." The beam flips downward. "What in the hell are you two doing here?"

"Fixing the car," says Pepper.

"What car?"

"The one we're sitting in."

The beam rises again and travels along the planes and angles of the Mercedes-Benz, pausing for a loaded second or two on the three-pointed star at the end of the hood, before traveling lovingly along the swoop of the left front fender.

"Holy Christ," he says.

"That's what I said," says Pepper. "Or something like it."

He walks along the driver's side, running the beam along the sleek black metal before him. The glow reflects from his awed face. "Where did you find this?"

"Here."

"*Here?* In this shed?"

"Yes, here in this shed. Did you think the tide brought it in?"

Caspian circles the left fender. I brace my knee on the seat and rise to follow him as he goes.

"But that's impossible," he says. "Do you know what kind of car this is?"

"Of course we do," I say. "I don't know much about cars, but I do know a Mercedes when I see one."

He stops and meets my gaze. The wide-eyed greenness startles me. "Not just any Mercedes. It's a landmark, a 1936 Special Roadster. I don't think more than five or six of them were ever built. Don't even know how many survived the war."

"Well, at least one did," says Pepper.

"We're trying to fix it," I say. "Pepper is, anyway."

He continues his progress. "You would have had to have been European to get your hands on this. German, probably. You'd have had to know the president of the company. You'd have to be an aristocrat, someone at the very top. Is that a bullet hole?" He bends over the rear right-side fender, touches the metal with one finger, and straightens.

"Are you saying this is some Nazi's car?" Pepper asks.

"The Nazis weren't aristocrats. But something like that." He stops at the front passenger wheel and whistles, low and slow.

"Then how did it get here?" I ask.

He looks up. "That's a damned good question."

Thirty minutes later, Caspian is buried to the waist inside the hood of the Mercedes. Pepper has just returned from the Big House with an armload of flashlights, which she dumps on the floor. "Thank

God Granny's gone to her room already," she says. "Probably writing out my execution order."

"Whoever tried to fix this car should be prosecuted for crimes against humanity," says Caspian, muffled. His shirt is rolled up to the elbows; his jacket lies across the leather seat.

"Sorry," says Pepper. "I'm not very good at German."

"How do *you* know so much about it?" I ask.

He pops up, flashlight in one hand and wrench in the other. (Definitely a wrench.) A smear of grease obscures his cheekbone. "I spent eight years in Germany as a boy. I know this car like I know my own . . ." He glances at Pepper, then at me. "My own hand."

"Lucky for us."

"Lucky for the damned car, you mean." He disappears back into the engine. "I can't believe it. This car is a legend. It's like working on a Stradivarius."

"A what?" asks Pepper.

"A violin," I say. "The ne plus ultra of violins."

"What am I, a lawyer?"

"He means it's the greatest car in the world, all right?" I fold my arms and study the snug military fit of Caspian's trousers against his derriere. "The pride of the Nazis, apparently. And it just so happened to be hiding in Granny Hardcastle's shed."

"Surprise, surprise," says Pepper.

"Now, Pepper. Granny may be difficult, but she's not a Nazi."

"How do we know that? Look at old Joe Kennedy. He practically goose-stepped down the Mall when he was ambassador in London. You know, right before the war."

"And what do you have against Joe Kennedy, hmm?"

She folds her arms. "Nothing. I'm just pointing out what I *thought* was an obvious fact, that the older generation, our parents and grand-parents, well, some of them weren't exactly rioting in the streets against the fascists. Germany declared war on *us* after Pearl Harbor, don't for-get. Not the other way around."

Caspian pops up again and lays his wrench on top of the fender. "Well, you're damned lucky, ladies. You haven't wrecked it beyond repair, though God knows it looks like you've tried."

"What a relief," says Pepper.

"What a miracle, you mean." He spreads his fingers tenderly along the edge of the hood, like a caress. "All right. So what are your intentions here?"

"It's a *car*, Major. Not your teenage daughter, for God's sake."

Caspian fixes her with his cast-iron look.

"We just wanted to see if we could make it run again," I say. "A summer project to keep us busy. Idle hands, you know." I lift my hands and wiggle my fingers to demonstrate.

"Okay. Have you tried to find the rightful owner?" He puts a little emphasis on the *rightful*.

"There weren't any papers in the glove compartment."

"Finders keepers," says Pepper.

Caspian's face goes all exasperated, an expression I rather enjoy. He walks around the front of the car and opens up the passenger door. He has to slide in sideways, on account of his soldierly figure. He pops open the glove compartment.

"See?" Pepper is triumphant. "No papers in sight."

Caspian lifts himself back out of the car. "Well, you've got to find the registration, or it's not worth a dime. To you or anyone else. No one's going to buy a hot car."

"Who says we're going to sell it?" says Pepper.

He lifts an inquisitive eyebrow.

"All right. I'll tell you what." Pepper raises her alluring haunch and props herself on the hood like a living ornament. Her skin glows against the flashlight. "If you help us put this tin lizzie back together . . ."

"*Help* you?"

"Now, you know you can't resist."

It's Caspian's turn to fold his arms. He runs his gaze up and down the car again, sweeping fender to sloping trunk, and back up again to that luxurious cockpit. The lust in his eyes turns the air green. I feel a flutter in my belly, a shameful warmth between my legs.

"I guess I might as well hang around and make sure the job's done right."

Pepper leaps from her pose, flings herself against his chest, and loops her long arms around his lucky neck. "Caspian! You darling!" She kisses his cheek, an inch from his mouth.

The flutter in my stomach takes a sickly turn.

Caspian unwinds Pepper's arms. "You're going to have to follow my orders to the letter, understand? I'm in charge, here."

"Yes, sir." She salutes.

"No whining. No complaining about chipped fingernails."

"Chauvinist pig," says Pepper. "I never whine."

He goes on staring at her like a stern father, like the marine sergeant in charge of boot camp. "Keep your mouth shut except to say *Yes, sir*. Keep your ears open and you might just learn something about the best damned car in the world."

"Oh, my God." She closes her eyes and shivers. "Keep going."

I look at the two of them, five yards away from me on the other side of the swooping black Mercedes, face to beautiful face. She's working her wiles, he's pretending not to notice that the most alluring woman in the world is flirting right before him. But of course he notices. How could you—if you were a stalwart, red-blooded bachelor officer in the United States Army—how could you not notice a woman like Pepper?

I pick up the wrench from the edge of the fender and carry it to the toolbox.

"That's settled, then," I say, brushing the invisible dirt from my hands. My eyes are a little blurry. "Now why don't the two of you get started while I head back to the house. I think I've got a headache coming on."

"Tiny . . ."

"Good night, sis!" Pepper waves her hand, without looking at me, and takes the flashlight right from Caspian's fingers. "See you in the morning."

A knock on the bedroom door interrupts the promise of an hour's quiet contemplation. I tuck the manila envelope back beneath my silk slips and close the drawer. At my feet, Percy releases a shaggy sigh.

"Come in."

Granny Hardcastle opens the door and doesn't mince words. "Well. That sister of yours."

"That sister of mine." I shrug.

"I hope you had a word with her."

I straighten my back and turn around, bracing my arms against the chest of drawers. "Actually, Granny. Now that you raise the subject. I think you were abominably rude to her."

Granny, in the act of settling herself in the chintz armchair in the corner, flinches backward like I've struck her with a stick. She collapses the last few inches into the cushion. "I beg your pardon."

"Pepper's outspoken, I'll grant you that, but you practically accused her of sleeping with her employer. In an outrageously vulgar manner, I might add." My palms are sweaty against the chest of drawers, but I hold them fast. Hold the wood for dear life.

Granny's steely backbone could hold up the Chrysler Building. "Really, Tiny. I believe Miss Schuyler herself began the descent into vulgarity. I was only speaking to her in the language she understands best."

"Granny." I smile. "That sounds a great deal like *She started it.*"

Granny's flamingo lips press together so tightly, they disappear into her mouth. "My son and I were just discussing how out of sorts you've been lately. Not yourself. How you need a bit of rest to pull yourself back together before September."

"I need a lot of things, Mrs. Hardcastle, but rest isn't one of them."

"I understand Frank hasn't quite behaved as he should—"

"That's between me and Frank, Mrs. Hardcastle."

"—but every marriage goes through its troubles, Tiny. Its stages, if you like." Her lips soften into a smile. "I know my son may have been a little harsh with you. Like most men, he has certain notions of how wives should behave. But I understand how it is, believe me. My husband always had a weakness for a pretty girl; it's only natural, really. But there's no reason the goose can't have a little sauce, too, now and again, to keep up her spirits."

Oh, Christ. I was expecting any number of angles to Granny's lecture, but this wasn't one of them. My fingers curl around the edge of the top drawer. "I don't need any sauce, Mrs. Hardcastle. I just need Frank to . . . to . . ." Well, what *did* I need Frank to do? "To stop messing around with his campaign staff, right before my face, for starters."

Granny leans back in the chair and places her wise arms on the armrests. "Now, Tiny. We're women of the world, aren't we?"

"I don't know. Are we?"

"Let's not pretend you didn't know the bargain you were making, when you married Frank. Every woman makes a bargain when she marries. This is part of your bargain."

"No, it isn't. He promised me. He promised me it wouldn't be part of the bargain."

She waves her fingers, without lifting her arm. "Men make loads of promises, Tiny, in order to keep us happy."

I form my right hand into a fist and bring it down on the wood behind me. "No. That was the deal. You know my family. You know I grew up in the middle of a fashionable marriage, right smack in the middle, my mother taking lovers and my father turning the other way, and sometimes picking up a girlfriend of his own, and—"

"But it worked for them, didn't it? Don't your parents love each other?"

The question brings me up short. Because, tucked in there amongst all the bad memories—running into Daddy and some impossibly young secretary enjoying dinner at the Stork Club, walking in on Mums during a little afternoon splendor with the Russian emigré prince who was supposed to be appraising the art in the drawing room—yes, tucked in among the bad ones lived a few good ones, a few moments of crystalline contentment. The time we went on vacation in Europe, and I caught Mums dancing with Daddy in the middle of an evening downpour in the Tuileries, and the expression of joy on her face, and the expression of tenderness on his, turned my breath into smoke. And wonder. Because how could you forgive him for the secretaries? How could you forgive her for the Russian princes? How could you say to each other: *Oh darling, it's really all right that you had sex with someone else, that you made love with lots of other people? It's all right that you put your mouth on someone else's mouth and kissed it, that you undressed and joined your nakedness with someone else's nakedness, that you shared an orgasm in all its marvelous, messy glory with someone else.* How could you love someone and then engage in the most intimate of acts with another person?

Or did I know the answer to that question already?

"So maybe it works for them, somehow. But they aren't happy, not like ordinary people, not *contented* . . ."

"Is that all you want, Tiny? Contentment?" She puts one hand on each armrest and rises to her feet, and in her stance and her expression I see a much younger woman, the ambitious one who took her money and beauty and bought a blue-blooded Bostonian with it, and so created a potent alchemy of ancient social prestige and bottomless lust for power, the modern Hardcastle family. "Do you really want to be an *ordinary* person?"

I tilt my chin to meet hers. "There's nothing wrong with ordinary."

"You wouldn't have said that two years ago."

"Maybe I've learned a thing or two."

"Oh, Tiny." She places her hand on my shoulder, and good Lord, you wouldn't think a grandmother born in the previous century could still maintain a grip like that. "For God's sake. Listen to you. You're not seeing the big picture. This is larger than all that. This is *history*."

"Oh, Granny, really—"

"What happens to Frank if you leave him, hmmm? What happens to all of us? The family. The people of Massachusetts. The country, the world."

I open my mouth, but I don't know how to answer her. Her hand turns gentle on my shoulder, kneading me through the cotton sleeve like a mother would, if I'd had that kind of mother.

"You see? You've already made your choice, my dear," says Granny. "You can't go back."

The phone rings.

"I expect that's Frank," I whisper.

She glances at the telephone, releases my shoulder, and walks to the door. "Then I think you'd better answer it, hadn't you?"

I let it ring a few more times—*drrring drrring drrring*—into the solemn air. I think of those cartoons, where the phone actually jumps into the air, shocked by the electricity on the line.

"Hello?"

"Tiny, it's me."

"Hello, Frank."

His voice is low and subdued. "I spoke to Dad. Well, he came over and spoke to me."

I hook my fingers under the cradle and carry the telephone to the indigo horizon outside the window. Behind me, to the west, an unseen sun drops below the sky. To the left, the houses have put on their porch lights. Except Caspian's house, which is still dark and uninhabited. "And what did your father say to you, Frank?"

A deep sigh electrifies the line. "Tiny, you're wrong about Jo."

"*Please*, Frank."

"No, really. I admit, she's a pretty girl, we flirt a little, but that's all."

"I'm not an idiot."

"I'm not a liar."

"No, of course not. I'm not sure you would consider this a lie, a real one. You probably think it's a white lie, a harmless little fiction to keep your marriage going, to keep your wife happy, to keep anyone from getting hurt."

"Jesus. Is that what you think of me?"

I press my nose against the window. A film of fog creeps up the glass, obscuring my vision. "I don't know, Frank. I don't know what I'm supposed to think of you anymore. I don't know if I ever did."

Silence fills the receiver. I imagine Frank sitting at his desk in the office, staring at the blotter, wondering what to say. Which lie, possibly, to tell.

I continue. "The thing is, it doesn't really matter if you slept with her or not. If you're telling the truth or not. The point is that it *could* be true. That it's been true before. That it *will* be true someday, maybe not now, but in a year or two, when we've had a fight or you're under strain or you're away on a trip or something. Some excuse to let things slip. And then some pretty girl gets the better of you. It *will* happen. It will happen repeatedly. I know it will."

"That's not fair, Tiny."

"No, it's not fair. It's really not. Because the other thing is, the *harder* thing is that you're a good man. You're a smart man and a good man. You'll make the world a better place. You'll do great things, one day."

"I can't do them without you, Tiny."

Another long pause. I count the pale shadows of the rollers washing ashore, one after the other, all the way across the Atlantic Ocean to our little patch of Hardcastle beach.

Frank ventures: "Do you want me to come out there?"

"No. You need to keep the campaign going."

"This is more important. I need you, I've always needed you, I need you to keep me straight—"

"Well, I'm not ready to see you yet."

"Tiny—"

"I have to go, Frank. I have to think. Good night."

I hang up before he can reply. I set the telephone back down on the nightstand and take my shoes off, one by one, and then I slip through the door and down the stairs in my bare feet.

Outside, the sand is still warm. I dig my toes in to the knuckles.

A moon has appeared out of nowhere, a hazy half-moon, just bright enough to pick out the curls of foam on the beating ocean ahead. Down the line of Hardcastle houses, someone is having a party, playing some music. The Beatles. The bass chords rattle the air, overlaid by the high pitch of teenage giggles.

I form my arms into a circle before me and arrange my feet into first position.

It's not easy, dancing on the soft piles of sand near the dunes. I have to force out the party music and listen to the notes in my head. My legs aren't what they were. I stay on the pads of my feet, I concentrate on posture and extension rather than the movement itself. The movement always comes last, the icing on the cake, the skin over the frame.

But the muscles do warm, eventually. The memory returns, and while I can't raise my legs as high as I once could, and I can't quite launch myself aloft with the same power, I can still leap. I can still spin, perfectly balanced, rhythmic and fearless, and when I finish, panting, staring out at the ocean while the waves tumble over each other, I find I am myself again, Tiny Schuyler, perched on the brink.

I turn back to the Big House, and as I do, I catch sight of a light through a second-story window of the Harrison cottage, overlooking the beach: the corner bedroom that belongs to Caspian.

"Tiny. Fancy running into you here."

I jump probably as high as the chimney stack.

"Tom. My goodness. You startled me."

"Just out for a walk." He's carrying a drink in one hand, a cigarette in the other.

I sniff. Actually, it's not a cigarette.

He holds the joint up. "Drag?"

"No, thanks."

"No, of course not." His teeth are white in the moonlight. He nods at the Harrison house, at the light in the corner bedroom. "Looks like someone's still up, anyway. Dreaming about stabbing little Oriental babies with his bayonet."

"I thought grass was supposed to make you mellow, Tom." I cross my arms.

"Yeah, well. He just pisses me off, that's all. The way everyone worships him. It's like they're blind, they don't see." He swishes his ice, drinks, swishes some more. "What about you?"

"What about me?"

"I mean, you see through it, don't you? You're not a robot."

"Oh, I'm a robot, all right." I make jerky movements with my arms. "A true believer."

Tom takes a step closer.

"Where's Constance?"

"Watching the kids. You've heard the news, right?"

"What news?"

He holds up his joint with thumb and forefinger and smiles as he takes a drag. "Connie's pregnant. Due in March."

"Congratulations."

"Yeah, I may not be Frank Hardcastle, but I'm good for something, right?"

"You know what, Tom? I think it's time you went home to your wife."

"Yeah, you're probably right." He holds out the joint again. "Come on, Tiny. Just one little taste. Loosen you up. You'll be a new woman."

"No, thanks."

"It's better for you than this stuff." He jiggles his drink.

"I said, no thanks."

"You're so fucking scared, Tiny. Just imagine what life would be like if you were a little bit braver."

There is a pain in my chest, a sharp squeeze, like they say you get when you're having a heart attack. I reach out and slap Tom across the cheek: a little too low, more jaw than flesh, not quite the dramatic noise I was hoping for.

But still. A slap.

Tom's eyes bug out a little. "Hit a nerve, did I?" he says.

"Go to hell."

"I like it. I like it when you get pissed off. Come on, let's get pissed off together. Let's tell the whole fucking family where they can shove—"

I turn around and stride through the sand, in the direction of the house.

"Tiny! Come back!" Tom is laughing.

I walk faster, into the gap between the porch lights, kicking up sand as I go. I breathe in angry little gasps, furious at the ruins of my evening.

A hand snags my arm, and I open my mouth to scream.

"Everything okay?" says Caspian.

I look up and relax into his grip. *Home,* my brain assures me. *Safety.*

Though of course, this isn't safe at all. Not the least bit safe, meeting Caspian here like this, unexpectedly, under a darkened sky, in the pocket of shadow between our two houses.

"Fine. Just Tom being Tom."

"I saw," says Caspian.

I realize he's wearing a plaid dressing gown crossed over a white T-shirt. My pulse hits my neck. "You were watching me?"

"It's good to see you dancing again." He nods at the beach, and I follow his gaze. There's no sign of Tom now, as if he's dissolved into the sea. Maybe I imagined the whole thing. But I can still smell the weed. I can still hear the jingle of ice. Caspian says idly, "Should I go after him?"

As if to say, *Shall I kill him for you?*

"God, no. It's not worth it."

"What was he saying to you?"

"He wanted me to smoke a joint with him."

"Stupid ass."

"He said . . ." I hesitated.

"What?"

"Oh, you know. The usual rant. That you bayoneted babies and all that."

Caspian lifts his hand to his hair. "Well, I didn't."

"I know."

This is so unexpectedly easy, talking to Caspian in the intimacy of darkness, beyond the sight of any other eyes. Even the moon is hidden behind the roofline of the Big House. Caspian's hand remains on my arm, cupped around the elbow, just the right pressure and location that a straight young matron like me couldn't really feel guilty about it. His breath smells of toothpaste, warm and minty sweet, and I think of him standing at the sink, getting ready for bed. I think of him rising from the sea this morning, the shape of his missing leg between his knee and the jetty below. That gap of empty air, which contains so much.

"Are you okay, Caspian?" I say. "Are you going to be okay?"

He knows what I mean. "No, I'm not okay. But I'm alive."

"I keep imagining you in that helicopter—"

His hand drops away from my elbow. He looks back at the beach, in the direction of the jetty. "Well, don't. Because I don't actually remember it, myself."

"Any of it?"

"Not until I woke up in a Saigon hospital a week later. So you see, I'm lucky. I'm pretty fucking lucky. Luckier than I have any right to be. And once I got over feeling sorry about my leg, feeling sorry about my buddies who didn't make it . . . not that you ever really get over that, you just find a way to live with it . . ." He looks back at me, and though we can't see each other very well, I feel the touch of his gaze as if he's laying his hands on my face.

"Yes?" I whisper.

"I came home," he says. He reaches out and brushes my chin with his thumb, and *this* touch is guilty, no question about it. This is how a lover touches you. "Good night, Tiny. Keep dancing out there."

He turns and disappears into the sand.

I hold myself still, staring at the patch of shadow where he used to stand, and I think, this pain, this squeezing in my chest, I wish it *were* a cardiac attack. Because anything would feel better than the way my heart is beating now.

Caspian, 1964

She hadn't eaten, so he made her an omelet with chopped tomato and plenty of Cheddar cheese.

"I won't be able to eat it. I'm too nervous," she said.

He lifted the edges of the egg with a spatula. "You have to eat, Tiny. Look at you."

"What's wrong with me?"

"Nothing's *wrong* with you. But you're not carrying an extra ounce."

"I can't eat when I'm anxious." Her voice was small and determined, a girl working up her nerve. She stood near the darkened windows in a neat powder-blue suit. As outfits went, it hardly seemed like the kind you wore to run away into a new life. The matching powder-blue hat was perched on top of her suitcase, next to the door.

"Well, eat this." He slid the omelet onto a plate and poured a glass of milk. "Got to be up early tomorrow. You'll need it."

She sank into the sofa and accepted the plate. He set the milk on the lamp table next to her. "Thank you," she said, without looking at him.

"Hey." He crouched down in front of her and tapped her knee. "You're okay with this, aren't you? You're sure?"

She pushed her fork into the omelet. "I'm sure. I sent him the letter, didn't I? No turning back." The plate wobbled under her attack. She gripped it with one hand, stuck the egg into her mouth with the other, and chewed bravely.

"Hey," he said again. "Will you look at me?"

She lifted her eyes. Her mouth was still full, as if she couldn't seem to force the omelet down.

He smiled. "That's better. You're not nervous of me, are you? Because that would hurt. Really hurt, Tiny."

Tiny swallowed at last and worked up a smile. "No. I just . . ."

"Just what?"

"Well, I just don't want you to think I'm throwing myself at you, that's all. I appreciate your helping me out. Giving me a lift out west. But I don't— I know you have a life of your own. I'm not asking for anything more." Her gaze dropped back down to her eggs.

Now that he was close, he could smell her again, and her fragrance had changed along with her clothes. She'd washed out the scent of his shirt and his apartment. She'd showered again in her own apartment, showered with her own soap and her own creams. She smelled like flowers and baby powder, like a girl's bathroom.

He put his hands on his knees, to keep himself from touching her. "Well, do you *want* anything more?"

"I—" Her face flushed. "I don't know how to answer that."

Cap studied her in the lamplight, studied her ladylike blue suit and her dark hair curling obediently around her ears, her eyelashes shielding her from penetration. Her force field had assembled back around her. But it wasn't a force field, after all, was it? It was more like a shell, an exquisite painted-on version of herself, made of habit and nature, a girl who hated to disappoint others. He wondered why he ever thought she was stiff. Only the shell was stiff, not the woman inside it.

She poked at her eggs. "What are you thinking?"

"I'm thinking I'd like to photograph you again."

"Dancing?" She looked up.

"No. There's not enough light, anyway. Just sitting here, like this. We'll call it *Bride readying for her big day.*"

"But I'm not getting married."

"I'm not talking about a wedding."

She placed her fork at a five-o'clock angle on her plate and reached for her milk.

"Tiny," he said. "It's just me. You don't need to be nervous."

She tilted her milk glass and stared inside. "Maybe I just need something stronger."

"No. Clear head, clear conscience."

She widened her mouth into a smile. Her teeth were—of course—white and perfect, honed by the very best Park Avenue dentists. "All right, Caspian. Take my picture again, since you can't seem to help yourself."

While she finished her omelet and drank her milk at the table, he closed the curtains and turned on all the lamps. He'd put her on the sofa, right next to the arm, so she could lean against it for support. He dragged over a floor lamp and adjusted the shade.

"You should open up a studio," said Tiny.

He took her empty plate and glass and put them in the kitchen sink. "I told you, it's just a hobby. I already have a job."

She arranged herself on the sofa. "Shall I touch up my lipstick?"

"Not a chance. Just put your feet up on the cushion. Maybe lean your elbow on the arm." With deliberate methodology, he prepared the camera: changed the lens, chose the film, screwed in the flashbulb.

"Take off my jacket?"

God yes.

"Only if you like," he said.

Her blouse was cream-colored and made of silk. It draped expensively against her body, revealing a single strand of small pearls around her throat, the same shade as her skin. "Is this all right?" she asked.

He lowered himself in front of her. "You're beautiful. Look at me. You don't need to smile, just . . . Tell me more about your sisters."

She rolled her eyes. "What do you want to know about my sisters?"

"What they're like. The trouble you used to get into."

"*They* got into trouble, not me. They're only eleven months apart, Pepper and Vivian. They— Oh, that flash. Could you turn it off?"

"Sorry. Let me see if I can bring in a little more light." He carried over the lamp from the desk in the corner and placed it on the side table. "Keep talking."

"Well, they're birds of a feather. Maybe Pepper's more a free spirit. She's the older one. They went to Bryn Mawr together, though Pepper barely graduated last year, and Vivian got high honors. The ceremony was just last weekend, actually. She looked dazzling in her white dress."

"I'll bet."

"That's it, really. They're both independent, but Vivian's always known what she wanted."

"And what's that?"

"To be a journalist. She's starting a job at the *Metropolitan* magazine in New York, when the summer's over. She'll probably be running the place in a year or two."

He smiled and moved to another angle. "I think I like your sister."

"You wouldn't be the first." She puffed a bit of scornful air from her nose: another girl, and you'd have called it a snort. "She and Pepper, they aren't shy. I'll bet they've had dozens of lovers already."

"Dozens?"

"Well, at least a dozen between them."

He set down the camera. Tiny looked across the room at the wall of photographs. Her brow was creased, her large eyes narrowed into almonds. The corners tilted upward just a fraction, unlike her mother's.

"What about you, Tiny?" he asked. "Any lovers? Other than your fiancé, I mean."

"He's not my fiancé. And if you can't guess, I'm not going to tell you."

"Fair enough. A lady has her secrets." He lifted the camera again.

She turned to face him, and in a million years, forests and glaciers advancing and retreating across the continents, species flourishing and disappearing, he could never have predicted what Tiny Schuyler said next.

"When Pepper was twenty, she had a photographer take her picture in the nude."

His fingers froze on the camera lens. "Did she, now?"

"She showed me the photographs. She looked beautiful, of course. Pepper's the most beautiful of all of us. The most daring. I asked her why she did it. Whether she wanted to be a model or an actress or something, or just to scandalize my parents. Do you know what she said?"

His pulse was off and running again, plucking staccato against his skin. "No idea."

"Just because she felt like it. She wanted to know what she really looked like, without any clothes or mirrors. Just her. Her true self."

"I see."

She raised her knees and hugged them to her chest. She was still staring at the wall of photographs, her head tilted to one side. "I was just thinking . . ."

He loved her expression, loved the way the lamplight grabbed the thoughtful curve of her eyelashes. "Yes?"

"How hard it is to tear down the barricades. No, that's not it. I mean the way we act. You lay down these tracks, even though you know it's not the right track, even though you can see what track's the right one. But you don't know how to get off yours. You know how you *want* to behave, what you *want* to be, the change you need to make—the thing you need to stop doing, or start doing—and yet you stay on your old track. You can't find the switch that takes you to the other one. You can *see* the change, the desired state, but you can't quite touch it. Like my mother, wanting to be good."

"So what's the desired state, Tiny? Your desired state."

"Not to be so stiff. Not to be so scared."

"Of what?"

"Doing the wrong thing." She drew a massive breath into her lungs and turned her head toward him. "I think I'm ready now."

"For what?" he whispered.

She lifted her fingers to the buttons of her blouse. "Keep clicking."

"Actually, I'm out of film."

"Well, go get another roll."

He rose obediently and found his camera bag. His ears rang, like they'd been stuffed with wire, the way he sometimes felt in an ambush. He loaded another roll of film and snapped the case shut. When he turned around, Tiny was naked, wholly and delicately naked, bent over her legs, rolling down her stockings. Her clothes lay in a heap on the floor, brassiere and girdle on top.

"Is this really what you want, Tiny?" he asked.

She lifted her head and dropped the stocking into the pile. She still wore the pearls. "Yes."

"All right. Lean back against the arm of the sofa. Relax your shoulders. Turn your hip a little, back toward the sofa. Just the hip. That's it." Her breasts were larger than he imagined, beautifully shaped, puckered at the tips despite the warmth of the apartment. The lamplight inhabited her skin. He hoped he could capture its translucence, the singular liquid glow beneath her surface, but he knew the limits of film. The curve of her rib cage, the hollow of her hip bone, the uptick of her lips into the tiny crescent at the corner: you could force these inanimate details through the layers of lens and aperture and imprint them faithfully on a strip of plastic, to be forever preserved in their exact present form, like fruit in a jar. The breathing woman, the quality of her skin, lived only in his head. His bones. His chest, where his heart beat and beat, pumping out the minutes of a May evening.

As he fell into a rapturous silence, moving about, changing angles, Tiny's body stretched out, inch by inch. She extended one sinewy leg like a cat, and then an arm above her head, dangling over the end of the sofa. She tilted her face and looked at him, wise and sideways, as if she— innocent Tiny, immaculate Tiny—knew things he could only guess.

His thumb, moving to advance the film, kept going and going. End of the roll.

He lowered the camera. "That's it. Do you want me to load another?"

"No, that's enough, I think." She watched him quietly.

He rose to his feet and walked to the bedroom, where he found an old dressing gown and returned to the living room. He kept his eyes on the slice of upholstery next to her cheek while he draped her with his robe, like a Victorian piano whose curving limbs must not be exposed to the rapacious male gaze. She clutched it modestly to her bosom, propping herself on her elbows, and Cap turned his back so she could wrap herself back up in privacy. While the silk whispered behind him, belting her in, he rewound the film and removed it from the camera. "Here you are," he said, turning slowly, holding it out to her.

She plucked it from his fingers and rolled it about in her palm. Her hair had loosened up in all the stretching and posing, and it tumbled past her temples as she gazed down at the small and potent cylinder. Its extraordinary contents.

She handed it back to him. "You take it."

"Me?"

"Yes. A memento."

"Don't you want to know how they turned out?"

She shook her head. "That wasn't the point, really. Go on, take it. I trust you."

He closed his fingers around the roll. "That's a lot of trust."

She shrugged. The dressing gown was green and old-fashioned, silk like they used to make them, and it lay beautifully on her pale skin, picking out the spikes of tiny color in her brown eyes. It was far too big, of course. She'd rolled up the sleeves, and the extra material overflowed the snug cinch of the belt. She knitted her fingers together and stared at his hand. "There was another reason," she said.

"Another reason?"

"My sister. Pepper. Why she had those photographs taken." A rueful chuckle. "The real reason, probably, knowing her."

"Oh?"

Tiny unclasped her fingers and wrapped one hand around his fist, trapping the film inside.

"She wanted to sleep with the photographer."

"I see. Was she successful?"

"She wouldn't tell me. But judging from the photographs, I don't see how he could have resisted her."

"Except he's supposed to be a professional. Not to take advantage of the situation." Cap uncurled her fingers and walked to the darkroom, where he set the film on the counter and stared, gathering his breath, at the array of photographs still attached to the drying lines: Tiny suspended in a starburst of an arabesque; Tiny's leg stretched upward to an impossible height, not a toe out of line; a blurred Tiny swirling past the lens; Tiny's face sculpted by the sunlight from his window. His white shirt collar against her neck.

He grabbed the edge of the counter with his fingertips and squeezed his eyes shut.

"It wasn't taking advantage," said Tiny, from the doorway. "It was what she wanted."

"She was vulnerable."

"She put herself in that position, knowing it was vulnerable. Her eyes were open." *Swish, swish,* went his robe against the darkroom floor. A warm hand rested flat upon his right shoulder blade. "I left him, Caspian. I broke off the engagement. I've started a new life, right here, at this second."

"You don't need *me* to do that. You don't need anyone except yourself."

"But I *want* you. So much it hurts."

His knuckles gleamed white against the counter. He bit down against his lip, because he was about to say something stupid. Stupidity filled his mouth and ran out his eyes, and it tasted like salt.

"I know what you're going to say," she went on. "You're right, I guess. I shouldn't just jump from one man to another. And yes, you'll be off to the other side of the world in two weeks, and yes, I don't really know you, and what happens if you don't come back, and what happens when you do. That's all true. But you're *not* taking advantage of me, Caspian. I just want to make that clear. It's the other way around. I saw you and I wanted you, I think I even loved you, yes, I *do* love you. I'm thoroughly in love with you, you can't imagine how much. Since I first saw you in the coffee shop, and now more, because you turned out even better than I dreamed. And I want to drive to

California with you, like we said, and I want to drive across the country as your lover. *Not* your friend, your lover. I've been a good little daughter and a good little sister and a good little student and a good little girlfriend and a very, *very* good little fiancée, and I just want to leave all that behind and be your lover, no, I want you to be *my* lover, be my good little lover, and let the rest of it, everyone's ideas of what I *should* be, go to hell. I want to jump to the other track before it's too late. Before I wind up as someone's good little wife. Someone's perfect little fucking wife. Smiling for the camera."

He released the counter and touched her hands, which had crept around his waist.

"This is the switching point, Caspian," she whispered in his shirt. "This is me, switching tracks."

"I guess that's one thing to call it. A new one on me. We could start a new slang. *Let's go back to my place and switch tracks.*"

"Unless you don't want to. In which case, I'll just grab a blanket and sleep on your sofa. But I think you want to."

Want to.

"I'm just trying to do the right thing here. What's best for you. That's all I've been trying to do, since you first showed up on my doorstep in your red fucking dress."

"Oh, I see. And has it ever occurred to you, Mr. Noble Intentions, that I just *might* be able to decide what's best for me, all by myself?"

Cap turned, and luckily the light wasn't on, and she was dressed in shadow, or the sight of her face might just have obliterated him. Her hands linked behind his waist, strong as chain, and she leaned back as far as she could. Looking up at him. Smiling, probably. Jesus.

"I mean, really," she said. "This is the twentieth century."

And there it was, a snap in his chest, the audible noise of his best intentions cracking in half and cracking again, a chain reaction of thick cracks causing hairline cracks, causing the whole goddamned works, the whole vast machinery of his human willpower, to crumble downward into his abdominal cavity, where it lay pretty much useless.

He wrapped his hands around the back of her head. "And you've decided this is what's best for you."

She nodded her head against his fingers.

"This is what's best for me."

He leaned down and kissed Tiny Schuyler, right in the middle of her waiting mouth.

Tiny, 1966

The car lies in the driveway like a sleek black shark, a Cadillac coupe. The tailfins are neat and sharp, and the top is down to absorb the noontime sun.

Pepper whistles. "Ooh, I hope it's a guilt present from Frank."

I think of my sapphires and diamonds, tucked away in the bedroom safe. "I think he's already given me one."

"There's always room for another. A philandering husband is the gift that keeps on giving."

I wipe my greasy fingers on my handkerchief and tuck it into the pocket of my dungarees. Back in the shed, Caspian is still hard at work, absorbed in the inner workings of the Mercedes-Benz engine. Pepper and I have promised to bring him back a sandwich and a cold Coke from the icebox. "I don't think so," I say. "He just gave me a new car a few months ago." When I told him I was pregnant again.

"Visitors, then?"

I look down at my stained dungarees, my smeared shirt. "I hope not."

"Let's go in the back door, just in case."

But we're no match for Granny Hardcastle's five senses, which might be fading individually but still form a powerful sucking vortex when they rotate in synchronous orbit. Whether it's the sound of the door, or the vibration of the floorboards, or the hot ocean breeze wafting briefly through the air, Granny calls out, as we turn the corner to the staircase: "Tiny, darling! I have someone I'd like you to meet."

I exchange looks with Pepper. "Do you mind if I freshen up first?" I call back.

"I'm sure what you're wearing is suitable."

Pepper lays a hand on mine, atop the newel-post, and speaks in a low voice. "Want some backup?"

"Go on ahead. I'll be fine."

"Call me if you need me," she says, heading for cover up the staircase, and I smile up after her, because my God, we do have our differences, but isn't it reassuring to know a Pepper is right there when you need one?

The French doors to the terrace are shut tight, protected by thick striped awnings, and the living room is cool and dark. A man rises from the chair across from Granny, medium in every detail: medium height, medium brown hair, medium round features. I wonder if I've met him before. He has a face you couldn't remember. I hold out my hand. "Good afternoon. Tiny Hardcastle. Forgive my appearance; I've been outside."

"Mrs. Hardcastle." He smiles a medium smile. "A hot one out there, isn't it?"

I brush back a tendril of hair from my temple. "Yes, it is. Would you like a cool drink?"

He gestures to the table next to his chair. "Already have one, thanks."

"Tiny," says Granny, "this is Dr. Keene. An old friend of the family. He's one of the best psychiatrists in Boston."

I look at Granny. I look back at Dr. Keene.

"I beg your pardon?"

Dr. Keene goes on smiling relentlessly. "Your grandmother is too kind."

"She's my husband's grandmother."

"Yes, I know that. Your father-in-law suggested I stop by."

I settle myself on the arm of the sofa and arrange my hands together in the crease of my thighs. The fabric is tough and durable beneath my fingers, making me feel just a bit more tough and durable all over. "Did he? I can't imagine why."

"He thinks you're under some strain, my dear."

"Oh, really? That's very kind of him, really, but I'm sorry to have put you to any trouble. I don't require a shrink, at the present time. A *drink*, from time to time—my God, don't we all—but not a shrink."

"Tiny, really." Granny is horrified.

Dr. Keene remains on his feet, studying me. Still the gentle professional smile. "It's all right, Mrs. Hardcastle. Many patients are resistant to treatment. It's a sign, in fact, that treatment is needed."

"Well, that's convenient," I say.

"Now, Mrs. Hardcastle." He means me, not Granny. "There's nothing to be scared of. I'm here to help you, believe me. Think of me as a friend of the family. That's what I am, after all."

I rise from the sofa arm. "I don't need any help. I didn't ask for any help."

"You don't have to do anything. Just sit down with me for a bit. Maybe we'll take a drive in my car, get some fresh air."

"It's a lovely car," says Granny.

I glance out the front window to the black Cadillac coupe, lying like a shark in the driveway. The chrome at the tips of the tailfins reflects the high noon.

"That's all right. I have my own car."

"Then let's go talk somewhere. Somewhere you feel comfortable, Mrs. Hardcastle."

"We're talking. I'm comfortable."

"You don't look comfortable at all, Mrs. Hardcastle. You look anxious and upset. If we talk, I can help you. I can write you a prescription, maybe give you a few days' rest somewhere."

"I was resting just fine out here, until you walked in."

Dr. Keene turns his head to exchange glances with Granny.

"Tiny," says Granny, "why don't you take Dr. Keene upstairs to your room? He can examine you, maybe give you some pills."

"I don't want any pills."

"You prescribed me something wonderful, didn't you, Dr. Keene? When my husband died."

Dr. Keene takes a step toward me. "Your father-in-law says . . ."

"My father-in-law can go to hell." I fold my arms across my chest.

He nods at my elbows. "You're putting yourself in a defensive posture. That's not necessary, I assure you—"

"I don't want you near me, Dr. Keene. I certainly don't want you in my bedroom. In fact, I'd like to ask you to leave."

"Are you certain of that, Mrs. Hardcastle?"

"Quite certain."

Another glance at Granny. "I'm afraid I was instructed specifically not to leave without treating you, Mrs. Hardcastle."

"This is my house," I say. "You are here at my pleasure. Not my father-in-law, not my husband's grandmother. I'm a grown woman, and I can make my own decisions."

"I hope you won't make this difficult, Tiny," he says, in an even, lyrical voice that should sound soothing, and instead strikes my ears like a threat. He takes another step toward me, and his stance is that of a predator.

I hold my ground. "I'd like you to leave, Dr. Keene."

Granny lurches to her feet. "I knew it! Dr. Keene, you've got to do something. You see what we're talking about. She's not herself, she's—"

"Please be quiet, Mrs. Hardcastle, and let me handle this. I've encountered this kind of resistance many times."

I'll just bet you have, I think.

I check the angle to the staircase, to the back door, to the front door. The house feels hollow, empty, as if Mrs. Crane has left, as if the entire complement of Hardcastle family and retainers has melted into the floorboards. The hairs are rising on my neck. *Get away*, my brain screams.

"Again, Dr. Keene." Somehow my voice remains calm. "I'm going to have to ask you to leave."

Another step forward. "I'm afraid I can't do that, Tiny. I have my orders."

"Mrs. Crane!" I call out.

"I gave her the afternoon off," says Granny.

"Dr. Keene—"

A body appears at my elbow, out of nowhere, accompanied by the scent of fresh perfume and an air of crackling purpose.

"Excuse me. What seems to be the problem?"

"Pepper." I turn to my sister in relief. Backup. "Dr. Keene, this is my sister. Dr. Keene is a *psychiatrist*, Pepper. He was just leaving."

"No, I—"

Pepper thrusts out her hand and grasps that of Dr. Keene, almost before he can offer it. "Why, Dr. Keene! I'm so sorry to miss you. A friend of my sister's is a friend of mine."

"I'm sorry, Miss—?"

"Schuyler. Pepper Schuyler." She keeps her hand in his. Covers it, in fact, with her other hand, which is long and slender and tipped with scarlet. If you didn't know any better, you'd think Pepper's hands are purely decorative. "I'm a special assistant to a certain senator in Washington, the junior senator from the great state of New York. You've heard of the senator, surely? He used to be attorney general of the United States. Just imagine that. The nation's tip-top lawyer, and, boy, does he love a good fight."

"Of course I've heard of the senator." The good doctor alternates his gaze between the two of us.

"You were just leaving, Dr. Keene?"

He tugs at his hand. Pepper doesn't let go. I glance down, and there are her scarlet fingernails, curling into the tender underside of his wrist. My God.

"Dr. Keene?" she says. "Or should I call up my boss for a friendly chat?"

"That's not necessary," he says. "I can return at a more convenient time."

I clear my throat. "See that you do. Down, Pepper."

My sister releases the medium Dr. Keene. He sighs, straightens his cuffs, and turns to Granny, whose face has turned a bright shade of Palm Beach pink. "Mrs. Hardcastle?"

"I apologize, Dr. Keene, for the behavior of my . . . my . . ."

"Think nothing of it, my dear." He picks up his jacket from the back of the chair and pats each pocket. "In fact, I believe I've learned a great deal from the hostility of the patient's response."

"What? What have you learned?"

Dr. Keene finds his keys and slings his jacket over his shoulder. "I recommend the most absolute quiet. She should be encouraged to remain in this house. In her room, if possible. I should go so far as to say that she shouldn't be allowed to leave until I return."

"Return? I don't believe I invited you back," I say.

But Dr. Keene is already heading for the door. He pauses with his hand on the knob and looks back at me, smiling benignly. "Forgive me, Mrs. Hardcastle. As I understand it, I don't require your invitation."

P epper opens up the icebox and takes out the pitcher of iced tea, made fresh that morning by Mrs. Crane and still swimming with lemon slices. She pours it into one of the two tumblers sitting on the scarred wooden counter. "You want something stronger in that?"

"No, thanks."

She hands me a glass and clinks it with her own. "You'd think they'd renovate."

"What?"

She gestures her head to encompass the wooden counters, the free-standing cabinets, the enamel Hotpoint electric range resting on its curling Victorian legs. "Probably a hit at the St. Louis World's Fair or something. Not even the Schuylers would put up with a kitchen this old."

"It confers prestige, I suppose, if you can't find it anywhere else."

"Prestige schmestige. Let's go outside."

It's Wednesday, low tide, and the sand bakes under the sun. The beach is wide and hard. Three of the wives are huddled in their folding chairs, under an umbrella, while a few kids splash in the surf nearby. I angle away from them, toward the jetty, where the boats bob untended at their moorings, waiting for the men to return, or the teenagers to stir themselves.

"You need to get out of here," says Pepper. "You just need to leave."

"I can't just leave."

"Why not? You're like fucking Hamlet. Pull the plug. Get the hell out. I'll help. I'll pack your bags for you."

I keep walking, down the length of the jetty. The sun burns my skin; the condensation from the lemonade trickles over my knuckles.

"So you're just going to stand there and take it?" says Pepper. "Let them lobotomize you? Pat you on the head and give you a bottle full of happy pills?"

I reach the end of the jetty, set down the lemonade, and pull off my sandals.

"Jesus," says Pepper. "You're not going to jump, are you?"

"It's not that simple, Pepper."

"I hope the hell not."

"The thing is, it's not so bad, is it? Playing along. I'll bet ninety-nine percent of women would trade places with me in a heartbeat. Ninety-nine percent of women surveyed would just love to be Frank Hardcastle's wife. If he wants to screw around with a pretty girl or two, why, they'd just turn their heads away. Look at all this." I wave my sandals at the beautiful hard beach, the gray shingles of the Big House, the windows twinkling in the sun. "It's mine. The good life."

"Are you crazy?"

"Frank's a good man, Pepper. He could even be a great man. He just has a weakness, that's all. He loves me, he really does. He's called me every day, he sends flowers. He's worried sick."

"Then why doesn't he come out here himself, instead of sending the family doctor to lobotomize you?"

"That wasn't Frank. That was his father."

"What's the difference?"

"A hell of a difference." I turn to face her. I imagine I can feel Granny Hardcastle's gaze through one of the windows, staring at us, watching my every tic. "Frank's father went through this. His wife left him, and that's why he never ran for office himself. He couldn't stand it if the same thing happened to Frank. The end of everything."

"Then little Frank Junior should have kept his naughty pants zipped."

"You don't understand. If I left Frank, if I divorced Frank, they'd find a way to ruin me. This Dr. Keene today. He's the shot over the bow. The warning shot."

"Screw them. Screw their warning shots. Live in infamy. Infamy's a hell of a lot more fun than this, believe me."

I shake my head. "That's what I used to think. It looks good, until you're there. And then you realize what they're saying about you, you realize how many people you've disappointed, how selfish you've been. How you've failed everyone."

"I don't give a damn about that."

"Well, you're Pepper. And I'm Tiny. And I care. I just *care*. I can't help it." By now, there are tears trickling down from the corners of my eyes, and I don't try to stop them. "I can't help it, Pepper. I just don't have it in me. I tried once, and I don't have the strength to disappoint them. Not in the end, I don't."

"Who's them?"

"*Them?* It's *everyone*, Pepper. It's you and Vivian and Mums and Daddy. Frank and Granny and Constance and *everyone*, people I haven't even met, people who walk down the street and read newspapers and see pictures of me and think, oh, she's not that pretty, look at her nose, she's too skinny, she's not skinny enough, she's too tall, she's too short, she's stuck up, she's stupid, she's in it for the money, I hear he cheats on her, I hear she cheats on him, I hear she sneaks out for a smoke, I hear she's a Goody Two-Shoes who never took a puff in her life. Everything. Everyone. You don't know what it's like. You don't know what *shame* is like. I've tried not to care, Pepper. I've tried so hard. But I can't help it."

Pepper takes my sobbing face against her collarbone. "Oh, Jesus. You poor thing."

"I can't do it again, Pepper. I can't go through that again."

"Go through *what* again?"

I lift my head from her wet skin. "I have to show you something."

H oly cats." Pepper angles the photograph to the light from the window. "Nice tits. I mean really lovely. I didn't know you had a bosom that lovely. You should show them off a little more."

"Pepper!"

She lifts her gaze from my reclined black-and-white image and looks me straight between the eyeballs. "Who took these?"

"Caspian."

"*Caspian?* Caspian *Harrison? Major* Caspian?"

"That's the one."

"Holy cats. *Caspian.* Did you sleep with him afterward?"

"That's my business."

"So you did. Well, screw me. I'm . . . wow. The good major." Pepper closes her mouth and turns back to the photograph. "And when did all this happen?"

"Two years ago."

"Two years ago? But that's—two years ago—that's when you got married, wasn't it?"

"Just before the wedding, to be exact. Two or three weeks before, something like that."

Pepper lets out a whistle, long and low, making her cheekbones pop out above her pursed lips. "Tiny, Tiny. To think you wore white. Cold feet, was it?"

"Something like that."

"Have you done it since? Since he got back?"

I snatch the photograph away. "Of course not!"

"So why are you showing me this now?"

I reach for the manila envelope and shove the photograph back inside. My nakedness disappears from sight. "Because remember when I had you sell that bracelet, a few weeks ago?"

"Sure I do. I— Wait a minute." She snatches back the envelope. "You're being *blackmailed*, Tiny? Caspian *Harrison* is *blackmailing* you?"

"Of course it's not Caspian. Give that back!"

But she's already opening the flap, already sliding out the contents. The photograph, the note. "Jesus. Oh my God. This is like a movie. One of those gangster movies—"

"This is not a movie. This is real life, *my* life, and if this ever gets out, it won't matter whether I leave Frank or not, he'll be ruined, and it will be my fault, to say nothing of *my* life being ruined—"

"Why will *your* life be ruined? *Frank's* career will be over, sure, but that's no more than he deserves, the cheating bastard."

"Oh, Pepper. Think. Think about it. Think about this photograph being splashed across the newspapers for every man Harry to look at."

She fans herself slowly with the contents of the envelope. Her face is a little flushed beneath the olive tan. "Could you open a window or something?"

I walk to the window overlooking the beach and lift the bottom sash. A rush of hot wind catches me in the stomach. "It's warmer outside, actually."

"At least it's fresh."

I lie down on the bed, back to front, and prop my feet up on the wall above the headboard. My stomach growls, wondering where lunch has got to. I fold my arms across my rib cage to muffle the sound. The shock of Dr. Keene is receding at last, taking the rest of my emotions with it. The brain left behind is unnaturally sharp, unusually cold. Ready for action.

"If it's not Caspian, then who is it?"

"I don't know. Someone who found the photographs."

"Well, screw him. Go to the police."

"I can't do that. Frank will find out."

"So what if he does?"

"Pepper, Caspian's his cousin. How am I supposed to tell Frank I slept with his cousin?"

"You never told Frank?"

The fan overhead is rotating at low speed. I imagine myself grabbing hold of one of the blades and going around and around, like a carnival ride. I can almost feel the air rushing against my cheeks. "Not exactly. A little. I think he guessed the rest, except about Caspian. But he's never spoken to me about it. He never seemed to care. He was just . . . He was just glad I came back. Glad I changed my mind and went through with the wedding. A gentleman, you might say."

"What does Caspian say?"

"About the blackmail? I haven't told him."

"Why not? He took the pictures, goddamn it!"

"I just can't, that's all. He might tell Frank, or Frank's father."

"Do you think so? He seems pretty square to me."

Round and round, getting me nowhere. "Oh, he might. Trust me. It's the Hardcastle way. The family comes first, when the chips are down."

"I think you're wrong, there. I think he's his own man."

I swing upward to sit on the edge of the bed, gripping the comforter with my fingers. "I said, *trust me.*"

Pepper folds her arms. She's starting to look a little rounder now, Pepper. If you look closely, you can maybe even see a trace of fullness at her belly, about the size of a man's spread palm, beneath her cotton shift. A wide scarf holds her hair back from her face, and I'll be damned if the sculpture of her cheeks hasn't taken on a layer or two, a coating of new clay. "Just what the hell happened between you two?" she asks.

"It doesn't matter now." I hoist myself up and turn around to face her, sitting cross-legged in the middle of the bed. "The point is what I'm going to do now."

"Did you reply to *this* little valentine?"

"No. Not yet."

Pepper drums her fingers against the envelope, which dangles from her crossed arms. A plain manila envelope, the kind you see in offices everywhere. The photograph and note are still outside it, pinned to the manila by her scarlet-tipped thumb. Her head tilts to one side as she watches me. Her face is half in shadow, half alight with the golden glow of an afternoon beach streaming through the window. "You have no idea who this guy might be? No idea how he got his hands on the photographs?"

"Caspian says he packed up the photographs, before he left for Vietnam. An attic or a closet somewhere."

"Well, anyone in the family could have gone in the attic, right? Two years is a long time."

"But why would anyone in the family be blackmailing me?"

"That bitch Constance. She's no friend of yours. You should hear the stuff she says, behind your back."

"She loves Frank more than she dislikes me," I say absently. My head is tilted, my eyes are fixed on Pepper's thumbnail, which covers my slender black-and-white hip at the edge of the photograph like a scarlet fig leaf. "Could you give me that photograph for a moment?"

She hands it to me. "What about her husband? Tim?"

"Tom."

"He's got a chip on his shoulder the size of Plymouth Rock. I'll bet he—"

"This photo was developed in a shop," I say.

"What's that?"

I look up at her. "There's a time and date stamp on the border. It was processed in a professional lab."

"Well, of course it was."

"You don't understand. Caspian develops all his own film. He has a darkroom in his apartment."

Pepper frowns at me. "Let me see that."

I hand her back the photograph.

She holds it up to her nose, squinting a little. Surely my little sister doesn't need reading glasses, does she? Wouldn't that be a hoot. Pepper, wearing glasses. She reads out, "Eleven twenty-two a.m., May the fourth, nineteen sixty-six," and looks up at me. "Is that a clue, Mr. Holmes?"

Already I'm putting on my sandals. My brain is buzzing, my veins are fizzing with something. Hope? Purpose, maybe. Doing something. I head for the door.

"I don't know. But I'm going to find out."

"Are you, now? And how do you plan to do that, Miss Scaredy-Cat?"

I pause at the vase of flowers on my chest of drawers. Hyacinths, delivered yesterday with a handwritten note: *To my darling wife. I love you. Frank.* They're a lovely shade of blue, unearthly, each tiny petal poised in dewy perfection. But when I bend my face to smell them, the scent is almost too faint to catch. As if they've left their essence behind in the hothouse.

I straighten from the flowers, take the envelope from her fingers, and tuck it under my arm.

"I'm going to talk to Caspian."

For lack of anything more, I address Caspian's feet. They're shod in old army boots and stick out from beneath the elegant swoop of the Mercedes-Benz rear fender like a pair of gigantic leather bookends.

"What's that?" he calls, in a metallic voice. "You've got the sandwiches?"

"Would you mind coming out of there for a moment? I can't stand here shouting."

Caspian scoots out slowly, foot by foot, clad in worn Levi's and a stained old shirt. He's lying on one of those wheeled planks, like mechanics use. He straightens to a sitting position and braces his boots against the floor so he doesn't roll. "Is something wrong?" he asks, when he sees my face.

"The photographs," I say.

He doesn't ask which photographs. "What about them? I told you I boxed them up. I checked on them, when I was back in town. They're still there."

"I know. I mean, I'm sure they are. I mean the other photographs.

The ones you took of me on the sofa." My lips are thick and clumsy; the words seem to stick in them.

Caspian frowns. "Those? That's just film. I never developed them."

"What did you do with the film?"

"I mailed it to you, of course. Before the wedding." He rises to his feet. "Didn't you get it?"

I almost can't hear him, through the beat of my own pulse in my ears. "Where did you mail it to? Which address?"

"To your apartment. I didn't want to take a chance that Frank would find it and get curious. Why? What's going on?"

"Nothing."

He reaches for my arm. "Tiny—"

I shrug him off and take a stumbling step backward. "It's nothing. I was just wondering."

"Did someone—"

I turn to the door, to the wedge of open sunlight, but Caspian bolts in front of me and takes me by the arms. "Hold on. Wait a moment."

I stare at the buttons of his shirt. "Please let me go."

"You're in trouble."

"No more than usual."

"Tiny, I'm here to help you. To serve you. That's why I'm here, the only reason."

"Don't you think you've done enough already?"

Caspian flinches and drops his hands, as if I've turned into molten metal. I gather myself and look up at his face. A black smear lies across one cheekbone, rubbed there by a dirty hand. His forehead is dark with grease.

"You're one of them," I say. "You're a Hardcastle. You're part of this whole racket. Frank's campaign staff, carrying him into the White

House with your bare hands. Never mind who gets hurt along the way. The end justifies the means, doesn't it?"

"You know that's not true. I don't give a damn about Frank's ambitions."

"Then why are you campaigning with him? Why are you all protecting him like this?"

You wouldn't believe a man with one leg could stand so still. You'd think he was made of stone, or wax, the way he looks down at me, or maybe through me. Not even a single dark pupil flexes against a green Harrison iris. I could count his eyelashes.

"Well?" I say, because I am not going to stand down this time, I'm not going to fade away. "Why do you defend Frank? Why do you let them dress you up in your uniform and your medals and . . . and *use* you like that?"

"I'm not."

"Oh, really? Then what do you call it?"

He blinks at last and lets out a heavy sigh. He steps out of my way and makes for the car. I turn and watch him as he picks up a wrench and sinks back down to sit on the wheeled platform. "This," he says fiercely, holding up the wrench. "Me, here." He gestures around the shed, toward the door. "The ceremony in Washington, the hotel the other night. You think I'm doing it for *Frank*? Helping Frank? Protecting *Frank*?" He shakes his head.

"What, then? Tell me. For God's sake."

He leans backward on the wooden platform and stares at the ceiling. "When you're done thinking about it, come and find me."

A flutter disturbs the air, and the mother starling ducks in through the shed door and rushes to the nest in the roof beams. The baby starlings stir, opening their red throats, wide with anticipation.

I let my gaze fall to Caspian below them. His knees are raised, the left one a bit larger than the right. His hand with the wrench lies across his wide chest, moving slightly with the rhythm of his breath. His wide chest, which once sheltered me, which then traveled across the world and bled out into the jungle mud, which was hoisted almost lifeless into a helicopter while I wrapped Christmas presents in my tasteful Back Bay living room.

I step across the dusty floor and sink to my knees next to him.

"I'm here now, aren't I?" I say.

He rolls his head and looks at me, without speaking. Exactly the same eyes, the same cheekbones, the same jaw, the same Caspian. Except for that scar on his forehead, curling around his brow.

I reach out a brave hand and touch his knee. "Does it hurt?"

"You mean now?"

"Now. Whenever."

"Sometimes. A lot of the time. But not now."

I lean forward and kiss the edge of his broad patella. The denim is hot beneath my lips and smells of oil. "I am so sorry. You don't know how much. If I— I just keep thinking, over and over, it's *my* fault, if I hadn't—"

Caspian sits up. "It's not your fault."

"You wouldn't have taken that second tour—"

"Then something might have happened in the first tour. You never know what might have been. You just never know."

His breath is close to mine. His breath and my breath.

I lean my cheek against his knee, facing the wide old boards of the shed wall. Above us, the baby starlings exclaim delight at being fed. "I'm sorry. I'm so sorry. Your beautiful leg."

"It's just a leg, I told you."

"I screwed up, didn't I? I screwed up so badly. You should have found another girl."

"There isn't another girl, Tiny. Not in the wide world."

He doesn't touch me. Thank God, he doesn't touch me one bit. I stare at the wall, holding his knee under my cheek, and at last the starlings settle down and I rise to my feet and walk wearily to the door, where I pause, bracing my hand on the post. The sun burns down on my hair. Before me, the bracken is clearer now, pushed aside by dozens of hands over the past few weeks. The grass is beaten down into a path. It's a wonder Granny Hardcastle hasn't noticed.

I turn back. "There's one thing. Something I've been meaning to ask you."

Caspian is lying down again, knees still raised, about to roll back under the car. His head is shadowed by the fender. "What is it?"

"Something that reporter mentioned to me. He said he was looking into something about Frank. Some incident when Frank was at Harvard. His junior year, I think he said. I told him I didn't know anything about it."

Caspian swears softly.

"I see. So there is something. Something no one's told me."

"I don't know much about it myself."

"But you do know. The family knows. You're protecting him."

Caspian lies there quietly with his head under the front fender of the Mercedes. He fiddles with the wrench. "I didn't know if they'd told you or not."

"Are you going to tell me now? Or do I have to find out for myself?"

"Why don't you ask Frank?"

"Because Frank isn't going to tell me the truth. Or is he?"

Caspian sighs. "All right. I *could* tell you what I know, which isn't much. But I think you need to ask your husband instead."

"And why is that, Caspian?"

He rolls back under the car and starts to clank around with his wrench. "Because it's not my place. I'm not here to push you off the ledge, Tiny. The ledge is your choice, I can't touch that. I'm just here to catch you if you jump."

I stare at the soles of Caspian's strong boots, at his legs visible to the knee before they disappear into the undercarriage of the Mercedes-Benz. My hand clenches around the manila envelope, crumpling the edges.

"Do you mind if I borrow your car?" I say. "I can't find my keys."

Caspian, 1964

Funny thing, falling in love. You can't quite explain the difference between this—kissing the girl you love, having sex with the girl you love—and all the kissing and the sex that came before. You can't describe the difference between her flesh and that flesh, her hips and those hips, her gasp and those gasps. You can't parse the qualitative and quantitative aspects of the experience, the units that make up the whole, any more than you, the untrained viewer, can explain why the *Mona Lisa* is the *Mona* fucking *Lisa*. You just stand back and take it in and say, *Wow, so this is art*.

You lie back in your bed, you hold her chest next to your chest, her ribs next to your ribs, her breath and your breath, and you say, *So this is love*.

"I want to see Mount Rushmore," said Tiny. This wasn't entirely out of the blue. They'd been lying there for a while, talking about this and that, because discussing the sex they'd just had was like discussing the *Mona Lisa*, too big and too complicated, and maybe a little too new and sacred too. Anyway, what did you say, after an hour like that? What were the words? *Are you all right?* As if he hadn't been paying attention the whole time, as if all the action were one-sided: his lust casually dismantling her virginity. *I love you?* Banal, compared to what he actually felt, the complexity of his entanglement with the person lying in his arms, invading the pores of his skin.

So they stuck to what could be communicated through words, what actually needed saying.

Like the trip out to California. Their new track, laying itself out ahead.

"Mount Rushmore's in South Dakota," he said. "If you still want to see the Grand Canyon, it's going to be hard to do both."

"We have two weeks, though."

"I guess we'll see how it goes. But you may have to make a choice."

"That's okay. I like making choices, it turns out." She ventured a hand across his chest, up one pectoral and down the other, winding up curled around his opposite shoulder, and it was strange, antigravitational, that a touch so light, a skeleton so fragile, should hold him so securely in place in his own bed.

She stared at her hand, wholly unaware of its magical power, and continued. "I was thinking I might try to teach dancing, once I'm out there. I'll never be good enough to dance professionally, I mean with a real company, a prestigious company, and anyway that's a hard life. Lots of backstabbing and bleeding toes. But I could teach kids, like I did with my little dance company in Boston. Maybe open my own studio."

"Sure you could. That's a great idea. Plenty of little ankle biters out there, these days, that's for sure."

"Good. So that's me. What about you?"

The moon had come out, a friendly half-moon, not too bright. He stared at the white ceiling, at the fan rotating ponderously. His own bed. His ordinary bed, except it was rumpled beyond repair, sheets and blankets all twisted up and hanging to the floor, an unholy mess, and for the first time in his life he didn't care, he wasn't tempted to jump up and straighten and tuck everything back into the wholesome flat prairie his father taught him. His ordinary bed, except he lay here naked with Tiny in his arms, *Tiny*, and they'd just had sex together, he and Tiny: he'd entered her body with his body, she'd taken him joyously into herself, and his nerves were still sparkling, his brain was still foggy with pleasure and disbelief. With the scent of her breath. "You know about me. I'm a soldier. Leave ends in sixteen days, then I get on a plane, a fat old noisy deathtrap of a troop transport, first class all the way, and go back to active duty."

"And how long are you signed on for?"

"I'm an officer, Tiny. A career officer. I'm on until I resign, or retire. But the tour lasts a year, officially."

"An officer?" She lifted herself up and looked down at him, and the fearless intimacy of her naked and dangling breasts made him sing a little, inside his chest where she couldn't hear. "I didn't know that. Are you commissioned? What rank?"

"Captain."

"Ooh, a captain! Why didn't you tell me?"

He shrugged. "You were already head over heels. Didn't want you to go off your rocker or anything."

She fell back laughing. "Oh, my God. My mother will die, absolutely die."

"She'll probably get me court-martialed, knowing her."

"*Knowing* her?" Tiny stopped laughing and lay still against his ribs. "How do you know my mother, Caspian?"

"Because she was there at your apartment, when I came looking for you."

Tiny shrieked. "She *what*?"

I can't believe you didn't tell me," Tiny said. "You took my picture like that, you *slept* with me, and you didn't happen to mention that you'd met my mother an hour before."

"I didn't see how that was relevant to sleeping with you."

"*Men.*"

He added, "Anyway, that wasn't sleeping."

They were driving Caspian's old Ford down Route 3 to the Cape. His idea. *Does she know your name?* Tiny had demanded, and *Yes, of course,* he'd answered; and *So she knows where to find you,* said Tiny, and *Well, I gave her my card,* he'd said, in the most natural way in the world; and *Why the hell did you do that?* screamed Tiny, and *Don't worry, she doesn't know you're with me,* he'd told her soothingly; and *Trust me, she'll know it in a few hours, when he gets the note I put through his mail slot and dials up Mother, and Mother comes marching over to batter down the door,* she'd said.

He'd leaned back on the pillow, put his hands behind his head, and considered the matter: weighed the satisfaction of letting Mrs. Schuyler batter down his door to discover the precious Tiny lying luxuriously deflowered in his arms, versus the wisdom of postponing such a confrontation until Tiny was ready to face it, and the downstairs neighbors weren't around to call the police.

"I have this place on the Cape," he'd said at last. "My mother's place, an old family house. She left it to me and my sister, when she died. About an hour away, at this time of night."

This time of night: the car crashing through the moonlight, the grass shimmering silver by the road. He'd put the top down, because that's what you did when you drove to the Cape in the middle of a silvery May night with the woman you loved.

"Don't get funny," she said. Her arms were crossed over her chest, and a ladylike silk scarf tethered her hair. She sat primly in the passenger seat, her legs tangled at the ankles under her powder-blue skirt.

"Come here." He held out his right arm.

She considered the arm, considered the chest to which it was connected. She brushed her fingertips down her skirt and edged grudgingly in his direction.

He dragged her into the middle seat and kissed the top of her head. "That's better."

She fell asleep at once, nestled sweet-smelling in his shoulder, and as the car rolled along, and the salt wind and the moonlight stirred the hair at the top of his head, he thought that he would probably never be happier than this moment, that you couldn't achieve any greater contentment than this, any more sublime confluence of sensation. Before life fell apart again.

I n the end, they swung into the sandy driveway of his mother's beach house an hour and a quarter later, because Cap drove a little more slowly than usual, prolonging the ride. He cut the engine and stared at the old shingles, at the white trim catching the moon. How long had it been? Maybe a decade. So hard to schedule his few family visits to coincide with the height of summer.

He nudged Tiny. "Wake up, sweetheart." He'd never used that word before, but it fit, at this moment.

"Hmm?"

"We're here."

Tiny lifted her head. "The Cape?"

"Mmm." He climbed out of the car and held out his hand. She

stumbled out after him, untying her silk scarf, straightening her skirt. "Let's get you to bed."

"What time is it?"

"One o'clock or so."

"It feels later."

He found the key in the birdhouse and opened the door. The familiar smell surrounded him: wood and weather, mildew and salt and lemon polish, towels drying in the sun. Childhood. The place was tidy, exactly as he remembered: the family sent someone over every so often for dusting and repairs, kept the gardener on his rounds. There was his mother's chair, next to the knobbled fieldstone fireplace, covered in a ghostly white sheet. The electricity was probably still off. He used a flashlight from the car to find the hurricane lamp in the pantry and light it with a long match.

Tiny still stood in the hallway, blinking sleepily. She took off her shoes and dropped them by the door.

"Bathroom?" he said.

She nodded.

"Go upstairs and turn right. The door at the end of the hall. Water should be on by now, because of the gardener, but the boiler's not lit, obviously, so it's going to be cold. I'll just get the suitcases from the car."

He heard the water trickling through the pipes when he came back in. He carried the suitcases upstairs to his room and set the hurricane lamp on the bedside table. The curtains were closed. He pulled them wide to the moonlight and yanked up the bottom sash of the window. The cool air rushed in, the rhythmic wash of the ocean. He watched the faint undulating phosphorescence of the surf until the water stopped and the bathroom door creaked in the hall behind him. He turned and lifted away a few sheets from the furniture. A pale fog of dust rose and settled.

"Is this your room?" Tiny asked from the doorway.

"Yes. Slept here as a kid. I can push the beds together, if you like."

"That's not necessary. Which one is yours?"

That's not necessary. A little ungentlemanly fall of disappointment in his chest.

He pointed to the single bed closest to the window. "Right there. I'll just use the bathroom while you get changed."

The water in the tap ran ice-cold. He splashed his face and brushed his teeth. His reflection was paler than he expected, or maybe it was the moonlight. He scrubbed his skin with a towel and headed back to the bedroom, where Tiny had blown out the hurricane lamp and burrowed into his bed.

He arrived on the old hooked rug in the center of the room, hesitating. The bed wasn't built for two.

"Well, come on," said Tiny. "I'm not getting any warmer in here."

Under the sheets, she was naked and fresh, delicate in his arms, miraculous. He kissed her collarbone, her beautiful neck. "You're not too sore or anything, are you?"

"We can find out."

He'd never really liked the term she used, *making love,* but he liked it now. Like *sweetheart,* it fit somehow, it carried the scent of truth. The sweetening of his heart when he touched her skin. The enlarging of this store of love inside his chest, when she touched his skin, when he balanced himself on his palms and locked them carefully together. No, she wasn't too sore. She'd never felt better, she said, and he thought of the photographs he'd taken—the ballet ones, interestingly, not the naked ones—and he raised her elastic right leg to his shoulder.

"Oh!" she said, surprised and pleased.

Like the drive along the highway, he made it last as long as he could; but like the drive, it had to end sometime, didn't it, drenched in moonlight and the salt scent of the pulsing ocean outside the window. "How dangerous is it, really? Tell me the truth," panted Tiny, damp and hot below him in the mattress, her chin hooked over his shoulder, her arms still clenched around his back. (*It* meant Vietnam, he surmised.)

"Am I going to make it back, you mean?"

"Don't say it like that."

He concentrated on lifting himself off her—conscious of her dainty frame, which must surely be crushed under his bulk, though she didn't complain—without falling over the side of the bed. She turned on her side, making room. Her back to the window.

"The odds are good, if you keep your head down," he said.

"Will you promise to keep your head down?"

"If you ask me nicely."

"What does that mean?"

He pulled her in a little more snugly. "It means I can't make any promises, can I?"

He'd said that line before, more than once, but he meant something different this time. Something more to do with her freedom than his. He knew for a fact there wouldn't be any other women, no matter how brutal and barren things got out there in the jungle, the way he knew he could do without hot water and cold beer when he put them out of his mind. But Tiny? He couldn't ask her to wait. He couldn't ask her to take on the chaste and peripatetic life of an army wife, just like that, on the basis of a few weeks' unstudied passion.

Look what it did to his mother.

"Okay," she said. "But you'll know where to find me when you get back."

He rested his cheek against Tiny's soft hair and thought about getting back, next year. He thought about the possibility of reunion. He thought the unthinkable, about maybe changing his line of work. Selling his photographs or something. Money wasn't the problem. He had money, at least. Enough to support a wife and kids in a little house in San Diego, near the ocean. Spend summers at the Cape, right here in his mother's old place, just like when he was a kid. Happiest time of his life, until it ended.

"Don't worry, I'll find you," he said at last, but she was already asleep.

It wasn't the few bars of charcoal dawn that woke him, changing color outside the window, but the absence of Tiny from his side.

He called her name. No answer.

He listened for the sound of water trickling in the pipes, for the vibration of her footsteps on the old floorboards. The hollow next to him was cool, but at least the hollow was there. She couldn't have been gone long.

Cap was a man of action, but at that moment, he didn't want to act. His body lay slack and heavy in his old single bed, unwilling to stir. An unsettling premonition struck him: if he rose from this bed, if he threw off the sheet and blankets that had sheltered the two of them during the night, he'd break the spell. He'd return them both to the ordinary world, to their ordinary lives, and the past three days would have been nothing but a dream. A parallel universe. An unstable element, created by a team of curious scientists, existing for a second or two in a laboratory before breaking apart.

Tiny, he said again, more loudly, but the house remained silent.

He had no choice.

He flung away the covers and launched his feet to the floor. The boards were cold and hard against his skin. At the window, the curtains were still open, the bottom sash still raised. The ocean breeze had turned positively chilly, more suited to the beginning of April than the third week of May. In another week, the houses along the shore would be filling up, the businesses would open their shuttered fronts. The beach outside his house and his cousins' houses would, by the end of June, have witnessed football games and swimming races, sailing competitions and fishing matches. Always competition. They were always winners and losers in his family.

At this moment, though, while a pink sun struggled to rise above the heavy gray horizon, the beach contained only a single tiny figure, wrapped in a blanket, smoking a cigarette, facing the ocean. The breeze moved her tousled dark hair. She stood at the edge of the ragged wet lines marking the reach of the surf, so that when the white foam washed toward her, it sometimes found her toes and sometimes not quite.

I am in love with you, he thought, and then, an instant later, the more permanent, the more certain *I love you.*

For an instant, he contemplated crouching down and shouting the words from the open wedge of the window. But of course you didn't spoil the moment like that. You didn't wreck her serenity with a brash display. Anyway, she probably couldn't even understand him, while the surf crashed in her ears.

So he stood a moment or two longer, leaning against the window frame, marveling at her. Marveling that he'd found her, that she wanted him, too. In the growing pink light, he saw the dissolution of his own doubts, the emergence of a truth, whole and clean. He saw, in cinematic detail, the infinity laid out before them: two weeks of honeymoon bliss, crossing the country in his car with the top down, staying in motels and campsites and eating at roadside diners and coffee shops, making love to rattle the heavens, to make the angels weep. A year of hell, writing back and forth, exchanging photographs, while a ball of virtuous longing took up residence in the pit of his stomach. Then homecoming, reunion, a house in San Diego near the ocean. Small but pretty. Her ballet studio, his photography. Kids, friends, family. Christmas Eves. A couple weeks back east every summer, maybe, or as long as they both could stand.

Mornings like this, poised in the dawn, in which he would make her coffee and bring it down to the beach, where she'd be waiting for him, and they would stand there wrapped in a shared blanket, drinking coffee, not saying anything. Waiting for the wondrous day.

He turned from the window, found his undershirt and trousers, and headed downstairs to tell her.

Tiny, 1966

drive with the top up, because that's what you do when you're sneaking out of the family compound under the suspicious eyes of your in-laws.

I can't find my keys, I told Caspian. That was true, if a little misleading. Actually, the keys to my Cadillac have gone missing from the drawer in the pantry where I always place them after a drive, *always*, and I suspect I'd be wasting my time if I tried to look for them.

Half an hour along the highway, I'm glad the top is up, because the usual afternoon thunderclouds arrive early, all black and towering, and five miles out of Plymouth the first fat drops fall *kersplat* on the windshield, scattering the dust. Après them, the deluge.

There's nothing like the clamor of a downpour on the raised canvas top of a convertible. You feel as if your head is stuck inside a dwarves' mountain mine, an incessant rolling clatter, like metal on stone. You think it's the end of the world, possibly. How could the sky release that much water and survive? But eventually the decibels climb back down, the horizon swallows the clouds. The sun comes out, mollified, just as you pull the car up to the curb outside your husband's campaign office on Boylston Street.

"Mrs. Hardcastle!" Josephine is surprised to see me. So surprised, in fact, that her confident young face actually fills with color. "We thought you were at the Cape."

"I'm sure you did." In ten precise tugs, one for each finger, I take off one white cotton summer driving glove and then the other. My pocketbook is hooked over my elbow. "I was looking for my husband."

"Frank— Mr. Hardcastle's giving a speech in Cambridge this afternoon."

"Will he be back here before returning to his hotel?"

She looks down at her desk and shuffles through a paper or two. "I'm not sure. Scott's with him; he has the schedule."

"Really? He didn't ask you to accompany him?"

A pair of young women at the back of the office raise their heads to stare at us. Josephine's cheeks take on a little more raspberry. "He asked me to stay in the office this time. It's not a big speech."

"I see. May I take a look at Scott's desk? Perhaps he's left a copy of the schedule there."

"Right over there by the window, Mrs. Hardcastle."

Frank's campaign headquarters are carefully plain, a bureau of the people. The walls are decorated with campaign memorabilia and cheap American flag bunting. There are no private offices, except for a large meeting room at the back, and the battered brown furniture is all secondhand. A massive Xerox machine fills a space in the corner, next to the storeroom. Scott's desk sits in the opposite corner, overlooking the Boston Public Library, immaculately organized. There is a leather blotter, a silver cup for pens and pencils, a plastic telephone in avocado green, a ceramic ashtray, empty metal in and out trays. A cubby at the end contains a few stacks of paper, a notepad, a manila folder labeled PRESS RELEASES, another labeled DAILY BRIEFINGS, and another labeled

SCHEDULES. I open that one. WEDNESDAY, JULY 25TH, 1966, announces the paper on the top of the stack.

MORNING

9:00 coffee at American Legion (see notes)

10:45 coffee at Carpenters Local 111 (see notes)

AFTERNOON

2:15 Lunch at the Union Oyster House with Barry Gorelock

3:00 Speech at Austin Hall, Harvard Law School (arrival 2:30, see notes)

EVENING

6:00 Reception and dinner, the Harvard Club (see notes, guest list attached)

I check the clock on the wall next to the storeroom door. A quarter past three. Should I make the drive out to Cambridge? Do I have time? Frank usually sticks around after a speech, if he hasn't got anything pressing afterward, talking in his shirtsleeves, listening. Frank's a good listener, actually, when he wants to be. When he's campaigning for your affection. He looks you right in the eye, like there's nothing more fascinating or moving in the world than your little problems. It's almost irresistible.

My gaze falls back to Scott's desk, as if to find an answer to my dilemma. A couple of cigarette butts lie in the ashtray, interrupting the general cleanliness. Next to them is a stamp roll on a pewter dispenser, half-finished. A few stamps drag on the wooden surface of the desk, as if the coil was tugged too hard the last time it was used.

I reach out and touch the foremost stamp with one finger. George Washington.

A s a child, I hated trouble like a cat hates fleas. My sisters were always happy to take advantage of this particular weakness. When I got up in the middle of the night for a glass of milk and caught Vivian just sneaking in, reeking of cigarettes, she'd say: *I'll tell Mums you were the one who broke her perfume bottle,* or *I'll tell old Roby you forged Mums's John Hancock to see that ballet with the senior class* (Mrs. Robillard was our headmistress at Nightingale-Bamford), and that was that.

But here's the curious thing: the trouble in question didn't have to be *my* trouble. Do you remember that time I walked in on Mums in the library with her Russian prince? Mums raised her beautiful tousled head from the sofa cushion and said, *For God's sake, Tiny, the door was closed, you silly child, you should have knocked,* and the shame rained down on my thin shoulders. *My* fault, that I had disturbed her; *my* fault, that I had discovered her fault. If I hadn't opened that door, everything would be fine. The tree falling in the woods, with no one to hear it. And I am always careful, now, to knock on a closed door. I am always afraid of what I might find on the other side. Whose shame might be transferred to my shoulders.

So on this lengthening July afternoon, as I race down the streets of the Back Bay in Caspian's familiar Ford, my hands clench the steering wheel and my stomach lurches in fear. If it weren't for the anger, I'd stop right here. I'd pull to the curb and put my face in my hands and cry and cry, shaking in every sinew, since no one is here to watch me.

Josephine has informed me that Scott lives in an apartment on

Back Street, not that far from where I lived in the years before I married Frank. Providential, really. It means I don't have to think as I flash past the familiar blocks, the friendly trees. I don't need to count the streets, to read the signs. The Ford stops and starts and turns almost by itself, and when I find a car-sized gap on the curb around the corner, between a Chevrolet and a dirty orange ten-year-old Oldsmobile, I slide perfectly into place on the first pass.

The super doesn't appreciate my summons. He pushes open the outer door and takes me in, smart little hat to rounded leather toe, and scratches his white cotton belly. "What's the matter, lady? I work the goddamned night shift. I don't need this."

"I'm from Mr. Maynard's office. His place of employment. It seems he's left an important document inside his apartment this morning."

"Why can't he come here himself and get it? The dumb cluck."

"Because he's out in Cambridge on business at the moment." My palms are damp inside my gloves; my heart is beating so hard and so fast, it's going to splinter my ribs. *Trouble.* I'm going to get in trouble for this.

"Aw, Jesus. I'm not supposed to let you in, lady."

"Really, sir. Do I look like some sort of criminal to you?"

The super glances at the pocketbook on my elbow, at the white gloves on my slender hands. "No, I guess not."

"Please, then." I melt the frigid muscles of my face into a smile. "I'd be most grateful. We really do need that paper."

He slumps his hairy shoulders in defeat. "All right, all right. Hold on, will you?"

A hunch, that's all it is. A hunch, based on the flimsy presence of a roll of George Washington stamps on Scott Maynard's desk, on the ready supply of plain manila envelopes in the Vote Frank campaign office, on the frequent access of Frank's campaign staff to our house on Newbury Street, where the precious roll of Caspian's film might or might not have ended up. He's young and broke—the shabbiness of this brownstone suggests *that*, at least—and when you're young and broke, you'd maybe think blackmailing the boss's wife is a harmlessly profitable trick, wouldn't you? She's not going to tell her husband, and you're certainly not going to let those photographs out in the wide world to destroy the candidate's career. The rich little bitch can afford a few grand, can't she? All those pretty jewels on her neck. Young Mr. Maynard makes a little dough to keep body and soul together, and no one gets hurt, right?

The super's keys jingle on his hips as I follow him up the dirty steps, flight after flight. The stairwell smells of garbage and damp carpet, and the higher we climb, the warmer the air grows. By the time we reach the top floor, a rotting inferno encloses us. Not that the super seems to care. He fumbles for his keys while the sweat crawls down his neck and into the thatch of fur at the top of his back. A surge of nausea crosses my belly. I hold my hand to my mouth and breathe in the hyacinth scent of my gloves.

"The fuck," mutters the super, and then: "Bingo." He shakes the key free of its neighbors and sticks it in the lock. "Here you go, lady. Don't be too long, all right? I gotta sleep."

"I won't disturb you, I promise. Thanks ever so much."

The first thing I do in Scott Maynard's apartment is open the nearest window. The air outside has freshened after the thunderstorm, and in comparison to the fetid heat at the top of the stairwell, the back alley is a spring garden. I breathe a few gusts deep into my lungs, and when the nausea recedes, I turn to lock the door and survey my surroundings.

Well, young Mr. Maynard is no Dorothy Draper, but his apartment—like his desk in the campaign office—is small and neat, containing only a scrap of a kitchenette and a square table for eating, a chest of drawers, a sofa, a bed, a few lamps. I check the chest of drawers first, but it's all on the up and up, just tidy stacks of underwear in the top drawers and folded pajamas and shirts further down. In the tiny bathroom, there's no room for more than a comb, a toothbrush, and a jar of Brylcreem.

I have just opened a promising cardboard box in the single closet when a voice drifts through the wall, and a familiar jingle of keys sends me scooping up my pocketbook and diving into the closet atop the shoes.

There is no knob on the inside of the closet door. I pull the barrier toward me, as close as I can, but a fine crack of light still streaks across my yellow skirt. I gather up my knees and bury my burning face between them. The shoes dig into my bottom, my pulse pounds at my temples. The edges of Scott Maynard's three or four suits part around my hat.

He's probably stopped here to change into one of those suits, hasn't he? Maybe a fresh shirt, too, before tonight's reception and dinner at the Harvard Club. In another moment, he'll open the closet door and reach for the hangers on the rod, and his gaze will drop and find the white tip of my shoe, the length of my leg in its nude stocking.

I wait for the sound of the faucet, or the refrigerator door as he fetches a cool drink with which to refresh himself. I hope he doesn't notice the open window behind the sofa. Men don't notice details like that, do they?

But no such domestic noises reach my ears. Instead, I hear voices. Frank's voice.

You know those dreams, where some murderer comes into your room with a knife in his hands, and you want to scream and run away, but your limbs are frozen and your throat is frozen and you just stand there, paralyzed, watching your own murderer approach, hating your own body for betraying you like this, for failing to protect you from this elemental harm? I mean, really. Millions of years of evolution, and you can't even run away from your own murderer?

I think I'm having one of those dreams.

"We only have an hour," says Frank, muffled, imprecise, but still undeniably Frank through the wooden door of Scott Maynard's closet. Through the slim crack of daylight.

Scott says something back, something I can't quite hear because his body is perhaps turned away, or his voice is perhaps not as well-known to me as that of my husband.

Then the wet, familiar pause of a kiss.

"Oh, God," Frank groans.

I want to close my ears at the despair in Frank's voice, Frank's voice as I have never heard it before, raw and anguished and alive, alive, *alive*.

But I can't close my ears. I cover them with my hands, but it's no use. I hear the rustle of clothing, the creak of sofa springs. Someone cries out; I think it's Scott. I take in a mouthful of linen skirt and crush it between my jaws. "Jesus," Frank sobs softly, "Jesus Christ. Jesus Christ. Oh, God. Oh, God." Over and over he invokes his Savior. Scott's voice joins him, suppressed, because you don't want the neighbors to hear, do you? You don't want the police barging into the middle of all this.

And then it's over, a final cry from one, a groan from the other, a wooden rattle and a thump, collapse. I think they must be on the floor.

My teeth bite into my skirt. I can't cry, I can't sob. They'll hear me if I do.

"Jesus," Frank gasps. "Oh, Jesus."

Scott says something back.

"I know." Frank is crying. "I know. God help me."

The tears fall silently down my cheeks. Not for me—I'm beyond the reach of pain, I've spun bang out of this universe and come to rest in some nether dimension of excruciating numbness—but for Frank. Frank, on whose immaculate surface I have skated for eight years, unable to find the hairline crack that would lead me to the world underneath. No wonder.

I can hear them panting together on the other side of the door. A desperate syncopation that slows, breath by breath, into harmony.

"You okay?" Frank asks tenderly.

Scott murmurs something.

Frank says, "God. I can't do this anymore. It's killing me."

This time, Scott's voice is clear. "I love you."

There is a long silence. Scott's face is vague in my memory, next to the iridescent Josephine. I recall dark hair, dark eyes, an aloof smile, eyebrows that hooked at the ends. A nose that seemed to condescend to me, the candidate's mere wife. How does Scott look right now, to my husband's enraptured eyes?

"I love you, too," Frank says, in a wholly different tone than the comforting *I love you*s that I, Christina Hardcastle, his wedded and lawfully bedded wife, receive from him daily. As if the sentence originates from some section of Frank that lies against his heart. And then, in despair: "I can't help it. I can't. I can't stop."

I sit absolutely still, absorbing Frank's shame. The floorboards creak; the clothing rustles. There is a rush of water from the bathroom, and footsteps. "Thanks," someone says, I can't tell whom. I wipe my wet face against my skirt.

A silence begins, long and intimate.

"I'm sorry," says one of them, I don't know how much later. I think it's Scott.

"It's not your fault." Definitely Frank.

"I should just quit. Quit the campaign and go to work in another city. Another fucking *state*."

"Maybe you should." More silence, and then: "No, don't. Scott, no."

"Come on."

"Scott, no. I'm done, I can't. My wife. I just can't."

But they do anyway, whatever it is they do. Quieter this time, voluptuous, while I stare at the thread of daylight and inhale the sweaty woolen scent of Scott Maynard's suits, enrobed in shock, waiting and waiting for them to finish. I need to vomit. The tears have dried up by now, and the sinews have thawed, but I'm still trapped in my tiny closet, unable to leave.

'm standing in a telephone booth on Cambridge Street. I don't know how I got here. I remember crawling across Scott Maynard's floor and throwing up in his toilet. Shock. My limbs stiff. I remember brushing my hair with his hairbrush, splashing my face with his water. Closing the window, turning the lock on the knob before I closed it. Stairs. Caspian's blue convertible Ford, sitting around the corner, as if nothing's happened.

Then a blurriness of driving, the streets of Boston passing before my eyes.

I stare through the glass at the gray walls of Massachusetts General. A doctor walks by, dressed in blue-green scrubs, holding a cup of coffee. I think of Vivian's husband, a pediatric surgeon of what they call *exceptional promise*, who will soon be completing his residency at St. Vincent's in Greenwich Village. Mums frets that he'll be offered some brilliant post somewhere else, somewhere across the country where you can't get a decent martini. A handsome man, Vivian's husband, a really nice guy, saving kids' lives left and right. She calls him Doctor Paul sometimes, like it's some sort of private joke between them, and he laughs and kisses her when she does. He worships her, really. Vivian, my incorrigible sister Vivian, thoroughly in love and married and respectable. Who'd have guessed? She writes a regular column in the *Metropolitan* now, a real must-read, sly and gossipy and elegant. Maybe you've seen it. They have a rambunctious one-year-old boy, on whom Mums dotes with an improbably idolatrous devotion, and another baby due this winter. A sunny apartment near Gramercy Park, not too far from the hospital, a few blocks away from our cousins the Greenwalds. A lovely, leafy, luxurious corner of Manhattan.

Why the hell did I ever leave New York City? At least in Manhattan, the queens aren't afraid to let you know it. You don't end up marrying them by mistake.

Then my brain goes static again, unable to bear the strain. I pick up the receiver, slip a dime through the slot, and ask the operator to put me through to the *Boston Globe* switchboard.

"Jack Lytle," he says brusquely.

"Mr. Lytle. It's Christina Hardcastle."

"Jesus. Yes. Hello. What can I do for you?"

"I need to speak to you, Mr. Lytle. In private. Is there somewhere we can meet?"

An instant's pause. "Where are you?"

"On Cambridge Street. Across from the hospital."

"Whoa. All right. Everything okay?"

"Everything's fine."

"I'm driving in from Dorchester. Can we meet somewhere on Charles Street in twenty minutes? There's a coffee shop on the corner of Chestnut."

"I . . . I hate to put you to any trouble."

"No trouble at all. I was about to head downtown anyway, this dinner of your husband's."

"Oh! Were you invited?" My voice is bright with small talk. I lift my gloved fingertips and tap an arpeggio against the glass.

"Well, you know. They like to have press there at some of these speeches."

"Well, that's . . . that's very nice. I'll see you in twenty minutes, Mr. Lytle."

"Can I ask what this is about, Mrs. Hardcastle?"

"No," I say. "No, you may not."

Jack Lytle orders coffee. I order water and ask him if he has any cigarettes. He tosses me the pack and lights us both up.

"You sure you want to hear this?" he says.

"I think I know what you're going to say, if that's what you mean."

He looks long, then back at me. "All right. The way I hear it, Frank Hardcastle was summoned to the office of the dean of Undergraduate Studies in March of 1960 to answer rumors that he was having an affair with a professor." The coffee arrives. Lytle adds cream and sugar—a lot of sugar—and says, as if it needed saying: "A *male* professor."

"I see. And?"

"And that's all. No official reprimand, no public record of any kind. Everyone in the dean's office at the time denies a meeting ever occurred."

"So it might be a rumor."

He sucks on his cigarette. "It might. But I'd say my source is pretty solid."

"You can't tell me who it is?"

"No. Sorry."

I play with the tips of my gloves, which lie alongside my pocket-book on the Formica table, a little dirty from the phone booth. The cigarette burns between my opposite fingers. I think, *This is like a play. I'm some actress playing Christina Hardcastle onstage. This isn't really* me. *This can't possibly be* my *life. If I just keep going until the end of the scene, keep playing my part, the curtain will drop and the audience will applaud and I can go back to my real life. Back to Cape Cod, where I will start the whole summer all over again.*

Even better: back to Boylan's Coffee Shop, where I will start the past two years all over again.

Lytle observes me for a moment, the seasoned journalist, and then speaks up into the silence. "Any reason you're coming to me now?"

"Yes. But I'm not going to tell you."

"Fair enough."

I look up and meet his gaze. "So. I suppose the rest of the story, the thing you're trying to establish, is that the Hardcastles paid every-one off to make the story die. They had the professor deny everything, Frank deny everything, anyone who had any knowledge of the affair deny everything." I lay the cigarette, untouched, on the edge of the ashtray. The smell is making me somewhat ill. "Then they set about looking for a girlfriend. For a . . . I don't know. What's the word? I'm sure there's a word for me."

He clears his throat. "A beard."

"A beard. That's it. And Frank threw himself into it, got himself a reputation as a ladies' man, because it isn't as if he's not attracted to women at all. He just . . . He just . . ." My throat pinches down on the words.

"He just likes men more," Lytle says quietly, flicking ash into the tray.

"I'll bet they hand selected me," I say. "Then they groomed me for it. They made me think I needed *them*, instead of the other way around."

"You're perfect for the role. Perfect in every way."

"They were so grateful to me. As long as I behaved myself, as long as I went along with everything, they were so grateful."

"Well, they would be, wouldn't they? Everything depends on you."

I fall back to my gloves, my pocketbook.

"So what are you going to do about it, Mrs. Hardcastle? You've got a pretty big decision to make. A crossroads, as we hack writers like to put it."

"Yes, I do."

"Can I ask you a question? Do you love your husband?"

"That's a very personal question."

"It's relevant, though, isn't it?"

Behind the counter, the waitress is eyeballing us as she wipes away at some smudge next to the register. Her hair is pulled back in a cap; her lipstick is a little too bright for the fluorescence above. I think of Em, the waitress at Boylan's who always knew how warm I liked my apricot Danish, who never blinked an eye when I asked her if she knew where Caspian lived. "Always knew you had taste," she said, that was all.

I never did go back to Boylan's, after the wedding. I wonder what Em is doing now.

Lytle stirs his coffee and watches my face, patient as a slender clean-cut Buddha in a formal dinner jacket. Oh, damn, he's good at this, isn't he?

Well, then. Answer the question. Do you love your husband, Mrs. Hardcastle? Do you love Frank?

I speak softly to the Formica. "I think so. I did, anyway. I do. I love him, I always have, just not the way . . . I think . . ." I look up again. "I think he'd make a wonderful congressman. I really do."

"And that's the trouble, isn't it?"

I finish my water and stub out my cigarette. "Can I ask *you* a question, Mr. Lytle?"

"I guess it's only fair."

"What's the point of all this? Why are you looking into my husband's personal affairs?"

He shrugs. "Because I'm a journalist, Mrs. Hardcastle. It's what I do."

"But you're the only journalist following this particular story."

Lytle picks up his spoon and taps it against the side of his coffee cup. "You know, here's the truth. I feel for the guy. I really do. I know you're too mad to look at all this from his side . . ."

"Oh, I can see it from his side, all right."

He angles his eyebrows at me. "But it's not easy, when the great ambition of your life stands in perfect one hundred and eighty degree opposition to the natural urges of your own body. When you have to hide your true self from everybody, including your own wife. Because at some point, the bill's going to come due. You're going to have to pay, one way or another."

"I doubt that's even occurred to Frank," I say. "He's a Hardcastle. When you're a Hardcastle, everyone else pays."

Lytle finishes his coffee in a gulp, crushes out his cigarette, and reaches into his pocket. "Can I give you a lift somewhere? You don't look so good. You need to eat something. Call up a friend, have a good cry."

I touch my cheek. My fingers are cold; the skin beneath is hot. "I'm fine."

He lays a couple of quarters on the table and straightens his immaculate dinner jacket. The look he casts me is warm with pity. "Don't forget, Mrs. Hardcastle. You're holding all the cards. You can make Frank or break him. Don't let those bastards make you think you're the one caught in the corner, here."

I don't know what expression I return Jack Lytle for this little piece of practical advice, but he answers with a shrug and a shake of his head. He glances down at the two quarters on the table, sweeps one of them back into his pocket, and sends me a conspiratorial wink.

"Unless they've got something on *you*, of course."

I n the phone booth again. It takes ages to get Caspian on the line. "He's in the shed," I've told Mrs. Crane, and then I have to describe the shed and its location, have to tell her to look for Pepper if she can't find Caspian. Pepper will know where he is. I beat my dime against the metal side of the telephone, waiting for the operator to tell me to deposit more money.

"Tiny?" His voice is urgent. "What's the matter?"

"I need you to tell me something, Caspian. The truth. Did Frank invite himself to the medal ceremony, or did you ask him? I mean, did the Hardcastles invite you back, or the other way around?"

There is a yawning chasm of a pause.

"Tell me quick, Caspian. I don't have a lot of spare change."

"They asked," he says. "And I said yes."

"Why did you say yes, Caspian? You have to tell me."

"You already know why I said yes."

"I need you to *tell* me, Caspian. In words."

He speaks quietly. I picture him in the library, talking into the corner so the walls will absorb his voice. "Tiny. The truth? Because I missed you, missed you worse than I missed my leg. Because I was worried sick about you. Because I figured that since I wasn't any closer to getting over you, after two goddamned years, the next best thing was to be near you. Even if I couldn't touch you."

"To watch over me."

"Yes."

The operator tells me to deposit another dime. I obey, with shaking fingers. I lean my head against the top of the box and let out a heavy tear-soaked breath.

"Tiny? Are you all right? Where are you?"

"Caspian, listen to me. I don't deserve you. I don't deserve your love and your loyalty and your goodness. I made the worst mistake in the world, but I'm going to make it up to you. I'm going to deserve you this time. I'm going to be strong, so strong and brave you won't even recognize me. And then I'll come back and *tell* you how much I . . ."

"What are you talking about? Tiny, what's happened? Where are you?"

"I'm in Boston. I'll see you in the morning, all right?"

"Tiny! What's going on?"

"I'm leaping, Caspian. I'm leaping off the ledge."

Click. I'm out of dimes.

'm standing before the door of my house on Newbury Street. My wedding gift from the Hardcastles. I've driven here in Caspian's blue Ford convertible, driven here like a madwoman with the top down, my hair flying, and the numbness is gone, the shell of brittle fear, and I am alive, alive, *alive.*

Alive and furious. I will change into my most smashing gown, swipe on my brightest lipstick, fasten on my most glittering jewels, and drive straight back to the Harvard Club. Before I can change my mind, before the Hardcastles can find me and change my mind.

I'm going to leap off the ledge, and I don't give a damn what lies beneath.

I stick my key in the lock and push it open. A light switches on in the living room, to the right of the hall.

"Tiny, my dear."

My father-in-law steps through the archway into the entrance hall, followed by Dr. Keene, whose face hangs downward with professional regret.

"Thank God," says Mr. Hardcastle.

Caspian, 1964

The air was even colder than Cap imagined, as he stepped out through the screened porch to the soft sand. He wished maybe he'd stopped to make that coffee after all, but how could you make a decent cup of joe with no electricity, no hot water, and last year's leftover grounds crusted at the bottom of the can? They'd stop to eat on the way back out. There must be someplace convenient to eat breakfast between here and the Massachusetts Turnpike. They'd take the Mass Pike to Albany and consult a map. Whether to head in a southerly route or stick to the north. Mount Rushmore or the Grand Canyon.

He climbed up the dunes. His feet sank deep into the cold sand, numbing his skin. The sunrise had spread across the horizon now, gold-tipped pink against the washed-out sky, filling the beach with liquid new light. He searched for Tiny's blanketed shape at the edge of the surf, the small fog of her cigarette, but there was nothing there.

Just the ocean rolling in, wave after wave.

A surge of unreasonable panic overtook him: Could she swim? Had a rogue wave overtaken her somehow? Or had she walked in deliberately, weighed down by the woolen blanket, for some buried reason that Cap, in all the raw and tender discovery of last night, was unable to plumb?

But then he saw her footsteps, hollowed into the sand, heading to the right in a straight, purposeful line.

He scrambled over the crest of the dunes and down to the harder sand of the beach itself. And, yes, there she was, at the end of that long straight line of footsteps, standing now before the house that belonged to his grandmother, the Big House, the one that would pass down to his uncle Franklin and then to his cousin Frank, the heir apparent, future head of the family, who was getting married to a Park Avenue heiress in two or three weeks.

No doubt Tiny was familiar with houses like this, big shingled colonials with sun porches at either end and spacious terraces out back made of Connecticut bluestone. She could appreciate the multitude of chimneys, the elegant weathering of the shingles, the white-ribbed symmetry of the shutters. The understated scale of the place, so that you didn't quite realize how big it was until you walked through the front door and stood in the entrance, and the generous dimensions of hallway and stairway, of the drawing room (to the right) and the dining room (to the left) stretched out around you.

Not that his mother's house was shabby, not at all. It was spacious and polished, well upholstered and well equipped. More livable, really; more like a real family summered there, and not a public one. But nothing like the Big House, because his mother was only a daughter and Caspian only a lesser cousin.

Tiny stood before the Big House like a connoisseur, motionless, taking in every detail. She took in a last draw of her cigarette and dropped it into the sand next to her feet. The blanket had slipped below her shoulders, which were bare. He wanted to come up behind her and put his arms around her waist and kiss those bare shoulders, and then pull her into the sand and make love to her right there, on the blanket, in the sunrise.

But before he could reach her, Tiny herself turned in his direction, and the expression on her face startled him.

"What's the matter?" he called out.

"You knew!" she screamed. She clutched the blanket at her breast with both hands. "You *knew!*"

"Knew what?"

She let go of the blanket with one hand and gestured to the house. "Franklin's house! His grandmother's house! You *brought* me here! You brought me *back* to them! You're *one* of them!"

He planted his feet in the sand and stared at her, dumbfounded. The reddish strands in her hair, lit by the sunrise. The panicked width of her eyes. Her pale lips. He thought, I can make sense of this. I can figure this out.

"Did you think I wouldn't recognize this place, in the dark? Why didn't you just take me to Brookline and deliver me like a package?"

Brookline. Franklin. Grandmother.

Wedding. In two or three weeks, he couldn't remember exactly. At St. James's on Madison Avenue, reception to follow at the Metropolitan Club. To a well-bred girl from one of the best New York families.

To Christina Schuyler.

"How much did they pay you?" she screamed. "Did they give you permission to sleep with me first? Do they know about *that*, Caspian? Or is that our little secret?"

The pieces of sunrise broke apart from the sky and fell to the sand around him. Above the quiet roar of the ocean came a new noise, a different roar, that of a well-tuned engine revving its way carefully along a narrow road, and four tires crackling against the gravel.

Tiny shrugged the blanket back around her shoulders and turned her face to the circular drive before the Big House, half of which was just visible around the corner of the sun porch.

Cap followed her gaze to a bright yellow roadster, which rounded the end of the oval and stopped at the verge next to the ocean path. Without having laid eyes on it before, he knew the car belonged to Frank. Fast, sleek, elegant, well-bred. A suitable car for an heir apparent. For a prince in waiting.

But the figure that rose up from the driver's side didn't belong to Franklin S. Hardcastle, Jr. No flash of golden hair glinted in the sun, no broad white-shirted shoulders propped open the door. Instead the hair was dark, like Tiny's, and the shoulders were covered by a navy-blue jacket that Cap knew, without being close enough to see, was made of fine wool bouclé and trimmed in white.

"Tiny!" called Mrs. Schuyler, across the new dune grass and the untouched sand. "Thank God."

Mrs. Vivian Schuyler, 1966

The photograph on the front page of *The Boston Globe* is enough to rend your heart, if you have the kind of heart that isn't pickled in vodka and finished off with a squeeze of lime.

NO IMPROVEMENT YET IN CONDITION OF CANDIDATE'S WIFE, reads the sorrowful headline, and below it, poor Franklin Hardcastle, Jr., sits in a hospital waiting room, the really anodyne kind with the white walls and the beige plastic seats and the yellow plastic flowers. His blond head is cradled in his hands. His handsome face is craggy with worry. It looks as if some naughty newspaper photographer broke into the hospital wearing doctor's scrubs, and snapped the devastated Frank unawares, but Mrs. Vivian Schuyler of Fifth Avenue, New York City, knows better than that. She wasn't born yesterday. She flips right past the front page and keeps on going until she reaches the society column. The familiar names there are so reassuring. This is what's permanent. This you can count on.

The taxi makes an abrupt right turn. Mrs. Schuyler looks up—she's never troubled with motion sickness, not her—to find the neat white columns and tidy green lawn of the Woodbridge Clinic looming through the windshield. "Here already," she says. "What a clever fellow you are."

The driver grunts through his nose and stops under the porte cochere. Mrs. Schuyler hands him a worn ten-dollar bill and opens the door herself. A pair of flashbulbs explode nearby, but she's been expecting them, and doesn't flinch.

"Mrs. Schuyler! Mrs. Schuyler! Is there any update on your daughter's condition?"

She takes off her sunglasses and smiles vaguely at the men and their cameras. "I've just come to visit my daughter. I know as much as you do."

The portico is wide and clean, studded with trim potted boxwoods. Outside the shelter of the overhang, a few urns of scarlet geraniums soak up the August sunshine. The overall effect is one of precision and conspicuous good taste, the sort of place to which you could turn in relief when your well-bred daughter-in-law has a nervous breakdown, a fit of fashionable hysteria.

The driver places her small blue suitcase next to her feet. "Thank you," she says, and lifts it up. "No need to wait."

As she approaches the front door, the reporters fall back. No doubt they've been given a perimeter of decency to observe. From inside, she hears a faint pair of heated voices, not quite shouting. She puts her hand on the knob and swings it open, and another flashbulb pops over her shoulder.

The voices halt midargument. Mrs. Schuyler steps across the threshold, suitcase in hand, and looks from one astonished figure to the other, comely nurse and broad-shouldered visitor.

"Why, Major Harrison," she says. "What a lovely surprise."

A s Mrs. Schuyler expects, the private waiting room of the Woodbridge is furnished with considerably more luxury than the public one, and Major Harrison fills every inch of it.

"Do stop pacing," she says, taking out a cigarette. "I never figured you for the pacing type."

"I'm not." He stops and turns to her. A tasteful watercolor decorates the wall behind him, a beach at sunrise. The contrast between delicate beach and bristling soldier is almost too much to bear.

"I don't suppose you have a light," she says.

"They're not allowing visitors. I've been arguing myself hoarse with that damned nurse. They've got her in a room somewhere, and only Frank and his father are allowed in. And that doctor, Dr. Keene. Pepper's arguing with *him*. She talked her way past the nurse this morning and Keene had her thrown right back out."

"That's my girl." She finds the lighter in her pocketbook and puts her cigarette between her lips. Major Harrison bends forward and takes the silver Zippo from her hand and lights her cigarette absently, without thought. "Thank you," she says, just as absently.

He resumes his trailblazing on the Oriental rug. "I'm going crazy. They say they've had to sedate her, that she's not even coherent. Something's up, something's happened, and I can't figure out what. She called me two nights ago—"

"Called *you*?"

"Don't strain yourself. There's nothing going on. She trusted me, that's all. I'd finally won *that* back, at least." He braces his hands on his hips and speaks to the wall.

"Does her husband know?"

"What the hell am I supposed to say? *I was your wife's lover, the one she ran away with for the night, right before your wedding? The one she ditched to marry you, after all?*"

"And you still love her."

He sinks one hand in his short hair. "You have no idea."

Mrs. Schuyler finds the ashtray on the corner table, hiding in the lee of an enormous vase of fragrant yellow roses. "She didn't ditch you, Major Harrison. If that makes it any easier. During the drive back to Boston, she asked me if you'd known who she was, all along, and I said yes. I told her you'd already split for San Diego and left her to Frank." She shrugs. "All my fault."

She braces herself for an explosion of rage, but it doesn't arrive. Instead he sighs, puts his hand at the back of his neck, and shakes his head. "Yeah, I figured."

"Well, I thought I was doing the right thing. I thought it was for the best. I didn't know you from Adam, and I knew Frank and the Hardcastles, and I knew Frank loved her, really loved her, and I thought she'd be happy. That she'd found her true calling. Of all my girls, she was the one who could pull it off."

"So much for maternal instinct."

"Indeed." Mrs. Schuyler fills her lungs slowly and blows the smoke back out, taking time to think. Major Harrison shifts position to look out the window at the smooth green lawn, eyes keen, as if he's scouting out some disputed enemy territory. She drops her gaze to his legs and tries to remember which one is human and which is machine. She certainly can't tell from here. A strapping man, Major Harrison. Full of vengeful purpose right now, as still as marble, breathing in her smoke without a flinch. She can't blame Tiny for wanting him. Why *has* he come back, after all? Just to screw his cousin's wife again, or something more? What a mess, what a goddamned mess. She should have seen it coming. Tiny never was like her mother, was she? She can't just conduct a nice simple pleasant affair, no one gets hurt, no one's life turns upside down, no one gets dragged to the Woodbridge Clinic in the middle of a congressional campaign. "Do you have any idea what happened?" she asks. "When she called you the other night?"

"She was in Boston." He pauses and looks at her at last, green-eyed and livid, and even she, Mrs. Vivian Schuyler of Fifth Avenue in New York City, whose taste runs elegantly to Russian princes and other women's husbands, even *she* can't quite keep her bones from shivering.

Major Harrison continues. "Pepper says someone was blackmailing her, someone who'd gotten their hands on some photographs I'd taken two years ago—"

"Oh, for God's sake. You kept *photographs*?"

"These particular photographs I hadn't even developed. I'd mailed the film back to her, to her apartment on Dartmouth Street, just before I left for San Diego."

"Well, it so happens she never returned to that apartment, Major Harrison. She came straight back to New York with me until the wedding, and the movers boxed everything up and sent it to Newbury Street."

"I see. An inside job, then. It figures. This goddamned family."

Mrs. Schuyler leans back against the sofa and dangles her arm over the side. A pretty reproduction it is, a genuine imitation Chippendale, upholstered in green and smelling of old roses. The rest of the room follows suit. You might be in a Beacon Hill mansion, except that the furniture on Beacon Hill is the real deal, as old as ancestors. To be perfectly honest, Mrs. Schuyler is just beginning to prefer a cleaner look, herself. Just beginning to get a little impatient with the past, with all the old habits that have come so naturally before. She was born into a family much like the Schuylers—much like the Hardcastles, for that matter, at least the Hardcastles before Granny brought in all that lovely money—and she's slept on some century-old bed or another since the hour she was born. (At home, of course, because hospitals, like sexual fidelity, were terribly middle-class in those days.) "Don't worry," she says. "I can deal with the blackmail later. The point is, why did she break down? There must have been something, something specific."

"Frank was stepping out on her."

"Well, of course he was. Did she think he wouldn't?"

He makes a strange sound, a strangled groan, and whips around with astonishing agility to pound his fist against the wall. Not so hard that it goes through, but hard enough to make Mrs. Schuyler jump on her Chippendale cushion. He growls: "I could *kill* you all, sometimes. What you've done to her. All of you."

"Do you think I don't know that?"

"She just wanted to please you," he says. "She just wanted you to be proud of her. Just a little bit, that's all she asked."

"I was proud. I am proud." She turns away and stubs her cigarette into the tray, stubs and stubs, long after it's gone out and turned blurry in her eyes.

"It's my fault, too, I guess. I never fought back. I never should've let you drive away with her. I should've broken down the door." He looks up, toward the door of the waiting room, which is closed. "I should break down her door right now. I don't believe for a minute she's sick. They've taken her, Mrs. Schuyler. That doctor, Dr. Keene. Pepper says he was at Cape Cod the day before, trying to get her to go away with him. Tiny knows something, and they don't want her to talk."

"Knows what?" says Mrs. Schuyler, as innocently as she can, though her heart is beginning to jump now, her heart is launching into her throat at the words *They've taken her*.

What, exactly, does Tiny know?

Major Harrison is staring into his large hands, which fist and flex before him, like the primitive brute he is. Not that Mrs. Schuyler minds a little primitivism, now and again. "I don't know, exactly. But right before she left for Boston, she was asking me about—"

"About what?" Mrs. Schuyler untangles her long legs and leans forward on the sofa. "About what, Major Harrison?"

"There was an incident at Harvard, the year before she met Frank. Nobody ever talks about it. It was hushed up pretty fast. But I've had my suspicions."

Mrs. Schuyler spreads out her hands, palms down, and stares at her fingers. She's relieved to see they're not shaking. Her gloves are still on, her white cotton summer gloves that protect her complexion from the sunshine. Liver spots are so unseemly, such a telltale sign that one's not as young as one was. That one's charms are wearing as thin as one's aging skin. "Have you, now," she says quietly.

His shoes scrape against the floor. "Why? Do you know something?"

"I know a lot of things, Major. It's part of my job. Also"—she looks up—"I happen to be dear friends with the ex–Mrs. Franklin Hardcastle, Senior. Tiny's mother-in-law."

"Aunt *Liz?*"

"Oh, you know her name, do you? Yes, she was exiled to New York, as you'll recall. She lives a few blocks down. We have lunch. She's a lovely woman. A better woman than I am, not that I mean to damn her with faint praise, as the saying goes."

"Jesus Christ."

"Yes, so you see, I believe it's rather important that we——"

The door swings open and hits the opposite wall with a soft bang.

"Mrs. Schuyler!" exclaims Frank, darting across the rug to take her hand. At the same instant he touches her fingers, he notices Major Harrison standing next to the wall, tall and silent. His head swivels, not quite sure which to address first: Mrs. Schuyler's hand or his cousin. "Cap? What are you——" He looks back at Mrs. Schuyler. "I didn't know you knew each other."

"Oh, we go way back, the two of us," she says. "How are you, Frank? How's my daughter?"

"Better, I think. The sedatives seem to be working, thank God." He casts another glance at Major Harrison, a glance of weary curiosity. His skin is pallid, his eyes strained. Even his hair has given itself up to worry, lying lank and unpolished against his skull. "She was hysterical before. Hysterical, paranoid, trying to escape. The way she fought those orderlies, I couldn't believe it. She thinks Dr. Keene wants to murder her. I've never seen her like this. I don't know what to do."

Major Harrison makes a noise in his throat.

"I'm sorry." Frank shakes his head. "How do you know each other again? What's— Is something going on, here?"

Major Harrison swings his fist out sideways to meet the wall. "She's not sick! For God's sake! Don't you see what's happening? You're her husband, you're supposed to take *care* of her!"

A flush spreads over Frank's cheeks. "I *am* taking care of her! What the hell are you talking about? What the *hell* do you know about my wife?"

"More than you think!"

"What are you even *doing* here, Cap?" Frank turns to face his cousin and assumes an aggressive stance. His hands turn into fists.

Major Harrison says coldly, "I'm concerned for her. As her friend. As someone who knows what this family is capable of."

"And what the hell does *that* mean?"

Mrs. Schuyler rises. "Gentlemen. If you don't mind, I believe I'd very much like to visit my daughter."

Dr. Keene is very, very regretful. "I very much regret that Mrs. Hardcastle isn't in any condition to receive visitors." He waggles his unremarkable head back and forth.

"Nonsense," says Mrs. Schuyler. "This is not a parlor on Beacon Hill. She's not receiving *visitors*. I'm her mother, and I want to see her."

"That's not possible, I'm afraid." He rests his hand protectively on the doorknob behind him. He intercepted them only a moment ago, when Mrs. Schuyler was just inches from the door herself, and interposed his slim white-coated body between the two—door and woman—with expert grace, as if he's been accustomed to these sorts of maneuvers for all of his professional life.

Frank speaks up behind her in a reasonable voice, a politician's voice, smoothing the way for compromise. "Dr. Keene, surely we can allow Tiny's own mother to see her. The sedatives seem to have taken effect. She just wants to make sure Tiny's comfortable."

"A natural urge." Dr. Keene smiles. "But in these delicate psychiatric cases, we can't exercise too much caution. The slightest trigger can set off another episode. Mrs. Hardcastle needs the most absolute quiet right now."

Absolute quiet. You can hear it behind the door, a sepulchral absence of sound. Mrs. Schuyler thinks of her dream, a few nights ago, and a premonition rises up like bile in the back of her throat. She needs a drink to force it back down. Mrs. Schuyler has never liked silence, anyway; she's deeply mistrustful of people and places that make no noise at all. Sound is life. Silence is the opposite.

Absolute quiet is the absolute worst of all.

She pitches her chin at the old familiar angle and raises her eyebrow in the old familiar way. The actions help to keep her heart steady, her adrenaline in check. "Surely, Dr. Keene, we can bend the rules a teensy half-inch, don't you think? I'd be most grateful for even the smallest glimpse of my daughter. I promise I wouldn't disturb her, not a bit."

For an instant, the flicker of temptation touches his eyes. Then it's gone. "I'm sorry, Mrs. Schuyler. Perhaps in a day or two, when she's had a chance to rest. Not that I can make any sort of guarantee, in so serious a case as this."

"Listen here," growls Major Harrison.

Frank cuts him off. "Dr. Keene, as Mrs. Hardcastle's husband, I have the right to make decisions like this—"

"Actually, Mr. Hardcastle, and with all due respect," says Dr. Keene, still smiling, "that's not precisely true."

"Not true? How can it not be true? I'm a lawyer, Dr. Keene, and I know precisely what—"

"As a lawyer, then, Mr. Hardcastle, perhaps you should have taken a little more time to examine the admittance papers before you signed them." Dr. Keene releases the doorknob, removes his glasses, and wipes them with a handkerchief from his breast pocket. "Your father, who will be paying for her care here, has the power to make those decisions on her behalf."

"*What?*" says Frank.

"What the *hell*?" says Major Harrison.

"That's impossible," says Frank. "I want to see those papers. That's illegal and unconscionable, and I'll fight you all the way to court if I have to—"

But Major Harrison is already muscling his way past them all, lifting Dr. Keene away from the door as he might remove a potted plant from his path. He grabs the doorknob. It's locked. Without hesitation, he steps back, raises one leg, and releases a kick of pistonlike strength.

The wood splinters. The door flies open.

The room is empty.

From the look on Dr. Keene's face, he's as surprised as anybody. Mrs. Schuyler takes a grain of comfort in that thought.

Fleeting comfort, because in the next instant, he's running to a telephone in the hallway and picking up the receiver. She can't hear the words, though, because Frank is shouting in panic, and Major Harrison has grabbed her hand and tows her down the hall, the opposite direction, toward the back of the building.

Her shoes totter against the slick floor. She gasps out a question—*What on earth?* or *What in the devil?*, she's not sure—but it's lost in the scramble. They reach the end of the hallway, a T junction.

"You go that way, I'll go this," says the major. "Look for Pepper!"

"Pepper?"

"She's with Pepper! Trust me." He takes off down the left-hand hallway, and Mrs. Schuyler, too shocked to do anything but obey that commanding officer's voice, takes off her shoes and runs down the other. The passage is white and empty, lined with doors. Should she check any of them? What in the hell is she looking for, anyway?

Pepper. Pepper and Tiny.

And what does she do with them if she finds them?

She rounds an antiseptic corner and collides with a man's broad back.

The two of them tumble to the ground. The man grunts in surprise.

"I'm so terribly sorry," she begins, sarcasm at the ready, and the man turns his face toward her. His hair is graying, his eyes are blue. "Why, Franklin!"

"Vivian!"

His eyes dart to the nearest door, a few feet away. An image flashes back in Mrs. Schuyler's brain, the instant before she collided with him. He's got his hand on that knob, he's closing that door.

She turns her head. "Major!" she calls out.

"Quiet!" Franklin Hardcastle grabs her wrist.

"Take your *hand* off me!" she snaps, but for once in her life, a man doesn't obey her. Instead, he tightens his grip, he squeezes her slender wrist, and such is her fury at this ungentlemanly conduct, she jerks her hand away. She jerks with heroic force—she, Mrs. Vivian Schuyler of Fifth Avenue, who lunches at the Colony Club and shops at Bergdorf's—because her *daughters* are behind that door, she knows it in her blood, her *daughters*, and by God there is no cad on earth who can stop her from reaching them.

Hardcastle falls to the floor and lunges for her ankle. She raises her other hand, the one that still holds her shoe with the tall heel, and she bangs him on the head with it, as she might rap an impertinent dog with a newspaper.

In her maternal rage, she must have got him good, maybe found his eye with a righteous stiletto. He falls backward, and she reaches for the door and flings it open.

A small room appears before her, an office of some kind, and in the chair slumps a delicate-boned woman in a white nurse's uniform. Her head rests on the desk, cradled by her arms.

"Tiny!" Mrs. Schuyler darts forward, and something heavy crashes into her side. She sprawls to the floor.

"Mums?"

Mrs. Schuyler grabs her upper arm and looks up indignantly. "Pepper?"

"What are you *doing* here?" Her middle daughter, dressed improbably in a white nurse's uniform, drops a metal chair on the floor.

"Help me up, for God's sake! Is she all right?"

Pepper's hand closes around Mrs. Schuyler's upper arm, which is white with pain, and hauls her upward. "She's fine! She's just high. I don't know what the hell they gave her, but it doped her into seventh heaven. I found a couple of nurses' uniforms in the staff closet and managed to sneak into her room when they left with the drugs, the grand escape plan, but not soon enough. I had to drag her down the hallway, and fucking Hardcastle found us. Hit me, the bastard." She rubs her cheek.

Mrs. Schuyler rounds the corner of the desk and touches her daughter's white back. Behind them, the summer light strikes hard against the Venetian blinds. The room smells stuffily of old wood. "Tiny? Oh, darling. My God, that bastard——"

A thump interrupts her. Tiny lifts her head. "Mums?"

In the doorway, Hardcastle is struggling with someone, a broadshouldered someone, for whom he's no match at all. An instant later, he drops back to the floor. Major Harrison muscles past him and staggers around the desk to kneel in front of the floppy Tiny and take her hands. "Jesus. Is she all right? Tiny, talk to me."

"Caspian. Darling." She smiles. "Why are you so pink?"

He turns his head to Hardcastle, who has grasped the doorframe and is launching himself to his feet. "I'm going to fucking kill you," he says.

"Are you threatening me?" Hardcastle says.

"Right after I get her out of here, I will physically rip you apart——"

"And what are you going to do with her, hmm? You *can't* get her out of here. There are reporters everywhere. A guard in the lobby. She can't leave here without my signature."

Tiny turns her sleepy head to her father-in-law. "You, sir, are a jackass," she says, "and I want a—a what-do-you-call-it——"

"Divorce?" says Pepper.

Tiny smiles like an angel. "Yes! Divorce. And then I will kill you and feed you to Percy."

Mr. Hardcastle throws up his hands. "You see? She's gone straight out of her mind. She's staying right here."

Mrs. Schuyler straightens, pulls off her gloves, and fixes her eyes on the trickle of blood smearing the orbital bone of Hardcastle's left eye. "She hasn't gone out of her mind. She's fighting you back, you old bastard, and I'm proud of her."

"She's nuts, and she's staying right here."

"I'm her mother. I'll walk right out of here and explain to those reporters what you're doing, and, by God, your precious son will never be elected to so much as the sanitation board."

"No, you won't," he says. "Because if you *try* to take her, if you think for one instant you can remove my daughter-in-law from this clinic, you should know I've acquired a set of photographs from a certain young lady in the campaign office—"

"Dad?"

Hardcastle turns.

Frank stands in the hallway, just outside the door. His blue eyes are wide and white rimmed; his hand presses against the edge of the doorframe, as if it's the only thing holding him up.

"Frank—" Hardcastle begins.

"Dad, what's going on?" Frank's voice is calm, if a little higher-pitched than usual. A little uncertain, for once in his life, of the ground beneath him. "What do you mean, photographs? From *Josephine?*"

Hardcastle inhales long and loud: a parent about to explain things to an exceptionally young child. He speaks soothingly. "Your wife is sick, Frank. She's had a breakdown. She—"

"Is that true?" Frank shifts his gaze to Mrs. Schuyler, to Tiny, and to Major Harrison, who has risen to his feet and placed a protective hand on Tiny's shoulder. "Cap? Why are you here? Dad?" He turns back to his father. "Why *can't* we just take Tiny home now? Why do we need to lock her up here?"

"Son—"

"Tell me, Dad. Tell me what's going on here."

Pepper interrupts in a fury. "Oh, I'll tell you what's going on here, Frank Hardcastle," she says. Valiant Pepper. She's holding her cheek with one hand, her fierce heart in the other. The nurse's cap lies upside down on the floor, by her feet.

That cheek will need ice, Mrs. Schuyler thinks. Where are they going to find ice? She curls her arm around Tiny's shoulders, touching Major Harrison's hand on the other side. Her scarlet manicure against his neat soldierly fingernails. The premonition is rising again, but this time it doesn't taste like bile. It has a saltier taste, the taste of pity.

Pepper raises her other hand and stabs her finger in Frank's direction. "I'll tell you what's going on. Tiny told me herself, before they pinned her down and stuck that last syringe in her. You see, my big sister caught you doing it with your little boyfriend the other day—"

"*What?*"

"And I'll bet Daddy found out. I'll bet Daddy's having you followed. Aren't you, Daddy? I'll bet this Josephine reports to you, doesn't she?"

Nobody stirs. The sound of shock bounces from the walls and echoes about the furniture. Hardcastle's mouth is slack, grasping for a denial he can't quite seem to locate. The room has turned suffocating. In the heat, Mrs. Schuyler's silk stockings itch against her legs, not that you'd ever reveal a detail like that, at a time like this, and when your legs are perhaps your most alluring feature. Her hand moves to cover that of Major Harrison, coiled like a spring atop her daughter's tiny white shoulder. To keep him steady. Not to strike.

"Christ," whispers Frank. "Dad?"

"Son—"

"It's true, isn't it?"

"No, I—"

"Dad. Dad." Frank shakes his head. He looks at Tiny; he lifts his hands and stares at his palms like he doesn't recognize them. Across his face, the Venetian blinds form a horizontal pattern of sunshine and shadow. "My God," he says. "What have I done?"

The poor man, thinks Mrs. Schuyler. He can't even comprehend it. He's doesn't even know what this is, what it means, when the bill comes due.

Hardcastle's jaw moves. "Son, it's for your own good. Someone had to—"

Frank's right hand closes into a fist, which he swings with almighty force into his father's stomach.

"Go to hell," he whispers.

Hardcastle drops to his knees. Major Harrison starts forward, an officer's instinct, either to save him or to finish him off.

But Frank doesn't even glance at his father. He strides around the corner of the desk, where Tiny sits, straight-backed, her hands braced on the sides of the chair. The round nurse's cap tilts drunkenly onto her temple. Frank kneels before her and straightens it.

"Frank," she says. "Franklin. You hit him."

"I'm sorry," he says. "I'm so sorry."

"You're always sorry. But you don't mean it." She closes her eyes, as if the lids are too heavy. "You can all go to hell."

"I will," he says. "You can stick me there yourself. Just let me get you out of here first."

Mrs. Schuyler glances at Major Harrison, who's hauling up Hardcastle's defeated body by the collar. "I'm all right," the older man gasps.

A sliver of gray hair falls onto his cheekbone. He scrabbles for the hand holding his collar, but Major Harrison isn't letting go.

Mrs. Schuyler's fingers fall away from Tiny's shoulder. She takes a single step back, relinquishing command, and the sunshine on her dress feels delicious. Frank slides his arms tenderly around his wife's body and lifts her from the chair.

"What are you doing?" cries Hardcastle. He lunges toward them, hand outstretched, but Major Harrison jerks him back like a puppet.

"I'm taking her home." Frank doesn't look at his father. He doesn't look at anyone: not Mrs. Schuyler, not Pepper, not the anguished face of Major Harrison. Not even Tiny, nestled in his arms. Her eyes are closed anyway. He stares ahead, glassy and determined, his forehead pale with sweat. "I'm taking my wife home," he says, and he carries her small, sedated body past them all and through the door to the hallway beyond, and nobody moves to stop him. Nobody makes a sound. His footsteps clack deliberately down the linoleum, softer and softer, until they disappear around a corner.

Pepper looks at Major Harrison. "You're not going to stop them?"

He shakes his head. He looks as if someone has just inserted a metal claw into his chest and torn apart his rib cage, bone by bone. He bends to turn the fallen chair upright and throws his uncle into the seat.

Mrs. Schuyler, a little unsteady herself, eases her posterior into the chair Tiny has just vacated. She wants a cigarette, but she's left her pocketbook somewhere. She crosses her legs and drums her fingers on the desk to disguise the trembling.

"Mr. Hardcastle," she says, "I believe you said something about photographs."

The look he returns her is thick with hostility. "Yes, I did. Obscene ones, taken by some dirty photographer, and that little whore Josephine found them—"

"I took those photographs," says Major Harrison. "They're mine. I want them back."

"*You* took them?"

Major Harrison puts his hand back around the crumpled apex of Hardcastle's collar. The scar on his forehead shines white against his tanned skin. "I want them back, Uncle Franklin. Now."

"You took *those* photographs?"

"That's what I said."

There is a long, cold silence.

"You fucking bastard," Hardcastle says. "Your own cousin. You little—"

Harrison tightens his hand and leans down to Hardcastle's ear. "I *want* them *back*." He pronounces each word as if it deserves its own sentence.

"You bastard. You're not getting them back. And if Frank can't get his wife back under control, if she breathes a single word of any of this, if *any* of you do—"

Major Harrison jerks back on the collar. "I'll kill you. Do you think I won't? I'll hunt you down. I'll—"

"For God's sake," says Mrs. Schuyler. Her fingers have stopped trembling now, thank God. Maybe that was the trick. You didn't need a cigarette or a drink; you just needed to wait it out. "Enough of this ridiculous man talk. This nonsense about killing and hunting. You're making my head ache. Franklin, my dear, give the fellow back his photographs, please."

Hardcastle looks at her as if she's crazy. As if she's just commanded him to row down the Charles River in his tidy white briefs. His skin is really too flushed, she thinks. Drinks too much. It's a fine line between one too many, and just plain too much.

Trust her, she knows.

"You heard the lady," says Pepper. "Give her the snaps."

"And? I haven't got all day." Mrs. Schuyler taps her watch, the old gold Cartier her husband, Charles, gave her for Christmas, just after Tiny was born. Her favorite.

"I'm not going to give you the photographs, Vivian," he says. "You can threaten me all you like with your thugs—"

"Major Harrison is not my thug." She offers up a smile to the major's green-steel eyes. "Though he's welcome to the position, if he likes. There's always an opening."

"You're wasting your time," says Hardcastle, smooth-voiced and resonant. The Venetian stripes lie like prison bars against his skin. He's still bleeding from her stiletto, and Major Harrison holds him by the scruff of the neck, but he talks like he's won the game, like he's won the set and match. He talks like a world champion, like someone who doesn't know what it means to lose.

Ah, but that's not really true, is it?

He *does* know. He's lost before. A real heartbreaker.

Mrs. Schuyler smiles again, a different kind of smile. She wishes she could draw this moment out to an infinite length, that she could spend the rest of her life luxuriating in the anticipation of what comes next. After all, she's worked hard for it. Lunches here and cocktails there, friendly little favors performed and confidences shared and pathways smoothed, until she finally drew out what she wanted. She had what she needed. She had insurance.

Because you never know when you might need insurance, one fine August day.

"My dear Franklin," she says. "When was the last time you spoke to your ex-wife?"

He blinks. "My ex-wife?"

"We are such dear, dear friends, Liz and I." Mrs. Schuyler leans forward across the desk and takes Hardcastle's cold hand between her fingers. "In fact, she tells me everything. She told me, for instance, why her marriage ended. Such a sordid little story. I was appalled. And then she told me how much you had to give her to keep her mouth shut."

Hardcastle's face turns a slow shade of white.

To his left, Pepper bursts out into the brightest laughter. She leans her hip on the desk and laughs and laughs and laughs.

Tiny, 1966

When I saw Frank deliver that commencement address at Harvard, all those years ago, I knew he'd be president one day. I just knew. You could see his future lie about his shoulders like a mantle; you watched his destiny beam from his eyeballs. In the gleam of his teeth, you caught a flicker of elation. He spoke, and you flew into the air, carried along by the breath of his optimism, by his jaunty vigor, by the words that assured *You are good; we are greater; we can do this together.*

I remember how the sun shone down on his hair that day, the halo of promising gold, and I think of it now as I stand by his side on the ballroom stage at the Copley Plaza Hotel, gazing at him with all the rapture of a wife whose husband has just been elected representative of the 8th District of the Commonwealth of Massachusetts to the 90th Congress of the United States of America.

Below us, the audience of campaign donors and staffers and journalists and friends stands on its feet and beats a crescendo of triumphant applause. I can't see them very well; the lights are too bright on my face, the flashbulbs too blinding. The air is packed with cologne and cigarettes and nervous perspiration, and the orchestra behind us is playing "America the Beautiful," heavy on the trumpets, terribly stirring. Frank's hand squeezes mine, dry and confident. His jacket is off; his shirtsleeves are rolled up. He's just loosened the knot of his red silk necktie. It's half past ten at night, and Frank Hardcastle is ready to get down to business.

He looks down at me, smiles, and bends his head to kiss me on the lips. The audience roars. It's just the two of us up there, the brand-new congressman and his glossy wife. Frank's father wasn't invited. Josephine and Scott have left the campaign. (We made a deal, Josephine and me: I agreed not to prosecute her for blackmail, and Josephine agreed to donate her new diamond stud earrings to a charity auction for the families of wounded soldiers.) I'm wearing a patriotic liberty-blue cocktail dress and a pair of small pearl earrings. I've gained back most of the weight I lost in August, and I suppose I look a little more robust now, not quite as liable to be flung up into the power lines by a stray gust of early November wind.

"Thank you, darling," Frank whispers in my ear, and I return the squeeze of his hand.

He turns back to the audience and holds up his other hand, his right hand, the one that's not holding mine. The masses simmer down before us. Frank leans into the microphone. "Thank you," he says, and his voice is magnified, eight thousand times richer and more presidential than the thank-you he just delivered into my ear. Like he really means it. Thank you, everyone. Thank you for your support, for your belief in me. I couldn't have done it without you.

There is another surge of applause, and Frank holds up his hand to quell it. The flashbulbs pop against his forehead. His face contains just the right mixture of confidence and humility. Yes, you voted for me, you supported me; you wonderful folks, you; but I deserved it. I deserve your vote and your support, because I'm just a little bit better than you, aren't I? Smarter, more eloquent, better-looking. I'm Franklin Hardcastle, and I can solve the world's problems, if you'll just give me that chance, ladies and gentlemen.

And you know what? Maybe he can.

By the time Frank reaches the suite upstairs, I've already showered and changed out of my liberty-blue cocktail dress. The dewiness of my skin feels newly born. I haven't touched a drink tonight; no, not a sip of champagne, not a single stray puff from a sneaky cigarette. I want to be fresh and clearheaded. I want to remember every minute.

He says good night to the bodyguard (there is a bodyguard now) and his chief of staff (there is a chief of staff now) and closes the door behind him. His smile dims a little as he gazes at me. I rise from the edge of the bed, in all my glory.

"You were wonderful," I say. "I was so proud. I *am* proud. You did it."

"*We* did it." He walks up to me, takes my hand, and kisses it. His hair is still sleek and undisturbed; not a single lock falls forward. "I couldn't have done it without you. Thank you. I mean that."

"I told you I'd see it through to the election."

"You did. You're a trouper, Tiny." He kisses my hand again. "Every moment. Like that dress you wore tonight, I couldn't take my eyes off you, nobody could. You charmed them, you won them over. Like you were born for it."

His blue eyes drown me with admiration, and I bask in it, I really do, because how can you resist the admiration in Frank Hardcastle's blue eyes? When all that razzle-dazzle is focused straight on you, igniting your skin, bang kaboom. His other hand touches my waist, warm and secure, the way a husband touches his loyal wife at the end of a triumphant day, a landmark day, the day he's elected to national office by the people of Massachusetts.

I slip my fingers out of his grip and step away. His hand falls to his side.

"But I'm not, Frank. I *wasn't* born for it. I wasn't born for you. We both know that."

Frank closes his eyes and sighs toward the carpet.

I say, "I'm sorry. I made a mistake, that's all. I thought I was one thing, and it turned out I was another. A better thing, I like to imagine."

"Well, I wish I could have changed your mind. I wish I could have deserved you."

"Frank, it's not me you have to deserve. It's *them*, the people who elected you. I promised I wouldn't serve the papers until after the election, and I kept that promise. So now it's your turn. You have two years to prove that you're the only thing that matters, that you can be who you are and still do the job they've given you. Two years. My gift to you, for doing the right thing and sticking up for me in that clinic. And now I'm sticking up for myself."

He opens his eyes and takes my hand again, the left hand. He studies the empty space, where my wedding ring used to sit, until half an hour ago. The welt is still there, a little red. I catch the scent from his clothes, the gentle waft of cigarettes from the ballroom downstairs.

"I'm grateful," Frank says. "You didn't have to do that for me, after what my family did to you. What I did to you."

"I did, though. I had to square it with myself, that's just the way I am. I don't want to look back and regret anything. What if you go on to do some good? To make history? Because you can, you know. You have that power, you're one of those people. You were born with a rare set of talents. And I can't go through life wondering whether my mistakes—ours—might somehow have made the world a lesser place."

"I keep thinking . . ." He pats my hand between his. "I keep thinking, I can't help it, if only we'd had that baby, after all. You know what I mean? Because if you had a baby—"

"You would still be the same person, Frank. A baby wouldn't have changed *you*. It would only have changed me."

"But maybe we would have tried harder to make it work. Don't you think? If we had a baby counting on us, on the two of us."

"But we didn't, Frank. We lost that chance. So I have no one to act for except myself, and this is how I choose to act. I choose to leave you."

He still holds my left hand, not quite ready to give me up. His eyes are soft and pleading, in a way that's become familiar to me, over the past few painful months of confession and remorse and resolve. His and mine. The new Frank, replacing the old. Or maybe it's just the old Frank, the *real* Frank, emerging beneath the one I married. I hope so, anyway. I hope he emerges from this a better man, a man of integrity, the man I kept glimpsing but couldn't find. I hope he doesn't waste this parting gift of mine.

"There's nothing I can do to change your mind?" he says.

"There's nothing you can do. I can't ask you to be someone you're not. I hope you won't expect *me* to become someone I'm not."

"I do love you, Tiny. It was never that. The honest truth, I love you more than ever. I just wish—"

I rise on my toes and kiss him on the cheek. "I love you, too, Frank. I love you the same way you love me. And I wish you all the best, and if there's anything I can do for you, even after the divorce, I'll do it. I'll stand by you. I'll always support you."

He lets go of my hand, and his arms fall around my waist. The room is dark, only a single lamp lit, and we stand there quietly, husband and wife for the last time, embracing in the pool of gentle yellow light. And I think, this is good. This is how it should be. All partings should be like this.

Fifteen minutes later, I'm driving along the highway in my Cadillac, driving with the top down. The moon is cold and hard above me, not quite full, and the wind smells of frost. I huddle inside my thick wool coat and sing along to Dusty Springfield on the radio.

You know, it wasn't that bad. At the time, I thought I hated it, the stages and speeches and lights, the pop of unceasing flashbulbs, the parsing of words for reporters, the endless bland phrases. I hated getting up and knowing I had a schedule of events ahead of me, a long day of glossiness. But there were good moments. Talking to people. Laughing with that waitress at the diner in Wellesley, sharing coffee with that housewife who knits beautiful woolen scarves while the kids are at school, to make a little extra on the side. I bought one myself. I'm wearing it now. I hope she buys herself a treat with the money, but she'll probably get a new winter coat for the oldest boy, sixth grade, who's growing like bamboo. That's what women do.

Because you learn things when you talk to people, especially people who aren't like you. You learn what a goddamned polyglot race we are, we marvelous human beings. Some people are friendly, some people are gruff. Some want security, others want independence. Some want the government to run things; some want to run things on their own. Some people need a helping hand, some people need a kick in the pants. Some want to live and die in the same small town; some want to ramble the wide world. Some are content with little; some cannot stop striving. Some want to lie beside a true love, to worship a single god; some crave a universe of loves, a universe of gods. I could go on and on, the differences between them, between me and you, between you and the woman sitting next to you at the hairdresser, wearing that dress you'd never wear in a million years, reading that book you wouldn't touch. The genius of politics, of people like Frank, is to link them all, understand them all. To represent them all, not just the ones you agree with. The ones who think and act like you do.

I don't know. I couldn't do it. But it was interesting, all the same. I'm just glad it's over. This time, for good.

At one o'clock in the morning, the highway is frozen and deserted. It's just me and Dusty, holdin' and squeezin'. I can drive as fast as I like, and I do. I race along the acres of bitter pavement as if the past itself is chasing me. The roar of the engine vibrates my marrow; the rush of speed lightens my veins. The salt wind invades my wool hat and numbs my ears. My eyes water a few cold tears. I almost wish I could keep driving forever, that I could draw this moment out to an infinite length. That I could spend the rest of my life luxuriating in the antici-pation of what comes next.

At last I round the corner of the drive, and the porch lights illu-minate the trees. I'm not cold anymore. My blood is as light as air. A tall figure crosses the glow of the headlamps. He's opening up the car door almost before I've stopped. He reaches inside, sets the brake with one hand, and lifts me up with the other. He places me carefully on the hood. Percy bays for joy at our feet.

"You waited up," I say.

"You think I could sleep?"

We kiss and kiss while the engine runs; we kiss as if kisses are going out of business. As if a new shipment of kisses has finally arrived, after two and a half years of empty shelves and rationing. Caspian's warm mouth melts away the coldness in mine. He sinks into the driv-er's seat, drawing me on his lap, and shuts off the engine. His fingers touch my cheek, my chin, as reverently as a pilgrim before his idol.

"Let's go inside," he says.

The electricity is off for the winter. Caspian's made a fire in the living room and brought in blankets and pillows. *It's not the Ritz,* he says, pulling me down, and *I don't need the Ritz,* I say, cradling his face in my hands, *I just need you.* He says, *And a nice hot fire?* and I say, *Well, that's lovely too.* And then we stop talking, because while we've seen each other regularly at campaign events, he in his uniform and I in my tweed suits and heels, we haven't held each other, we haven't kissed each other in two and a half years, and you can't find any words to describe a longing that deep. You can't find any words to explain what it means when you hold him and kiss him at last.

Afterward, I get up and make cocoa on the gas stovetop in the kitchen, so Caspian doesn't have to strap his leg back on. I settle in the crook of his shoulder and think what a pleasure it is, to make midnight cocoa for Caspian while he stretches himself like a wounded lion before the fire and watches me come and go. To hand him his mug, which he accepts gratefully, without any awkward shame. Percy, curled up on a square of red wool blanket next to the hearth, lifts his head from his forelegs, and I swear he smiles at us.

"Did you think I wouldn't come, after all?" I say.

"No, I knew you would come. I just didn't believe it until I saw the headlights."

I love his smell. I love the warmth of his skin beneath my cheek, the solidity of bone and muscle, the safe and soundness of him.

"Is Pepper still here?" I ask.

"She left today. She's driving to Boston and loading it on the car train to Palm Beach, for the auction."

"How does the car look?"

"Amazing." He shakes his head. "I almost cried when she drove it off. The sound of that engine. I'll hear it in my dreams. Loved that car like my own soul."

"Almost as much as you love me?"

"It's a close call." He squints his eyes at the ceiling. "But, yes. Almost as much as I love you."

I set down my mug, half-finished, and kiss him again, and again we make love in the blankets, next to the fire, and by three o'clock in the morning, all the drapery is parted, all layers shed, and the nakedness is as good as I dreamed. Maybe better. He stays inside me and holds my hair in his hands, and he says, "I have a question. But you don't have to answer it."

"Mmm." I'm almost asleep. How could you not fall asleep, as warm and sated as that, as stretched and full, still throbbing deliciously in all your nooks and crannies? Anyway, I can't imagine what question can possibly still lie between us. Like sweethearts separated by war, we've written to each other every day, we've explained and teased and vowed. Haven't we already dragged all our furniture into the sunshine?

He fills his palms with my hair, empties them, and fills them again. Weighs and measures me. "When I heard . . ."

"Yes?"

"When I heard you lost a baby. That September."

We lie on our sides, still connected. The firelight curls over his skin. I wrap my leg more securely around his hip. "No," I say.

"No, it wasn't mine?"

"No. I would never have done that. I've made a lot of mistakes, God knows. But I wouldn't have married Frank if I'd been carrying your baby."

The fire pops behind me. I stare at the hollow of Caspian's throat and wonder what he's thinking. Whether he's grieved, or relieved.

Whether he wanted that baby, or not. Whether he—like me—is pondering the mysterious workings of biology, the possible inadequacies of my womb. Calculating our odds. Speculating what joy or hope or heartache still lies before us.

And he has already lost so much.

"I want to give you everything," I say. "Everything you deserve. I don't know what I'll do if I'm not enough."

Caspian doesn't tell me not to feel that way. He doesn't tell me to be someone I'm not. Instead, he kisses my forehead and lifts himself up. He reaches out for one of the blankets and tucks it around us. The wool is thick and warm, a Black Watch plaid scented by decades of cedar. He gathers me back into his arms, facing the fire, and rests his chin on the top of my head.

"It's going to be all right," he says. "We're going to be all right."

When I wake up, the fire is out and Caspian is gone. The room is filled with a slow gray light, the birth of dawn. I slide my hand into the hollow beside me, and I wish I could trap the trace of sacred warmth that remains there, to capture it in my flesh so I'll never be cold again.

I call out Caspian's name, but my voice isn't working properly yet, and the word only travels a few feet. Well, never mind. It's hot and lovely underneath this immense weight of plaid blankets—there must be four or five of them, and I close my eyes and imagine Caspian layering them anxiously over me before he left—and besides, he'll be back here soon. I'll just sleep a little longer. God knows I need it, after a night like that.

But there's no undoing the dawn, is there? My mind tingles behind my closed eyes. I can hear the distant trickle of pipes, a muffled thump or two, the scratch of Percy's loyal claws against the wooden floor, as Caspian readies the house and loads the car. Night has spun out, and we'll be leaving soon, and haven't I been waiting for this departure all autumn? All my life?

I open my eyes and push back the covers. The air freezes against my skin. I rise to my feet, gather a blanket around me, and pad softly across the living room to the terrace door.

Outside, the world is gray and new and ice-cold, and the ocean is quiet. The sand numbs my feet. I tuck the blanket closer and watch the gentle white-tipped tide, the empty shore. The Hardcastle cousins are back at work and home and school, building the future. The footballs and sailboats and cocktails have been put away until next summer. Even Tom is back at work in his cramped office at Tufts, finishing up his folk studies, while Constance keeps house and swallows her happy pills. I rise to my toes, because the sand is so cold and because I want to dance, dance.

The extravagant motion of my legs keeps parting the blanket, shocking me with cold, making me shiver, but I keep going anyway. I fight back. When I see Caspian's tall figure crossing the terrace toward me, Percy dogging his heels, I finish off with a series of high-legged fouettés, just showing off. His smile is wide when he reaches me. "You're nuts," he says.

"I'll bet it turned you on."

"Sure did."

He's carrying another blanket in one hand and a pair of coffee mugs in the other. He hands me the coffee and draws me up into his arms, facing the ocean, and he wraps the blanket around us both. The coffee is hot and strong. I sip it slowly.

"You were up early," I say.

"I couldn't wait any longer."

"Car's all packed?"

"Whenever you're ready, Tiny."

His arms are thick, his voice is steady. After a minute or two, the shivering melts away, and only my feet are cold. Percy settles on them with a sigh. We stand there wrapped in a shared blanket, drinking coffee, not saying anything.

Waiting for the wondrous day.

Pepper, 1966

The Florida sun sits in her bones, and Pepper Schuyler doesn't want to move. Doesn't want to flick a single fingertip, in case she might disturb the cocoon of heat that surrounds her.

Funny, you're supposed to get all hot and bothered when you're pregnant, aren't you? Pepper's sure she heard that somewhere, that your body temperature rises by a degree or two, or something like that. Well, she feels the opposite. She hasn't been warm, really *warm*, since August. As if the greedy little fetus inside her is sucking up all the heat and energy she can possibly manufacture, leaving nothing for poor, elegant Pepper to live on.

"Mrs. Schuyler?"

Pepper cracks open a reluctant eyelid.

The white-jacketed attendant doesn't look pleased to see her. "Mrs. Schuyler," he says again, in a way that implies he isn't fooled by the *Mrs.*, not one little bit. Maybe it's the absence of a ring on her finger. Anyway, even worse: "There is a gentleman to see you."

"A gentleman?" Pepper opens the other eye. Her heart smacks against her ribs, *gathump gathump*. "What does he look like?"

The attendant frowns at her moxie. Moxie is not a quality to be admired within the pale-walled sanctuary of the Breakers, even when the sun pours down and the cocktails are served. "He is of medium height, madam, wearing a blue suit and carrying a briefcase."

Pepper nibbles her lip. The attendant is quite tall. "What color were his eyes?"

"I'm afraid he was wearing sunglasses."

"What color was his hair?"

"Gray, I believe." The attendant's eyes shift for just an instant to the gentle golden summit of Pepper's belly, rising between the two halves of her pink bikini.

Pepper releases a long sigh.

"He insisted the matter was of pressing urgency, Mrs. Schuyler, or I wouldn't have bothered you." The attendant's eyes return to her face, carefully bland.

Pepper reaches for her robe. "All right."

She rinses off her feet at the edge of the beach and slips on her Jack Rogers sandals. She stops at the front desk to see if she has any messages. "Just one," says the clerk, handing her slip of paper. "A telephone call."

Pepper squints at the brief white square and crumples it in her palm. "Thank you."

By the time she's changed into her green Lilly shift—two sizes bigger than her usual and one of the only things she can fit into at the moment, short of some hideous maternity tent—and made her way to the porch, the gentleman's brow is damp with perspiration, and his fingers are tapping with impatience around his trickling lowball glass. He rises quickly to his feet and removes his sunglasses. "Mrs. Schuyler?" he says, glancing at the dancing green monkeys that stretch across the middle of her dress.

"You've found me." She holds out her hand.

"I'm Daniel Thorne. From the auction company."

His palm is damp. She withdraws quickly. "Oh, of course! Have you seen the car? Is anything wrong?"

Mr. Thorne motions to the wicker armchair opposite. Pepper settles into the cushion and crosses her long legs. At least she still has her legs, even if the rest of her has gone to hell. Big belly, big breasts. Even her cheekbones are starting to disappear. Thank God there's plenty of cheekbone to spare.

"Nothing's wrong. Nothing's wrong at all. Quite the opposite, actually. We were all stunned when the vehicle was delivered. Everything we'd dreamed. Really a most remarkable—er . . ." He trails off, distracted by her stomach. What is it with people? Pepper wants to scream: *It's a baby, for God's sake, it's just a baby, we all started out like this!*

"Yes, I know," she says. "Really remarkable."

"And the provenance."

"Fascinating, isn't it? It took us some time to find the papers, as you know, but I think everything's in order now."

"Yes. The law is quite clear on the subject of abandoned property. There's no difficulty there, I assure you." He takes a drink and pats his forehead with his handkerchief.

"So what *is* the difficulty, Mr. Thorne? Or have you interrupted my afternoon sunbathing just to congratulate me?"

He drops yet another panicked glance to her belly. "Congratulate you?"

"On the car, Mr. Thorne." Pepper smiles and gazes longingly at the drink in his hand, which perspires luxuriously onto his fingertips.

"Oh, yes. Of course. The thing is, Mrs. Schuyler, we've had an offer for the car."

"An offer? But the auction isn't until Saturday."

"Sometimes, in the case of an automobile this special, we receive private offers before the public sale. A sort of preemptive strike, when the buyer is particularly keen."

"Oh, really? From whom?"

"The buyer wishes to remain anonymous. She's made the offer through her lawyer."

"She?"

"A woman, yes. That's all we know." He finishes the drink and reaches into the inside pocket of his jacket. "The offer is substantial. I don't mind saying it's the most generous offer we've ever received."

"Well, it's an extraordinary car."

"Indeed it is." He hands her a folded piece of paper. "But I think you'll agree, a number like this is hard to pass up."

Pepper accepts the paper between her manicured forefinger and her manicured middle finger. She unfolds it, stretches out her arm until the ink stops swimming, and reads all the zeros.

"Jesus Christ," she says.

Mr. Thorne laughs. "That's what I said."

Pepper stares and stares. She squints and holds the paper a bit farther away, just to be sure. Three hundred thousand dollars.

Take the car and sell it, Tiny said. *It's yours. Sell it and start your new life. They won't dare object. Mums has them by the balls.*

But three hundred thousand dollars? Who on earth would pay three hundred thousand dollars for a car, a hunk of metal and leather, no matter how extraordinary? A woman, Mr. Thorne said. A woman who wants to remain anonymous. A woman who has that kind of money to throw around, she might be anyone. She might be pulling a trick of some kind. She might have her own reasons, just like Pepper has hers.

Pepper reads the number again, zero by promising zero, taking her loving time with each one. Three hundred thousand dollars. You could start a hell of a new life, you could go somewhere and raise a baby in the sunshine, somewhere no one could find you. You could become an entirely new woman, the woman you maybe always wanted to be.

Or it might be someone's way of paying you off, when you've refused to be paid off, again and again. Someone's way of keeping you delicately under his thumb, safe and sound.

Between the columns of the long Breakers porch, the ocean gathers and crashes. The surf is busy today. The tide is on the point of turning.

She looks back up at Mr. Thorne's sweating face.

"I accept."

ACKNOWLEDGMENTS

In *The Secret Life of Violet Grant*, Vivian Schuyler dismisses her oldest sister in a few lines: "Neither of us could politely stand Tiny, who by the grace of God had married her Harvard mark last June, and now lived in a respectably shabby house in the Back Bay with a little Boston bean in her righteous oven. God only knew how it got there."

As soon as I wrote that paragraph, I knew that perfect little Tiny was hiding a very big secret, and that my next book would be about her. I am enormously grateful for the entire team at Putnam who not only went along with this impulse, but cheerfully encouraged it to fruition. Many thanks to Chris Pepe and Laura Perciasepe, editors extraordinaire, for their enthusiasm and expert advice, and to Ivan Held for his eternal commitment to putting our best book forward. I can't say enough about publicity and marketing wizards Katie McKee, Mary Stone, and Lydia Hirt, who make every release seem like the only book in the world, and to Meaghan Wagner, who keeps everybody on the same page. You are the unsung heroes, and I appreciate your passion more than I can say.

Special thanks are due to my crack team of author buddies, who have made my life so much richer, and who have offered cheers, advice, and commiseration in perfect measure. Karen White, Lauren Willig, Eloisa James, Linda Francis Lee, Bee Ridgway, Susanna Kearsley, and all you other dearies, near and far: I love your talent and your kindness, and most especially how they exist side by side.

I couldn't write and remain sane without the love and support of my family and friends, and most especially that of my husband, Sydney, who thinks every book is my best one yet.

No words are sufficient to describe how my literary agent, Alexandra Machinist of ICM, supports my books at every single step of the journey. I don't know what benevolent hand led me to try my luck with her five years ago with the manuscript of *Overseas*, but I've never once regretted placing my dreams in her hands. She is the best of the best.

Finally, to the booksellers, librarians, bloggers, and readers who have taken my books to their hearts and their bedside tables: a thousand thanks. It's an honor to live on your shelves. Please keep in touch.

Tiny Little Thing

BY BEATRIZ WILLIAMS

DISCUSSION QUESTIONS

1. The novel is structured almost like a conversation between Tiny and Caspian, with alternating chapters in the present (Tiny) and past (Caspian). However, Caspian's chapters are written in third person, while Tiny's are written in first person. Why do you think the author chose to write the novel in this manner? How does this affect how you connect to each of the characters?

2. From the moment she appears in the novel, Pepper is presented as the opposite of Tiny. Pepper says what she thinks, and men lust after her perfect body: "Nature's just devious that way, giving Pepper all the sex appeal, as if to lock us in our preordained places and watch, breathless, to see if we can break loose." Throughout the novel we learn about Tiny's struggle to break loose from her shell as the perfect obedient wife, but in what ways might Pepper be stuck, too? Is she just as trapped in this role nature gave her as Tiny is in hers?

3. We learn early on that Tiny dislikes having her photograph taken, and yet photography plays a pivotal role in both narratives. Why

do you think Tiny has an aversion to being photographed? What did you think of her description of the photo call at the fund-raiser, and how it affected her? How does this compare to her photography sessions with Caspian? Why do you think the author made photography such a central issue, given the historical context of the book?

4. Frank appears to be the perfect husband, but he of course has a secret. Do you feel sorry for Frank at all? Is he a pawn in his family's games, a victim of sorts, or is he just as driven as the rest of the Hardcastles to achieve political success and power no matter whom he hurts?

5. When Tiny realizes that her husband is cheating on her, she loses her cool and finds it completely unacceptable. However, Granny Hardcastle implies that Tiny did know, or at least should have known, what she was signing up for when she agreed to marry a politician. Do you think Tiny did in fact know what she was getting into when she married Frank, and if so does she have any right to be angry about the life she chose?

6. We see signs of Tiny rebelling against her in-laws early in the novel with acts as small as adding a splash of vodka to her lemonade. But at what point do you think she turned a corner, admitting to herself that the life she chose isn't what she dreamed it would be?

7. When Tiny is younger, her father gives her love advice: "You want to be happy? Marry a man who can take you places. Marry a man you can be proud of, a man with a future ahead of him. A woman's never happy if she can't respect her husband." This is the sort of

advice a young woman might expect to hear from her mother, but perhaps not from her father. How does the meaning behind such advice on love change when it is coming from a man's perspective?

8. When Tiny reflects on Frank's and other politicians' charisma and "razzle-dazzle," she says, "you might call it artificial, a masquerade, but really it isn't. The mask is part of the person. That's why it's so compelling." Do you agree with this statement? Is the "mask," the face someone puts on for the world, part of the person? Can you never fully take it off?

9. Caspian is a soldier, but he is also a photographer. What do you think this hobby says about his character and his ambitions?

10. When Pepper arrives in Cape Cod, Tiny is skeptical that they will get along. However, as they spend more time together, they become closer and Tiny begins to feed off of Pepper's confidence and outspoken nature. Do you think that Tiny would have had the courage to break free from the Hardcastles if Pepper had not come to Cape Cod?

11. In the end, Frank keeps his wife by his side through the election, and Tiny lives happily ever after with Caspian. Do you think that all of the characters got what they deserved in the end? Why or why not?

12. Tom makes it very clear at the Hardcastle dinner table that he opposes the war, and by extension everything Caspian stands for. Tom is a character we are meant to despise, but do you admire him at all for speaking out against the Hardcastles? Further, what

similarities do you see between Tiny and Tom, two characters who married into the Hardcastle family?

13. By the end of the novel, do you think Tiny has completely rid herself of her "good girl" personality as she embarks on a life with Caspian? Do you think it's possible for a person to fully shed a defining characteristic like that, or is it too ingrained?

14. Granny Hardcastle is a force to be reckoned with. She has strong opinions about the supporting role Tiny needs to play in her family as Frank's wife, yet she is an independent and outspoken woman. Do you think Granny Hardcastle is to be admired in some respects, or is she simply a villain?

15. Toward the end, Vivian and Pepper claim their own chapters in a novel that until this point revolved around Tiny and Caspian. Why do you think the novel breaks its pattern and shifts its focus to these characters for the final scenes?

16. At the very end, Pepper accepts an offer for the car she restored with Caspian and Tiny. Who do you think this mystery buyer is and why did Pepper accept the offer? Is she simply submitting to the same manipulative power structure that Tiny fought to escape, or does she have a strategy of her own? Why do you think the author left her fate so ambiguous?

Read on for a sneak preview of
the next captivating novel from Beatriz Williams

ALONG THE INFINITE SEA

Available now from Putnam

Overture

"To see all without looking;
to hear all without listening."

CÉSAR RITZ
King of Hoteliers, Hotelier of Kings

Annabelle

All you really need to know about the Paris Ritz is this: by the middle of 1937, Coco Chanel was living in a handsome suite on the third floor, and the bartender—an intuitive mixologist named Frank Meier—had invented the Bloody Mary sixteen summers earlier to cure a Hemingway hangover.

Mind you, when I arrived at Nick Greenwald's farewell party on that hot July night, I wasn't altogether aware of this history. I didn't run with the Ritz crowd. Mosquitoes, my husband called them. And maybe I should have listened to my husband. Maybe no good could come from visiting the bar at the Paris Ritz; maybe you were doomed to commit some frivolous and irresponsible act, maybe you were doomed to hover around dangerously until you had drawn the blood from another human being or else had your own blood drawn instead.

But Johann—my husband—wasn't around that night. I tiptoed in through the unfashionable Place Vendôme entrance on my brother's arm instead, since Johann had been recalled to Berlin for an assignment of a few months that had stretched into several. In those days, you couldn't just flit back and forth between Paris and Berlin, any more than you could flit between heaven and hell; and furthermore, why would you want to? Paris had everything I needed, everything I loved, and Berlin in 1937 was no place for a liberal-minded woman nurturing a young child and an impossible rift in her marriage. I stayed defiantly in France, where you could still attend a party for a man named Greenwald, where anyone could dine where he pleased and shop and bank where he pleased, where you could sleep with anyone who suited you, and it wasn't a crime.

For the sake of everyone's good time, I suppose it was just as well that my husband remained in Berlin, since Nick Greenwald and Johann von Kleist weren't what you'd call bosom friends, for all the obvious reasons. But Nick and I were a different story. Nick and I understood each other: first, because we were both Americans living in Paris, and second, because we shared a little secret together, the kind of secret you could never, ever share with anyone else. Of all my brother's friends, Nick was the only one who didn't resent me for marrying a general in the German army. Good old Nick. He knew I'd had my reasons.

The salon was hot, and Nick was in his shirtsleeves, though he still retained his waistcoat and a neat white bow tie, the kind you needed a valet to arrange properly. He turned at the sound of my voice. "Annabelle! Here at last."

"Not so very late, am I?" I said.

We kissed, and he and Charles shook hands. Not that Charles paid the transaction much attention; he was transfixed by the black-haired beauty who lounged at Nick's side in a shimmering silver-blue dress that matched her eyes. A long cigarette dangled from her fingers. Nick turned to her and placed his hand at the small of her back. "Annabelle, Charlie. I don't think you've met Budgie Byrne. An old college friend."

We said *enchantée*. Miss Byrne took little notice. Her handshake was slender and lacked conviction. She slipped her arm through Nick's and whispered in his ear, and they shimmered off together to the bar inside a haze of expensive perfume. The back of Miss Byrne's dress swooped down almost to the point of no return, and her naked skin was like a spill of milk, kept from running over the edge by Nick's large palm.

Charles covered his cheek with his right hand—the same hand that Miss Byrne had just touched with her limp and slender fingers— and said that bastard always got the best-looking women.

I watched Nick's back disappear into the crowd, and I was about to tell Charles that he didn't need to worry, that Nick didn't really look all that happy with his companion and Charles might want to give the delectably disinterested Miss Byrne another try in an hour, but at that exact instant a voice came over my shoulder, the last voice I expected to hear at the Paris Ritz on this night in the smoldering middle of July.

"My God," it said, a little slurry. "If it isn't the baroness herself."

I thought perhaps I was hallucinating, or mistaken. It wouldn't be the first time. For the past two years, I'd heard this voice everywhere: department stores and elevators and street corners. I'd seen its owner in every possible nook, in every conceivable disguise, only to discover that the supposed encounter was only a false alarm, a collision of deluded molecules inside my own head, and the proximate cause of the leap in my blood proved to be an ordinary citizen after all. Just an everyday fellow who happened to have dark hair or a deep voice or a certain shape to the back of his neck. In the instant of revelation, I never knew whether to be relieved or disappointed. Whether to lament or hallelujah. Either way, the experience wasn't a pleasant one, at least not in the way we ordinarily experience pleasure, as a benevolent thing that massages the nerves into a sensation of well-being.

Either way, I had committed a kind of adultery of the heart, hadn't I, and since I couldn't bear the thought of adultery in any form, I learned to ignore the false alarm when it rang and rang and rang. Like the good wife I was, I learned to maintain my poise during these moments of intense delusion.

So there. Instead of bolting at the slurry word *baroness*, I took my deluded molecules in hand and said: *Surely not.*

Instead of spinning like a top, I turned like a figurine on a music box, in such a way that you could almost hear the tinkling Tchaikovsky in my gears.

A man came into view, quite lifelike, quite familiar, tall and just so in his formal blacks and white points, dark hair curling into his forehead the way your lover's hair does in your wilder dreams. He was holding a lowball glass and a brown Turkish cigarette in his right hand, and he took in everything at a glance: my jewels, my extravagant dress, the exact state of my circulation.

In short, he seemed an awful lot like the genuine article.

"There you are, you old bastard," said Charles happily, and *sacré bleu*, I realized then what I already knew, that the man before me was no delusion. That the Paris Ritz was the kind of place that could conjure up anyone it wanted.

"Stefan," I said. "What a lovely surprise."

(And the big trouble was, I think I meant it.)

First Movement

"Experience is simply the name
we give our mistakes."

Oscar Wilde

Pepper

PALM BEACH • 1966

1.

The Mercedes-Benz poses on the grass like a swirl of vintage black ink, like no other car in the world.

You'd never guess it to look at her, but Miss Pepper Schuyler—that woman right over there, the socialite with the golden antelope legs who's soaking up the Florida sunshine at the other end of the courtyard—knows every glamorous inch of this 1936 Special Roadster shadowing the grass. You might regard Pepper's pregnant belly protruding from her green Lilly shift (well, it's hard to ignore a belly like that, isn't it?) and the pastel Jack Rogers sandal dangling from her uppermost toe, and you think you have her pegged. Admit it! Lush young woman exudes Palm Beach class: What the hell does she know about cars?

Well, beautiful Pepper doesn't give a damn what you think about her. She never did. She's thinking about the car. She slides her gaze along the seductive S-curve of the right side fender, swooping from the top of the tire to the running board below the door, like a woman's voluptuously naked leg, and her hearts beats a quarter-inch faster.

She remembers what a pain in the pert old derrière it was to repaint that glossy fender. It had been the first week of October, and the warm weather wouldn't quit. The old shed on Cape Cod stank of paint and grease, a peculiarly acrid reek that had crept right through the protective mask and into her sinuses and taken up residence, until she couldn't smell anything else, and she thought, *What the hell am I doing here? What the hell am I thinking?*

Thank God that was all over. Thank God this rare inky-black 1936 Mercedes Special Roadster is now someone else's problem, someone willing to pay Pepper three hundred thousand dollars for the privilege of keeping its body and chrome intact against the ravages of time.

The deposit has already been paid, into a special account Pepper set up in her own name. (Her own name, her own money: now, that was a glorious feeling, like setting off for Europe on an ocean liner with nothing but open blue seas ahead.) The rest will be delivered today, to the Breakers hotel where Pepper is staying, in a special-delivery envelope. Another delightful little big check made out in Pepper's name. Taken together, those checks will solve all her problems. She'll have money for the baby, money to start everything over, money to ignore whoever needs ignoring, money to disappear if she needs to, forever and ever. She'll depend on no one. She can do whatever the hell she pleases, whatever suits Pepper Schuyler and—by corollary—Pepper Junior. She will toe nobody's line. She will fear nobody.

So the only question left in Pepper's mind, the only question that needs resolving, is the niggling Who?

Who the hell is this anonymous buyer—a woman, Pepper's auction agent said—who has the dough and the desire to lay claim to Pepper's very special Special Roadster, before it even reaches the public sales ring?

Not that Pepper cares who she is. Pepper just cares who she *isn't*. As long as this woman is a disinterested party, a person who has her own reasons for wanting this car, nothing to do with Pepper, nothing to do with the second half of the magic equation inside Pepper's belly, well, everything's just peachy keen, isn't it? Pepper will march off with her three hundred thousand dollars and never give the buyer another thought.

Pepper lifts a tanned arm and checks her watch. It's a gold Cartier, given to her by her father for her eighteenth birthday, perhaps as a subtle reminder to start arriving the hell on time, now that she was a grown-up. It didn't work. The party always starts when Pepper gets there, not before, so why should she care if she arrives late or early? Still, the watch has its uses. The watch tells her it's twenty-seven minutes past twelve o'clock. They should be here any moment: Pepper's auction agent and the buyer, to inspect the car and complete the formalities. *If* they're on time, and why wouldn't they be? By all accounts, the lady's as eager to buy as Pepper is to sell.

Pepper tilts her head back and closes her eyes to the white sun. She can't get enough of it. This baby inside her must have sprung from another religion, one that worshipped the gods in the sky or gained nourishment from sunbeams. Pepper can almost feel the cells dividing in ecstasy as she points herself due upward. She can almost feel the seams strain along her green Lilly shift, the dancing monkeys stretch their arms to fit around the ambitious creature within.

Well, that makes sense, doesn't it? Like father, like child.

"Good afternoon."

Pepper bolts upright. A small and slender woman stands before her, dark-haired, dressed in navy Capri pants and a white shirt, her delicate face hidden by a pair of large dark sunglasses. It's Audrey Hepburn, or else her well-groomed Florida cousin.

"Good afternoon," Pepper says.

The woman holds out her hand. "You must be Miss Schuyler. My name is Annabelle Dommerich. I'm the buyer. Please, don't get up."

Pepper rises anyway and takes the woman's hand. Mrs. Dommerich stands only a few inches above five feet, and Pepper is a tall girl, but for some reason they seem to meet as equals.

"I'm surprised to see you," says Pepper. "I had the impression you wanted to remain anonymous."

Mrs. Dommerich shrugs. "Oh, that's just for the newspapers. Actually, I've been hugely curious to meet you, Miss Schuyler. You're even more beautiful than your pictures. And look at you, blooming like a rose! When are you due?"

"February."

"I've always envied women like you. When I was pregnant, I looked like a beach ball with feet."

"I can't imagine that."

"It was a long time ago." Mrs. Dommerich takes off her sunglasses to reveal a pair of large and chocolaty eyes. "The car looks beautiful."

"Thank you. I had an expert helping me restore it."

"You restored it yourself?" Both eyebrows rise, so elegant. "I'm impressed."

"There was nothing else to do."

Mrs. Dommerich turns to gaze at the car, shielding her brows with one hand. "And you found it in the shed on Cape Cod? Just like that, covered with dust? Untouched?"

"Yes. My sister-in-law's house. It seemed to have been abandoned there."

"Yes," says Mrs. Dommerich. "It was."

The grass prickles Pepper's feet through the gaps in her sandals. Next to her, Mrs. Dommerich stands perfectly still, like she's posing for a portrait, *Woman Transfixed in a Crisp White Shirt*. She talks like an American, in easy sentences, but there's just the slightest mysterious tilt to her accent that suggests something imported, like the Chanel perfume that colors the air next to her skin. Though that skin is remarkably fresh, lit by a kind of iridescent pearl-like substance that most women spent fruitless dollars to achieve, Pepper guesses she must be in her forties, even her late forties. It's something about her expression and her carriage, something that makes Pepper feel like an ungainly young colt, dressed like a little girl. Even considering that matronly bump that interrupts the youthful line of her figure.

At the opposite end of the courtyard, a pair of sweating men appear, dressed in businesslike wool suits above a pair of perfectly matched potbellies, neat as basketballs. One of them spots the two women and raises his hand in what Pepper's always called a golf wave.

"There they are," says Mrs. Dommerich. She turns back to Pepper and smiles. "I do appreciate your taking such trouble to restore her so well. How does she run?"

"Like a racehorse."

"Good. I can almost hear that roar in my ears now. There's no other sound like it, is there? Not like anything they make today."

"I wouldn't know, really. I'm not what you'd call an enthusiast."

"Really? We'll have to change that, then. I'll pick you up from your hotel at seven o'clock and we'll take her for a spin before dinner." She holds out her hand, and Pepper, astonished, can do nothing but shake it. Mrs. Dommerich's fingers are soft and strong and devoid of rings, except for a single gold band on the telling digit of her left hand, which Pepper has already noticed.

"Of course," Pepper mumbles.

Mrs. Dommerich slides her sunglasses back in place and turns away.

"Wait just a moment," says Pepper.

"Yes?"

"I'm just curious, Mrs. Dommerich. How do you already know how the engine sounds? Since it's been locked away in an old shed all these years."

"Oh, trust me, Miss Schuyler. I know everything about that car."

There's something so self-assured about her words, Pepper's skin begins to itch, and not just the skin that stretches around the baby. The sensation sets off a chain reaction of alarm along the pathways of Pepper's nerves: the dingling of tiny alarm bells in her ears, the tingling in the tip of her nose.

"And just how the hell do you know that, Mrs. Dommerich? If you don't mind me asking. Why exactly would you pay all that money for this hunk of pretty metal?"

Mrs. Dommerich's face is hidden behind those sunglasses, betraying not an ounce of visible reaction to Pepper's impertinence. "Because, Miss Schuyler," she says softly, "twenty-eight years ago, I drove for my life across the German border inside that car, and I left a piece of my heart inside her. And now I think it's time to bring her home. Don't you?" She turns away again, and as she walks across the grass, she says, over her shoulder, sounding like an elegant half-European mother: "Wear a cardigan, Miss Schuyler. It's supposed to be cooler tonight, and I'd like to put the top down."

2.

At first, Pepper has no intention of obeying the summons of Annabelle Dommerich. The check is waiting for her when she calls at the front desk at the hotel, along with a handwritten telephone message that she discards after a single glance. She has the doorman call her a taxi, and she rides into town to deposit the check in her account. The clerk's face is expressionless as he hands her the receipt. She withdraws a couple hundred bucks, which she tucks into her pocketbook next to her compact and her cigarettes. When she returns to the hotel, she draws herself a bubble bath and soaks for an hour, sipping from a single glass of congratulatory champagne and staring at the tiny movements disturbing the golden curve of her belly. Thank God she hasn't got any stretch marks. Coconut oil, that's what her doctor recommended, and she went out and bought five bottles.

The water turns cool. Pepper lifts her body from the tub and wraps herself in white towel. She orders a late room-service lunch and stands on the balcony, wrapped in her towel, smoking a cigarette. She considers another glass of champagne but knows she won't go through with it. The doctor back on Cape Cod, a comely young fellow full of newfangled ideas, said to go easy on the booze. The doctor also said to go easy on the smokes, but you can't do everything your doctor says, can you? You can't give up everything, all at once, when you have already given up so much.

And for what? For a baby. *His* baby, of all things. So stupid, Pepper. You thought you were so clever and brave, you thought you had it all under control, and now look at you. All knocked up and nowhere to go.

The beach is bright yellow and studded with sunbathers before a lazy surf. Pepper reaches to tuck in her towel and lets it fall to the tiled floor of the balcony. No one sees her. She leans against the balcony rail, naked and golden-ripe, until her cigarette burns to a tiny stump in her hand, until the bell rings with her room-service lunch.

After she eats, she sets the tray outside her door and falls into bed. She takes a long nap, over the covers, and when she wakes up she slips into a sleeveless tunic-style cocktail dress, brushes her hair, and touches up her lipstick. Before she heads for the elevator, she takes a cardigan from the drawer and slings it over her bare shoulders.

3.

But the elevator's stuck in the lobby. That was the trouble with hotels like the Breakers; there was always some Greek tycoon moving in, some sausage king from Chicago, and the whole place ground to a halt to accommodate his wife and kids and help and eighty-eight pieces of luggage. Afterward, he would tell his friends back home that the place wasn't what it was cracked up to be, and the natives sure were unfriendly.

Pepper taps her foot and checks her watch, but the elevator is having none of it. She heads for the stairs.

On the one hand, you have the luxurious appointments of the Breakers, plush carpets and mirrors designed to show you off to your best advantage. On the other hand, you have the stairwell, like an escape from Alcatraz. Pepper's spindly shoes rattle on the concrete floors; the bare incandescent bulbs appear at intervals as if to interrogate her. She has just turned the last landing, lobby escape hatch in sight, when a man comes into view, leaning against the door. He's wearing a seersucker suit—a genuine blue-striped seersucker suit, as if men actually wore them anymore—and his arms are crossed.

For an instant, Pepper thinks of a platinum starlet, sprawled naked on her bedroom floor a few years back. *Killed herself, poor bimbo,* everyone said, shaking the sorrowful old head. *Drugs, of course. A cautionary Hollywood tale.*

"Nice suit," says Pepper. "Are they making a movie out there?"

He straightens from the door and shoots his cuffs. "Miss Schuyler? Do you have a moment?"

"I don't think so. Certainly not for strangers who lurk in stairwells."

"I'm afraid I must insist."

"I'm afraid you're in my way. Do you mind stepping aside?"

In response, Captain Seersucker stretches his thick candy-stripe arm across the passage and places a hand against the opposite wall.

"Well, well," says Pepper. "A nice beefy fellow, aren't you? How much do they hire you out for? Or do you do it just for the love of sport?"

"I'm just a friend, Miss Schuyler. A friend of a friend who wants to talk to you, that's all, nice and friendly. So you're going to have to come with me."

Pepper laughs. "You see, that's the trouble with you musclemen. Not too much in the noggin, is there?"

"Miss Schuyler—"

"Call me Pepper, Captain Seersucker. Everyone else does." She holds out her hand, and when he doesn't take it, she pats his cheek. "A big old lug, aren't you? Tell me, what do you do when the quiz shows come on the TV? Do you just stare all blank at the screen, or do you try to learn something?"

"Miss Schuyler—"

"And now you're getting angry with me. Your face is all pink. Look, I don't hold it against you. We can't all be Einstein, can we? The world needs brawn as well as brain. And the girls certainly don't mind, do they? I mean, what self-respecting woman wants a man hanging around who's smarter than she is?"

"Look here—"

"Now, just look at that jaw of yours, for example. So useful! Like a nice square piece of granite. I'll bet you could crush gravel with it in your spare time."

He lifts his hand away from the wall and makes to grab her, but Pepper's been waiting for her chance, and she ducks neatly underneath his arm, pregnancy and all, and brings her knee up into his astonished crotch. He crumples like a tin can, lamenting his injured manhood in loud wails, but Pepper doesn't waste a second gloating. She throws open the door to the lobby and tells the bellboy to call a doctor, because some poor oaf in a seersucker suit just tripped on his shoelaces and fell down the stairs.

4.

"I thought you wouldn't come," says Mrs. Dommerich, as Pepper slides into the passenger seat of the glamorous Mercedes. Every head is turned toward the pair of them, but the lady doesn't seem to notice. She's wearing a wide-necked dress of midnight-blue jacquard, sleeves to the elbows and hem to the knees, extraordinarily elegant.

"I wasn't going to. But then I remembered what a bore it is, sitting around my hotel room, and I came around."

"I'm glad you did."

Mrs. Dommerich turns the ignition, and the engine roars with joy. *Cars like this, they like to be driven,* Pepper's almost-brother-in-law said, the first time they tried the engine, and at the time Pepper thought he was crazy, talking about a machine as if it were a person. But now she listens to the pitch of the pistons and supposes he was probably right. Caspian usually was, at least when it came to cars.

"I guess you know how to drive this thing?" Pepper says.

"Oh, yes." Mrs. Dommerich puts the car into gear and releases the clutch. The car pops away from the curb like a hunter taking a fence. Pepper notices her own hands are a little shaky, and she places her fingers securely around the doorframe.

Just as the hotel entrance slides out of view, she spots a pair of men loitering near the door, staring as if to bore holes through the side of Pepper's head. Not locals; they're dressed all wrong. They're dressed like the man in the stairwell, like some outsider's notion of how you dressed in Palm Beach, like someone told them to wear pink madras and canvas deck shoes, and they'd fit right in.

And then they're gone.

Pepper ties her scarf around her head and says, in a remarkably calm voice, "Where are we going?"

"I thought we'd have dinner in town. Have a nice little chat. I'd like to hear a little more about how you found her. What it was like, bringing her back to life."

"Oh, it's a girl, is it? I never checked."

"Ships and automobiles, my dear. God knows why."

"You know," says Pepper, drumming her fingers along the edge of the window glass, "don't take this the wrong way, but I can't help noticing that you two seem to be on awfully familiar terms, for a nice lady and a few scraps of old metal."

"I should be, shouldn't I? I paid an awful lot of money for her."

"For which I can't thank you enough."

"Well, I couldn't let her sit around in some museum. Not after all we've been through together." She pats the dashboard affectionately. "She belongs with someone who loves her."

Pepper shakes her head. "I don't get it. I don't see how you could love a car."

"Someone loved this car, to put it back together like this."

"It wasn't me. It was Caspian."

"Who's Caspian?"

Pepper opens her pocketbook and takes out her compact. "We'll just say he's a friend of my sister's, shall we? A very good friend. Anyway, he's the enthusiast. He couldn't stand watching me try to put it together myself."

"I'm eternally grateful. I suppose he knows a lot about German cars?"

"It turns out he was an army brat. They lived in Germany when he was young, right after the war, handing out retribution with one hand and Hershey bars with the other."

Mrs. Dommerich swings the heavy Mercedes around a corner, on the edge of a nickel. Pepper realizes that the muscles of her abdomen are clenched, and it's nothing to do with the baby. But there's no question that Mrs. Dommerich knows how to drive this car. She drives it the way some people ride horses, as if the gears and the wheels are extensions of her own limbs. She may not be tall, but she sits so straight it doesn't matter. Her scarf flutters gracefully in the draft. She reaches for her pocketbook, which lies on the seat between them, and takes out a cigarette with one hand. "Do you mind lighting me?" she asks.

Pepper finds the lighter and brings Mrs. Dommerich's long, thin Gauloise to life.

"Thank you." She blows a stream of smoke into the wind and holds out the pack to Pepper. "Help yourself."

Pepper eyes the tempting little array. Her shredded nerves jingle in her ears. "Maybe just one. I'm supposed to be cutting back."

"I didn't start until later," Mrs. Dommerich says. "When my babies were older. We started going out more, to cocktail parties and things, and the air was so thick I thought I might as well play along. But it never became a habit, thank God. Maybe because I started so late." She takes a long drag. "Sometimes it takes me a week to go through a single pack. It's just for the pure pleasure. It's like sex, you want to be able to take your time and enjoy it."

Pepper laughs. "That's a new one on me. I always thought the more, the merrier. Sex *and* cigarettes."

"My husband never understood, either. He smoked like a chimney, one after another, right up until the day he died."

"And when was that?"

"A year and a half ago." She checks the side mirror. "Lung cancer."

"I'm sorry."

They begin to mount the bridge to the mainland. Mrs. Dommerich seems to be concentrating on the road ahead, to the flashing lights that indicated the deck was going up. She rolls to a stop and drops the cigarette from the edge of the car. When she speaks, her voice has dropped an octave, to a rough-edged husk of itself.

"I used to try to make him stop," she says. "But he didn't seem to care."

Dear Reader,

I love what I do. I'm lucky enough to pursue the world's second-oldest profession—storyteller—and such is the power of my gratitude, I sit down and pursue it every day, zealously, with joyous passion. As a result, in addition to the book you're holding in your hands, and the other Beatriz Williams books on the shelves of your favorite bookstore, I also write historical fiction under the pen name Juliana Gray.

My newest Juliana Gray book is called *A Most Extraordinary Pursuit*, and it kicks off a brand-new series set (mostly) in Edwardian England, starring a very proper, very resourceful young woman named Emmeline Truelove, who serves as personal secretary to the august Duke of Olympia . . . at least until he dies, under somewhat mysterious circumstances, and his heir cannot be found.

Of course, even a resourceful woman like Truelove can't solve a cross-continental mystery on her own, so she enlists (or rather, is forced to enlist) the help of Freddie, Lord Silverton, who seems at first to be just the sort of glamorous, brainless Edwardian bachelor who won't be any help at all, except when it comes to ordering wine. She's also visited by an unwelcome stowaway on her voyage of discovery, who might or might not be the ghost of a certain member of the Royal Family, and seems bent on offering unsolicited marital advice at every turn.

I hope you'll enjoy this excerpt from the early pages of *A Most Extraordinary Pursuit* and I invite you to follow Truelove on her journey—which, I assure you, only grows curiouser and curiouser as she draws closer to the heart of the mystery, and the fate of Olympia's extraordinary heir. Of course, Truelove's real journey takes her deep into her own soul, and a yearning that may take another book or two (and a few more adventures with Freddie and the new duke) to fully explore . . .

With warmest wishes,
Beatriz Williams (writing as Juliana Gray)

You might wonder why a man so distinguished as the Duke of Olympia chose to employ a humble female, not related to him by blood, as his personal secretary. I can only say that His Grace was a man of great loyalty, and his affection for my father must have guided his choice. In any case, from the moment he offered me the position, two days after my poor father's funeral, I wrung my last nerve in an effort to prove—to the duke and to the world—that I was not a charitable endeavor.

The Duke of Olympia hadn't wanted a grand state funeral. He had told me this five years ago, on the occasion of Queen Victoria's mortal dissolution, while we waited in the black-draped gloom of his London study to depart for the official solemnities at St. George's Chapel in Windsor: a pageant in which England's dukes and duchesses must necessarily play their role. I remember well how the two of them stood in the glorious ermine-trimmed robes due to their rank, dwarfing even the great scale of the room—His Grace stood nearly six and a half feet tall, and his wife, though more than a foot shorter, carried herself like a giant—and how the duke then asked for a glass of port. I poured one for each of them, and as the duke accepted the libation from my fingers, he said, "It's a damned business. I suppose these rituals are good for the public, but I'm damned glad I shall be dead for the occasion of mine."

The duchess had put her hand on his arm and said, in a voice of great emotion, "Not for many years."

To which he had patted her affectionate fingers. "I trust, when the fateful hour arrives, you and Miss Truelove will ensure that as little fuss as possible is taken with my mortal remains. If I had wanted a cortege through the streets of London, I should have elected to become prime minister."

So when His Grace expired without warning in the middle of his favorite trout stream—about a mile from the door of the stately pile that had served as the seat of the Dukes of Olympia since the Glorious Revolution first raised the family to the prominence it enjoys today—there was no magnificently solemn procession through the streets of Whitehall, attended by heads of state. The duke's remains arrived at the nearby church of St. Crispin on a caisson pulled by a single horse, and were borne to the humble altar by his grieved grandsons, the Duke of Wallingford and Lord Roland Penhallow; his natural son, Sir Phineas Burke; and three nephews by marriage, His Highness the Prince of Holstein-Schweinwald-Huhnhof and the Dukes of Southam and Ashland. The county gentry were invited, of course—who could possibly deny them the pleasure?—along with a handpicked selection of friends and relations who might reasonably be expected to conduct themselves with the necessary gravity.

But while the church was filled, it was also small, and when we proceeded to the internment in the family plot, I observed that every last face among us hung with an oppressive weight of grief for this man—this colossus—we had known and admired and occasionally loved. Her Grace the dowager duchess stood veiled on the edge of the newly turned earth, supported by the Duke of Wallingford, the step-grandson to whom she had become especially close, and though her back remained straight, her shoulders curved slightly inward, as if they had begun to warp under the burden of her loss. They had married only twelve years ago, when the duke was already a widower of many decades, and while the marriage had come late in life, and occasioned much sniffing among the more narrow-minded of the duke's contemporaries, it proved as intimate and loving a union as any I had ever witnessed. I shall never forget the sight of the duchess's face when the unhappy news was brought to her at last, at the end of a frantic afternoon's search for her missing husband: the slow way in which her mouth parted and her expression crumpled, as disbelief gave way to despair.

I remember thinking, at the time, that no one would ever mourn me so utterly.

The minister, an elderly man whose own father had first baptized an infant Olympia into the Church of England, wasted few words on the internment itself. It was February, and the wind was bitter with the promise of snow. The air smelled of loam and rot and annihilation, the extinction of a century that had begun with the bloody triumph of Waterloo and was now concluding with the burials of Victoria and Maestro Verdi and, in his turn, the grand old Duke of Olympia.

I watched the polished wood descend into the rough and barbaric earth, and a kind of panic swept over me: not of grief, exactly, but the sense that a candle was sputtering out, which could never be lit again.

By contrast, the reception afterward was almost jovial. I thought this was exactly as His Grace would have wanted it, and after all, only a natural reaction of the human spirit when it comes in from the cold to a brightly lit room, furnished amply with refreshment.

I flatter myself that we did the old lion proud. He had always appreciated the civilizing effect of good drink and fine food, and the dowager duchess and I, in consultation with Norton the butler and Mrs. Greenly the cook, had chosen the funeral meats with loving care. By the time the guests arrived in carriages and motorcars from the churchyard, the servants had laid everything out on an enormous trestle table along one side of the great hall, while the footmen circulated to ensure that nobody's glass remained empty for long. Had everyone not worn an uncongenial black, it might have been a Christmas ball.

"Not quite the thing for a funeral, one imagines," said my companion, as he surveyed the assembly. "I believe that's Lady Roland by the punch bowl, squinting her disapproval."

"We did not design the menu with Lady Roland's opinions in mind," I said.

"We?" His eyebrows lifted.

"I am—I *was*—the duke's personal secretary."

"Oh! My dear. What a dismal sort of job. I suppose you're glad *that's* over."

"I quite liked my position, as a matter of fact. The duke was a generous employer, if exacting."

"Exacting!" He laughed. "Yes, I daresay that's the charitable way to put it. I'm Freddie, by the way."

"Freddie?"

He leaned over my wine. "Frederick, if we must be proper about it. Have you really organized all of this?"

"With a great deal of advice, of course."

"Oh, of course. One mustn't allow anyone to know how capable we are. This wine is excellent, by the way. I applaud your taste. The last of His Grace's seventy Lafite, is it?"

"Yes. You're familiar with it?"

"I don't know much," he said, tapping his temple with one forefinger, "but I do know wine. One's got to be an expert about something, and it might as well be something that gives one pleasure. I say, were you really Olympia's secretary? You don't look like a secretary."

"How does a secretary look?"

"Certainly not like a charmingly constructed young female. Isn't paid employment supposed to be improper and that sort of thing? Have you got to work one of those nasty typing machines?"

"On occasion, when His Grace's personal business demanded it."

Freddie—Frederick—I could hardly call him by either name, so I called him by none—looked at me keenly over the top of his wineglass, which had now fallen dangerously empty.

"I say, you *do* look dashed familiar, though. Have we perhaps met?"

"I don't recall. Did you ever have personal business with the duke?"

"Personal business? Haven't the foggiest. Probably not."

"Then I imagine we haven't met before."

In truth, I would have remembered if we had. I shall not go to such lengths as to call this Freddie an Adonis—the term, I feel, is tossed about too carelessly these days—but in those early days of the century, he possessed the lucky beauty of youth in spades, beginning with a helmet of sleek gold hair and ending in a well-polished shoe, with all manner of blue eyes and straight noses and lantern jaws arranged at regular intervals in between. His shoulders extended sturdily from a somewhat disordered collar. He had a quick, lean way of moving himself about, which he disguised by his lazy expression. If anything, he stood a bit too tall for convenience, but perhaps I quibble; I sometimes suspect I am overparticular when presented with specimens like this self-professed Freddie. At any rate, as I regarded the radiant totality of him in the great hall of the Duke of Olympia's country seat, I expected he was probably very good at the tennis, had left Oxford with a dismal Third in History, went down to Scotland every August to kill grouse in a Norfolk jacket and leather gaiters, was engaged to marry an earl's daughter, and had a mistress waiting for him in a flat in Kensington, to which he motored back and forth in a two-seater automobile.

How this brainless, glamorous creature had come to rest in my proximity, I couldn't imagine.

"And yet," he said, "I can't quite shake the feeling."

"What feeling, sir?"

"That we've met before." A footman passed; Freddie, still frowning, stretched out his glass for servicing. "Do you go to London?"

"Only when His Grace is—was—in town."

"Belong to any clubs?"

"Not your sort of clubs."

"House parties?"

"I have generally preferred to remain at home when Their Graces are called away on social visits."

"I say. How amazingly dull. Well, chin up. You're free now, eh?" He nudged my upper arm with his wineglass, which was already half-empty again.

"Free? I'm in mourning."

"Well, but after a decent interval, I mean. Surely the old chap's left you a nice little remembrance, so you can run off and see the world and all that sort of thing. Smoke cigarettes and gad about in ocean liners, quaffing champagne by the bucketful."

"I haven't begun to think about it."

"Oh, come now. Admit it, it's been in the back of your mind, all this time. Why else do we put up with the old duffers, eh? The pot of gold at the end of the rainbow." He leaned close again and winked, and in the copious candlelight—the duke had not yet begun the project of electrifying Aldermere Castle before he died, and perhaps five hundred fine beeswax candles illuminated the great hall this February night—his eyes looked a little too bright.

"Yes," I said. "Exactly so. And if you'll excuse me, sir, I'm afraid I must speak with the butler about the wine."

"The wine? What's wrong with the wine?"

"I suspect there's too much of it."

He laughed at me, and I was about to turn away, when his expression changed to one of recognition. He snapped his fingers. "Now I remember!"

"Remember meeting me?"

"No, alas. Remember that I was supposed to summon you to the library for a desperately important meeting."

"A meeting? With whom?"

"With whom? Why, herself, of course. The dowager duchess. Wants a word with you, on the chivvy." He shut one blue eye and stared through his wineglass at the ceiling, as if admiring the optical effect. "Better you than me, if you're asking. But then, nobody ever does."